The Way
of the Outcast

a novel
by Alexey Osadchuk

To my Dear Reader, with gratitude,
Alexey Osadchuk.

Mirror World
Book#3

Magic Dome Books

The Way of the Outcast
Mirror World, Book # 3
Second Edition
Published by Magic Dome Books, 2017
Copyright © A. Osadchuk 2016
Cover Art © V. Manyukhin 2016
English Translation Copyright ©
Irene Woodhead, Neil P. Mayhew 2016
All Rights Reserved
ISBN: 978-80-88231-17-2

Table of Contents:

Chapter One

Warning! You are not logged in!
Would you like to log in?

The message glowed an acid red. I felt as if I was about to press the proverbial nuclear button.

Well, it might not come to that but still. Some people I know would have given a lot for access to some of Mirror World players' accounts.

This was another considerable drawback of Daily Grind accounts. The Bronze plan allowed you to access your char from your computer without having to climb into the immersion capsule. Even though the only feature available in this mode was the player's Dashboard, the mere fact was enough to make you rub your hands with glee.

Now I could at least check my email or copy my screenshots to a memory stick. My girls had been pestering me to show them Boris and Prankster but

I'd never managed to get around to it.

What a shame I didn't have computer access to the auction. You had to have at least a Silver account to have those kinds of perks. Never mind. I'd have to work with what I had.

Vicky had stayed true to her word. We'd gotten the loan. Much to our joy, the money had already been wired to the respective German and Japanese bank accounts. Christina's growing new heart had been paid in full.

When I saw the money transfer confirmation, I felt as if someone had pulled out my backbone.

Sveta, my wife, was crying. It had been ages since I'd seen her like this. She'd always been the strong one. But that day emotions got the better of us.

What a shame I couldn't have been with them. Damn this occupational therapy! After twenty-eight days of lying motionless in the capsule, my body was pretty much useless.

My eyesight was even worse. For the first two days I thought I'd gone blind. Strangely enough, it didn't scare me. I had somehow distanced myself from the fact. The main thing was, we'd done it. The rest was paperwork. In any case, by the evening of the third day I had already been able to enjoy sunset views from the comfort of my wheelchair. Even the fact that my new glasses were much more powerful didn't bother me. It was well worth it.

I knew it wasn't over yet. I'd say, it was only the beginning.

The total of the loan was awesome. The bankers had been well and truly generous with us.

They'd offered me exactly what I'd asked for: a quarter of a million.

Most of it went on Christina's hospital bills. Having gotten that out of the way, I immediately paid what I owed to Shantarsky's bank and closed my account. I didn't give a damn about my long-term credit history there. I didn't even want to think about that person.

Next item on my spending list was my Bronze account. That had cost me fifty grand. Plus another five for saving all of my character's stats. My professions, my gear, my levels and Rep points, my race and my pets — all was present and correct.

What a shame I couldn't change my name though. This was one option Mirror World didn't have. If you were born Olgerd into that world, Olgerd you would stay.

If you fancied changing race, this wasn't a problem provided the money was right. There was virtually no attribute you couldn't change if you didn't mind the price tag. None but a player's name, that is. Having said that, the game offered countless short-term anonymity options — again, if you were prepared to pay.

Actually, the five grand I'd paid for saving my stats included their discount. Regular players had to pay more. Vicky had been especially generous that day. According to her, I'd been lucky to have come when I had. Half a year previously, the interest rate wouldn't have been so, ahem, interesting.

Talking about the interest rate, we'd agreed on 11%. *Agreed* was actually an exaggeration. She simply told me that this was the best they could do. She admitted they were trying to accommodate me as it was.

The amount was mind-boggling. I managed to make them agree to my paying it back within ten years. Thirty-five hundred a month. Dmitry had been right: Mirror World was the only place where I could earn this kind of money.

I signed the contract without hesitation. All in all, I'd have to pay back over four hundred thousand. I didn't care. I'd reached my main goal. Christina would live!

And the loan... well, I'd have to look into it. I already had a few ideas.

Oh, and one other thing. The insurance.

Before I signed the contract, I'd had to insure my life and my health. Now if anything happened to me, the bank would still get its money back. Still, a stone-faced Vicky made it clear they were not at all interested in this scenario. Which was why my next login was to be performed from their state-of-the-art module center under the supervision of several medical professionals.

That made sense. First I needed to do what I had to do. I could always die afterwards. Something told me that they would be perfectly comfortable with *this* scenario. At first I'd thought it was my paranoia playing up, but no: both Dmitry and Sveta told me more or less the same thing.

So as of now, I was going to take care of myself. I had to make full use of their occupational therapy facilities. I shouldn't even think of any more extended-immersion gigs. I really had to start visiting their gym and swimming pool. Dmitry had promised Sveta to keep an eye on me in order to make sure I did it. He'd looked as if he'd meant it, too.

Login successful!

Excellent. Admittedly, the game developers took their clients' data protection very seriously. I couldn't just open my Dashboard: I needed an ID authenticator, or 'an IDA' as Dmitry called it. It was a small gizmo that looked a bit like a smartphone with a computer connection.

Once you entered your password, the gadget would ask you to press your thumb to its sensory panel to take a fingerprint reading. That done, you had to sit straight without blinking as the camera scanned your irises.

Next, the box would ask you to pronounce certain words. According to Dmitry, this was to check your voice tone and also to see if it betrayed any fear or anxiety. You might be entering your Dashboard at gunpoint, you never know. If the system smelled a rat, it would forward the data to security operators at the main server. Putting it plainly, this was one hell of a useful little machine.

Right. I was logged in. I did a quick check of my stuff just to see if everything was there. It was okay.

Next.

My inbox kept winking its little light at me as if saying, *Come on, master, check me already!*

Heh. No points for guessing what's inside. Lady Mel's representatives had already contacted Dmitry, asking him very nicely why I hadn't showed up at work. They were obliged to be nice to us because my contract specified that I got paid on extracted value. Basically a freelancer. I sort of rented her mines and declared the resources I'd farmed for remuneration. I didn't have a set wage. I didn't owe anything to anyone and kept my own schedule. This had been the first condition I'd discussed with Weigner. What if I had to drop everything and rush to my sick daughter's side? So this was one of the contract's main clauses, as far as I was concerned. And had I not known anything of my bosses' agendas, I might had even felt touched by their consideration.

Once Dmitry had offered his explanations, they'd stopped bothering him. For a Mirror World player, occupational therapy is sacred, especially following a month-long immersion job. Actually, the girl who'd called him had tried inconspicuously to find out which center I'd been taken to. To which Dmitry, brusque as usual, reminded the girl that as a company worker he had no right to disclose sensitive information. And if anything like that happened again, he'd be forced to report the incident to the security team.

When Dmitry had told me all that, I'd been surprised by the fact that the secretary — or whoever that girl was — had seemed to have really chickened out. She began offering excuses saying they were worried about their best worker and wanted to know if he needed any help. Yeah, right. Messing with the

Glasshouse's bosses wasn't a healthy idea.

I found the thought both scary and reassuring. I felt like a tiny remora fish accompanying a Great White: so far, the shark didn't seem to be interested in the little fishie but still could snap at me at any moment. The pros of the situation: other smaller sharks seemed reluctant to approach. Cons: my shark, even if it chose to ignore my culinary qualities, could with a single shake of its tail dive to the deep where I couldn't follow her, leaving me to be ripped apart by smaller predators.

I opened my mail.

There. Just as I'd thought.

Three letters from Weigner and another one from my new so-called friend, Tanor. Uncle Vanya too had dropped me a line.

Quite a backlog in only forty-eight hours.

Heh. I'd better start with Uncle Vanya, then.

Hi,

What the hell happened to you? We wanted to meet, no? You're never available. We're a bit worried.

Let me know when you're back online.

Your share of the Darkies loot is safe with me.

Right. This was pretty much clear. The guys must have smelled a rat. I needed to decide how to answer their questions. Never mind. This was nothing serious. Once I was back in game, I might write to him and tell him I'd been in therapy. If I did it now, they'd put two and two together and see right through my account-changing game.

Now Weigner.

The tone of his three letters grew exponentially in various stages of hysterics. The man was panicking. He must have had his bosses on his back. Well, this demanded a similar "therapy letter" from me just to calm him down. I'd have to write it later. Not now. I might mention the phone call to Dmitry too, just to reassure Weigner. I had no idea what his role in the Steel Shirts clan was but he was okay.

And last but by no means least, Tanor's message,

My dear Olgerd,

Judging by your sudden and prolonged disappearance, I'd venture a guess that your immersion period has run out. To the best of our knowledge, you'd stayed in game for almost a month trying to raise the necessary Reputation points with Mellenville. It would be logical to surmise that you're currently in occupational therapy.

I don't for one second doubt that the bank has refused your loan application. Just as I told you, basically.

What a shame. All this time wasted. Don't you think?

Never mind. You need to get some rest now. Take your time. Get your strength up. We're looking forward to seeing you back.

If, by some chance, you log in earlier than expected, I just want to let you know you don't need to worry about the money. The sum you need is already here, awaiting you.

We could meet IRL if you wish to discuss all the details. I'm pretty sure you need the money now. Just let us know where to find you and we'll be there.

Do you remember me telling you about our clan's state-of-the-art module center? We could transfer you there anytime — today if you so wish.

I've just been told that our clan's treasury has a complete brand new Master gear set waiting for you! They say it's the best you can get. Don't you think it's cool?

Hope I've managed to cheer you up a bit,
Looking forward to greeting you back,

Tanor

He cheered me up, yeah right. You could say that.

So their clan had started with the proverbial carrot. They're doing their best not to pressurize me into anything. They have the money ready; they'd even found some nice gear for me. So they thought the bank hadn't given me the money? Actually, it was good. The small shark was readying to attack the little fish, not yet seeing the huge fanged monster it was skirting.

Let them think they had me in their pocket. In the meantime, we'd play for time. Dmitry could easily pull the wool over their eyes for another week, telling them I was still in therapy and wasn't allowed to go online. By the time they decided to turn to the proverbial stick, I had to be ready.

I had a week to master the Combat class. The

stronger I was, the higher my chances of survival in No-Man's Lands.

The good news was, my new immersion would be nothing like the first time when metaphorically speaking I'd taken a leap into the dark, blindfolded. Now I'd seen it all. I'd tried and tested myself in the game. I'd witnessed what combat classes could do. I now had a lot of advantages compared to first-time newbs.

If I wanted to succeed, I had to do some quality research on combat classes. I couldn't study all of it, of course: the Net was absolutely bursting with information, some of it helpful, most of it useless. I decided to limit myself to the most popular resources.

Take the Mirror World Wiki, for instance. It had virtually everything you needed to know about the game. Naturally, no one was going to share any truly yummy bits of intel but even so, according to Rrhorgus' son Max, it was "chock full of cool stuff".

"You could say that," I mumbled, staring at all the charts and diagrams on the computer screen. "I don't know where to start."

Funny I'd never visited it before. Having said that, these sites were so numerous these days that you could make neither head nor tail of it all.

"I'll get used to it," I said, just to cheer myself up.

Even if I managed to work out the very basics, that in itself would be a considerable result.

What a shame I couldn't access my class stats! You had to be in full immersion to do that. According to Dmitry, it was a security measure.

Which left me with a problem. The Wiki had nothing on Ennans: nada, zilch, zero. In other words, the only person who was qualified to add entries about Ennans was yours truly.

So I had to switch to my "cousins": the dwarves and gnomes.

Now... where were they?

A click of the mouse summoned a fearsome-looking bearded dwarf. In his powerful suit of armor, he looked twice as big as he really was, which in turn made his head seem disproportionally small.

And how about gnomes? Same, really. If anything, they appeared even more menacing.

Now let's check the classes available to me.

I wanted the standard package. Close combat, magic attacks, distance weapons, this sort of thing.

Close combat was more or less clear. I wasn't going to be much good at it, period. I couldn't even imagine myself brandishing a dwarven battle axe or a gnome's hammer. Besides, what was the point in having heavy weapons if I had my Boris? Despite his zero level, he already had a whole cartload of Stamina points. And once his experience began to grow... and once I bought him a purpose-built set of gear... what would happen then? Oh no, forget close combat.

This wasn't the problem. Problem was, I'd be constantly on my own — and far behind enemy lines, too, surrounded by the most dangerous wildlife that existed in the game. I had to decide how best to capitalize on everything I already had. Which was quite a lot, actually.

Had I been a member in an established and —

which was equally important — strong group, I wouldn't have had to ponder over this dilemma. But as it was, I had to start thinking about creating my own team which, although small, had to be promising.

Judging by the bits of description I'd managed to piece together from all sorts of sources, all mounts were basically fighters: strong, fit and extremely tenacious. In gamers' lingo, they were tanks. In other words, having Boris in my group, I could forget close combat: I just didn't fit in the picture myself — neither as a heavily-armed warrior nor as a light ambidextrous one.

In all honesty, my first urge was to concentrate on magic classes. That way, Boris could make mincemeat out of our enemies while I could heal and support him. But in thinking so, I'd completely overlooked our last but by no means least team member: Prankster. Providing magic support for the group was apparently his job — as part of his pet class. At least that's what all Mirror World experts said. The phrase used by the Wiki, "a healer and a buffer rolled into one", seemed to describe Prankster's potential perfectly well once I'd managed to translate it into normal human parlance. To put it short, the higher my level, the more useful would my little menagerie be.

I had a tank. I also had a buffer/healer. Now I had to decide how *I* could fit into it.

Oh, well. Let's have a look.

I clicked through to a picture of a gnome in light armor. He clenched a monstrous crossbow fitted with optical sights and a complex set of gear wheels. A bagful of bolts and screws dangled from his belt.

I immediately thought about the Caltean attack in the Citadel and the gnome fighting the "hedgehog". He'd been the last man standing, perfectly alive when all other players including the top-level wizard had already kicked the bucket. He'd even managed to bid a hasty retreat when the going had gotten tough.

I liked this crossbowman. He was light and agile. A distance weapon: exactly what our little group needed in order to be full of surprises. That's settled, then.

I needed to check out this class with other races, too, to find out all its pros and cons: what weapons they could use, etc.

The gnome was more or less clear. Now the dwarf.

A stocky black-bearded guy, clenching an *arbalest*. Same as a crossbow: different name, slightly bulkier and heavier.

Humans and Alves were archers; Dwandes excelled at dart throwing. Large races didn't seem to have this class at all.

Having spent a good half-hour studying the facts, I'd finally come to the following conclusion: if one wanted to use distance weapons, he couldn't do better than choosing the Alven race.

Undoubtedly, forest dwellers had their drawbacks. Their gear was flimsy to say the least. If an Alven archer was forced to engage in a hand-to-hand, he wouldn't last long. Even a dart-throwing Dwand could make quick work of him.

Still, their gear's shortcomings were more than compensated by excellent Range, Precision and Rate of Fire bonuses. No other race had anything like them.

A gnome crossbowman's gear was virtually the same as that of a Human swordsman but the former had serious problems in regards to his Range and Rate of Fire. Still, if a gnome's bolt hit the target it could deal just as much damage as a proverbial cannonball.

Humans really didn't impress in any of these respects. Their domain was magic and witchcraft. If I'd understood it well, Humans were the best wizards in Mirror World.

The further I read, the fewer illusions I had about the information's seemingly chaotic nature. Everything had in fact turned out very logical and organized.

There was a certain balance between classes and anti-classes. This in itself made the gameplay much more interesting and, let's be honest, more intelligent. Once you'd chosen Mirror World, you had to be ready for a learning curve. Now I had some idea of the sheer amount of guidebooks and manuals a potential player had to peruse before even entering his new virtual home. You couldn't expect to conquer this world by sheer enthusiasm. An arrogant newb wouldn't last five minutes against more advanced and prepared ones.

Normally, at this point I would be racked by doubt. How sure was I that I had to get into it all? Was I even up to it? Playing was one thing but this wasn't my case. I was about to become the epicenter of a future war the likes of which Mirror World hadn't yet seen.

In any other situation I'd have already had my brains in a twist with worry. But right now I felt something totally different. I wouldn't say I wasn't afraid. Still, this wasn't *fear* fear. I felt a little anxious but that was normal, I suppose.

Also, this strange mix of emotions betrayed some sort of fighting spirit. How strange. I'd never have thought I'd experience something like this.

An insistent incoming call distracted me from my research. The phone's panel lit up with the word, *Brother*.

I pressed *Accept*. "Hi there."

"Hi," Dmitry's voice was typically brusque and serious. "How are you?"

"Fine today. I'm busy now studying your leads."

"Wrap it up, man. End of boot camp. Time to go to the front line."

"Great. You coming?"

"No. I might burn your cover."

"You think they'd stoop so low as to spy on somebody in the real world?" I asked, doubtful.

"They might," Dmitry said with confidence. "We'd better play it safe and bide our time. As soon as they find out you're off the hook, all hell will break loose. So this week you'll have to work hard, I'm afraid. Make sure you don't overexert yourself. Knowing your tendency to self-destruct..."

"I'll be careful, I promise."

"Good," he heaved a sigh. "Now, location. Have

you decided on anything?"

"I have. The Nameless Isles."

"Good choice. There're at least twenty of them there. Easy to get lost. Their mobs are low-level, too. A newb location. You'll level up to 30 easy."

"Sure. And what's even better, there're no Steel Shirts there."

"The fact that they use their own lands to level up their recruits says nothing," Dmitry warned. "Keep your eyes peeled. Good luck!"

"Thanks, man."

"You've done good," he added. "The Nameless Isles are a good choice. Over and out," he hung up.

I nodded to myself. Indeed, the Nameless Isles were a godsend.

When I'd first tried to come up with a plan, I'd asked myself: where was I supposed to begin? No-Man's Lands didn't sound too promising. I couldn't expect to level up my current char properly there. Hoping for a streak of good luck wasn't an option.

All Lands of Light had been carved up between clans who were bound to notice my presence pretty soon. I'd even had a crazy idea to fly over to the Dark side at night and level up there. But that was risky.

My grand plans had ground to a halt.

That's when I'd turned to Dmitry for advice. He explained that when the game had still been in its infancy, the developers had come up with special locations they used to help combat classes grow and evolve. Those nurseries were some sort of training ground for inexperienced players, complete with low-level mobs and simple quests issued by NPCs.

That was all good and well, with one drawback, or so players said. The developers had apparently decided to add a fly to the ointment simply to make sure life wasn't all fun and games for newcomers. Nothing critical: just slight fluctuations in weather conditions. At North Ridge, for instance, there were occasional ground frosts and snowfalls. The Snake Desert had hot spells. And the Nameless Isles were known for their rains. Well, rains — more like sunshowers.

But newbs in their starting clothes hadn't appreciated weather fluctuations. They'd absolutely flooded Support with protests and complaints saying that the game developers were applying pressure to players, forcing them to buy expensive runes, elemental protection or even cloaks. The developers had turned a deaf ear to their pleas — for which I was now eternally grateful.

Over time, the flood of complaints had subsided. Newb locations stood abandoned.

How had it happened?

Easy. After the end of the clan wars, all Lands of Light had been divided between the strongest clans. New castles had been erected in locations with neutral climates, promptly surrounded by new towns and villages. Now why would you suffer in silence, freezing to near death or getting soaked when there were more comfortable locations available?

Dmitry had forwarded me the classified login data. Apparently, the old newb locations had only 2% of all game logins. The remaining 98% players chose to log in to clan-controlled territories.

That was perfect.

According to Dmitry, I had the choice of three types of locations: cold, hot or rainy. And as much as I hated the latter, I'd had to choose it in the end.

Having no Anti-Heat protection, I'd immediately rejected the Snake Desert. For a while I'd been quite serious about the North Ridge: I'd already had rain up to here. Besides, I'd already had my Anti-Frost protection, anyway — I'd installed it before my first trip to No-Man's Lands.

But that was before I'd seen the map.

The North Ridge was a long narrow hill range stretching all along the border, smooth-sloped and gently-rounded. The Nameless Isles, however, were a smattering of islets big and small in the southern part of the Great Ocean. It offered much better protection from any prying eyes.

I'd also found out that the North Ridge was exactly where the remaining 2% of players chose to log in. Apparently, I wasn't the only person averse to humidity. Then again, how was I to know?

Never mind. Enough research. Time to go downstairs. My module awaited me.

I rode the elevator alone, studying my gaunt aspect in the mirror. I'd seen corpses with better complexions. Having said that, compared to my first day offline I was as fit as a fiddle. I could even walk unassisted now. I had no need for crutches anymore.

The elevator dinged softly, announcing its arrival at the first floor.

The corridor was flooded with light.

It was busy here. So many operators! Their lab

coats were everywhere. You could tell this was a VIP center.

Having said that, if the game developers weren't entitled to it, who was?

Would they kick me out of here once I'd completed my mission? Or would they allow me to stay? Too early to even think about it.

This center was exactly why I'd had to move town. Dmitry had simply ordered me to do it. After I'd told him about the bank's offer and the fake Pierrot, my brother had grown even more focused. Without him, I wouldn't have gotten very far at all.

"Olgerd?"

I turned around. A girl stood behind me. About twenty-five, lab coat, pale-blue doctor's hat. The name tag on her chest said *Irene*.

I nodded. "That's me. Hi."

"Hi. You ready?"

"Sure."

"Let's go, then."

My new "coffin" wasn't too far. We reached the end of the corridor, then entered a hall.

There were other capsules there, all closed. They looked like nothing I'd used in the past. Even though I was no technical expert, I could see these were the latest top-of-the-range models.

"There it is," she pointed at the only open capsule.

The familiar purple goo welcomed me, enveloping my body. "Mind if I ask?"

"Absolutely," she said without taking her eyes from the screen.

"Is it my imagination or has something changed? I feel as if I've been dropped into jelly. Just please don't use science speak."

She smiled. "This is the latest model. To put it plainly, in earlier versions we had to use a gel bed which vibrated-"

"-to prevent bedsores," I helpfully offered.

She nodded. "Exactly. But now we have this special type of gel which envelops your whole body, sending electric impulses through it. Which is a very healthy idea. And as a bonus, it adds new sensations to your virtual experience."

"Oh. I'm curious."

I'd have dearly loved to ask her a few more questions but she beat me to it,

"That's it, Oleg. Let's initiate the immersion procedure."

Her delicate fingers ran over the screen, tapping the invisible keyboard. The lid began to lower.

"Good luck," Irene smiled. "Enjoy your immersion!"

"Thanks," I whispered back.

A few moments later, the already-familiar void embraced me.

Silence. Darkness.

I glimpsed a flicker of light approaching faster and faster, accelerating toward me.

Before I could even blink, the light took me in.

Still no sounds. I looked around me. Where was I?

A round room, about five paces wide. A stone floor. Torches burning on the walls. No windows.

I raised my head. Powerful wooden beams supported a gloomy vaulted ceiling. This could be one of the Citadel's towers, only without their characteristic arrowslits.

Greetings, Olgerd! Welcome back to Mirror World!

In order to fully experience the beauty of our world, complete the registration of your Bronze account!

Register now: Accept/Decline

Accept.

Congratulations! Your registration is now complete!

Would you like to choose a new class?

Absolutely.

My heart missed a beat. Even though I'd already made up my mind, I had a nasty feeling I'd forgotten something important.

Generating your character's settings and characteristics should take less than a minute. Please wait.

Of course. This was a new race. Did that make me some sort of pioneer? Never mind. I could wait. The halo around my head won't fall.

Jesus. Their minute was taking quite a while.

Sorry about the delay! Your character's settings have been reset.

Would you like to continue: Yes/No

About time! I heaved a sigh and pressed *Yes*, ready to face an exhaustive list of various combat classes.

Wait a sec. What the hell was this? Was it some kind of mistake?

A holographic image of my Ennan char clad in a simple starting kit appeared at the room's center. But it wasn't his clothes that had thrown me. I had all my gear safe in my bag. It was the class list. It consisted of only one entry:

Army Mechanic

My hands shook as I went through the settings. It couldn't be. What, only one class?

I looked at my Ennan. He stood there legs akimbo, hands on his hips, grinning from ear to ear. Who the hell did he think he was?

Wait a sec... what on earth was this? I took another look at my first weapon dangling from his belt.

Damn. I looked up at the powers that be and heaved a fatalistic sigh. "A *slingshot?* You have to be joking, right? You want me to conquer No-Man's Lands with a freakin' slingshot?"

Chapter Two

Calm down, Olgerd.

Take a deep breath. No need to panic.

Inhale. Exhale.

Like that... good.

Now let's have a look.

A mechanic, so what? So I hadn't gotten an archer or a crossbowman. What was my problem? That they didn't have suitable classes?

Big deal. Take Narchs, for instance: they had four arms, of all things. I dreaded to think how they managed, but apparently they did. Quite successfully too, judging by the Plateau battle. Very efficiently, if I may say so.

Oh, and here was a parchment scroll containing my Lore Info. It was ancient and yellowed.

It happened in early fall, just as I traveled the foothills of the Steely Mountains. I was visiting my

---

friend Rold from the Tinkh people. His folk were nothing really special. Just some Ennans living in a village. They kept themselves to themselves. Never took part in any feuds or clan wars. They worshipped the Lord of the Underworld.

Contrary to what people usually think, their clan lived by trade, not by mining or smithing. It might actually have been one of the reasons for their isolation.

So one night as he sat by the fire warming his aching joints and smoking his best old pipe, Rold told me about some tragic recent events.

As it turned out, one of the oldest clans in the whole of the Steely Mountains had recently ceased to exist. The Tinkhs didn't know much about what had happened there. Some said that the Der Swyor miners had come across a rich vein. Others said that the clan leader had behaved disrespectfully at the last Elders Council. But my friend Rold, he thought that it was all about Master Grilby who must have uncovered the ancient secret of raising people from the dead.

Here the text paused. The whole of the next paragraph was blurred as if whoever had written it had spilled some liquid onto the parchment. Whether he'd done so accidentally or for a reason, I couldn't say. I moved on to the next paragraph.

...the clan's warriors put up a valiant resistance. But what could they do against the Alliance's army? There were fifty attackers to each defender. Many a hero found his death that tragic day. You need to give

the Der Swyors justice: they fought as one man. According to Rold, a handful of common workmen barricaded themselves in the Tower of the Winds and successfully held the enemy back for a while. His story left a lasting impression on me.

That was the end of this so-called Lore Info. Actually, no. There was a signature below,

The Chronicles of Arvein. Page 25.

The game developers weren't exactly generous with information. Or was it just me?

What a weird class description. If you thought logically, my mechanic just might be the descendant of those brave defenders of the Tower of the Winds.

Oh, well. I suppose it's better than nothing at all. There was only one thing I'd love to know. Had those tower defenders used slingshots against the enemy too?

Talking about slingshots. I remembered a YouTube video in which a burly guy fired a slingshot at cows' skulls, using steel bolts. I still remembered the loud snapping sounds and the popping of exploding bones.

Besides, somehow I didn't think it was going to disrupt the gameplay. Most likely, I was about to fit into the combat classes nicely, slingshot and all. Judging by the char's grinning mug, I was in for quite a ride.

Never mind. One problem at a time. What's with my characteristics?

On top of the existing Speed, Strength and Stamina, now I also had Health, Protection and Intellect. Next to the blue Energy bar I discovered a red one for Life, green for Experience and yellow for Knowledge.

Thanks to what I'd gleaned from the forums, I already knew that the Life bar corresponded to Health. It was the same mechanism as the correlation between Stamina and Energy. As your Health grew so did your Life bar.

I really needed to look into it properly. I had plenty of Energy; but judging by my Life reading, I could die from the first sneeze!

The bar was calibrated into forty units. Each Health point gave me 20 points Life.

Now, Strength.

Before, it only used to affect Energy regeneration speed. Now it was going to do the same for Life as well. The damage dealt, too, directly depended on its numbers. Which was definitely good news.

Protection was more or less clear. Knowledge, however, was a bit of a dark horse for me. Could it be some analog of mages' Wisdom? I really couldn't tell. I might need to try it out first.

The next hurdle was the absence of the so-called bonus points. The game developers must have decided — and rightly so — that those I'd received at registration were enough.

So the whole thing was a bit off balance, really. I had to enter a warrior's path with zero Protection and minimum Life. The weakest of the Nameless Isles mobs would be able to blow me over with a feather.

I also had some advantages, though.

First, my gear's stats were quite high for level 1. And second but not least, my little menagerie.

Also, according to forum messages, I was entitled to five bonus points to distribute as I saw fit with every fifth level gained. If I lived long enough to see that, that is.

Very well. My characteristics were more or less clear. Let's check my inventory.

Five icons were highlighted in my bag: two of Clothes, two Miscellaneous and one Weapon icon.

I started with the clothes. What did our generous admins have for me?

No surprises there. A leather vest and a pair of canvas pants, a standard newbie kit.

The vest added 1 pt. to both Health and Speed while the pants did the same for Strength and Stamina.

All this was a pittance, of course, compared to my Reflection kit even if you forgot the fact that it was hung with runes like a Christmas tree.

Any newb was bound to find their starting kit very useful, of course. Anyone but unfortunately not me, although I could admittedly use the extra point to Health.

Still, the game's rules dictated that if I wanted to wear this leather excuse for a garment, I'd have to remove some of my outerwear, breaking the set. Which would lead to the loss of both the precious Strength and Stamina points and my impressive Speed bonus. Putting it simply, one puny extra point to Health wasn't worth all the trouble.

Seeing as my new clothes were non-transferable, I might need to delete them from my inventory later simply not to clutter my bag. Having said that, there was no rush. I could always get rid of a potentially useless item.

That was me done clothes-wise. Now, weapons. Oh! How interesting. Apparently, my slingshot had a very cute name:

> *Name: a Minor Pocket Slingshot*
> *Category: Simple*
> *Weapon type: Main (non-transferable)*
> *Level: 0+*
> *Restriction: only Ennan race*
> *Range: +0.5*
> *Rate of fire: +0.5*
> *Precision: +0.5*
> *Damage: +1.0 ... +1.6*
> *Durability: 25*

Well, let's just hope I might procure something more impressive at a later date. I'd even agree to a Major Pocket Slingshot.

Now, Miscellaneous.

If the truth were known, forums said nothing about it. Normally, new arrivals received their bonus points, a set of tattered clothes and a basic weapon. No Miscellaneous items had ever been mentioned.

Then again, who knows? Did I really think that forum members shared all their gaming secrets? Highly unlikely.

Now. Item one, a small leather case.

Name: a Standard Tool Kit
Pcs: 4

Nice name, simple and informative. Wish I could say the same about its contents.

Sharpthorn, 1
Wambler, 1
Measurometer, 1
Fix Box, 1

Their logic was understandable. Being a mechanic, I had to use some sort of tools. Only I didn't have the slightest idea how I was supposed to defeat even the lowest-level monster by brandishing a measurometer or, God forbid, a wambler? The best I could do was probably load my slingshot with the sharpthorn, then immobilize the enemy by giving him a whack with the Fix Box, just to be on the safe side.

Relax, Olgerd, I said to myself. It could have been worse. Of course I was upset, seeing as I'd looked forward to choosing a standard combat class. On the other hand, I had to give my Ennan credit. So far, he'd never let me down.

The last item in my inventory aroused mixed feelings: a reluctant optimism tinted with perplexity.

Name: *A Pocket Book of Blueprints and Bind Lines*

The book was quite fat, its dirty brown cover worn and spotted with burn marks and engine oil. The spine was hanging on a thread. A fine net of cracks and little holes riddled the cover. I got the impression that either the book's previous owner hadn't valued it at all or he'd used it in a less than sterile environment.

I opened the book, about to start reading, but found nothing inside apart from some dimmed pages and a welcome message,

Greetings, Olgerd!
We're sorry. You can't read the book yet. Your Knowledge level is too low. Please try again later.

Yeah, right. *Please try again when you get smarter,* is that it?

In any case, I discovered a few empty pages at the end of the book. The tool case, too, had a lot of empty slots. I suppose that was their way of telling me that if I wanted to fill them up, I'd have to do it myself.

Never mind. I was done studying my freebies.

Greetings, Olgerd!
Would you like to complete account activation?

I cast one last look over my inventory and clicked *Yes.*

The magic torches dimmed. The holographic Ennan floated toward me, still grinning.

The darkness consumed me.

When I opened my eyes, I stood on the sea shore. Or should I say, on the Great Ocean shore.

Congratulations! Activation complete!
Welcome to the Nameless Isles!
Would you like to download and install our free app: Fact Sheet of the Nameless Isles?

The stench of brine and rotting algae assaulted my nose. The roaring of the surf and the sound of rain pattering on the sand mixed with the rustle of palm leaves and the hum of the empty bamboo stems in the wind.

Black thunderclouds hung low in the sky. The wind blew hard. The swell was rough. The downpour was every bit as bad as it had been back in Drammen.

Was it the admins playing with me? Or was this kind of weather normal here? In which case I could understand why no one was in a hurry to use this location.

I felt heavy, pressure pinning me down. I'd already forgotten how it felt to walk around naked. Mirror World never let you off the hook.

I needed to rectify the situation pretty quickly. I hurried to get dressed.

Congratulations!
You've received +1660 pt. To Energy!
Current Energy levels: 1700.

Much better. Even the rain didn't feel so wet anymore. The clouds overhead seemed lighter somehow. The ocean, too, wasn't as murderous as it had originally looked. Things were looking up.

Time to take my bearings.

The long strip of sandy beach was about forty of fifty paces wide. It arced like a sleeping snake between the ocean and the green wall of the jungle. Nice big beach. I liked it.

The sand was technically white but you couldn't tell its color straight away because it was mixed with tiny fragments of sea shells, dried algae, petty bits of driftwood and all sorts of flotsam and jetsam.

This definitely wasn't meant to be a tourist destination. Having said that, there's no accounting for taste. Personally, I wouldn't enjoy lying on the littered sand staring at the raging ocean.

The forest's edge didn't look too inviting, either. The location was probably prone to tornadoes, judging by all the uprooted palm trees.

Excuse me? Anyone hear me? Was this a newb location or what? I found it hard to believe this place was meant for beginners. It was spooky.

Success! The Fact Sheet of the Nameless Isles has been installed and is ready for use!

Very well. What did we have here?

The app was good. It contained the location's detailed map and its bestiary. Judging by which, the local wildlife was quite diverse.

The map also listed all the natural resources and the settlements of the local NPCs.

Now I could believe that this used to be a starting location once. I'd never received such detailed instructions during my first registration. Then again, Grinders didn't need this kind of info, did they? All they had to worry about was finding an employer and getting to work.

Now, however, my situation was quite different. The sooner I managed to adapt the easier I might find it in the future.

So let's start with the map.

Once synchronized, my satnav dutifully reported my bearings. According to it, I was in the northern part of this rather large location: on its smallest and furthermost island.

The nearest NPC village was on the biggest isle to the east. It looked more like a continent on my map.

I told my satnav to lay a course to the village. After a brief pause, it offered what it believed to be the shortest route.

Oh. To get there, I'd have to cross two more islands. It would have been much easier to just summon Boris. Still, I didn't want to attract any unwanted attention. Even though the sight of my gear didn't add to my inconspicuousness, still a Grinder dwarf who'd managed to scrape together enough small change to buy a Bronze account was a more common sight than a Grinder dwarf soaring in the sky astride a black Gryphon-like creature.

Never mind. A walk might do me good. I could have a good look around in the process, seeing as I was stuck here for a week at least.

Off we go, then, to face any unwelcome adventures!

I didn't have to go very far before I stumbled across an enormous fish carcass. It must have been at least twenty feet long. The smell... you can't even imagine.

Its stomach had been ripped open, rotting flesh and guts spilled everywhere. Had it not been for the rain, I would have smelled it much earlier.

I stood there staring at the gory scene. It looked believable indeed, as if I was on a God-forsaken desert island amid the ocean.

Distracted by studying the fish's fin, I failed to notice the footprints at once. They were triangular, about a foot and a half long and half as wide.

Well, well, well. If that wasn't... I was no expert, of course, but even I could tell a bird's prints when I saw them.

Mechanically I raised my head. If this place was inhabited by birdies of this shoe size, I should really keep closer to the trees.

Then again, that might not be the best option either. You never know what the jungle might have in store for a curious traveler. I'd had this nasty sensation of being watched the whole time I'd been on the beach. Every time I turned to face the forest, the feeling disappeared only to resume later.

So much for their newb location. It made me shudder. Even Spider's Grotto felt safe and comfy in comparison.

I was about to turn round and continue on my way when I finally realized something simple but paramountly important. My weapon! I hadn't even thought about checking it!

I just couldn't believe it. Hey, mobs and predators, come quick! Enjoy the juicy flesh of a reckless nerd, a worthy specimen of modern society!

My hands reached for the Minor Pocket Slingshot, still stuck under my belt. I didn't even know how to use it!

Actually, who hadn't used one at a tender age? I wasn't an exception. We didn't call it a *slingshot* then: we actually called it a *catapult*. It had been a long time ago though... in real life, too.

I had no idea about slingshot ballistics in the virtual world. But this wasn't a question I should be asking myself. Why oh why hadn't I even thought of testing my only weapon first and foremost? Olgerd, Olgerd. You're a dork to end all dorks. Think that someone like you was about to venture into No-Man's Lands!

Right, time to rectify my blunder.

I closed my left hand around the slingshot handle, made of dark wood and fitted out with what looked like an ordinary elastic. The pouch in the back was made of a piece of leather. That was basically it.

The only little thing lacking was finding some ammo. Seeing as my inventory listed nothing of the kind, I might need to forage around for something suitable. Not forage even. There was plenty of ammo lying literally underfoot.

That small pebble over there might do nicely.

You've received an item!

Name: A Beach Pebble

The moment I placed the pebble into the pouch, the system told me something very interesting,

The Minor Pocket Slingshot is loaded!
Missile: a Beach Pebble
Fit for Purpose: Yes
Range: +0.6
Rate of Fire: +0.4
Precision: +0.4
Damage: +1.0 ... +1.1

Aha! The little pebble had increased Range but negatively affected both Rate of Fire and Precision. As well as Damage.

Very well. What if I pick up a smaller one?

I lay a new pebble into the pouch.

The Minor Pocket Slingshot is loaded!
Missile: a Beach Pebble
Fit for Purpose: Yes
Range: +0.8
Rate of Fire: +0.6
Precision: +0.6
Damage: +0.8 ... +1.0

How interesting. The new pebble had improved all stats apart from Damage. It had dropped quite considerably. Which was exactly what I didn't need.

What if I took a bigger stone? Like that gray rock over there...

The Minor Pocket Slingshot is loaded!
Missile: a Beach Pebble
Fit for Purpose: Yes
Range: +0.3
Rate of Fire: +0.3
Precision: +0.3
Damage: +1.8 ... +2.2

Well, that made it pretty clear. A heavier "missile" improved Damage but lowered all other stats. All I had to do now was put it to the test. Meaning, I needed an enemy.

A powerful roar came from the rainforest, making every hair on my virtual body stand bolt upright. Did they say we should be careful of what we wish for?

Chapter Three

The roaring resumed, closer this time, accompanied by what sounded like the cracking of branches and whole tree trunks being swept from the creature's path.

I could already see palm tops sway in the thick of the woods. This was something very big, very loud and very angry. And it was heading for me.

I cast an unenthusiastic look at my slingshot. "I've had enough. To hell with secrecy!"

...Boris appeared just as the mysterious monster barged out of the undergrowth, crushing the bamboo trunks and palm trees unlucky enough to happen in its path.

I bent down, scooped a handful of pebbles and sprang onto Boris' back. In one powerful wingbeat I was out of the newb killer's reach.

I could see the feathers bristle on the scruff of Boris' neck.

"Some newb location, eh?" I slapped his powerful neck. "Sorry I had to drag you into this, kiddo."

He didn't hear me, too busy watching the huge beast which was now furiously spinning in place on the beach.

"I know the feeling," I whispered to Boris while I was studying the creature.

He was quite a sight, I had to admit. At least twenty foot tall, he had a massive body, a rectangular head, large paws, a fat hairless hide, a long crocodile tail and a pair of long curved fangs.

He didn't look as if the game designers had invested much thought into him. They must have taken a croc, a wild boar, an elephant and a rhino, then clicked through the randomizer. The result was a mutant from hell.

And how were you supposed to fight such specimens? With a slingshot, too.

Actually, why was he so angry, spinning and jumping on the spot? A couple of times he even dropped to his side. The place where I'd stood only a few seconds ago now resembled a ploughed field. Interestingly, he didn't seem to notice me at all. I wasn't even in his aggro zone. What was the matter?

"Kiddo, mind going down a few feet?"

Boris cast me a sideways look, as if to say, 'You aren't serious, are you?' Still, he promptly obeyed.

Once we'd descended a bit closer, everything had become clear. The beast couldn't care less about me. He was under attack himself.

His assailants looked weird like everything else

in this so-called newb location. They had skinny monkey-like bodies covered in hairless skin of a dirty gray hue. They had long front legs and short hind ones. Not the nicest of guys. Not to even mention their heads.

I'd once happened to visit a client on business. He had this large fish tank in his office in which he had piranhas swimming around. The guy had a very nasty habit of making his visitors watch the fishies' meal times. Admittedly I'm not a lover of such scenes but that day I couldn't very easily have said no.

Now too, as I watched the bald "monkeys" throw themselves at the beast, I had a vague *déjà vu* feeling. Same fish heads packed with needle-sharp teeth. Same sharp, twitching motions.

I'd love to know what had affected this particular game designer's creativity. "Boris, mind going down a bit more? They can't see us, anyway."

He obeyed, allowing me to survey the scene in greater detail. As I studied the local uglies, the system helpfully informed me about their nature.

The game developers hadn't invested much imagination into the giant beast's name, either. He was simply a Stomper. The fish-headed monkeys were Swamp Monks.

According to their respective descriptions, the Stomper was the location's biggest mob in the area and Swamp Monks were the deadliest. They were fast and very smart; besides, they always hunted in packs.

Their levels made me wonder, for the umpteenth time, if I was indeed in the right place. The Swamp Monks were all level 20. Stomper was 30. This way I might just as well have gone to No-Man's Lands. There was something wrong here. Something very wrong.

As I thus indulged in navel-gazing, the fish-headed midgets were gradually overpowering the roaring giant.

I counted at least ten of them. They were swift and dexterous. There seemed to be a system in their attack. They'd done it before, that's for sure. Five of them clung to the Stomper's back, trying to bite through his thick hide and the powerful muscles protecting his spine. The other five bustled around the mob's feet, shrieking and snapping their sharp teeth.

Even a nerd like myself with zero hunting skills could see they were trying to distract him.

The beast was clearly tired but still trying to sink his long fangs into his attackers. He was too slow though. In his situation, he should either move little and try to preserve his energy or duck back into the woods where the monkeys would find it harder to move. Still, the game developers must have cut a corner in his Intellect department.

Gradually his roaring changed, sounding more like a whimper. The Monks chirped with glee: one of them must have finally gotten to the creature.

No idea why I did what I did next. It could be the giant's helplessness — or it could have been the Monks' nasty cheering that must have reminded me of something from my past. It didn't matter. I attacked them.

The moment I lay the first pebble into the

slingshot, I received the first unpleasant surprise. A new message materialized, its letters acid red,

Warning! The Air Attack restriction has been activated!
-20% to Damage dealt to ground targets.
Keep leveling and gaining experience, and one day it will change!

What was that, for crissakes? What did they think they were doing? They'd clipped our wings in mid-flight!

First they'd given me this ridiculous weapon, then sent me to this so-called newb location, and now this? What kind of sick joke was that?

Calm down, I said to myself. No good falling apart. Let's think logically. The slingshot might explain itself later. It might actually prove to be a worthy weapon every bit as good as some exquisite Elven Bow... or at least I hoped so.

As for this place, I might have to look into it once I logged out. They couldn't expect a newb to start playing against mobs twenty times his or her own level!

This restriction, however — setting all emotions aside and thinking logically — actually made more sense than anything mentioned above. As a zero level, I was bound to be subject to restrictions.

To sum it all up, if the gameplay's logic was anything to go by, I was in for lots of discoveries and unpleasant surprises.

As I was thus collecting my thoughts from the

information overload, the Stomper was already on his last legs. Digital legs, but still. Naturally he was going to respawn in due time but that was yet to happen — provided I failed to step in. This wasn't the right moment to ponder about the future. I had to act fast. Stupid as it may sound, if I didn't help him now, I might repent my indecision at my leisure.

"Boris, mind circling them for a bit? Slowly. I need to take good aim."

I grabbed the slingshot's pouch with my thumb and index finger.

The sling pulled taut.

My hand froze alongside my right eye.

I took aim.

I'd long decided on my first target: an especially brazen Monk who'd sunk his teeth into the giant's neck, showering him with blood from a severed artery.

Before letting go of the pouch, I smiled at a sudden thought. Funny, really. The slingshot was actually the only weapon I knew how to use. I'd had a whole childhood of experience.

The smooth little rock escaped my hand with an unexpected force, sending a brief vibration from my weapon hand to my left shoulder. Wow. This was something I'd never seen happen as a child!

In one powerful pop, just like in that YouTube video, the little bastard flew off the Stomper's neck.

The system message was another surprise.

You've attacked a level 20 Swamp Monk.
Damage dealt: 40
Keep on fighting!

~ 43 ~

How freakin' much? Forty points? Didn't its stats say one point of something? Not that it made too much difference to the nasty midget, not with his levels. Still, for my zero level forty points damage was way beyond my dreams. What could have caused it?

Wait a sec.

I knew it! I wasn't just any zero level, was I? My gear stats, that's what must have done it. This was the 116 Strength points of my Reflection kit in action. And that's with their 20% restriction, too.

Naturally, had I been standing down there on the beach, the Monks would have made quick work of me. But I'd rather swap the considerable extra damage for the safety of Boris' back.

Actually, judging by the stats' description, my mount was supposed to receive part of my XP without detracting from it. Ditto for Prankster. So it wouldn't be a bad idea to summon him too. He could sit on Boris' neck and learn the ropes.

Prankster materialized on my shoulder and immediately leaped onto his big buddy's head, paying no heed to me. Why should he? The unfolding show below was much more fascinating.

My attack hadn't gone unnoticed. The Monks knew we were there. The one I'd shot down was angrier than the rest: a couple of times he'd even tried to jump in the air to get at us.

He could jump, I tell you. If he were intelligent enough to climb onto the Stomper's head and repeat his attempt from there, he might just have made it. I told Boris to climb a bit higher.

The Stomper's column-like hind legs gave way

from under him. The Monks shrieked their triumph. For a split second they'd forgotten all about me, the whole pack assaulting the monster.

Big mistake.

My second pebble hit the most forward one right between the eyes just as he was about to sink his teeth into the Stomper's throat.

You've attacked a level 20 Swamp Monk.
Damage dealt: 35
Keep on fighting!

Screaming his indignation, the Monk tumbled to the ground. Immediately — much to my surprised relief — the Stomper joined in the action. With one swing of his giant head, the wounded Monk lay broken on the sand.

That was it.

One down.

The following message admittedly pleased me,

You've killed a level 20 Swamp Monk!
You've received Experience!
Congratulations! You've received Achievement: David and Goliath
Reward: +2% to Physical Damage dealt by you
+1% to your chance of receiving Knowledge in combat.

This was another thing that differed from my old Grinder account: I could receive Achievements now. Forums spoke at length about this important phenomenon. If you disregarded all the emotions and boiled it down to the facts, they made Achievements one of Mirror World's sacred mysteries. No one could tell how many types of them there were nor offer any kind of chart or classification. The Achievements system seemed to be a fickle and unpredictable beast. Or, as the local old-timers put it, *highly randomized.*

Both mine and my beasts' green XP bars continued to fill up. This was a good sign. I seemed to be doing everything right.

The funny thing was, I hadn't received any XP for my first shot. Simply attacking a monster wasn't enough, apparently. You then had to win the fight. Losers didn't receive XP. So if the Stomper managed to finish off my first target, that would be excellent.

The loss of a pack member must have reminded the other Monks that their victim was still going strong. I made a mental note to steer clear of the giant in the future. You wouldn't want to fool around with a creature that could swat a 1000 pt. Life mob like a fly.

The Stomper put the Monks' hesitation to good use. He scrambled to his feet and staggered toward the forest.

"Good decision, buddy. These idiots won't be able to get to you so easily in there."

Judging by the Monks' squeaking, they didn't like this latest development at all. They sprang onto the Stomper, redoubling their efforts.

"Thanks for turning your backs to me," I said, loosing off another pebble, the biggest I had. Like an infuriated bee, it sank into the back of my first target's head just as he was climbing the retreating Stomper's leg.

The pebble had stripped the little bastard of 50 pt. Life.

Sensing my support, the Stomper swung round. His left foot made a sound like a sink plunger as it stamped the wounded Monk deep into the sand.

Two down!

My XP bar was already half-full. Excellent. That's the way to do it.

The wounded Stomper seemed to have gotten second wind. He was really on a roll. Two more Monks went down. Who'd have thought he had so much left in him still!

Despite having lost nearly half their pack within the last few minutes, the Monks persisted albeit not as enthusiastically anymore. Six isn't the same as ten, after all. Also, I got the impression that the Monk I'd assaulted first had been their pack leader. Without him, their new attack was pretty disjointed. They paid for it straight away, losing the fifth pack member to the Stomper's powerful jaws as he attempted to get to the giant's throat.

I singled out the most active one. He seemed to be trying to organize his teammates. I had to give the midgets their due: having lost half their force, they were still on the offensive.

With a loud release of the sling and a resounding clap, another rock escaped my Minor Slingshot, followed by an angry squeak as it found its target.

You've attacked a level 20 Swamp Monk.
Damage dealt: 20
Keep on fighting!

Not very generous, was it? Apparently, the lower Damage must have had something to do with the shorter range and the smaller slug. Still, for the Stomper it had been plenty. Left for a brief moment without their new leader's guidance, the four remaining Monks lost two more fighters to his powerful blows.

That was that. You could say we were four against their three. We were in the majority!

Before I could celebrate the fact, my unexpected ally lost his footing: either due to the loss of blood or simple carelessness. It didn't matter anymore. I watched as he slowly collapsed to the ground to the Monks' cheerful squealing.

Waving their front legs with glee, they charged at him.

No idea what had come over me. I was probably angry I'd failed to help him. Or just mad at him for having screwed up so stupidly just when victory was within our reach. I really don't know.

I loosed off all the remaining pebbles in one long burst. I didn't even need to take aim: they were all within an arm's reach of each other.

Of course my pebbles were like mosquito bites to them. Still, they served their purpose. Once again the Stomper managed to surprise me. In one desperate thrust he rose on his hind legs, then dropped onto the approaching enemies.

That was the end of it. He'd just swatted them like as many flies.

Congratulations! You've received a new level!
Current level: 1
Reward: +10 to Knowledge.
Current Knowledge: 10/40
Congratulations! You've received Achievement: One Soldier Can Make a Battle.
Reward:
+1% to Physical Damage dealt by you;
+1% to your chances of knocking your opponent unconscious in battle.

I looked at my pets. "You okay, guys? First blood to us."

The system obligingly dished out their respective XP. We were growing! I just loved it.

I stroked Prankster's little head. "You know what, guys? I think I start to like this place."

Boris turned a few circles over the motionless Stomper, then began to descend. I told him to land next to my first slain Monk.

Close by, they looked even uglier than from a distance. Add to that the unbearable stench of rotten fish. Bah. It must have been my brain playing up.

As I looked at the Monk, I had a growing suspicion that the game designers weren't a 100% mentally stable. The creature was a half-finished sketch of a fish mutant apparently arrested in its development just as it had entered Mirror World.

Suppressing a bout of nausea, I stopped and

crouched next to it. Right, what did we have here? My first reward... or *loot* in game speak.

Items received:
An Eye of a Swamp Monk, 1
A Tooth of a Swamp Monk, 3
A Clot of Slime from a Swamp Monk, 1

I was surprised how clean the actual process was. I didn't have to grope inside this ugly monkeyfish's guts. The system did it all for me. The moment I agreed to pick up the items, they miraculously appeared in my bag while the Monk's body began to vanish into thin air. Good news. No idea how I'd have managed without this function.

Having studied the remaining six bodies, I'd acquired more teeth, slime and other obnoxious substances including a few vials of Venom of Swamp Monk. I just hoped that some of this was worth something.

"Right. Seven checked, three more to go."

Had Dmitry not reminded me that all slain enemies had to be checked for loot, I would never have thought about it. It took some getting used to. Which I probably would. It looked as if I might be doing this quite often.

I warily approached the Stomper lying motionless on the sand. You never know what he might do.

I stopped a few paces away. Now I could see clearly that my intervention had been pointless from the start. The giant had been doomed the moment he'd been attacked. The edges of the numerous bites covering his body were turning black even as I watched. This must have been the Swamp Monk venom taking its toll.

The poor giant was shuddering, his wide barrel-shaped belly rising and dropping as he struggled to gasp his last breaths. It was a miracle he'd lasted as long as he had.

His red Life bar hovered at 80. Apparently, some inner force just wouldn't let him die peacefully.

I raised my head to the sky. "You over there! Quit torturing him, will ya?"

No one seemed to have heard me. And if they had, they were probably sitting there laughing their heads off.

"It's all right, man," I whispered, digging my hand into the sand. "It'll all be over in a minute. Oh... this one looks good enough."

The large pebble was much heavier than those I'd used earlier. It looked ugly and out of place in the pouch of my slingshot. I didn't care. This was irrelevant. I just hoped the system would recognize it as a suitable projectile.

Yes!

The Minor Pocket Slingshot is loaded!
Missile: a Beach Pebble
Fit for Purpose: Yes
Range: +0.1
Rate of Fire: +0.1
Precision: +0.1
Damage: +3.6 ... +4.8

Good enough. At this close range, neither Precision nor Rate of Fire really mattered.

I pulled the sling taut.

The Stomper lay on the sand with his eyes closed, his body convulsing faster.

Time to do it.

The sling made its popping sound.

The system showered me with an avalanche of messages, congratulating me on my new levels, Rewards and Achievements.

I didn't bother to read through them. I just wasn't in the mood. "You're free now, buddy."

Mechanically I accepted whatever loot I was due.

I might have spent some time moping about. Still, Mirror World isn't the right place for this sort of nonsense.

Boris behind me emitted a threatening hiss. I swung round.

The last thing I noticed before the lights went out was a pair of murky fish eyes.

Chapter Four

The lights came back on rather quickly. I must have been unconscious for a few seconds at the most. Still, this had been enough to realize I'd just died my first virtual death.

What did I feel? Nothing, really. I hadn't even had the time to get properly scared.

Where was I now? The gloomy beach was nowhere to be seen. Judging by the walls of rock towering around me and the stalactites hanging from the ceiling, I must have been inside a small cave.

A crystal altar rose at its center. A bright blue flame burned bright inside it, illuminating the insides of the cave.

I tried to move but couldn't. A system message appeared before my eyes,

You're dead.
Use the Altar's Force to resurrect: Yes/No.

Unhesitantly I accepted the offer.

Congratulations! You've resurrected!
Good luck to you, O Reincarnated One!
You've received Achievement: New Life!
Reward: +1% to Protection from Physical Damage!

Excellent. I could move again.

The altar's blue light expired, submerging me into darkness. Not the scary pitch dark of the logging in, just the regular gloom of an underground cave. My Ennan eyesight adapted to it in no time.

I cast a studying look around. A narrow passage gaped in a far wall. This was probably my exit route.

Very well, then. I was finished in here.

I dove into the crevice. Below it lay a narrow rock passage.

"So much for the light at the end of the tunnel," I chuckled as I stepped into it. After few more steps, I finally faced freedom.

No matter how much I'd have loved to step out into the soft sunlight to the birds' gentle singing, I ended up under the same incessant rain pouring from the heavy skies.

I was in the jungle. Everywhere I looked, there were palm trees, bamboo and giant ferns wound with creepers. A moss-grown cliff rose behind me.

A faint trail ran from the cave entrance into the forest.

I shrugged. "Oh well. I'll be off, then."

Still, before I went anywhere I had to work out what had actually happened back at the beach. Not that it was going to take a lot of time. Adventures could wait.

I perched on a large boulder by the cliff and cast a look around. Everything seemed nice and quiet.

Let's do it.

I opened the logs and scrolled down until I came to my killing Stomper.

Got it.

You've attacked a level 30 Stomper!
You've dealt a critical hit!
Damage dealt: 83
You've killed a level 30 Stomper!
You've received Experience!
You've received a new level!
Current level: 2
Reward: +15 to Knowledge
Current Knowledge: 25/40
Congratulations! You've received Achievement: A Hill and an Ant.
Reward: +1% to Energy Regeneration
+1% to your chance of receiving Knowledge

My XP bar was 98% full. Which meant that if I won my next fight I might even make level 3. I'd only taken a few shots and I was already level 2! Having said that...

Yes! It worked! My little beasties had made a new level too! Boris was almost level 2 already. Prankster lagged behind somewhat but he boasted a new ability. Let's have a look.

Congratulations! Your pet has received a new level! It's become stronger, sturdier and much more dangerous for your enemies!
Main characteristics:
Name: Prankster
Race: Black Grison
Type: Relic
Level: 1
Satiety: 90/90
Life: 3/20
Stamina: 0
Health: 0
Damage: 1,9 ... 2,6.
Abilities: Healing Wave I
The pet will use its ability to cast a spell allowing its master to restore 5% Life. Cooldown: 2 min.
Experience received: 10% of the owner's combat experience without detracting from it.
Nourishment: The owner can feed his pet at any given time by sharing some of his Energy with it.
Warning! A pet's level can't exceed that of its owner!
Available points: 5

Okay...
Apart from his new ability — which was good news in and by itself — Prankster had only received a few new stats. His Satiety levels had grown. He now had a Life bar and a Stamina stat. Plus he had been granted five points which I was going to distribute for

him shortly.

Now, his abilities. Finally I could see Prankster's entire ability chart. Admittedly all of its icons were still inactive but at least I knew that his next ability branch would open at level 15. Which was better than knowing nothing at all, I suppose.

The first advantage of a relic pet was having six abilities. Regular pets could only have four.

Next. Prankster could fight already at level 1: I wouldn't have to level him up to 30 in order to open Damage.

The next advantage applied to both Prankster and Boris. It concerned what Mirror World players called a "death penalty". If my mount or pet died in battle the way it had just happened to them only a few minutes ago, I could only summon them after a three-hour penalty period. That was a bit of a hassle but admittedly better than the six hours imposed on regular pet owners.

I closed Prankster's window and moved on to Boris. Unlike Prankster, he'd already received his first ability; the next one would open at level 20.

His system messages couldn't have pleased me more,

Congratulations! Your pet has received a new level! It's become stronger, sturdier and much more dangerous for your enemies!
Main characteristics:
Name: Boris
Type: Hugger the Night Hunter
Class: Relic

Level: 1
Satiety: 1000/1000
Stamina: 10
Health: 0
Life: 3/200
Damage: 5,6 ... 6,8.
Abilities: Flight. Riding a Hugger increases your speed 30%. It also allows you to carry two additional heavy items.

Experience received: 20% of the owner's combat experience without detracting from it.

Nourishment: The owner can feed his pet at any given time by sharing some of his Energy with it.

Warning! A pet's level can't exceed that of its owner!

Available points: 5

I wasn't going to distribute his available points quite yet, either. Once I logged out, I'd have to spend some quality time online looking into it, then make an informed decision. There was no hurry, especially considering I couldn't summon my little menagerie for another three hours, anyway.

I found this fact quite disturbing. I was too used to having a plan B (read: being able to soar up into the sky) whenever the going got tough. And it looked like now I had to rely solely on myself. Oh. Plus the Minor Pocket Slingshot.

Never mind. No good winding myself up. I needed to distract myself with something.

Actually, I still hadn't checked my loot.

"Let's have a look," I mumbled, opening my

inventory.

Aha. How interesting. The Swamp Monks had predictably left me some teeth, slime and venom. But Stomper, on top of two fangs, had also bestowed a proper item on me.

What was it, then?

Name: A Bone Bracelet of a Swamp Monk Warrior
Effect: +25 to Speed
Restrictions: none
Level: 20

This was the first real item I'd won in battle. And judging by its name, it stood to reason Stomper had at some point managed to alienate the Monks by swallowing one of their warriors.

The absence of restrictions was good news, as opposed to the item's level 20. I'd so have loved to put it on straight away. No such luck.

"Hi, you all right?"

I jumped at the sound of a stranger's voice. Blinking the messages out of my eyes, I raised my head. A red-skinned Narch towered not two paces away from me. Nickname: Dreadlock. Level: 0. Judging by his full set of herbalist gear, he too used to be a Grinder.

The hilts of two swords peeped from behind his back: both rather simple, by the looks of them. I'd seen enough swords both in Mellenville and the Citadel to know a thing or two about them.

There was something else about him I hadn't

noticed at first. Another pair of hilts peeked from behind his belt. But of course. He had four arms, didn't he? So naturally he needed four weapons. Admittedly they added a touch of danger to his otherwise harmless appearance.

I immediately thought about the Plateau battle. There, red-skinned Narch assassins looked suitably bloodthirsty: their eyes glowing with malice, froth dripping from their fangs, a curved saber in each of their four hands... Scary.

Dreadlock looked like a fine specimen of his race. Tall with broad shoulders, not an ounce of fat anywhere. This was the kind of guy who only waited for a command to slice you into shreds.

"I'm fine, thank you," I cracked a friendly smile.

He nodded. "I see. I wasn't really sure. Things happen. One's first death is never easy."

"Ah. How very thoughtful of you."

Then it dawned on me. "Did you say *first death*?"

He shrugged. "Yeah."

I frowned. Paranoia crept up, entwining my heart and growing new shoots generously nurtured with suspicion. "How do you know this was my first death?"

He grinned. "I don't. Or rather I didn't. Just an educated guess. Only newcomers resurrect at this altar, you see. Then again, you might just have happened to walk past. Or you might have had an appointment here. And what's more, now that I know your level, I'd have rather supposed the latter. The fact that you confirmed my initial suggestion is remarkable in itself. How did you manage to do two levels in your first fight?"

"By accident," I admitted, making a mental note to watch what I was saying.

He only chuckled.

"Can I ask you a question?" I hurried to add.

"Sure," he chuckled again, baring some very sharp fangs. "I suggest we talk as we walk. You *are* going to the village, aren't you?"

I sprang from my rock and theatrically brushed the non-existent dust from my pants. "I'd love to keep you company!"

"Excellent. Off we go, then."

When we left the cliff behind, Dreadlock finally asked, "What did you mean when you said you made two levels by accident? Mind telling me how it happened? Oh, sorry, you were going to ask me something, weren't you?"

I nodded, trying to fall into step with his giant stride. "I was. Actually, our questions have a lot in common."

"Shoot, then. It's even better this way."

"What did you mean by saying it was my first death? What has that got to do with the altar?"

"I see," he nodded. "*When all else fails, read the freakin' manual.*"

"Meaning?"

"Meaning I don't think you've ever got down to reading the location guides, have you? I can imagine your shock when you discovered the high-level mobs."

"You don't mean it's normal!"

"Normal? More like lunacy on the part of the

game developers. All forums are still arguing about the legality of all this. What killed you?"

"A level-20 Swamp Monk."

He nodded. "I see. It means you'd entered the location via the beach. Me, I was first smoked in the jungle. Didn't know what hit me. That's why I was so surprised when you said you did two levels before you died."

"Pure chance," I said. "I heard some noise and kept a safe distance. It was good timing. Some sick cross between a hippo and an elephant ran out onto the beach chased by some Swamp Monks. I was so scared I started shooting at them. Luckily for me, the monster then stomped to death a few of them. Unfortunately, I celebrated too soon."

"I see," he said pensively, casting a brief glance at the slingshot behind my belt.

I knew of course my story was too clumsy but I hadn't had time to think of anything better.

"Actually," he said, "had you kept your starting gear on, you might have received more XP."

"Excuse me?"

"The thing is, apart from recognizing a player's level, the system can also read his or her stats. By this token, our respective gear kits make us look more like level 17 or even 18."

"Oh. I read nothing about that, either."

He shrugged. "It's all right. I'll send you some useful links later."

"Thanks a lot. Why did they do it?"

"You mean the high-level mobs smoking newbs or the XP restrictions?"

"Both, actually," I offered, utterly embarrassed

He nodded his understanding. "As for the former, there's an old interview with one of the company's analytic department experts. You can still find it online, I think. Well, according to him, a newb's first death is highly important. In their first years in the Glasshouse, the developers aimed to scare players out of their minds for a start. Just as a trial measure. Like, if this doesn't scare you, go ahead but be warned! Now of course their philosophy is entirely different. Mirror World is too much part of human society now. The game owners don't care much anymore. Thousands of new registrations every day, what do you think? Most new players choose to start in calmer locations, anyway. So they left the old nurseries for adrenaline junkies like ourselves."

"How nice."

"As for your other question," he went on, "the company was apparently flooded with complaints from new players over their decision to allow Grinders to keep their character's stats and gear when upgrading. For a fee, of course. The company was too greedy. The outcry it caused among new players, you can't even imagine! Like, *it's not fair, we start the game from scratch and they...* blah blah blah. I bet the damage you dealt came as a pleasant surprise to you."

I only nodded.

"You see. So no wonder newbs in their starting kits weren't happy. The developers were forced to meet them halfway by introducing changes to Mirror World's entire combat system. A lot of the players regretted being so vocal, I tell you! Too late. So basically, now the system calculates the entirety of a player's stats and dishes out XP accordingly. Luckily, it doesn't apply to achievements."

"How interesting," I said, ducking to avoid yet another tree branch blocking my way.

"Actually," Dreadlock said, ramming through the thickets like a tank, "don't be too surprised if no one takes you on a raid. Lower levels won't want you because your presence in the group will strip them of their share of loot and XP. Higher levels won't invite you because you can't really help them much. Crafting gear kits have considerably lower stats than combat ones. So if you're planning on using your own gear, at least for the time being, be prepared to become a lone wolf, heh!"

"Great tip. Thanks. All of your advice has been very helpful. And I was considering dumping my starting gear!"

"You can always do that. Waste not, want not."

I grinned. "My point entirely. In this game, every scrap of cloth or piece of paper might prove useful. And my bag has only so many slots in it."

"Exactly," he chuckled. "It gets cluttered in seconds if you're not careful."

As we forced our way through the mesh of intertwining vines, branches and leaves, the system bestowed another message upon me,

Welcome, O newcomer! A long and dangerous road lies before you. Watch out! Your every step may-

Yeah, right. I closed the lengthy message without even reading it, agreeing to the unavoidable offers of free app downloads.

Judging by Dreadlock's focused stare, he'd just done the same. We exchanged knowing stares like Glasshouse old-timers and simultaneously winked to each other.

I quite enjoyed the feeling of not being a total newb anymore. Doubtless I still had a lot to learn; but let's face it, I'd seen much worse locations than this one.

The trail turned another bend. Now I could make out a small bay in the distance and the outlines of little lopsided huts.

Dreadlock stopped, closed his eyes and drew in a huge breath. His already barrel-like chest expanded to twice its original size. He blew the air out, opened his eyes and bared his sharp fangs in a bloodthirsty grin,

"Here we are! Can you feel adventures coming?"

I decided against telling him what exactly I felt at that particular moment. No good ruining his mood. Smiling modestly, I just nodded my agreement.

As we approached Azure Village, I began to realize that whoever had named this little settlement must either have been overly optimistic or a real joker.

A stockade snaked slapdashedly around the village, grinning its crooked rotten teeth like some giant monster. A matching gate stood wide open, listing to one side. A watchtower surprised me more by its sheer existence than by its atrociously bad quality.

There were no guards in sight though — neither by the gate nor on the watchtower.

We stepped through the gate.

We welcome you, O traveler, to Azure Village, the old outpost of the Fort!

As far as I remembered, the Fort was situated at the center of the main island. Apparently, there were several outposts in total — five, according to some forum posts, but only one of them was considered safe. And the Fort itself was the location's main instance.

The local NPCs were in fact all that was left of the former garrison, still attempting to defend this last plot of land that once used to belong to Mellenville. Judging by the dilapidated huts and the overall desolation, very soon the jungle would consume this miserable excuse for an outpost too.

Dreadlock stopped and turned to me, offering his hand. "Here we are, Sir Olgerd. Nice meeting you."

I shook his strong hand. "Likewise, Sir Dreadlock! Thanks for keeping me company. And for the tips."

"That's nothing. Can I add you to my friends list?"

I nodded. "Absolutely."

We exchanged friend invites and more handshakes.

"One more tip," he said. "There's a pole at the center of the village. I suggest you make it your resurrection point and try not to venture too far from it at first as you hunt."

"Why not?"

He chuckled. "It may sound strange but the first death is also the easiest. You probably didn't notice that you'd kept all your stuff even though the gameplay demanded you were left stark naked."

I scratched the back of my head. "True. I still have all my clothes."

"You do," he nodded. "No more freebies, I'm afraid. Now you'll have to do a corpse run double quick the moment you resurrect before some smartass helps himself to your stuff."

"Got it," I nodded. "Will do."

"Good," he grinned. "Right, I think I'm gonna give Sarge a miss for the moment. I've got friends waiting for me in another location. Good luck!"

He slapped my shoulder with one of his four hands and headed toward the sea. I decided to follow his advice and set off in search for the pole he'd mentioned. No good delaying something important like this.

When I turned the corner of one of the huts, a gut feeling forced me to look back. I peered through a sloppy row of bamboo stakes which apparently served as the main building material here. My new friend was staring after me, oblivious of the fact that I could see him. Which was good. Because I really didn't like what I read in his stare.

Chapter Five

"It had all started when they'd found gold on that wretched island," old Sergeant Crux said, baring the yellow stumps of his teeth.

He looked more like a street bum than a valorous Mellenville warrior. He was disheveled with a scraggly beard, his eyes red with either lack of sleep or constant alcohol abuse. He wore a tatty old army tunic.

I'd been forced to sit and listen to his soliloquy because this guy apparently was the location's key NPC.

"So you know how it goes," this excuse for a sergeant sniffed and spat on the ground. "The moment there's gold found somewhere, the place starts crawling with opportunists. Mellenville officials promptly sent in a prospecting expedition. But less than a year later, it became clear it wasn't worth the diggers' wages. The vein proved to be very poor, but at first it had indeed showed promise. They'd even managed to build the fort and the outposts. The expedition wasted some more time looking for more resources on other islands until finally they threw in the towel and announced they were leaving for the continent."

He rasped out a cough and went on, "They left our garrison on the main island in order to protect this miserable location. Gradually they forgot all about us. Just one of those things. What with epidemics, pirate raids and wild beasts' attacks, our ranks kept shrinking. The forest continued to reclaim the island. So it went on until finally something happened that no one could have expected. Later our wizard managed to work out what it was all about, but by then it was too late. The process had already gained momentum, you see."

He heaved a sigh. "If I told you these islands' entire history, I'd be at it all day. To put it short, our idiot architect had ignored the warning signs we'd discovered in the island's hinterland and laid the fort's foundations right on top of an ancient pagan shrine. He never asked himself why his workers were dying like flies. Who cares about prisoners, anyway? Because that's who built the fort: prisoners. Murderers, rapists and pillagers. Their bodies were simply thrown into deep holes nearby. So finally the fort was built. The architect got his share of praise. He packed up his stuff, very pleased with himself, and went back to his posh house in the center of Mellenville," the Sarge kept frowning and clenching his fists as he told me about it.

"Finally the day came which was the start of our undoing. Ask our guys if you don't believe me. That day, one of our recon groups returned to the fort. You'd think it's normal, wouldn't you? Problem was, they'd been missing for over a month."

I decided to add my two cents to the conversation, "That's a good reason to celebrate, isn't it?"

He cast a sideways look at me, his eye bloodshot. "So we thought too. Being lost in the jungle for a month is no joke! But when we opened the gate... you could forget celebrating!"

"Why?" I had a feeling I knew the answer already.

He shook his head. "They weren't our guys, were they? It was them all right but only their decomposed bodies... raised by some evil ancient magic. It was all because of Zeddekey, may he burn in hell! Our wizards had told him not to disturb the old shrine. He hadn't listened, had he? He did everything his own way, the bastard!"

As he continued to shower curses on the hapless architect, I racked my brains trying to remember where I'd heard the name before. Zeddekey... Zeddekey...

Wait.

But of course! Zeddekey's Catacombs which riddled the ground under the Citadel, the local instance that Tronus had recommended me to visit.

Funny this Zeddekey had left his mark here as well. The only difference was, he was a legend back on the continent while here everybody seemed to curse his name.

The walking dead here, the bloodthirsty ghosts of dead builders there... this Zeddekey definitely had a bone to pick with the forces of the afterlife.

As I thus reminisced, the Sarge had already moved on to cursing the architect's ancestry, each and every one of them, until finally tuberculosis got the better of him, sending him into a choked bout of coughing.

Gasping, he spat on the floor. His spittle was veined with blood. "My days are numbered, I'm afraid," he croaked.

"No way," I said with an encouraging smile. "You're gonna outlive us all."

He shook his head. "Leave it. What was I about? Oh yes. Our zombie scouts. My brother-in-law was among them. It's not that I liked him that much, not at all. Still, he didn't deserve it. No idea how I'm going to face my wife now."

He scratched the back of his head, deep in thought. "We smoked the zombies double quick. Not the first time, thank God. A lot of our guys had been over the Black Stream, and those lands are absolutely packed with all kinds of evil. The wizard helped a lot too. We bid our slain brothers farewell, then burned them all on a ceremonial pyre, as tradition dictates. We were about to go back to the barracks when a night watch kid came running and screaming, "Zombies! Zombies!" We talked some sense into him and hurried to the walls. They were everywhere! Eyes burning, teeth clattering, reaching their fetid hands out to get you..."

He paused. "Quite a few of them had been our soldiers. We could tell by their gear. Dead fortress builders, too. There were others — they looked like human beings only they weren't. They must have been the bodies of all those who'd ever died on this island. The wizard said it was some very old magic. He wasn't up to it. He also said — I still remember it — that one day the fort would fall. Said it was better to leave now than waste soldiers' lives."

He stopped and stole a glance around. "Me and my corporals, we tended to agree with him. Time was an issue. As soon as the zombies cut us off from the outposts, we'd be left without food or water. But our Captain had other ideas. He started yelling at the wizard, calling him a traitor and threatening he'd have him chained to the wall, the idiot. Not that the wizard paid any heed to him. But the look he gave us... It still burns a hole in me. It's as if he was looking at corpses. Me and my men, we got real scared. And the Captain just wouldn't leave it alone, would he? He was trying to set us up against the wizard. Too young, too stupid. Too different from the rest of us. You tell me: who are sergeants? That's right, they're yesterday's soldiers. And this, excuse my French, snotnose, had only just let go of his mommy's apron strings. A so-called knight! They receive rank according to their nobility status..."

He fell silent, staring ahead of him. "The rest of that night was relatively trouble-free, if you don't mind zombies perambulating in front of the fort walls. But closer to the morning we realized that the wizard had left and taken part of the garrison along. The night watch were the only ones left. I don't blame them. Not really. I might have done the same. Strategically he'd done the right thing, taking the bulk of the garrison out of the encirclement. It wasn't his fault it didn't quite go as he'd planned. By the evening, they were already back. Dead."

I obediently listened as he told me the rest of the story: the surviving garrison's miraculous escape and their subsequent struggle for survival at the last remaining outpost. I'd read it already at some forum or other, anyway.

As he spoke, my thoughts kept returning to another very important problem. How could I level up in the shortest time possible? Because time was an issue. I had too many obligations to fulfill — and quickly, too. Dreadlock had unwittingly given me an idea. I had to spend some quality time online looking into it. It might just work.

The Sarge was already finishing his tale. I screwed my face into an expression of mourning for his fallen comrades. The game's AI must have analyzed it and considered it appropriate, because the Sarge finally decided to dish out my first quest.

"Listen, Olgerd," he turned to me. "I can tell that you have your heart in the right place. You can see what's going on here. Every pair of hands is precious."

I looked meaningfully around me. He was actually right. Sure this wasn't the most popular of locations — what between the constant rain, zombies, Swamp Monks and other uglies — but still. According to Dmitry, players still came here, but I couldn't see anyone. Apart from Dreadlock and his mysterious friends, that is. The village looked abandoned. Could everyone be out doing quests, bound to return closer to the evening? Then again, who was I to complain? A deserted location was exactly what I needed.

"If you need help, Sarge, try me."

He gave me a toothless grin. "Jolly good, jolly good!" he rubbed his hands. "You've seen our wall, haven't you?"

I nodded.

"What I'd like you to do," he went on, "is to beat some stakes into the ground by the East gate. Think you could do that?"

New quest alert: East Gate fortifications!

Go into the forest and cut 20 stakes, then hammer them into the ground by the East Gate.

Reward: varies

Accept: Yes/No

On the surface this looked simple enough. Still, completing this quest would require my meeting all of the village's NPCs.

Firstly, I would need an axe made by the local blacksmith;

Secondly, I might have to see their store keeper and ask him for a spade;

And thirdly, I'd have to seek out the archer in the watchtower for directions as to exactly where to place the stakes. In return, every one of these chars would exact a service from me. So basically, I was in for quite a busy day.

I accepted the quest, bade my goodbyes to the Sarge and headed to the local smithy. According to the story book, Abel the blacksmith was about to return to the continent. By this token every newb in need of his help was immediately recruited as a porter, lugging cratefuls of tools, coal and steel parts — everything that the foresightful blacksmith could still salvage from the island — to the ship. Only then would Abel gift an axe to the lucky player — which, being a quest item, was basically worthless as it would disappear from your bag the moment you completed the quest.

I noticed him from afar. Little wonder: he was a good seven foot tall with a shoulder span to match and hands the size of sledge hammers. His head was as large as a beer keg trimmed with a black beard. He stood there knitting his eyebrows in thought.

"Good morning," I said.

"Hi," he mumbled, apparently not in the mood for talking.

"I need to speak to you," I insisted. "The Sarge told me to cut a few stakes-"

"What's keeping you?" he interrupted me. "Go and do it."

I shrugged. "I don't have an axe, do I? So I saw you and I thought you might have one for me."

"I might," he boomed. "But what's in it for me?"

"I haven't come to you empty-handed. Do you need help, by any chance?"

"Help?" he finally turned to me and gave me a long studying look. He must have been happy with what he saw because he grunted his approval. "I can see you're the working type. A digger?"

I smiled back. "You could say that."

He nodded. "Good. I do have a job for you. We're awaiting a ship from Mellenville to come and get us out of this wretched place. So I decided I'd better get ready. But I've got so much stuff! You can see for yourself. If you help me move everything to the shore, I'll make it worth your while."

New quest alert: Help the Blacksmith!
Help Abel to carry his possessions to the shore.
Reward: an axe
Accept: Yes/No

I accepted the quest and offered him my hand. "Deal!"

* * *

The quest didn't take me long: my gear's high Strength stats had taken care of that. I'd moved the entire contents of Abel's smithy to the shore in forty minutes flat. Had I been wearing a starting kit, it might have been a challenge.

It paid off: the system rewarded me with +10 to my Relationship with Abel and added a bonus on top.

"Great job!" he gave me an almighty slap on the back which very nearly knocked the living daylights out of me. "You're fast, aren't you?"

"I am," I suppressed a wince. "If there's

something else you need..."

"Agreed," he nodded, pleased. "Now my part of the deal."

Quest alert: Help the Blacksmith. Quest completed!
Reward: An Axe
Type: Quest item
Bonus reward: an Iron Necklace of a Shaman Swamp Monk

Their bonus wasn't much to write home about. Utterly useless, to be precise. Still, the sheer fact of receiving it felt good.

I thanked the blacksmith, walked a dozen paces away from his hut and perched myself on the edge of a half-rotten log.

Now. Let's have a look at my gifts.

The Shaman Monk's necklace may not have looked like much of a gift but still that wasn't a reason to ignore its properties.

A necklace was an overstatement, really. Nine bits of iron were strung together on the knotted dry stalk of some plant. Despite its primitive shape, this item definitely pointed at Swamp Monks evolving and developing intelligence. At least some of them were.

This excuse for a necklace offered its bearer +1 to Speed. Not that it was so important considering the item's whopping 1 pt. Durability.

As I fingered through the necklace, I noticed that one of the knots was about to come undone. Mechanically I decided to tighten it without even thinking of any potential consequences.

The strange-looking system message came as a surprise,

Warning! You're trying to alter an item's nature without possessing the necessary skills, recipes or blueprints!

Probability of ruining the item: 99%.

How interesting.

I could already see I was looking at another sleepless night at the computer screen just researching it all. Every day I was learning something new.

Very well. And what if I did try to "alter the item's nature"? If it got ruined, so what! I could live with that. It was worth the experiment. Especially considering the necklace was about to give up the ghost, anyway.

I gingerly pulled at the stalk's ends, slowly tightening the knot. Just a tiny little bit more...

As if!

Warning! You've destroyed an item: the Iron Necklace of a Shaman Swamp Monk!

You've received:

An Iron Bead, 4.

A length of reed string, 1.

Reward: +2 to Knowledge

Current Knowledge: 27/40

Well, well, well. Curiouser and curiouser.

Congratulations! You've received Achievement: Mr. Bungler.

Reward: +1% to your chance of receiving Knowledge.

I rolled the necklace beads around in my hand. Was I supposed to laugh or cry? Whoever called this clumsy misshapen bit of iron a *bead* must have had either too much sense of humor or too little imagination.

It was about an inch wide. Quite heavy, too. Where was the logic in that? A nine-bead necklace must weigh quite a bit — and still it was supposed to improve Speed, of all things.

Never mind. I shouldn't add to my mine of useless information. Neither the beads nor the reed string had any stats. But seeing as both had been mentioned, they might come in handy to someone. I might check the auction once I logged out.

Casting another glance over my unexpected riches I was about to shove them in my bag when I had an idea.

And what if...

My fingers closed around my slingshot's handle. Breathless, I chose the biggest bead and lay it into the pouch.

The Minor Pocket Slingshot is loaded!
Missile: an Iron Bead
Fit for Purpose: Yes
Range: +2.3
Rate of Fire: +2.5

Precision: +2.3
Damage: +6.7 ... +7.9

I felt my lips stretch in an involuntary grin. "Excellent!"

I quickly checked the remaining beads. Their stats were more or less similar. Pebbles were not a patch on them. Very good.

My experiment had proven very useful. Now I had four good slugs in case of an emergency.

And what if I tinkered with the bracelet too? Then again, what could it bring me — a scrap of leather or a fragment of bone at the most. Besides, it was brand new. I might actually be able to sell it once I was back on the continent. It might not fetch a lot but a few gold was still a few gold. Especially considering I knew nothing about its potential market value yet.

That was it, then. No experiments this time. I needed to read up on it first.

I weighed the beads in my hand. "Shame there're so few of you. You could have made my life so much easier."

Eh... I froze in place just as I was about to get up. "Actually, it might work. Did I assemble it for nothing?"

Consumed by this new idea, I stole a harried look around. No one. What I was about to do definitely wasn't meant for prying eyes.

I moved behind a dilapidated hut, just in case. With any luck, no one would disturb me there.

I reached into my bag and produced the

Replicator which had lain idle there all this time. It looked just like a school microscope minus all the buttons, gear wheels, lenses and other paraphernalia.

I'd already tried to use this wonder gizmo a couple of times but failed at each turn. Judging by its name, it was meant to copy or recreate — but what? No idea. You can't imagine the kinds of things I'd offered it: rocks, food, pieces of clothing... No way. Wonder if it might work now?

I laid the "microscope" in my lap. To begin with, I offered it several pebbles I'd picked up on my way to the village. Predictably, no response.

I returned the pebbles to my bag and moved to step 2, choosing the largest and roundest bead of all. Having said that... no. I'd better use the smallest one. If anything happened to it, at least I wouldn't regret it so much.

Right! Let's take a look.

Good job Sveta my wife couldn't see me now.

The moment I laid the little clump of iron onto the "microscope's" tray, the system generously offered a new message,

Warning! The object you have created is still unfinished!
Only fully finished objects can be replicated!

I grinned as I read the message out loud. This was just some sort of crazy Christmas!

Immediately I shut up and shrunk my head into my shoulders, looking warily around. The place seemed deserted. Right, Sir Olgerd, time to stop this nonsense and get your act together.

I just couldn't believe it! After all the trial and error I'd finally got a result!

I offered the remaining beads to the Replicator one after another, with the same result. The system recognized them all as objects built by me but as yet unfinished. How interesting. Having said that, I had indeed ruined the necklace. But if you looked at the matter from a different angle, both the beads and the piece of string had come about as a result of my manipulations with the necklace.

I brought the piece of string to the Replicator, just to double-check myself, and received the same message.

What did that imply? Firstly, now I could finally understand why the Replicator hadn't reacted to other objects in the past. And secondly, by destroying the necklace I'd apparently created something else, albeit "unfinished".

And what if... I rummaged through my bag for the murky Fragment of Blue Ice and offered it to the machine.

Warning! The object you have created is still unfinished!
Only fully finished objects can be replicated!

So it had recognized the Unworked Charm of Arakh, too! Why hadn't I tested it before? I simply hadn't had the time. First I'd met Tanor, then I'd had to talk to Max and his father Rrhorgus...

All I had to do now was decide how I could use

this.

Voices sounded behind the hut's wall, distracting me from all the thoughts and theories galloping through my head. I hurried to shove everything back into my bag and shrank deeper into the bamboo wall.

There were two speakers. As I listened, I realized they were talking about me.

"Oh, do shut up," one of them growled. Judging by the sound, the speaker must have been very big. "He must be around here somewhere."

"And what if he isn't?" the other voice squeaked. "What did the Chief say? We're supposed to keep an eye on him at all times!"

"Chief my ass!" the other one boomed. "Who does he think he is?"

"Cool it, will ya?" the second one squeaked. "I don't give a damn about your drama queen antics. If you think you're so tough you can challenge him, be my guest. Just leave me out of it."

"All right, all right," the other one hurried to agree. "Quit blabbing."

"I'm not blabbing," the second one insisted. "*You* are. We have an agreement. We rob the noobs and get the hell outta here. Just look at that toon! He walked right into our hands. Did you see his gear? How much do you think his full Digger kit will fetch at auction? You don't know, do you? Not that you know a lot. The Chief knew what he was saying: invite him to join our group and level him up to 10, and then.... But you've lost him, haven't you?"

"How can you lose him?" the first one boomed.

"He went to the smith to get himself an axe. Typical noob. If he's not there it means he's off to get a spade."

"All right," his partner squeaked. "Let's check the warehouse, then."

"Okay. It's better we take a shortcut through the woods. We'll get there quicker."

My heart was pounding fast and hard. *Here you are, Sir Olgerd. Out of the frying pan into the fire. How typical.*

I had no doubts they'd been talking about me. Who else might they have seen around here wearing "Digger's gear"? I should have actually taken a quick look at them. But never mind. Their voices were clue enough.

Talk about bad timing. Naturally, as long as I stayed in the village, no one was going to hurt me. Still, I wasn't looking forward to watching my back the whole time.

Change of plan, then. Time to leave the village and head into the depths of the island.

Chapter Six

I'd spent the last ten minutes lurking in the bushes watching the warehouse. I'd decided to catch a glimpse of the robbers. You should always know who you're dealing with.

The warehouse was the only structure in the whole village that you could actually call a "building". In sharp contrast with all the village huts, it had a tiled roof and stone walls lined with tiny barred windows.

I noticed my pursuers hovering a dozen paces from the entrance. Now why wasn't I surprised?

A Rhoggh and a Forest Dwand.

Both levels 20+: monstrous for this newb location. They should be on the continent playing with all the big boys but they were still stuck here — and I even knew why.

Interestingly, both had green tags. Whoever their Chief was, he paid good attention to detail.

So let's presume these two worked as a newb trap: cool guys in expensive gear who apparently knew the islands like the palms of their hands. They would think nothing of rushing a newb to level 10. Which was when players lost their immunity, becoming easy prey for PKs.

I doubted those two were PKs though. More than likely, both would be offline at the time of the actual killings. There must have been others, more suitable for the task.

Naturally, the owners of humble starting gear kits had nothing to worry about. But players like myself should start taking their safety seriously. My gear would go for at least a grand at any auction. Which was a lot of money.

The worst thing about it was, it was all strictly within the rules. If later I filed a complaint, the muggers would be put on the wanted list. That wouldn't make their names any redder than they already were. Even if they happened to run into the NPC police, it might not happen any time soon. After that, I'd be eligible for compensation, sure, but retrieving my stuff might already be a problem — and as for being reimbursed, the police fees might make a nice hole in any reimbursement payments. They wouldn't catch the felons for nothing. So basically, it was damned if you do and damned if you don't.

There were other reimbursement scenarios, though.

One of the most effective ones was through the hiring of an extorter from the better Fury-endowed players. A mercenary like that could teach the muggers a good lesson and retrieve some of your stuff in the process. Problem was, an extorter's fee was twenty percent of the articles stolen.

I didn't mind paying at all. The very fact that the extorter would bring justice to my enemies and get a lot of my money back was good news. That wasn't the problem.

The problem was, a professional-level extorter wouldn't take on a petty case (like mine undoubtedly was). Their job involved huge risks with the expenses to match. Besides, all extorters were already on every PK's black lists. Many enemies meant many problems: if they chose to take the risk, they had to make it worth their while.

For a moment, I even considered the crazy idea of allowing them to rush me to level 10. I promptly dismissed it though. Firstly, I was quite capable of making level 10 myself. This wasn't brain surgery.

Secondly, my little menagerie had to grow too. And to do that, they had to participate in combat. This was something that all forums were unanimous about. And as I wasn't really going to tell anyone about my beasties, joining groups wouldn't be a clever thing to do.

And thirdly and lastly, I just didn't want to get involved.

Right, enough admiring my noble thieves. I had to be on my way. I still had my Plan B to consider. Time was an issue: I had to think on my feet.

I was about to beat an inconspicuous retreat when the warehouse door opened, letting out a new player.

Judging by the funny hat and a staff in his hand, he must have been a wizard. Level 2. Interestingly, he was also an ex-Grinder. Profession: Fisherman. Even from where I stood, I could see the distinctive embroidered ribbons covering his clothes. He must have spared no expense on boosting his gear.

The greedy mugs of my new "friends" were about to explode with glee. No wonder: a new prey was literally walking into their hands. The Dwand stepped forward and said something to the newcomer. Shame I couldn't hear a word, but judging by the wizzy's sincere smile, he'd swallowed their story hook, line and sinker.

What followed next was a carbon copy of what should have befallen me. They began their spiel. The Rhoggh stuck out his chest as in, *I'm one tough guy,* as the Dwand kept talking, trying to pull the wool over the wizzy's ears. The wizard enthusiastically nodding his agreement. He probably thought how lucky he'd been to have met two top players in these backwaters. He was probably already counting his future levels.

Very nice, Olgerd. It was all well and good for me to sneer at him from the safety of the bushes. Had I not been lucky enough to overhear their earlier conversation, I too might have been celebrating their offer of "friendship".

I really should warn him, but not straight away. He might not even need my advice. An ex-Grinder, he was no spring chicken himself. It wasn't for nothing he'd chosen this location. Still, I should speak to him at the first opportunity, even if for my own peace of mind.

Time to log out, then. Much as I'd have loved to stay here a bit longer, I had to reconsider my initial plan. Besides, I had another hour and a half until Boris and Prankster's reappearance. Just enough time to do a bit of research.

I pressed *Exit.*

A flash blinded my eyes. I was back in the real world.

A SMILING MODULE CONTROLLER offered me my glasses. "Welcome back, Oleg! Feeling okay?"

"Actually..." I sat up on the edge of the capsule and glanced at his name tag, "Sergei, I'm fine, thanks. Surprisingly so."

"Excellent," he helped me to my feet. "It didn't take you long today. They warned me about your love of extended immersion sessions."

Yeah, right! I just love to hate them.

I chose not to answer. Instead, I said meaningfully, "Something has come up. I had to log out."

"I see," he said, peering at the computer screen. "Would you like someone to accompany you to your room?"

I hurried to wave his suggestion away. "No need to. I can make it on my own. You can keep the capsule running, by the way. I'll need it tonight."

"That's fine. The capsule is at your disposal 24/7," he assured me. "Going on an early-morning fishing trip?"

I sniggered. "Something like that."

My temporary abode was quiet and peaceful. I closed the door and hurried to the desk to boot up the computer. Then I headed to the bathroom for a nice long contrast shower.

After a quarter of an hour, I returned to my room fresh as a daisy. Now I could work.

I slumped into the chair and opened the email. What had we got here...

Another letter from Weigner. He must already be regretting ever signing me up. The Steel Shirts' leaders were good at applying pressure on their representatives. He needed to know when I was going to log in.

Uncle Vanya's message was typically brief,

WTF are you?

Rrhorgus wrote to let me know that all was quiet on the Western front. Apparently, no one was following him anymore. Tanor was probably thinking he had me in his pocket. Which was good news, I suppose.

Oh. My freshly-made friend had already sent me a message too. Let's have a look.

Hi Olgerd,

Sorry I completely forgot I'd promised you some useful links about the location. Here they are,

See ya,
Dreadlock

Oh well. I might have a look at them later. I had more pressing issues just now.

I didn't even notice the three hours of research fly past. Had it not been for my stiff neck and strained eyes, I might have stayed glued to the screen until the morning.

Grunting like an old man, I slumped back in the chair. My stomach promptly reminded me it was high time we had something to eat.

"All right, all right... I'm finished."

I'd promised both Sveta and Dmitry to take good care of myself: eating well, getting enough sleep and all that.

The local diner was one floor below. Still, on Dmitry's suggestion I had my meals delivered to my room. It was apparently common practice here. All you had to do was download the galley's app, tick the dishes you liked and place the order. Easy.

I opened it. What did they have for today?

A salad, a fish course and a bottle of water: excellent. Enough to quench your hunger but not too heavy on the stomach.

They brought my food in on a compartmentalized tray like those used in European clinics. Plastic cutlery, a damp napkin, everything vacuum sealed: space-saving, convenient and most importantly, cost-effective. It actually tasted good.

As I ate, I reread an old message in a forum discussion about what they called "item altering".

You can safely alter an item provided you're not a Grinder. Please note that the item has to be already hacked. You can't use a brand new one to do so.

Who would need that, might you ask?

Well, I do.

Let me explain. Let's presume I managed to lay my hands on a nice juicy thingy like an uber shield or a Jedi sword.

Imagine the thrill.

So I use this sword to chop down my enemies left, right and center. Time goes by and I start to realize it's losing its durability. And I already installed some real expensive runes on my favorite hole-puncher and had a wizzy cast a spell or two on it.

Shame, isn't it? It's all right if you've already outgrown the item and can sell it off at auction for a nice profit. But what if it's about to give up the ghost? Or even non-transferable? Are you still with me?

What's the point, might you ask. You can't get back the money you paid for it, anyway.

You're dead right there. But.

Let me counter your question with a question (for those who're yet to crawl out of their little holes). Which is a better choice: to mindlessly discard the item or fleece it for whatever it's worth even if it's only raw materials?

And while you're trying to come up with an answer, here's more food for thought. I personally saw a clanmate hack his shield and retrieve a few runes...

His report was followed by a flood of questions — mainly about the identity of his clanmate and the number of runes he'd salvaged. Quite a few commenters doubted the feasibility of his idea until luckier owners of altered items added their own evidence to the discussion.

How interesting. Apparently, game developers had thus tried to take the sting out of any potential loss of items, adding a consolation bonus of sorts. Which was good news.

I was about to reread the forum threads I'd already perused when my timer went off. That was it, then. Back into the capsule I go.

MIRROR WORLD MET ME with an evening twilight doused in a light shower. That was all right. Could have been much worse.

The warehouse yard was empty. The muggers had definitely chosen the wizzy. What a shame. I should really warn him at the first opportunity.

I decided against approaching the warehouse. Call me paranoid if you want. What if there was somebody lurking in the bushes waiting for me to come back? Oh no, sir, thank you very much. I might return in a couple of days or so.

But now my path lay in the opposite direction. I had to visit the third island.

Judging by the meager info I'd pieced together from different online sources, this patch of firm ground was arguably the least popular location of all the Nameless Isles. Which was exactly what I wanted.

The further away from the village I got, the warier I grew, casting cautious glances around me. I didn't need any problems here.

Finally I walked out into a small forest glade and listened hard. Silence. Nothing suspicious anywhere. It seemed all right. I could summon Boris now.

He materialized at my right side and immediately began swinging his eagle's head this way and that, searching out a potential enemy.

"It's all right, kiddo," I gave him a loving slap on the back of his neck. "There's no one here. We're going to boost you up a bit now."

I hurried to open his stats menu. I had five available points. Unhesitatingly I invested them into his Health. "Your Stamina is fine but you could use a bit of extra resiliency."

His Life bar grew fifty points. "I feel much better already," I told him. "Now, your friend!"

Prankster appeared instantly as was his habit. While he was prancing around the bushes, I distributed his bonus points. In stark contrast to Boris, his own Stamina glowed a big zero.

"You can continue feeding on my Energy until you level up a bit," I said. "So your Energy regeneration rate isn't that important. Your Health is, though."

That was me done pet-wise. Prankster now had 70 pt. Health compared to Boris' 250. Time to get going.

The sky was starless, the moon hiding behind the rain clouds. Perfect flying conditions.

In three powerful wingbeats, Boris took us high above the forest. Two more, and we were safely tucked away amid the black clouds. Ten minutes later, guided by my satnav, we were already landing on the rocky beach of the third island.

As soon as we touched down a few feet away from the waterline, I bent over to pick up some good pebbles for my slingshot. This was another reason I'd chosen the third island — there was plenty of ammo lying around.

I poured a handful of small round rocks into my belt pouch. They only took up one slot. I scrambled back to my feet and looked around, studying the beach. "Excellent. Just what the doctor ordered."

The whole island was the size of a football pitch covered in sparse undergrowth. No cliffs or tall trees: the visibility was excellent any which way you turned. Besides, it was a good ten-minutes' swim from the nearest island. Hopefully, no one was going to disturb us here.

The only thing I knew about this particular location was that it made up a minor part of the main quest chain, obliging you to visit the island and explore it. One of a gazillion pointless little quests dished out by the Glasshouse's NPCs. I just hoped that everything worked out as I planned.

Personally, I couldn't care less about those quests. My plans had suffered a dramatic overhaul. My initial idea of leveling up by buddying up with NPCs had already outlived its sell-by date, courtesy of the local PKs.

So now I was going to do what Mirror World old-timers called mob farming: smoking monsters till the cows came home, earning loot and XP in the process.

The island's inhabitants couldn't really pass for

monsters but they didn't look like cute little bunnies either. The location's bestiary classified Short-Tailed Carapaceons (which was the local beasties' moniker) as passive aggressive. In other words, they wouldn't attack you first but wouldn't suffer any BS from you, either.

They looked like regular crabs the size of an RV tire. Those higher in levels were bigger but they were as yet out of my league. Level 5 looked good for a start.

"One little crab by the sea so blue,

Along came another crab, and that made two," I sang.

Both Boris and Prankster gave me a funny look, their eyes pleading with me: *so these are the adventures you promised us? Smoking stinking crabs?*

"Absolutely, guys. What did you expect?"

Naturally, they didn't mean any of it. This was only my overwrought psyche playing tricks on me. The Reflex Bank building hung over my head like a proverbial sword of Damocles suspended on a horse hair. Which was about to snap.

Very soon I'd have to make my first payment. Christie's new heart had only started growing. And I had no idea if her little body would reject it or not. On top of which, I'd managed to attract the attention of the most powerful clan in Mirror World. Enough to drive you mad. Which might have already happened had it not been for Sveta's constant support.

As if sensing my state of mind, Prankster vaulted onto my shoulder in three long leaps and poked my cheek with his moist nose.

"It's all right, kiddo," I said. "I'm fine. Right! Time is money, whoever said that. Are you ready? Of course you are. Let's begin!"

We found the first crab a mere couple of feet from our landing site. I took it for a boulder covered in algae and all sorts of flotsam. Had it not been for the system message, I might have walked right past.

The crab sat there motionless, his large pincers stretched outward.

I froze a few feet away from it and told Boris to get ready. I forbade Prankster to get involved. Much better that he simply pranced around nearby, giving me an occasional heal in case the crab did get to my fragile cartoon body.

Wait! How could I have forgotten! I *was* a noob, really.

I hurried to reopen the system message and scrolled through, looking for the advice to make the third island my new resurrection point. I swiped *Confirm*. Now if I did manage to get myself killed, I'd resurrect right here on the island and not at the center of the wretched village I'd so promptly vacated.

"Phew! Let's get started!"

The crab snapped its pincers shut as if sensing trouble. Like, *come and get me if you can.*

I took another step and loaded my slingshot, casting a sideways glance at Boris. His powerful shoulder muscles pumped up.

In the meantime, Prankster leaped onto the largest boulder he could find and froze on top of it like a meerkat.

Actually, this was our first fight together. I

didn't count our little air raid on the Swamp Monks. That had been different.

"On my first shot!"

I drew back the sling with an already-practiced hand.

With a powerful pop, my first pebble rocketed off.

You've attacked a level 5 Short-Tailed Carapaceon!

You've dealt a critical hit!

Damage dealt: 150

You've killed a level 5 Short-Tailed Carapaceon!

I lowered the slingshot and watched, puzzled, as the still-uncomprehending crab disappeared into thin air. "Wait a sec. Is that it?"

I checked the logs. That's right. I'd killed him.

How about XP?

Oh. The green XP bar hadn't budged one bit. He'd left nothing behind, either. Zero loot.

So forum gurus had been right after all. Based on my gear, the system determined my level as 15 to 18. The crab was level 5. The only loot I could hope for was some quest item — provided I accepted the quest it came with. Quite logical, really, but it had been worth the try.

"Right guys, I think it's time for me to change into something more humble."

Regrettably I shoved my Reflection kit into my bag. I only kept the boots, the hat and the gloves. No one would make me run over the rocks barefoot. The starting pants and shirt glowed a miserable 1. Oh well. I probably looked like a card loser walking back home in the morning.

My stats plummeted. I sensed the long-forgotten pressure on my shoulders. One quickly gets used to the good things in life.

Now the system should recognize me as level 5 or 6. In theory, such a forced drop might suffice.

Let's see if it worked, then.

I caught sight of the back of another crab about fifteen feet away.

Boris was chomping at the bit, impatient to join in the combat. He was all shivery. Or was it his Mirror Soul reflecting my state of mind?

"Okay," I nodded. "You attack him first. Just be careful."

He darted off as if he'd been expecting this command all his life. In two long leaps and a wingbeat, he soared a good thirty feet into the sky and swooped down like a black shadow, dropping on top of the unsuspecting crab.

I blinked away the flood of system messages that followed and drew the sling. It had grown considerably tighter.

Whack!

The pebble hit the mob at the exact moment when Boris sank his beak into his back.

You've killed a level 5 Short-Tailed Carapaceon!

My XP bar jumped considerably. Interestingly, I got all the damage dealt by Boris and was rewarded with plenty of XP. My pets got their share: both had grown quite a bit. Which was very good news.

I also received some loot: an Eye and a Pincer of an Short-Tailed Carapaceon.

"Congratulations, guys! Great start!" I said to my beasties.

The dawn was already breaking when the system finally bestowed level 5 on me, awarding me with 5 bonus points.

Admittedly, after the first fifteen fights I'd felt pretty much at home with this combat thing. And during the thirtieth, I'd ignored the promise I'd made to myself earlier and removed all of my Digger gear. This sacrifice had resulted in a considerable XP increase. Initially it had made me feel vulnerable but I'd soon forgotten all about it in the heat of the fight.

Not that there was any serious danger to me, really. Boris was doing all the work. As the group's tank, he took all the opposition's hits upon himself. If the truth were known, he dealt the most damage, too. I couldn't do much fighting, not in those tattered pants and shirt so I mainly finished them off.

An hour later I had grown so comfortable I even allowed Prankster to participate. Surprisingly, his seemingly harmless bites considerably sped up the farming process.

And as for the loot... I had enough to start a crab stick factory.

Eyes, pincers, shells and even flesh — I might actually follow some forum members' advice and auction it all. These were useful resources, especially for cooks, alchemists and sorcerers. And not only them: there were tons of professions in Mirror World.

Besides, much to my joy, I'd managed to earn myself a steel ring and a bronze bracelet. The former gave +2 to Health and the latter, +1 to Protection. Neither had any restrictions to race or level, allowing me to appropriate both. My appearance of an inebriated card player began to morph into a shaggy Gypsy look: all I needed was an earring and a gold chain.

Now I was sitting on a rock taking a break from my martial exploits while considering how best to distribute the available 5 points. It might not sound like much, but if you think about it, you could do a lot with them. Only what would be the best way to invest them? Life and Defense were my weakest links, that's for sure. But then there was also Intellect...

Actually, it was a good job I remembered.

The yellow Knowledge bar was full to the brim: 40/40. That was interesting. What was I supposed to do with it now?

The XP bar was pretty much clear: 100% equaled a new level. The Energy to Life ratio wasn't brain surgery, either. But this Knowledge thing remained a dark horse.

I had a funny feeling that a rise in Intellect caused the Knowledge bar to grow. Which meant that it too depended on my participation in combat just like XP did.

What did that ensue?

Nothing really. I could make neither head nor tail of it. Having said that... Hadn't a certain system message mentioned Knowledge?

Yes! I knew it!

I pulled *A Pocket Book of Blueprints and Bind Lines* out of my bag. Hadn't the system given me the cold shoulder when I'd tried to open it?

I got my answer!

The book's front page wasn't dimmed anymore. There was a drawing at its center which looked suspiciously like a blueprint of something or other. Or rather, a draft, drawn with either a lump of charcoal or a very blunt black pencil. Unfinished as it was, I could still make out the outline of a large hammer inside some sort of dome.

As I took a closer look I realized the drawing could have been better. Even I with my zero experience in arts could see that.

A short caption under the drawing confirmed my suspicions. I smiled. I was actually right.

Name: A Blueprint of A Safety Bind Line I
Access requirements:
Knowledge, 40 pt.
Level, 5
Would you like to study the blueprint?

I clicked *Accept*.

Congratulations! You've studied a Blueprint: Safety Bind Line I

Having bestowed yet another Achievement upon me, the system then emptied my Knowledge bar entirely. Aha. I seemed to detect a pattern here.

Also, a small footnote appeared at the bottom of the sheet.

Name: Safety Bind Line I.
Description: Invented by Master Brolgerd during the First Underground War. Adds +10 to Durability when installed on weapons or ammunition.
In order to install the Bind Line, you will need:
A Sharpthorn
A Wambler
Warning! Building a Bind Line will deprive you of 50 pt. Energy!
Warning! The item's level cannot exceed that of the master installing the Bind Line!
Would you like to install the Bind Line: Yes/No

I glanced at the clock. That was okay. I still had time till logout.

I cast a look around and made myself comfortable on my rock. Let's try it.

Weapons and ammunition, they said? Very well. Let's start with the pebbles, then. This large speckled one would do nicely.

I clicked *Yes.*

I really hadn't expected what happened next. It was as if an invisible puppeteer had taken over me. The sensation was very similar to being controlled by the bot back in the mines.

I didn't try to resist. I was curious.

My left hand dug into my bag. My fingers closed over a square object. It felt like leather. I had a funny feeling I knew what it was.

That's right. The Standard Tool Kit complete with its mysterious contents.

Without letting go of the pebble, my right hand joined in the process. It reached inside the kit for the wambler, then transferred the pebble into my left hand.

The fingers of my right hand deftly secured the pebble in the tool as if in a vice. It felt as if I'd been doing it my entire life. Now the pebble was unmoving but could still turn on its axis like a mini globe.

Next. My left hand pulled the sharpthorn out of its pouch and inserted it into a small hole in the wambler's frame.

My hands froze momentarily while the system inquired if I indeed had 50 pt. Energy to spare. I confirmed. That was nothing for me now. I had more Energy than I could ever hope to spend.

A soft blue light enveloped the weird contraption my hands had just made. The pebble began to revolve. The sharpthorn sprang into motion simultaneously, like a curve plotter, covering the pebble's surface with a fancy weave of flourishes. Aha. So that's what it was then, this Bind Line. Those Ennans had some very weird engineers.

In a brief flash of energy, the pebble completed one last rotation and stopped. My hands came back to life, replacing the tools in their respective compartments.

All done. The pebble lay in the palm of my hand, covered in a rather simple decorative pattern.

Its shape had changed, too. Apparently, the installation had somehow made it more rounded.

Then again, it could be an optical illusion. The pattern simply made the pebble appear more regular.

Congratulations! You've received Achievement: The Stronger The Better.
Reward: +5 to Knowledge.
Current Knowledge: 5/40

And what about the item's stats?

Name: a Beach Pebble
Durability: 10
Warning! Every successful hit will now decrease the item's Durability 1 pt.

I reread the message and scratched my head. If I understood it correctly, I could now shoot this normally single-use rock ten times?

I hurried to my feet and cast a look around. No points for guessing if I could check it out straight away. Say, on that crab over there sidewinding itself toward the water edge.

My new projectile lay snugly in the sling pouch. It didn't look as if the slingshot itself had improved much. The elastic stretched with an unusual ease. Which was no wonder really, not after my birthday suit hunting session.

I took aim and let go of the pouch. The sling popped as it released.

Got him! Dead as a dodo.

I hurried over to the water's edge, jittery with impatience. The moment of truth.

It looked as if it had worked. The crab's body lay motionless.

Yess! My new slug was still there! Its Durability was 1 pt. less, just as the system had promised. Excellent. And most importantly, it solved so many problems.

With a sigh, I slumped back onto the rock. "It looks like I might stay here for another hour," I mumbled as I reached into my pocket for the first bead.

Chapter Seven

Congratulations! You've received a new level!
Current level: 12
Reward: +1 to Knowledge
Current Knowledge: 51/60

"That's it," I told my two furry sidekicks. "We're done here."

It was true. We'd spent three days on Crab Island as I'd christened it. As far as I was concerned, I could have stayed here forever.

Why not? Mobs were good. The location was decent — and most importantly, quiet. Loot wasn't up to much, true. But that was only a question of time.

I shouldn't complain, anyway. I had enough rings and bracelets to open a jewelry store. Crab meat was nothing to sniff at, either. I had my doubts it would fetch me much at auction but as they say, a penny saved is a penny gained.

What a shame they didn't have better mobs. Level 10 wasn't good enough for me anymore. I'd even thought I might need to go somewhere else to make level 12, so slowly had the XP bar moved in the end. The amount of loot had dropped, too, despite the fact that I'd stripped down to my pants.

Admittedly, I'd come to like this farming thing, especially when combat tactics had already been choreographed to perfection. It felt almost as quiet and peaceful as working down the mine.

Other players might have found it too boring but it suited me just fine. You did your quota and logged out. Back to real life, to your real-life family.

Last night when I'd made level 10, I'd finally decided to distribute the available points between Health and Protection. I'd also invested 1 pt. into Intellect and left one free for a rainy day.

I'm gonna tell you why. Once my Knowledge bar had filled up to 40, I reopened the Pocket Book of Blueprints, expecting to see something new. As if! Its pages remained dimmed.

I brought Knowledge up to 50, but it didn't help, either. As if being bloody-minded, the system had kept denying me access to new blueprints.

Today I'd added another point to Intellect and was now waiting for the Knowledge bar to reach 60. I just might receive something new and useful for all the trouble.

Never mind. Time to go back to the village. I had to see the Sarge. Our last meeting and my last quest: arguably the most complex and important in this entire location.

Sensing the change in my mood, Boris was already hovering by my side. Last night both he and Prankster had made level 10, to my unbridled joy. My little menagerie was growing strong!

"That's it, kiddo," I said, giving him a hearty slap on the back. "Time to say goodbye to Crab Island. Prankie!"

The little black Grison was already here. He leapt onto Boris' neck and stared at me impatiently, as in, *What are you waiting for, buddy?*

I grinned. "All present and correct! Off we go, then!"

* * *

We landed in the same forest clearing.

It seemed to be deserted. Good. I quickly deactivated the summoning charms. "Time you get some rest, guys. I'll go for a walk."

The village met me with an already-familiar shabby desolation. I hadn't met a single player on my way to the Sarge's shack. Would the game developers discontinue this location? Because if it went like this, in another year's time they wouldn't even have any NPCs left here: they'd all defect to somewhere else.

But if you looked at the problem from a different angle, the developers had spent a lot of money here. Why would they want it to go to waste? Especially as there'd always be some players like myself who'd have their own reasons for avoiding the limelight.

Finally I'd come to the Sarge's shack complete with the brave warrior himself. He noticed me from afar and cringed as if I'd pissed in his soup. Just look at him spitting everywhere!

"There you are, finally! Freakin' Santa's helper!"

We really weren't in the mood, were we? Then again, I could understand him. Had I had to stay in this wretched hole for even an extra month, I'd have been hating every living soul.

"Greetings, Sarge!" I gave him my best good-natured smile.

"You can shove them. What do you want?"

No, he'd definitely gotten up on the wrong side of the bed today. Forum posts had warned against this if you put your first quest off for too long. With every passing day, your relationship with the local authorities could suffer. You had to complete the quest to improve it.

"I've come to ask for my quest," I said bluntly.

He smirked and shook his head. "You're a funny bunny, aren't you? I already asked you to help. But no, you had more important things to do."

I shrugged. "Sorry. But you need to understand too. I'm a warrior and you're sending me to cut down some stakes as if I'm some kind of peasant. And not only that. Every toolmaker wants a piece of me. It's as if I'm doing it for myself. There're four of you here but you have more red tape than Mellenville Treasury."

I added this last bit about the toolmakers and red tape as an afterthought. If forum posts were to be believed, posing as an offended warrior was often enough to open a parallel quest. I even knew which one...

He cast me a long look, then chuckled, surrendering to my logic.

Quest alert: East Gate fortifications. Quest failed!

I heaved a sigh of relief. It had worked.

Not that that was a reason to celebrate. I'd just deactivated a major quest chain. Still, I couldn't do much about it. I wouldn't have been able to complete it anyway, not with all the local PKs hovering around. I wasn't in a hurry to part with my hard-earned gear.

"Well, Sarge, do you think you have something else for me to do? Something worthy of a warrior?"

He glared at me, then dissolved in a malicious grin. Judging by the curve of his toothless mouth, I was in for nothing good. He was fed up with me. Really fed up. Just like the forums had said he would be.

"The valiant knight is in the mood for heroic deeds?"

I nodded. "Why not?"

This seemed to have really pissed him off. "Very well. Here's something you can do. Kill the lich that's hiding in the Fort. That's a nice heroic deed for you."

He guffawed, almost hysterical, his furious glare drilling a hole in me.

I accepted the quest and turned to leave. I certainly had no desire to say goodbye.

"Get out of my sight!" he growled to my back.

"You'd better stay away until you're done!"

Your relationship with Sergeant Crux has plummeted!
From now on, you have no right of entry to the village. The local NPCs don't want to know you anymore.

Oh. This looked like a far cry from my original plan.

Which had been so nice and simple: to perform a quest chain issued by the Sarge and other NPCs, earning XP and Reputation in the process. *Then* the Sarge would have issued me one last quest: to mop up the Fort which was the location's only instance. Every villager would have given me a bonus item to use while their leader would have wished me luck in my endeavor — the wish which was in fact a Life-restoring buff.

Now I could forget all of that. All thanks to some greedy PKs.

If the truth were known, I'd have long abandoned my old plans and sweet-talking the local NPCs. I'd have found myself an island as far from here as possible and done my farming bit there, leveling up slowly but surely. Unfortunately, there was a problem. In order to leave the Isles, I had to complete the instance — and the Sarge was the one who issued this quest. One of the rewards for smoking the lich was a single-use portal scroll allowing you to port to any location on the continent, with the exception of its capital city.

And the lich in question was none other than the wizard from the Sarge's scary tale. The one who'd lured part of the garrison out only to return as a walking dead — or rather, a lich.

Some people had really sick imaginations. Liches, zombies... It made me feel hopelessly dated.

While I'd been reading up on two ways of getting the quest, I'd also researched the various ways of completing the instance. Compared to Spider Grotto it was nothing special. This was a newb location, after all.

The instance's main (and most unpleasant) feature was that the mobs' levels, including the lich himself, could change depending on the player's own. This was the developers' way of evening up the odds.

The instance consisted of four rooms: the gym, the kitchen, the dorm and the main hall now inhabited by the Fort's new owner. In order to simplify the task for the newbs, the lich was made vulnerable to physical damage. In other words, in order to release his soul, you only had to destroy his body. Easier said than done.

Predictably, all the rooms and corridors were packed with all sorts of undead critters. There were some pleasant surprises there, too, like treasure stashes.

As for the strategy and tactics... they weren't as straightforward. Ideally, you would do it in a group of five. But seeing as I was alone, I'd have to go there on my own. Never mind. I had a few surprises for the undead army.

I walked out of the village without looking

back. I wasn't ever going to return. I didn't feel too sorry about my failure to complete the "proper" quest chain. The more time I spent in the game, the better I was beginning to realize that not all was going hunky-dory in Mirror World. Not for me, anyway.

* * *

The Fort was situated on the central island, the largest of them all. I'd done a bit of research on it even though I'd never actually seen any images. Which I should have done.

As Boris approached the island, I expected to see some semblance of a village: a rotting stockade, listing watchtowers, that sort of thing.

Nothing of the kind.

When the gray rain clouds parted, revealing the looming outline of stone towers and narrow arrowslits, I nearly jumped. For a moment I thought that my satnav had taken me back to the Citadel. The resemblance was striking.

Actually, it was logical. Both fortresses had been built by one and the same architect. I'd forgotten all about it.

I stroked Boris' neck. "Don't land yet," I whispered in his ear. "Make a few more circles over the fortress first. We need to take a good look at it."

And the place was an eyeful, I tell you. Four giant bastions encircled by tall stone walls and a deep moat.

Everywhere you looked, you saw signs of desolation. Oh. This wasn't the Citadel with its host of players performing cleaning and maintenance jobs as part of their social quests.

"Now, kiddo, let's land somewhere nice and quiet. Next to those trees over there, okay?"

Boris spread his wings wide and glided down. Slingshot at the ready, I turned my head like an owl, ready to tell Boris to climb back up at any moment.

We landed without a problem. Big sigh of relief. We were no more than thirty paces away from the drawbridge.

I gave myself five minutes to take in the surroundings. Silence. Not a living soul in sight. I found it rather symbolical.

The rain grew stronger. Black clouds blotted out the sky. Large raindrops pelted the wooden parapet covers which had once been used to protect the Fort's still-living defenders.

Spooky.

This was a dead fortress.

A dead place.

I'd better walk to the gate alone. I deactivated the summoning charms. Before disappearing, both my pets cast me disappointed looks.

They were worse than children, really.

The road toward the Fort was paved with large rough cobblestones. Either Zeddekey had been stingy with building materials or the road had been built after him. Patches of grass peeked through the stones. The track was dirty and abandoned.

What a strange feeling. As I walked toward the

Fort, I got the impression that the walls themselves were moving toward me, trying to devour a humble traveler. The gloomy creation of the famous architect was both amazing and scary in its boundless strength. I could only imagine what soldiers must have felt, about to storm these impervious walls. Had they been scared? Disheartened? Had they realized they couldn't possibly defeat it? A little bit of all three, I suppose. That was another thing that made Zeddekey so good. The Fort's sheer sight was enough to discourage any advancing army.

I froze, admiring the ancient master's work. How many places like this one would I visit in Mirror World? And this was only a newb location!

Here is was, Zeddekey's magic, in all its glory.

Cheer up, Olgerd, old man. Not the first time.

"Awesome, eh?"

A calm voice behind my back was tinged with emotion. I swung round.

Instinctively my left hand closed around the slingshot while my right one pulled the pouch taut. Was it a new knee-jerk reflex that I'd begun to develop? Was the bespectacled nerd finally changing? Or was it a side effect of my 72-hour non-stop farming session?

Very possible.

"Sorry, man. I didn't mean to frighten you."

A player stood on the road just a few paces away from me.

Name: Vitar
Level 11

Race: Human

He raised his hands in the air in a conciliatory gesture. His arms shook with the cold rain. He only had starting pants on.

His blue eyes betrayed a mixture of compassion and curiosity. I bet. A slingshot wasn't something they saw here often. Still, he kept his hands raised, apparently knowing that there was no such thing in Mirror World as a harmless weapon.

I gave him a quick once-over, then switched my attention to the area around him.

He must have understood because he hurried to add, "It's all right, don't worry. I'm here on my own. There's no danger. And as for me..."

He spread his arms wide and turned about, splashing his bare feet through the mud, to show me he had no weapons on him. "You see, Sir Olgerd? I'm not your enemy. I hate violence, anyway."

"You'll have to excuse me too," I said, putting the slingshot away. "This place is spooky. You need to understand..."

"Absolutely," he said, lowering his shaking hands. "It was my fault. I should have made my presence known before addressing you."

He walked over to me and offered his hand. "Vitar."

"Olgerd," I answered his handshake. Our eyes met.

Wait! This was... oh no. I was too late, wasn't I? The wizzy! They'd ripped him off, after all. Bastards!

He must have read something in my stare

because he shrank back. "Everything all right?" he asked warily.

"Yeah, sure," I hurried to reassure him. "Did I frighten you too? Makes two of us, I suppose!"

He smiled cautiously. "You had this face..."

"Probably. For a moment, I thought I'd met you before. Only..." I made a show of looking him over.

"Of course! Only I was dressed then, is that what you mean?"

"Dressed as a fisherman."

"Exactly! And," he raised a meaningful finger, "I was wearing that stupid wizard's hat!"

I chuckled. "You said it. Who am I to argue?"

He burst into a cheerful loud laughter. It looked like I'd finally met someone normal. We might make a good team, you never know.

He must have misunderstood my stare as he hurried to explain, "Yes, yes, I'm dead broke. This is what happens when you become too full of yourself."

I frowned. "What do you mean?"

"Well," he said, even more humiliated, "I'm talking about my gear."

"I understand that," I hurried to add. "But you also said something about being too full of yourself."

"That's right," he nodded. "And might I add, I was also stupid and impatient. How can I tell you... Today I finally made level 10. And once I distributed all the new stat points, I really felt like I was some kind of Superman. The old location wasn't good enough for me anymore. So I came here and started smoking stronger mobs in my eternal wisdom. I even made another level but... I didn't even have time to celebrate the fact."

"Your quarry struck back," I concluded.

He sighed and scratched his rain-soaked head. I struggled not to laugh.

What a relief. I'd really thought that those village PKs had fleeced him. I'd even suffered a guilt trip for not having warned him when I could.

"I'll t-t-tell you m-m-more," he said, his teeth chattering, "I've b-b-been eaten th-three t-t-times... by the same m-m-monster..."

"What do you mean, by the same monster?"

"Th-thing was, the f-f-first time I di-died I was within the mob's aggro z-z-zone... and every time I re-resurrected, I tried to get to the chest with my stuff... But un-fortunately, he always g-g-gets to it first..."

"I see."

I made a mental note. This was a good lesson. At least I had Boris and Prankster who could distract any monster. Now Vitar, he hadn't been so lucky. It was pretty stupid of him to have ventured into the wilderness all on his own. At least he seemed to realize that now.

"D-d-dear Olgerd," the guy sounded embarrassed. "I wonder if you might have a bit of time for me? The monster I'm talking about, he was only level 12. We can do him easily between the two of us. You're a Godsend. I will reimburse you in full, I assure you. My stuff is very expensive. I'd hate to lose it. It cost me really a lot... I took out a loan to get it..."

I fingered my beard, thinking. All these extra adventures were the last thing I needed. On the other hand, how could I leave him without help? Okay, he'd been a bit greedy and paid for it — but he'd learned from his mistakes. I couldn't just turn round and leave him to his misery, could I?

I made up my mind. "What kind of mob is it?"

"It's an Armor-Faced Copperhead!" Vitar exclaimed, relieved. "Level 12! Between the two of us, we won't even feel it! He's nothing against us two!"

He cheered up, apparently reading my determination, very nearly pulling me into the forest by the sleeve.

"Wait a bit," I chilled him down. "I haven't agreed to it yet."

He kept grinning, knowing I wasn't going to let him down.

I ran a quick check of the bestiary. That's right. An Armor-Faced Copperhead, level 12. A fifteen-foot snake. Its abilities included a Venomous Bite: a nasty debuff aiming to gradually reduce the player's Life. I could actually try and smoke it. If push came to shove, I could always summon Boris.

I nodded. "All right. I'm gonna help you. Only let's make it quick. I've got lots of things to do. Where is it?"

Vitar very nearly jumped with joy. "Excellent! I'll owe you! It's over there..." he darted into the forest, showing me the way.

Darted was an overstatement, what with his starting clothes and all. Still, he moved much faster than I ever would in that kind of "gear". Apparently, being a Fisherman, he'd been leveling up Speed.

"Follow me!" he shouted, parting the undergrowth with his hands. "Follow me! It's right

___

over there!"

What's with all the shouting? Didn't he realize he'd attract all the snakes in the area? He must have gone slightly off his trolley with joy.

His bare back zigzagged in front of me. I had no problem keeping up with him but he barged on so recklessly that I began to lag behind. Soon he disappeared amid the greenery.

Following the sound of his voice, I leapt across a dirty puddle of water, ducked a bramble's greedy branches and promptly avoided the sharp bone-like limbs of a rain-drenched tree that resembled a fish skeleton.

Finally I reached a gap in the undergrowth where he'd disappeared only moments ago. I ducked in.

"I'm here!" he hollered at the top of his voice.

What was wrong with him? No, my first impression of him might have been totally wrong. I'd help him now quickly, then I'd be on my way. He was way too loud.

The first thing I noticed when I ran out into the clearing was the sheer number of chests lying in the grass. I saw at least five of them.

Vitar's behavior was strange, too. He stood at the other end of the clearing with his back to me — still hollering, telling all the forest that he was here.

And where was his mob?

I was about to ask when my body rose into the air, as if I was a fly stuck in some invisible jelly.

The system message descended on me like a ton of bricks:

Warning! Player Spitfire has cast a spell on you: Air Web!
Effect: You're immobilized
Duration: 15 sec

My attempt to open the inventory failed miserably. The summoning charms were also unavailable. How on earth had I managed to get into this?!

In the meantime, two more figures materialized at the center of the clearing.

Their name tags were red. Class: Robbers. Both were Alves. Both levels 20+. Nicknames: Sting and Gray.

My desperate attempt to struggle free proved pointless. That was it, then. As that guy in the Bible had said, "What I feared has come upon me".

I wanted to warn the wizzy and tell him to run when Gray's angry shout made me choke on my words.

"Vitar, you idiot! Shut up!"

Vitar swung round and dropped to his knees, whining, "Guys, please! You promised! You said you'd give me everything back! I did bring him to you, didn't I? Please!"

"Shut your filthy mouth," a third voice barked from behind my back. "What a pain in the ass."

"Spitfire, I want you to refresh the spell," the same voice ordered. "I don't feel like chasing him around the woods."

"It's all right, Boss," an invisible female voice replied from my right. "It's all under control. We still have a few seconds."

"Refresh it, I said! I need a word with him."

Warning! Player Spitfire has cast a spell on you: Air Web!
Effect: You're immobilized
Duration: 15 sec

Dammit! Just when I was readying myself to make a dart for the undergrowth.

Heavy squelching footsteps approached me from my right. The huge fanged head of a Rhoggh loomed up before me. His deeply set bestial eyes studied me as if I was his property. His wide jaws stretched in a grin, exposing two rows of sharp teeth.

Oh wow. Level 32! For a moment I'd forgotten my desperate situation. How long had he spent in this location? What kind of mobs had he used to level up?

His nickname — Gloom — glowed a fiery red.

"Just look at this nice juicy dude!" he barked.

"What do you want?" I asked. How very smart of me. I'm a master of the stupid question.

"What do I want?" he asked with theatrical surprise. "Same as everybody else, I suppose. To love and be loved!"

Sting and Gray guffawed.

"Now listen, Digger," the gang's leader said. "When you come round and get some loot together, come and see me. Off you go."

The last thing I felt before the lights went out was a huge bone hammer landing on top of my head.

Chapter Eight

"I'm an idiot! I should have known!" I circled my little room under Dmitry's watchful stare following me from the computer screen. "Who did I think I was — Mr. Smartass? My prided paranoia was having a day off! Why didn't it set my alarm bells ringing? I followed that wizzy through the forest without a single thought! Was I deaf and blind or something? He wasn't just yelling — he was calling his masters!"

"This is funny," my brother added calmly, offering his two cents. "They weren't expecting *you*, were they? They couldn't have been so smart as to calculate the exact time of your landing."

"Calculate, yeah right," I grumbled, slumping back into the chair. "No one could do that."

He nodded. "Exactly. They just chose a nice secluded clearing, sent their agents out in every direction and sat there waiting new..."

"New idiots?" I finished his phrase for him.

"Like myself, is that it? Just think that I spent all that time hiding and watching my own back, and what for? They've fleeced me like the proverbial lamb! Just because I felt responsible — for whom? Someone I didn't even know! He didn't give a damn about me and my problems! He couldn't care less about how *I* felt!"

New thoughts arrived one after the other, tearing my brain apart.

Dmitry maintained a tactful silence, allowing me to get it off my chest.

"The loss of all the expensive gear is only half the problem," I jumped back to my feet and resumed my pacing of the room. "I can't really blame Vitar or the robbers, either. The way they make their living in the game reflects their human nature, that's it. May God judge them. It doesn't mean I'm trying to justify their actions — they're lowlifes, as simple as that. But that's not the point. I'm angry with myself! How stupid. I should have smelled a rat. Now I've lost all that time."

Dmitry still didn't say anything. He opened a new pack of cigarettes and clicked a lighter. He didn't even look at me. Actually, I got the impression he wasn't even listening to me.

Strangely enough, his behavior had curbed my bout of hysterics. My anger began to subside, replaced by a peculiar peaceful feeling which I later recognized as apathy.

I slumped into the chair and closed my eyes.

His voice came after a pause. "Better now?"

I opened my eyes. "I think so."

"Good," he let out a puff of blue smoke. "Keep your hair on. You're not the first one and you're definitely not the last. Everyone goes through this, especially at lower levels. Some people die several times a day, losing everything they have. So what? You get up, wipe away the snot and keep going."

"What doesn't kill you makes you stronger," I repeated the Glasshouse's unofficial motto.

"Exactly. You're mad now but later you'll agree with me."

He stubbed out the cigarette. "It may sound trite but Mirror World adverts don't lie when they promise 'boundless opportunities to everyone'," he said with a sarcastic smile. "The game rules form a new behavioral model. Who are you in the real world? A skinny bespectacled nerd. Every bully can kick your butt without even noticing it. Any attempts to stand up for yourself — and you will try, I know you — might have negative consequences for your own body. The scope of your injuries will only depend on your opponent's weight class."

"What are you driving at?"

"I'll tell you now. Had your own level been closer to 25, to say nothing of your two pets, this PK encounter might have had a totally different outcome. And one more thing..."

He sat up and laid both his hands onto the table, which made him resemble Dad even more. "Your main mistake was, you were considering yourself small fry in this boundless virtual ocean. You were constantly on high alert for predators' attacks, forgetting that you too can grow a set of teeth. Your idea of 'quiet inconspicuous farming' was doomed from the start. You're being pulled into a powerful whirlpool of events; being passive just won't cut it. It's survival of the fittest out there. The sooner you realize it and, most importantly, the sooner you accept it, the faster you'll adapt to this new environment."

He leaned closer to the screen. "Listen, brother. You need to understand. You're not a Grinder anymore. You're a warrior. So behave like one."

"Warrior, yeah right."

"Cut out the sarcasm, will you? You know very well that I'm right."

He was. I had nothing to say to that.

Dmitry must have understood me. He cut his preaching short and moved on to the business at hand, "Have they taken everything *everything*? What have you got left?"

"Only my bag. And the Monks loot. I have the beads and some pebbles. That's all, I think."

"Gold?"

"They took the obligatory 1% of the money in my purse. I only had thirty gold there so it's peanuts. The rest of the money is in the bank. All the quest items and no-drops are with me. The slingshot, too."

"Lost a lot of XP?"

"Not really."

He nodded. "Normal. You and this Gloom guy have a big level gap."

"How did he do it, by the way?" I asked.

"By smoking Stompers, probably," Dmitry replied. "Or whatever. Lots of weird monsters out there. The location's bestiary is long out of date. The developers need to test new mobs somewhere so they keep adding occasional surprises for the newbs. But I don't think there's anything above level 30 there. The developers can't overrun the location's restrictions. How are your stats, actually?"

I shook my head. "So-so. Threes and fours mainly."

"Call it a C-student, not bad," he grinned. "Never mind. It'll all come back. You have your pets, that's the main thing. Have you decided what to do next?"

I rubbed my forehead. Then rearranged my glasses. "Nothing's changed, really. I need to do the instance. Luckily, there's no deadline. No one's gonna be in the way there. It might take longer, that's all."

"Good decision. You'll level up a bit and get some practice. You need to get the hang of your pets in combat too. Zombies are not the same as crabs. They won't stand in one place snapping their claws."

"I know," I mumbled. "Some newb location this is!"

He smirked. "You don't know the half of it yet."

I grinned back. The day's pressure seemed to have gradually subsided, all thanks to his natural positivity.

"One more thing," I said. "Please not a word of this to Sveta."

He nodded. "That goes without saying."

"And... I might need to stay virtual for a couple of days."

"If you say so."

I thought he might object. But he must have

realized that time was an issue.

I smiled. "See you, then."

"Good luck."

* * *

Two hours and a long conversation with Sveta later, I walked downstairs to my capsule.

Sergei the module controller seemed happy to see me. "Good evening, Oleg!"

"Hi."

"We received a message from you an hour ago saying you're in for an extended immersion."

"That's right."

"For how long?"

"Depends. At least a couple of days. Maybe three."

"I see," he nodded. "Then I have to ask you to come here first," he pointed at a white chair. "We'll fit you out with a catheter. Doctor's orders. He's prescribed you some vitamins and minerals in case of extended immersions."

Five minutes later, I was already lying in the capsule watching the lid of my "coffin" lowering slowly.

Darkness enveloped me.

Enter

The first thing I saw when they switched the

lights back on was the gray rocky beach of Crab Island. This was the game's resurrection point choice for me.

It was probably for the better. Good job I hadn't had the time to switch my resurrection point to the Fort. This place was nice and quiet — and it abounded with ammo. Which was an important thing indeed.

Rain pelted my bare back and shoulders. I still could sense some pressure weighing me down but way less than on my first day here. Level 12 began to show.

I did a quick check of my inventory, with a cooler head this time.

All I had left in my bag were the steel beads, a handful of pebbles and a few vials containing Monk slime and venom. The system's consolation gift. I gave a nervous shrug. All my hard-earned stuff and gear was gone — probably already shared between Gloom's gangsters.

I slumped to the ground. Immediately, the cold stone began to siphon whatever leftover warmth I still had in my body.

With the loss of my clothes, this had become a totally different ball game. Plus I couldn't buy anything from the warehouse keeper: the alternative quest branch had taken care of that. I wasn't welcome in the village anymore.

I could ask Dreadlock to sell me something but I had a funny feeling he had more important problems. When I'd hung suspended in the air, I'd managed to get a glimpse of the name tags on the other chests. Dreadlock's was there too. The robbers must have smoked his group minutes before my illustrious arrival. I should send him word anyway, but not now.

Trying to find a vendor among other players was a chancy and not particularly clever option.

One solution was to enter the instance and get some clothes there.

Now, my stats.

Protection, Speed and Health had 4 pt. each. Stamina and Strength, 3 each. Intellect: 2 pt. Not much, really. Almost the same as I'd had at the start of my first immersion. Once again I'd turned into a clumsy blob of flesh.

I used Health to bring Life up to 120. Energy was what really worried me. I only had 100 pt. left. I might need to "unplug" Prankster and switch him to autonomy mode, raising his Stamina. Luckily, he had 5 available points after having made level 10.

So I did. My little Grison was a free spirit now! Funny really: his Energy bar had 30 pt. more than that of his master. Me, I didn't even have my starting clothes: the rain had ruined them when I'd been busy doing level 8.

Seeing as my Stamina left much to be desired, I might have to wait before applying new Bind Lines onto pebbles. Every step of it took half of whatever meager Energy reserves I now had. Never mind. Single-use pebbles would do nicely for a start. Those by the water's edge were actually the best, almost uniform and just the right size.

That's sorted, then. I walked toward the ocean

gingerly, trying not to cut my bare feet on the rocks. It was remarkably quiet, the rustle of the rain the only sound I could hear.

A vicious-looking Ennan stared back at me from the water's rippling surface. What a sight. My beard stood on end, my hair so scraggly that a sea bird could make a nest in it.

My reflection curved its lips in a smirk. How funny. When I'd looked at it right now, this was exactly what I'd expected to see. Not the respectable citizen Oleg Ivanenko whom I'd seen in the mirror countless times before, but Olgerd the Ennan.

Chapter Nine

"Well, guys? Second time lucky?" I murmured, peering at where the drawbridge was supposed to be.

Boris shook like a dog by way of an answer, showering me with cold drizzle. All I could do was grin and bear it. It was so incredibly cold! My brain was seriously playing up. How could I convince my little gray cells that a bare-chested man pelted by the freezing rain and staggering under the tree-bending wind in the middle of the pitch-black night is actually warm and comfortable?

The night was indeed dark. Even with my famed Ennan eyesight I couldn't see much at all. Which was actually a good thing.

"Never mind. No good standing here chattering our teeth, is it? Let's do it!"

Boris couldn't agree more. The apprehension of combat made him tense up. He'd grown considerably: his Health was up 5 pt. and Satiety, 500. Besides,

~ 133 ~

every new level gave him +2 to Damage. So basically, he was our main hope now.

I gingerly rearranged my backpack and climbed into the saddle. "Off we go, kiddo. Just be gentle."

Softly like a cat he slid out of the undergrowth and darted for the drawbridge in long rapid leaps.

My slingshot was ready. I'd spent the last two hours collecting new pebbles on the beach.

The dark outline of the fortress loomed out of the darkness, its rusted portcullis grinning at me.

Whoever designed this stone monster was a genius. It really got to you.

As we were crossing the bridge, a new system message popped up,

Warning! This location can be too dangerous for players of your level! Solo players are advised to abstain from visiting the Fort.

I ignored it. As we approached the portcullis, another message appeared,

We strongly suggest you make the Fort your new resurrection point. Accept: Yes/No
Once you enter the instance, no other player can do the same unless he or she is a member of your group.

I clicked *Yes*.

There was no deadline for storming the fortress. I had all the time in the world. Also, the Fort defenders' levels were supposed to adjust to that of the player. Forums kept warning against some very nasty abilities the Lich received on reaching level 30. The loot was worth it, of course, but all the combat expenses might not be worth it.

I reread the Welcome message, simply to work up the nerve by reminding myself that this was still a game. The place was just too believable and spooky.

Never mind. Off we go!

I ducked under the half-lowered portcullis and stepped in. Then I stopped, allowing my eyes to adjust to the dark.

I stood in a long stone corridor. Narrow arrowslits lined the walls high overhead. I just hoped that a company of archers wasn't the Lich's first surprise.

I knew very little about fortifications — if the truth were known, I knew nothing at all. Still, a long-forgotten word had escaped the recesses of my teenage memories. Was it berbekin? Or barbican? Something like that.

The floor by the walls was littered with heaped-up rags.

I took a better look.

Nothing special. Just some useless stage props. I shouldn't expect anything of interest to happen straight away.

I kept going.

It was probably time to let Prankster out. It was more fun with the three of us.

He appeared in his signature lightning-bolt style. Was it my imagination or had my little four-legged friend grown a little? Then again, what's so surprising? He was level 10 already, after all.

Prankster didn't seem to like it here, either. His little nose was twitching, sniffing the air. He kept close to Boris without venturing too far on his own.

Finally the corridor ended, blocked with what looked like some steel bars ripped to pieces. The splintered halves of the fat door were shattered.

According to the Sarge, the wizard had been instrumental to the successful storming of the fortress. Which meant that he was responsible for all this mess. And in order to get back from the Isles, I was supposed to defeat him! Judging by the havoc he'd wreaked, I had my work cut out for me.

We cautiously threaded our way amid chunks of stone, door boards black with age and rusty fragments of the bars. Finally the corridor ended.

What did we have here? A small inner yard surrounded by tall walls. It felt a bit like sitting in a well.

Which meant that if any potential attackers successfully completed the corridor, their troubles weren't yet over. They entered this "stone well" where they were showered with arrows, rocks and other unpleasant surprises.

Having said that, hadn't our ancestors stormed fortresses just like this one with only a sword and shield? I could only envy their fearless spirit.

Boris growled, distracting me. I swung round. Aha. The first inhabitant of this giant graveyard.

A huge pile of rags lying by the opposite wall shifted.

My two group members took up their positions.

Boris stepped forward; Prankster moved to my right, ready to heal me whenever necessary. I strung my sling taut and stepped back.

In the meantime, this unknown and admittedly slow enemy had finally scrambled out of his hole. His hiding place was comprised of all kinds of junk: rotting leaves and smelly straw, pieces of tattered clothing and bones picked clean.

Finally he stood up to his full height.

Oh well. What a creature. Had I mentioned archers? Well, he was one, as large as life and twice as ugly.

The system, however, had its own name for him,

Name: a Walking Skeleton
Level: 12

Very well. As an archer, he wasn't really dangerous. Unless of course he could shoot his stringless bow one-handed.

Bits of tattered clothing still clung to his ribs and legs. An empty quiver dangled behind his back. The remaining piece of bowstring was caught on the bones of his right hand, the bow itself dragging along the ground behind him.

His eye sockets glowed with darkness. It reached deep into your heart, trying to break you, subjugate and enslave you.

Spooky.

The skeleton had already covered half the distance toward me.

"Boris, attack!"

In one smooth motion (practiced to perfection on the crabs), Boris soared several feet into the air, then dove onto the enemy. He nailed the undead to the ground and tore his skull apart in a few strokes of his powerful beak.

Congratulations!
We thank you, Sir Olgerd, for releasing the soul trapped in this poor body by ancient witchcraft!

That was it. I hadn't even had a chance to use my slingshot.

I gave Boris a slap on his back (he looked terribly pleased with himself) and bent over the pile of bones that the monster had left behind.

Not much.

Six arrowheads: four armor-piercing, two more for hunting. In my bag you go.

Next.

A copper ring with +3 to Speed. Hopelessly oxidized, with only 5 Durability left. Will do.

I slid the ring on my finger. Good enough. My Speed had promptly risen. 7 points, not bad!

That was the extent of it. Having said that, this was only the beginning.

My first opponent had died too quickly. It's true that the memory of his dead stare still gave me goosebumps but I'd admittedly expected something bigger. Even crabs had lasted longer. This skeleton must have been the developers' way of saying hello.

We crossed the inner yard without further ado.

Finally we entered the corridor leading to the gym. It was considerably lighter here. Which I suppose was good news.

Long-expired torches lined the walls. Cobwebs everywhere. The floor was littered with human bones and the omnipresent heaps of rotting leaves.

Nothing useful here.

The corridor took a slight curve. There I noticed a familiar heap of rags and other junk.

Another skeleton. No: two of them. They began moving in our direction, both just as slow as the first one.

"Boris — attack!"

He went for them head-on, scattering them like a bunch of bowling pins. By the time they had scrambled back to their feet and turned to face their attacker, I'd shot them calmly in the back. Boris had dealt them so much damage that I ran no risk of pulling aggro to myself. Which was exactly what we needed. Neither skeleton survived his second attack.

I checked whatever meager loot they had to offer.

Judging by the slowly disappearing scraps of military fatigues, these too used to be archers. They must have been the first to confront the undead attackers — only to add to the Lich's zombie army.

> *You've received:*
> *A Rusty Dagger, 1*
> *A Copper Ring, 1*
> *Arrowheads, 2*

Aha. My first close-combat weapon. The dagger's hilt was made of a rough piece of wood. Honestly, it looked like a kitchen knife — but it lay nicely in the hand. Its blunt leaf-shaped blade was encrusted with brown rust. Judging by all the notches and the porousness of the metal, its quality left much to be desired. Its Durability was a meager 7 points. Damage, however, was quite decent: 12 pt. In any case, now I had something to defend myself with if needs be.

The second copper ring added another 3 pt. to my Speed.

Loot was loot. Even if it would cost nothing at auction, at the moment every extra point to my stats was more than welcome.

We moved on.

The corridor seemed to go on forever. Another thirty feet, and more familiar outlines appeared from around the bend.

Two skeletons. No, not two... dammit! Four of the wretched things!

They walked toward me, swaying and shuffling their feet. Also archers. The last one held an intact bow in his left hand. This guy was our priority.

"Boris, we need to be careful. These guys are quite alert. And there's a whole lot of them."

We were going to repeat the already-tested scheme, adjusting it to suit the opponents' numbers. Boris would deal the first hit and move ahead in order to make the enemy turn their backs to us.

I cast a quick glance at my two pets.

Just look at those predators! Their eyes glowed

with excitement, their fur bristling, their tails swishing impatiently.

"Now!"

Boris leapt forward, knocking down two of the undead and sending a third one flying against the wall in one powerful sweep of his paw. The remaining archer slowly raised his bow. Luckily, it was just another stage prop — I could see neither arrows nor a quiver on him.

With a dull pop a pebble hit his right eye socket, razing half his skull.

You've dealt a critical hit!

I didn't expect what happened next. All right, so I was an idiot. I'd pulled aggro to myself, hadn't I?

I'd managed to strip him of some Health but that was way not enough. Boris in front was doing his best to distract the rest of the group. If I told him to come back, he'd bring them all to me.

Unexpectedly the archer began to walk faster. Not too fast, but he was definitely speedier than his buddies.

I promptly retreated. "You stay out of it," I told Prankster. "Only heal me if my Life drops to 70%."

70% was precarious enough. I didn't have much Life as it was.

My virtual heart was thumping, rapidly losing Energy.

What a stupid, unforgivable blunder!

Disregarding the pebbles, I reached for the first bead and lay it into the sling. Time to give it my all.

The sling popped. Another crit! Still not enough. The dead archer kept coming on to me. Darkness glowed in his only remaining eye, burning a hole in me. No good me lying to you: I was scared.

Mechanically I stepped back again, all the while realizing that the more I retreated the less damage I'd deal. But I just couldn't overcome my fear. Damn those game developers!

I took aim and released the sling. With the sound of crunching bone, the bead sank into his left shoulder, sending his bow-wielding arm flying through the air. Despite the loss, he kept coming. Was it my imagination or was his black glare glowing with ever more spite?

Somewhere in the dark in front of me, I could hear the snapping of bones and Boris' growling. It looked like he was busy right now.

Prankster hissed and hugged the ground.

"Don't even think of it," I told him, pulling the sling again. If I retreated any further, this battle would take ages.

I had to get a grip. These were only bits of program code. Believable artwork, nothing more. Nothing to fear. No need to retreat.

The distance between us kept shrinking. As if realizing I wasn't trying to run anymore, the archer walked ever faster.

Eight paces left.

Six.

Four.

I released the sling.

I hit him on the collarbone. Another crit sent

his Life into the red.

The hit was so powerful it swung him around, giving me time to fire again.

You've killed a level-12 Walking Skeleton!

My legs were shaking. My pulse was racing. I'd made it! With my miserable Life reading, the skeleton could have smoked me with one blow, sending me back to my resurrection point.

I'd have loved to have taken a short breather but I couldn't. I had to help Boris.

I ran around the bend and stopped. What a relief. Two of the skeletons were already vanishing into nothing while the third one was lying with his belly on the floor, struggling, while Boris sat astride him, methodically taking his victim apart bone by bone.

Soon he was trotting toward me, looking terribly pleased with himself.

"What took you so long?" I joked, then slid down the wall. "Enough. Time to take a break."

Chapter Ten

Dmitry had been right. Fighting even the weakest of skeletons was a huge learning curve compared to smoking Crab Island mobs. I'd learned more about combat tactics within an hour that I had in forty-eight hours of farming crab meat.

If I'd thought that I'd provided for any eventuality, I'd have been sadly mistaken. The gameplay gave me a good shaking as if I were a guilty puppy. I'd shot too soon, pulled aggro to myself and very nearly kicked the bucket as a result. My plan had been good; problem was, the big strategist who'd authored it had made a complete idiot of himself. It was a good job those skeletons were weak and awkward: had my first opponents been faster or higher in levels, I'd have been unlikely to escape with my life.

Never mind. Lesson learned. Shame about the beads' precious Durability, though. Wasting them so stupidly!

Now, the loot.

My skeleton had left, apart from the memories of our unforgettable encounter, only a bundle of bowstrings. Boris' opponents proved to be more generous.

You've received:
An Old Bracer, 1
A Copper Bracelet, 1
Arrowheads, 5
A Ragged Hood of an Archer, 1

No idea how other players might have reacted to this kind of loot, but in my situation it felt like Christmas.

Excited as a child, I picked the items up one by one, looking them over. I might have looked like a tramp who'd been rummaging through the local garbage dump, but this was my very own little victory.

This was what I liked about Mirror World. Everything here had a reason. In the real world, a rag was a rag; here, this tattered "Hood of an Archer" gave me +2 to Health. The bracer, this moldy piece of leather protecting my forearm from the chafing of the bowstring, added +5 to Protection while the oxidized strip of copper they had the audacity to call a "bracelet" boasted +2 to Stamina. Things were definitely looking up.

My possessions were growing while also improving my stats. This was a far cry from my Reflection kit but after all, this was only the beginning.

I put my new items on and sprang to my feet. The extra 40 Energy inspired me to battle on. My pets' eyes were laughing. I looked a sight, I had to agree.

Off we go, then! Big deeds await us!

Yet another bend finally took us out to the exit. I could see more staggering silhouettes in the light of the doorway. The last Rubicon. Beyond it lay the gym.

"Stay cool, guys," I whispered. "We're in no hurry."

The place was taken up by piled-up barrels, crates and pieces of crude furniture the Fort's defenders must have used to barricade themselves with. Judging by all the heaps of bones, skulls and rotting scraps of military gear, this "Rubicon" had cost the invaders dearly.

So much stuff! Unfortunately, these too were stage props. Nothing I could use.

I ducked in and began moving in short sprints from one pile to the next toward the doorway. My pets followed noiselessly.

I stopped next to a towering pile of boards which must have once been a farm wagon. It provided a perfect shelter from the undead ambling aimlessly in front of it.

Only two of them. Barely a mouthful for my Boris. Still, the doorway opened into the gym. The sounds of the melee were almost sure to attract more zombies.

Which meant we had to repeat our Diadem Serpent tactics.

I waited until the two zombies parted ways,

then signaled to Prankster. He darted toward the nearest skeleton, sank his teeth into his bony leg, then dashed back to us.

Just as I expected, the other skeleton continued sashaying toward the opposite wall without aggroing us. The moment he approached our makeshift barricade, Boris left him no chance.

You've received:
A Torn Boot, 1
A Rusty Hammer, 1

He must have been a builder or something. The system identified the hammer as a statless tool with 12 Durability. The Boot, however, offered +2 to Stamina, thus adding another 40 to my Energy stocks.

I tossed the hammer into my bag anyway. Waste not, want not. After a short deliberation, I also pulled the boot onto my left foot. I must have looked a sight but strangely I wasn't uncomfortable. Both Boris and Prankster curiously studied my big toe peeking out of the hole.

I shrugged. "So what? At least it can breathe," then turned to Prankster, "You'd better go get us the other one."

He sniffed, as if laughing, and disappeared over the barricade. The next moment he was already back, sitting on top of the tallest pile of junk as if saying, "Here's your delivery!"

This second victory garnered us a statless Lash and a Rope Belt with +3 to Stamina. That made 10!

Judging by the items, we must have released the soul of the wagon owner.

I put on the belt — which proved to be a length of ordinary rope — and headed for the gym doorway.

A weird noise was coming from behind it. I took a few more steps and peeked cautiously in.

My heart pounded, throbbing hard in my temples. This couldn't be. At least a hundred! This was a whole army!

The forums had warned, of course, that zombies were "numerous", but this! It looked like I'd be stuck here for a while.

Right, Olgerd, quit playing the drama queen. You'd better start thinking about how to get out of this mess.

I peeked out again, more daringly this time. There seemed to be no zombies next to the doorway which allowed me to take stock of the situation in my own time.

So, what did we have? A gym, about the size of three basketball pitches. The ceiling was high but not high enough for Boris to be able to fly freely.

I shouldn't forget that he could also scale walls: our last trump card in case the going got really tough.

The exit from the gym was located in the opposite wall: a huge door with a padlock. If forums were to be believed, it was guarded by a Ghoul — the first instance boss on our way. The name said it all. By killing him, a player received, on top of the usual loot, also the key to the padlock.

How interesting. All forum members agreed that he was the worst mob in the whole Fort, all thanks to some very tricky ability he seemed to have.

The ability's name was rather unpretentious: Sacrifice.

This is how it worked. Once activated, whenever the Ghoul was in danger, all the nearby skeletons and zombies hurried to his aid. As soon as the Ghoul's Life dropped to 50%, some of the zombies sacrificed themselves, healing him back to 100%. And seeing as there were over a hundred of them here, I had no illusions about the battle's outcome.

I quickly disregarded the idea of scaling the walls on Boris' back in order to promptly get to the exit and smoke him. This Ghoul just had too much Life. And I couldn't just get to the door: I needed the key to open it.

Which brought me back to Plan A: mop up the whole room by pulling zombies in ones and twos, and only then tackle the Ghoul himself.

I had my work cut out for me, didn't I?

The gym was divided into four sectors. I was in the first one, the nearest to the doorway. It resembled a riding ring — which it probably once had been.

Two more sectors ran parallel to each other, crowded with what looked like gym equipment and practice dummies.

Finally, the fourth sector was the smallest and the most dangerous one: a small corridor opposite, leading to the door and the Ghoul who guarded it.

Judging by all this, I had to admit that this creation of Zeddekey didn't at all look like an insignificant fortification on a God-forsaken island. Some of the richest land owners in Mirror World would have paid a lot of money for the right to own a stronghold like this. I had the impression that the game management had their own far-reaching plans for this location.

Let's start with the riding ring, then.

I surmised that the major part of the Ghoul's army was located there. They were the most numerous but luckily also the weakest. It consisted mainly of walking skeletons who must have once been the Fort's defenders.

"Your turn, Prankie," I whispered, stepping back toward the barricade.

Keeping in the shadows, Prankster darted toward the nearest group of two zombies who stood slightly aside from the rest. Judging by the broom and spade they were holding, they must once have been the local janitors. Had I not known I was inside a zombie fortress, I might have thought they were having a smoke break, talking unhurriedly. All that was missing was whiffs of cigarette smoke and the bored shuffling of feet.

Then they aggroed Prankie, shattering my mental image. Instead of friendly janitors, two decomposed corpses staggered toward me, contorting their gnarly bodies.

As soon as they approached the barricade, Boris attacked them. Soon I was already picking up the scarce loot. Both the broom and the spade were statless tools with very low Durability. The sheer numbers of undead workers must have been the developers' gift to new players planning to level up certain professions. I wouldn't be surprised if I came across a fellow Digger soon.

But a broom and spade? Even a hoarder like myself didn't need them. Then again, I had enough spare slots in my bag. In they go. The sweeper's canvas pants and the digger's dirty boot were a welcome gift, however: together they brought my Stamina up another 6 pt.

"Prankie, now bring us those three guys over there. We have a lot of work to do..."

Chapter Eleven

Congratulations! You've received a new level!
Current level: 17
Reward: +1 to Knowledge
Current Knowledge: 60/60

Finally! I could take a breather now. This had been the last skeleton group. I'd done three of the gym's sectors. All I had left to do was cross the little corridor and kill the Ghoul.

I slumped onto the gritty floor and closed my eyes. I'd been farming non-stop for a good part of nine hours.

Skeletons, loot. Skeletons, loot. More skeletons...

Actually, they hadn't been as numerous as I'd first thought. My fear must have tainted my judgment. I wasn't in the mood to open the logs but I must have smoked at least seventy or eighty.

If this was only the first stage, then it looked like I was stuck here for quite a while. Naturally, when you do it with a group of five, it doesn't take as long. Still, my solitude had its fortes which might actually outweigh the drawbacks. I was already level 17 even before I took on the Ghoul. Besides, the loot was all mine to keep. It was mainly zombie cast-offs, I agree, but nothing I couldn't use in my situation.

My earlier conjecture seemed to have been correct. Most of the skeletons had been workers of some kind. They'd dropped more tools than I could ever hope to use: I had fifteen or so hammers alone, plus several picks — of which I'd already chosen one for myself — and any number of spades, saws, hair combs, scissors, brooms, trowels, needles of every size, two fishing rods, several knives... my bag now looked as if I'd robbed a second-hand DIY store.

Some items had only 5 pt. Durability. They were of lamentable quality: rusted and pretty dented, their wooden handles cracked. The only redeeming feature they had in my eyes was the fact that they had no Profession restrictions. Anyone could use them.

Then again, was it really a redeeming feature? I somehow couldn't imagine a mine digger brandishing a pitchfork. Of which I already had three.

I was toying with the idea of getting rid of it all. Still, I had plenty of place in my bag. Store is no sore.

Some of the loot was good news. I finally got myself some clothes. It didn't matter that they were only good for the trash can: I wasn't wearing them for their style but rather for their contents: namely, their stats.

A leather pauldron and a worn gauntlet had considerably improved my Protection. Another copper bracelet and a faded shirt did the same for Stamina. A handful of copper and iron knickknacks — you couldn't in all seriousness call it jewelry — had positively affected both my Strength and Speed.

Finally, my pride and joy: a moth-eaten woolen doublet. +7 to Heath! If you didn't look too close at me, I could easily pass for a local.

When I'd made level 15, I'd received my five bonus points. I'd decided to wait before investing them into anything. I had it quite good at the moment.

Both Prankie and Boris were already level 14. One more level, and Prankster would get a new ability.

Also, I shouldn't forget that my Knowledge bar was full. Time to reopen the book and see if it had something to offer.

I hurried to pull the fat tome from the bag. Yes! Finally! Page Two wasn't dimmed anymore.

Wait. There was also a sheet of paper inside, folded in two.

The paper was yellow with time, covered in reddish brown spots. What was it doing here? It hadn't been there before!

I closed the book. My hands shook as I unfolded the paper.

Congratulations! You've found Master Brolgerd's Technical Notes.

Warning! You need to be a Mechanic to understand their meaning.

Would you like to study the notes? Yes/No.

Of course I would! What kind of question was that?

The system complied. Soon I was already perusing the ancient manuscript. It was written in a clear, neat handwriting — but judging by the sheer amount of ink spots covering it, whoever had written it was really in a hurry.

Having read a few lines, I realized that I'd been lucky enough to lay my hands on a description of some successful technical experiment.

As I read on, taking in the idea, I began to realize that Army Mechanic was the exact class someone like me needed.

By the simple method of trial and error, using various materials differing in their quality and nature and exposing them to the simultaneous effects of several Bind Lines, I have conducted the following experiment:

By taking a simple tool (the Fix Box), I applied to it three of the following high-grade Bind Lines:

Ph'av, the Binder of Facets
Ghoi, the Enhancer of Essence
Tarim, the Converter of Matter

By improving the tool, I aimed to build a mechanical creature that could function like a living

---

being. A creature like that could then be used to perform certain working functions, chores, etc.

The only person who'd have full power over such a creature would be its constructor himself. This can be achieved by creating an invisible Bind Line between the master and his creation...

As soon as I finished reading, a new system message came up,

Congratulations! You've received a new Ability: Creating a Mechanical Being.

Warning! Building a mechanical creature is a rather involved process which requires large amounts of energy as well as special materials of acceptable quality.

In view of this, we strongly recommend you abstain from activating this ability without due preparation!

All right. That much was clear. And what was on the next page?

Oh. It looked like a sectional blueprint of a mechanical beetle.

Yes! I was right!

Name: A Blueprint of a Scarab
Studying it will require 60 pt. Energy.
Would you like to study the blueprint?

Absolutely!

Congratulations! You've studied the Scarab blueprint by Master Brolgerd!
You've spent 60 pt. Energy
Current Energy: 0/60
Congratulations! You can build a Scarab now!

The message vanished. A small transparent icon appeared in the lower right corner of my control panel bearing the familiar picture of a beetle.

I opened his description.

A Scarab is the simplest mechanical being, Master Brolgerd's unique invention. Initially created to aid mine diggers lay tunnels under the Steely Mountains, the Scarab was later adapted for military purposes.
Skills:
Frontal Antler Ram Blow
Ordinary Blow
The loss of Durability triggers the Scarab's self-destruction by detonating its Energy resources.
Specifications:
The Scarab's level, Durability and Damage as well as the detonation's range are directly related to the quality and numbers of the materials used in its construction.
The Scarab's body is 100% metal.
The Scarab's builder should be prepared to share some of his Energy with it.
Tools required:
The Fix Box
Materials required: Metal

I finished reading and rubbed my tired eyes. What did they imply? I had the ability but I could only use it once I got back to the continent, was that it? Because I couldn't get the required materials anywhere here.

What a shame. Had I become a wizard, I would now be scorching my enemies with torrents of liquid fire or piercing them with arrows of ice. Instead, I was forced to stare at a useless icon of my newly-acquired skill.

"Wouldn't it be nice to add a new fighter to our group? Guys, what do you think?"

Neither Boris nor Prankster reacted to my words. Both slouched senseless at my feet, fast asleep. They were tired. They needed to replenish their energy levels before the decisive battle with the gym boss.

We'd searched the room already, checking for any secret stashes, but much to our regret found nothing at all.

The old forums said nothing about this kind of thing. No one was too forthcoming to offer any tips. Here in Mirror World, it was considered bad form to discuss stashes and hidden treasures. Everybody knew they existed but every player had to fend for him or herself.

"It's okay, guys. Sleep well. You've done a great job. I'll keep an eye on you."

It wasn't really necessary. According to the rules, the zombies could only respawn several hours after the boss' death. And it would be a good idea to put those hours to good use. You never know, all those secret treasures might reveal themselves to me during that particular period.

There were no skeletons left behind. The Ghoul's aggro zone was way out of reach. I could take a break too. Now was the perfect moment to stock up on my new improved ammo.

One of the skeletons — which must have been either a herbalist or a harvester, judging by his sickle — had dropped a necklace with +2 to Speed. This was nothing, of course, compared to my earlier trophy: a copper chain with +6 to Strength. And as according to the game's rules, I could only wear one necklace simultaneously, the latter one was at a definite disadvantage.

It was made of ten tear-shaped beads strung on a fine black thread. Its quality was immeasurably higher compared to the Swamp Monks' "jewelry" which didn't even deserve the name. This one had been made by human hand, you could see that straight away. Okay, maybe not exactly human but a sentient being's, nevertheless.

Its Durability was a meager 3 pt. Could my altering the item improve the beads' stats? I didn't care much about their shape. If you remembered the kind of boulders I'd used on the Monks...

Where was it now? Let's have a look... aha! Found it.

The necklace was heavy. Completely oxidized. The beads were massive. They were bound to improve Damage.

I studied the necklace for any obvious defects. It looked as if it had been broken quite a few times in the past, its thread all covered in knots. I wasn't a jeweler but even I could see they should have used a thicker one.

Finally I found what I'd been looking for: a loose knot, about to come undone. What if I tried to tighten it up... gently... yes!

Warning! You're trying to alter an item's nature without possessing the necessary skills, recipes or blueprints!
Probability of ruining the item: 99%.

I continued tightening the knot. It looked as if instead of altering it, I might just fix it. How would that affect its nature? Still, 99% of potential failure was a lot — even though it was exactly what I hoped for.

Warning! You've destroyed an item: a Copper Necklace!
You've received:
A Copper Bead, 8
Reward: +2 to Knowledge
Current Knowledge: 2/60

My losses: two of the beads and the thread itself. I wasn't worried about the latter, but the loss of two potential slugs wasn't good news. Still, I could live with it.

Now. Let's upgrade it. My recent Stamina boost had brought my Energy to 500. I could afford to use some to activate a Bind Line.

Where are those tools now? Time to use them!

Having parted with the required 50 pt. Energy, I watched, transfixed, as my hands secured the tear-shaped bead in the wambler. Flash! The new improved bead lay in my hand.

It felt weird. A bit like when I had first used the automatic parking system. You pressed the button and the steering wheel began to turn right and left on its own accord; all you had to do was step on the gas and press whichever buttons the computer told you to press. Admittedly, I'd done so with mixed feelings: the fear that I was about to hit something combined with the latest-technology thrill. Home sweet home...

But I digress. Wake up, Olgerd. This isn't home anymore.

I shook my head, focusing on the blob of copper in my hand. What did we have here?

Name: a Copper Bead
Durability: 10
Warning! Every successful hit will now decrease the item's Durability 1 pt.

Excellent. And Damage? +2! I'd been right, then. These were even better than the Monks' ones.

Let's do a few more. Another 350 Energy, and I'd have seven excellent bullets for my slingshot. Energy wasn't a problem. I could always bring it back up. But my chances of defeating a strong enemy would grow exponentially. In our line of work, every point could make a difference.

After a few minutes, my Energy bar dropped to

100, then began refilling — slowly but surely. If I only had some food or even elixirs! Not to mention Stamina stones. Gloom and his guys had well and truly fleeced me. I didn't even have a stale crust of bread left on me.

Never mind. Better not mention it.

I was about to place my tool kit back into the bag when I noticed that one of the tools in it was highlighted. Had I done something wrong? I needed to check.

Ah, so that was their so-called Fix Box. What a name. Those game designers had some funny ideas.

The Fix Box was a slim casing about five inches long and a couple of inches wide.

The moment I touched it, a small translucent panel appeared in my mind's eye. A vertical line divided it in two. To the left there were two gray cylindrical columns, reading 1%. They were marked respectively as Volume and Quality of Source Materials. Both looked very much like the charge icon of a cell phone.

To the right, there were four of my bag slots, containing the iron and copper beads and the two types of arrowheads.

So that's what it was, then! Did this mean I did have the resources necessary to build a Scarab, after all?

I could sense my own face dissolve in a smile. I rubbed my hands. Let's try it.

I highlighted an arrowhead and gingerly moved it into the left half of the panel.

One of the cylinders sprang to life, reporting

something. Oh. It looked like I celebrated too soon. Not even 0.5%!

Okay. And if I moved all of them at once?

Meh. Just over 11%!

After a moment's hesitation, I pressed *Confirm*. I didn't need the arrowheads, anyway. I'd been toying with the idea of using them for my slingshot but the system kept flashing an *Unfit for Purpose* message. In real life, that guy from the YouTube video would have found a way of using them. Which confirmed my suspicion that the game developers had only a very vague idea of how to use a slingshot.

Never mind. This was definitely better than nothing.

The Fix Box is 11.4% full!
Quality of source materials: 8.35%

Feeling like a hapless lab assistant, I studied the miserable results. Both were deep in the red. As I eyed them, I glimpsed a flash of bright green in the lower right corner. The first Scarab was ready for building.

That was good, of course. Its quality was a totally different question though.

Wait a sec... of course! I was an idiot! The Box's menu recognized the beads too, didn't it? And they'd been altered, right? What did that mean? It meant that item altering was the way!

I had a bagful of useless steely junk with me! Just think I was about to get rid of it all!

Grinning like an idiot, I slumped to the floor

next to the sleeping Boris and made myself comfortable. Prankster too was fast asleep, curled up on his friend's broad back. Each had about 50% Energy left.

"Sleep tight, guys. I'm gonna do a bit of magic. If everything goes well, we just might have a new group member."

Chapter Twelve

Warning! You're trying to alter an item's nature without possessing the necessary skills, recipes or blueprints!

Probability of ruining the item: 99%.

Warning! You've destroyed an item: an Old Sickle!

You've received:

A Rusty blade, 1

A cracked wooden handle, 1

Reward: +1 to Knowledge

Current Knowledge: 45/60

Congratulations! You've received Achievement: Breaking is not Making.

Reward: +1% to your chance of receiving Knowledge

The Fix Box is 100% full!
Quality of source materials: 8.15%

It looked like that was it.

I'd spent the last forty minutes "altering items' nature". 25% of all the metal junk was gone. I just hoped it was worth it. Then again, what did I have to lose?

Admittedly, the *'quality of source materials'* had fallen a little. It must have had something to do with the items' low Durability: most of them were a measly 2 to 4 pt. You couldn't make a silk purse out of a pig's ear.

In the meantime, my pets had restored their Energy. Ditto for myself. I just hoped it was enough to summon the new addition to my traveling menagerie.

I double-checked all the figures. I'd really done everything I could. So I pressed *Activate.*

My Energy dropped 250 pt. That was okay. Fair enough.

You've built the simplest mechanical creature: a Rusty Scarab!
New skill opened: Control
Current level: 1

Congratulations! You've received an Achievement: Beast Unseen!
Reward: +1 to Intellect
Current Intellect: 3

Congratulations! You've received Achievement:

Rusty Steel is Still Steel
 Reward: +1 to Intellect
 Current Intellect: 4

 Congratulations! You've received Achievement: Tin Pan Army General!
 Reward: +1 to Intellect
 Current Intellect: 5

As I read it, my back erupted in goosebumps. What was that now? Just by pressing a button, I'd opened a new skill and earned myself a considerable Intellect increase? And got myself three achievements in a row? Was it a one-off or was this normal in Mirror World?

I hurried to open the skill's description.

Control is a highly important skill for every army mechanic which allows him or her to control mechanical creatures.

The skill's level equals the number of the mechanical creatures the mechanic can control simultaneously.

The skill's growth depends on the frequency of its use.

Boris hissed furiously, distracting me from reading. I hurried to close the messages and swung round to the sound.

Jesus Christ almighty! What on earth was that?

Name: a Rusty Scarab
Type: a Mechanical Creature

Phew. "It's all right, guys. He's one of us."

I walked all around the strange beast, studying it. "Oh well. Only a mother can love someone like you."

His size surprised me. Considering the realistic amount of materials used, it didn't sum up. The metal junk I'd used had been nowhere near enough to have built this behemoth.

He wasn't that big but he was still about the size of a washing machine. I'd expected to see something much smaller. And I'd be lying to you if I said I wasn't pleased!

His body was large and fat, shaped as a squashed oval, the shallower part of it being his undercarriage. About waist high, he had six powerful legs and a rough five-pointed crest on the front of his head. His back was protected by an armored sheet of several pieces of metal fused together. The monster's entire body was covered in red spots of rust.

I opened his stats: very decent. Despite the word "simplest" in his moniker — and especially considering the low quality of source materials — the guy was quite impressive.

Name: a Rusty Scarab
Level: 8
Technical stats:
Protection: 35
Speed: 2

Durability: 750/750
Frontal Antler Ram Blow: 150.
Other Damage: 15
Blast wave damage: 450 (range: 6 ft.)

How cool was that? We had a second tank!

Immediately my mind offered me a very interesting tactical picture. The Scarab would enter combat first, dealing the first hit and pulling all of the mob's aggro to himself. As the mob tried to break the Scarab's metallic shell, Boris would enter the scene, followed by Prankster and yours truly.

I couldn't wait to try him out. Still, I needed to restore my Energy first. Once that done... Ghoul, just you wait!

Chapter Thirteen

We rattled and clangored all the way to the location boss in his corridor. It sounded just like the Just Married tin can concert. My scarab wasn't the stealthiest of creatures, that's for sure. No good taking *him* on recon missions.

I wouldn't be surprised if the boss gave us the key willingly, just to get rid of us.

The hero of all the racket sashayed next to me, undisturbed. His long steely antennae twitched in a most peculiar way.

Neither Boris nor Prankster seemed to mind the noise. They stole forward, silent and watchful.

Finally, the corridor. Somewhere in its recesses the boss lay in waiting.

We stopped. The silence felt good! I'd only walked a few feet but I'd already started to miss it.

Warning! You're about to face Ghoul the Gym

Boss!

This encounter might be too dangerous for players of your level!

Please turn back.

A moment later, as if in confirmation, the shadows parted, letting *it* out.

My voice broke as I whispered, "What a face!"

My two pets hissed their agreement.

The scarab didn't give a damn. He just stood there, motionless.

Very well, buddy. You go first. I activated the Ram Blow.

As the scarab rattled, accelerating, the Ghoul left the shadows, revealing himself to us in all his awesome glory.

Level 25. About ten feet tall. Broad-shouldered but stooping. His ape-like arms hung below his knees, giving the impression he was hunchbacked. Thin wispy hair framed a bald scalp, falling over his right eye. His left eye glowed with darkness. Green spittle dripped from his yellowed fangs. He was apparently anticipating a nice meal.

The scarab had already entered his aggro zone. He was only a few paces away from dealing the first blow. Finally the Ghoul registered the noise and reached out with his long arms.

"Come on, boy! Don't let us down!" I lay a copper bead into the slingshot's pouch.

The scarab complied. He rammed the ghoul's belly at full speed, critting him and stripping him of 300 pt. Life.

Surprisingly, the ghoul remained standing. Admittedly I'd expected my steely tank to sweep him off his feet but the Ghoul only staggered and stepped back.

Then he did something I hadn't expected at all. The ghoul scooped my scarab up in his powerful arms and sent him flying through the air.

Talk about strong.

The corridor echoed with the impact of metal against stone. The scarab lost 20% Durability. Uh oh. A few more knockdowns like that would finish him off, that's for sure.

Predictably, the scarab had pulled the aggro to himself. Growling, the ghoul staggered toward the heap of scrap metal writhing helplessly on the floor.

"Boris, your turn. Be careful. Make sure you don't aggro him."

His eagle eye glistening, the Hugger dashed forward. He would now attempt to peck him on the back, stripping him of Life point by an unhurried point without pulling the aggro to himself.

A 300 pt. crit was too good for words. I just loved my new skill.

"Don't you dare," I stopped the impatient Prankster. "Our job is to support the tank attack with intense gunfire."

Admittedly the damage from my slingshot was like a mosquito bite to him. But as the ancient Greek poet Choerilus of Samos had famously said, "Water can penetrate rock if its fall is incessant". Which was why, having used up my metal ammo, I switched back to beach pebbles.

It took the ghoul a good five minutes to work out how he could approach the scarab. Before that, he'd tried to pound him on his steel shell without dealing much damage. But now he repeated his first assault, sending the scarab flying along the corridor.

More rattling of steel. His Durability was now hovering at 15%.

But we'd put all this time to good use. Boris, with my humble assistance, had taken the shine off the ghoul's stats. His Life was in the red. We were winning. One last push!

The ghoul staggered toward the scarab and grabbed at his shell, jerking him into the air and lifting him over his head.

That was it, then. If my gut feeling was correct, we were about to lose a group member.

The ghoul confirmed my worst expectations. With a powerful thump against the ground, the scarab's Life plummeted to 1 pt.

Then several things happened at once.

Throwing caution to the wind, Boris landed a powerful blow — and a decent crit — on the ghoul's head. With a blood-curdling wail, the monster turned to face this new enemy — but failed to react promptly enough before the scarab's last skill activated.

An explosion shattered the corridor.

You've dealt a critical hit!
Damage dealt: 900
You've killed a level 25 Ghoul!
You've received Experience!
Congratulations! You've received a new level!

Congratulations! You've received a new level!
Congratulations! You've received a new level!
Current level: 20
Reward: +20 to Knowledge
Current Knowledge: 65/90.
Bonus points: 5
Available points: 10
Congratulations! You've single-handedly defeated the Fort's first Guardian!
You've received a reward upgrade!
New reward based on your character's class:
The Boots of a Fort Guardian
The Greaves of a Fort Guardian
Quest Reward: a Rune Key

Congratulations! You've received Achievement: Liberator of the Ghoul's Soul!
Reward: +5% to Energy Regeneration

I stared at all the messages in disbelief. My rise through levels was well-deserved and expected, considering that the system viewed me as a solo player. But two Blue-class items! No forum had ever mentioned it! And why should they? No one in their sane mind would walk around blabbing about these sorts of things.

I got me some new clothes!

I hurried to shed the two odd boots and reached for my new ones. Now...

We're sorry. Your level isn't high enough to use the item.

"What is it now?" I exclaimed. "How about the greaves?"

We're sorry. Your level isn't high enough to use the item.

"History repeats itself," I mumbled, swiping open the boots' description.

Name: The Boots of a Fort's Guardian
Class: Rare
Effect: +90 to Speed
Effect: +30 to Protection
Effect: +55 to Stamina
Effect: +55 to Health
Effect: +45 to Strength
Durability: 250/250
Restriction: Level 30
On collecting a full set, you will receive a bonus!

The greaves were more or less the same:

Name: The Greaves of a Fort Guardian
Class: Rare
Effect: +80 to Speed
Effect: +35 to Protection
Effect: +55 to Stamina
Effect: +55 to Health
Effect: +50 to Strength
Durability: 250/250
Restriction: level 30
On collecting a full set, you will receive a bonus!

If I understood the phrase "based on your character's class" correctly, the system's choice of characteristics targeted a shooter — definitely not a mechanic!

It must have been the slingshot. It had given me the false impression that an "army mechanic" was some kind of shooting class. The system must have made the same mistake. Now I could finally see the mechanic's fortes. The slingshot was just a useful extra to make sure the player had a weapon, however miserable.

Now I knew: my chars' main stats had to be Intellect and Stamina. Knowledge and Energy were my weapons. I also knew what I was going to invest all my available points into. No hurry, though. I could level up Stamina with runes and gear, but Intellect... I hadn't had a chance to look into it yet. I needed to study forums first. Then we'd see.

Wouldn't it have been nice to put on my new stuff! Still, according to Ecclesiastes, there was a time for everything. My time to gather stones hadn't yet arrived. I would make level 30 soon enough — and considering that normally Blue items were only available at level 70, I was lucky any way you looked at it.

Finally I noticed Prankster jumping and leaping around me in celebration.

"How could I have forgotten about you! You have a new ability, don't you, Prankie? Come on, show it to us!"

He and Boris had earned two levels each. Both were level 16 now. We were growing!

Ability: Reflection I
Allows your pet to cast a spell repelling 20% of
any physical or magical damage dealt to you.
Available points: 5

What an excellent ability. It worked similar to a magic shield, didn't it?

Seeing as Prankie was our buffer, we had to boost his Stamina first and foremost. 3 pt. would be plenty. His Life was quite important too, so I invested the remaining points into Health. His Life bar jumped up 20%.

Prankster was pleased. Just look at him! Bright-eyed and bushy-tailed — a sight for sore eyes!

Good. That was sorted. Now, scrap metal. We needed another scarab.

Chapter Fourteen

The Fix Box is 100% full!
Quality of source materials: 6.25%

Predictably so. Only 85% of the source materials were steel. I'd topped it up with scrap copper. At least now I knew that copper wasn't particularly welcome.

I'd done so for a reason. I still had enough scrap metal to make a third scarab with about 25% over. I was pretty sure that the last one would be a cut above the first. So I was saving him for the final battle.

Let's do it, then.

You've built the simplest mechanical creature: a level 7 Lame Scarab!

This one was one level lower. He was limping,

too. What about his stats?

Name: a Lame Scarab
Level: 7
Technical stats:
Protection: 13
Speed: 1
Durability: 650/650
Frontal Antler Ram Blow: 120.
Other Damage: 11
Blast wave damage: 390 (range: 4 ft.)

Oh well. All the stats had plummeted. Apparently, Quality wasn't just an empty word here. The difference between the two source materials was less than 2% — but look how it had affected the whole picture! Never mind. The third one was going to be just fine.

Actually, was it so necessary to wait? What if the second scarab died in the very heat of the battle? Wouldn't it be better to fill the Fix Box beforehand?

Good idea. I should feed it the choicest morsels I had.

After a few minutes of fiddling with bits of scrap metal, this is what I had:

The Fix Box is 100% full!
Quality of source materials: 10.34%

Much better. No wonder: I'd used all the steel parts of all the hammers, picks, scythes and pitchforks — everything that had more than 5 pt.

⊔urability. This last battle could be quite exhausting. My little army needed all the reinforcements I could summon.

I cast one last look around. "Right, are we finished here?"

I was about to put the key in the lock when my eye chanced upon a heap of old gray rags. Well, well, well. If this wasn't our first stash!

I walked over to it. Yes!

Congratulations! You've found the Ghoul's treasure!
Reward:
Life Elixir, 5
Vial of Power, 10
Energy Elixir, 5

Just what I needed! All the items were highlighted green!

Name: Life Elixir
Strength: Moderate
Effect: Restores 40% Life
Cooldown: 30 sec

The Energy ones were the same. But a Vial of Power... never seen anything like it before.

Name: a Vial of Power
Strength: Moderate
Effect: +40% to the force of the blow
One Vial is enough for one strike

How interesting. Let's just hope the sling shot counted as a strike. Another unpleasant surprise for the Lich.

Now I was definitely done here. Time to move on.

I sent Prankster the command to cast Reflection on me. In two turns of the key, the massive door creaked open.

"After you," I grumbled, letting the limping scarab in first.

The kitchen greeted us with silence. I could make out an occasional movement and noises somewhere out the back.

It wasn't a kitchen really — rather a mess hall. Plenty of space there. Long crudely made tables, lined with wooden benches. Judging by the large skewers heaped up by a huge fireplace, it must have been used to roast meat.

The place was a pigsty. The stone floor was covered in a thin layer of rotten straw spotted with dark blotches of red. Everywhere you turned, there was a layer of shattered kitchenware on the floor mixed with bones, pieces of tattered clothing and crude cutlery. Fat flies circled over heaps of what looked suspiciously like organic matter. I tried not to think what it could have been.

Slowly we walked to the room's center. Quiet wasn't the operative word: the new scarab made just as much noise as his predecessor.

The ceiling here wasn't as high as in the gym but it left plenty of leeway for Boris. I told him to get his bearings.

With two large hops, he reached the opposite wall. Hanging from the ceiling, he turned his eagle head this way and that, then froze, staring in the direction of the noise: apparently sensing the local inhabitants.

Outside, a thunderstorm raged. Framed by the windows, forked bolts of lightning illuminated the dark night sky. Can't say they boosted my morale. It felt like being cast in a horror movie. And this was only a newb instance in a starting location! I could only imagine what I'd have to deal with in No-Man's Lands.

We continued on our way, Boris walking the wall and ready to attack at a moment's notice.

One of the tables in front of us lay on its side. I could now hear the sounds very well. I'd heard them before in a hyena documentary: the crunching of bones and the tearing of dead flesh.

According to the forums, this part of the Fort was inhabited by rats who used to subsist on kitchen scraps. They must have switched to cooks themselves by now. The rats shouldn't be too numerous. The location boss was the Matriarch of the Pack. Not the most difficult of obstacles.

I took another step. The table was now about twenty feet away.

The munching and slurping stopped. Boris hissed, warning me we'd entered their aggro zone.

Something rustled behind the massive table. The next moment it flew effortlessly through the air. Holy mama mia!

So this was the designers' idea of a rat?

Each of the five monsters was the size of a bull terrier. One of them was even bigger: more like a mastiff. It must have been the Matriarch.

As the location boss, she was level 25. Her buddies were not too far off, level 22 each. Five pairs of black eyes focused threateningly on me.

Their jaws were covered in blood. No idea what they could have dined on. Better not to know. What had that ancient king said, "in much knowledge is much grief"? I couldn't agree more. I already had nightmares as it was.

The chief rat sized us up, then emitted a long hissing sound. Her soldiers clung to the ground, their muscular gray bodies circling us.

Aha. This mother of all rats had decided to surround us. She didn't seem to have any particular abilities compared to the others. Her hide was thicker and her hits were harder, that was the extent of it. Her high leadership skills were her only advantage. Rats fight in a pack, obeying their leader's every command.

The developers' purpose was clear: to allow players to confront a well-organized enemy. All those staggering skeletons didn't do much to improve one's combat skills. Not to even mention the crabs. Dmitry had been right: I was going to get in some excellent practice.

If forum gurus were to be believed, rat fighting tactics were directly the opposite of how I'd defeated the Ghoul. Trying to smoke the soldiers first wouldn't be the right thing. I had to start with their leader. The tank had to attack the Mother, pulling the pack's aggro to himself. Otherwise the pack leader would try to disperse the attackers, engaging all of them in battle and trying to first disable the least protected classes. In our case, that would be Prankster and myself. And judging by the rats' glaring viciously at me, they'd already made their choice.

"Dream on!" I yelled, then sent the scarab in.

He used the Ramming Blow to throw the Mother several feet into the air, pulling the pack's aggro to himself. An agonizing shriek assaulted my eardrums. A crit!

The chief rat had lost 250 pt. Life. Her buddies hurried to her rescue.

"Look at that one... she's lagging behind, isn't she? Boris, attack!"

He dropped onto the remaining rat, pinning her slimy gray body to the ground in his claws. His beak dug into her neck. For a moment, I even felt sorry for the poor thing — until it squirmed round and sank her crooked yellow teeth into Boris' paw.

He hissed with pain, momentarily releasing his grip. The monster struggled herself free and went for his throat — but I was ready!

My slingshot popped. The rat's head jerked as if she'd received a bullet. A crit!

Another shot to the head. Another crit.

That was enough for Boris to pin the disoriented monster back on the ground. His beak pierced the rat's gray flesh — in the throat this time. He ripped it open, letting out a cascade of hot blood.

One down.

I could feel my legs giving way under me. My

throat suddenly seized. Dark circles swam before my eyes. I wasn't used to seeing these sorts of scenes.

Just keep it together, Olgerd. Inhale. Exhale. Like that... good. No point falling apart now. This was only the beginning.

And how about our tank? He was still braving it. Still, he was on his last legs. Rats couldn't whack him against the wall the way the Ghoul had done. They had other methods — which in a way were just as effective. When they'd failed to chew their way through his shell, they went for his legs. The chief rat had almost gnawed one off already.

"Don't you dare! He's lame as it is!" I shouted, shooting my slingshot non-stop.

I decided not to risk Boris for the moment. The sight of the rat's teeth sinking into the scarab's leg was a little too much for me. My heart clenched. I knew he was only part of the program code but this world had already become part of me — to the point where I viewed both Boris and Prankster as my family.

Judging by the logs, the scarab gave as much as he got. He'd already dealt the Mama rat another ramming blow. He'd now pinned her against the wall and was busy methodically sinking his mandibles into her gray flank time and time again. Doubtful she had one whole rib left by now.

Within the next two minutes, I'd fired all the remaining beads into her. Her Life was deep in the red. Blood gushed from her mauled abdomen. The scarab didn't look much better. His Durability was at 5%. Half his legs were ripped off, with more rats hanging onto those still attached. Unlike their boss, they were brimming with Health and Energy. Even if the scarab's Self-Destruction stripped them of some, we'd still have three higher-level enemies to tackle.

What could we do? I was more than sure Boris could handle them. But at what price? They might hurt him real bad. They'd made quick work of the scarab, and he was made of steel. Should I mount Boris and shoot the mobs from the safety of the wall, maybe? Not really.

I was beginning to think I'd been overenthusiastic in coming here. Had it not been for my new skill, Boris would have had to die repeatedly before we completed the instance.

Oh well. The only way out was to build the last scarab and try to make him last the two remaining locations.

This one was about to explode.

But what if...

I jumped onto Boris' back and ordered him to climb to the ceiling. Prankster didn't leave my side.

In two powerful bounds, Boris managed to hang upside down over the fight scene.

Explosion. A crit. A powerful blast wave threw the squeaking gray bodies a good ten feet away from the epicenter.

You've killed the location boss: level 25 Matriarch of the Pack!

Left without a leader, her pack bids a hasty retreat!

You've received Experience!

You've received a new level!
Current level: 21
Reward: +10 to Knowledge
Current Knowledge: 75/90

Congratulations! You've single-handedly defeated the Fort's second Guardian!
You've received a reward upgrade!
New reward based on your character's class:
The Gauntlets of a Fort Guardian
Quest reward: a Rune Key

Squealing their indignation, the rats scattered in all directions. My quick thinking had just saved us an unnecessary scrap.

It might have happened, of course, that the rats were bound to this particular place — in which case we would have needed to build a new scarab and accept the fight before the Rats restored their Life stats. Still, it had all worked out just fine.

I waited a little more, then told Boris to come down. I needed to check the loot.

Another item for my Fort Guardian kit — excellent! The Ghoul had been more generous, though.

The gauntlets had similar stats — and unfortunately, the same restrictions. Never mind. Another nine levels and I could finally wear them.

The first rat I'd killed dropped a Rat Skin and some fangs. Utterly useless. I might see if I could find a taker for them at auction.

I looked around myself long and hard but

found no stashes here. It was probably because we'd failed to mop it up completely.

In which case, we could move on.

What did we have next? The barracks, followed by the main hall with the Fort's Boss.

I placed the rune key in the keyhole and began turning it. The rusty lock rattled and clanged. I pushed the door. It gave with unexpected ease, creaking its protest.

We found ourselves in a rather large room with another door in the opposite wall about thirty feet away.

There were two sentries posted at it. Both zombies, level 23. They differed considerably from the skeletons. Both had halberds in their hands — and they looked as if they knew how to use them, too. They wore leather cuirasses, greaves and bracers. Peaked helmets topped their heads. The gear was old and worn but it didn't make them any easier to handle.

They noticed us when we were about five paces away from the door. Both waved their halberds in our direction. As far as zombies went, their reaction times were quite decent. Not good enough to tackle a Hugger, though.

By the time they shuffled their crumbling boots to take a step forward, Boris was already on the ceiling right above their heads.

He kicked off, throwing his lithe body right at them. The undead guards collapsed in two heaps, rattling their bones. Boris didn't give them the chance to scramble back to their feet. His lightning attacks and powerful beak left not a hope in hell for the hapless zombies.

I was on my eighth bead when the system reported our victory. Still, I had nothing to celebrate loot-wise. As if mocking my efforts, all that the sentries had dropped were their halberds — while I'd had high hopes for their leather cuirasses or at least the bracers. Oh well. Never mind.

But once I studied our trophies, they didn't seem so hopeless. They might actually be worth something. The halberd's tip was a combination of a ribbed spear head and a battle axe blade with a sharp hook at its rear. The halberds' shafts were enveloped in steel to the half of their length. They even looked heavy. One had 11 pt. Durability and the other, 13. Virtually no rust; slightly porous but not obviously so. The metal was much better quality than what my bag was stuffed with. All I had to do was get myself more of those pokers.

Chapter Fifteen

It had taken us six hours to mop up the barracks. This time we'd had to deal with level-26 Zombie Guards. They hadn't been too numerous but had had to be handled individually because of their high levels. Thank God they didn't have a boss! Had they attacked us all at once like the rats had, we wouldn't have enjoyed it.

As it was, we'd used the already tested scheme: Prankster pulling them one by one, Boris and myself handling them. Take a breather, rinse and repeat. Now too, as we readied ourselves to face the Bone Golem — one of the two remaining bosses — I announced a break. We needed to restore and arrange a couple of things.

I'd managed to do another level. Both Boris and Prank were 19. There they were, snoring their heads off. They were tired, poor things. No wonder. We'd been walking around this fortress for the last forty-

---

eight hours.

I had no time for sleep. I reached into my bag, pulling out the hammer and the one remaining halberd. Gingerly I hit its shaft with the hammer.

Warning! You're trying to alter an item's nature without possessing the necessary skills, recipes or blueprints!
Probability of ruining the item: 99%.

Yes, I know, I know.

Warning! You've destroyed an item: the Rusty Halberd of a Fort Sentry!
Reward: +2 to Knowledge
Current Knowledge: 90/90

My Knowledge bar was full. Excellent. I made a mental note to check the Pocket Book of Blueprints at my first convenience.

This was the fifth halberd I'd destroyed — not counting five cudgels, six spears, three poleaxes and five swords. This should be enough to build two scarabs if necessary, plus an additional 40% Lame one if the going got really tough. If you added to this the metal I'd already loaded into the Fix Box, it was three and a half scarabs in total.

We'd have to tackle the Golem between the four of us. This little went without saying. Now that we could afford it, a steely tank would considerably increase our chances of success.

I rearranged a leather bracer on my forearm

and threw the hammer back into the bag. I'd indeed managed to get myself some gear off the guards. I now wore a thick padded gambeson — not exactly armor but it had come with some Protection points. Also a right-arm bracer and a leather knee protector. Plus a few iron rings and a bone charm. All of it utter junk but it had done my stats some good. Not that it really mattered. Once I got myself a full Fort Guardian's kit, we'd see who was the noob here.

The Pocket Book of Blueprints glowed green.

"Excellent," I whispered, pulling it out.

The third page wasn't dimmed anymore.

Name: *A Swarm of Fleas Blueprint*
Access requirements:
Knowledge, 90 pt.
Would you like to study the blueprint?

As if! One thing I really needed was some fleas!

I pressed *Yes*, anyway. The Knowledge bar promptly emptied.

Congratulations! You can now build a Swarm of Fleas!

A new icon appeared in the right bottom corner.

A Swarm of Fleas is a group of the simplest mechanical beings, Master Brolgerd's unique invention. Initially created to aid mine diggers fight underground monsters by transmitting deadly diseases, they were

later adapted for military purposes.
  Skills:
  Long Jump
  Bloodsucker
  Venomous Bite

  Specifications:
  The quality and numbers of the materials used in the Fleas' construction directly affect their following properties:
  Levels
  Damage
  Durability
  The colony's numbers
  A Flea's body is 98% metal and 2% toxic liquid
  The Swarm's constructor should be prepared to share some of his Energy with it.
  Tools required:
  The Fix Box
  Materials required:
  Metal
  Toxic Liquid

Oh wow. No wonder they'd decided to discontinue the Ennans! If these were the "simplest mechanisms", I dreaded to think what they might have invented at a later date.

A new tag appeared on the Fix Box panel: *Swarm of Fleas.* Apparently, each mechanical toy had its own stable.

And I'd forgotten all about the Swamp Monk's Venom, hadn't I? I had seven vials of the wretched stuff! All of them highly concentrated Blue-class items. Would that be enough to meet their 2% requirement?

Excellent. One vial was plenty. This stuff could go a long way.

Now the metal.

Even better! Three pieces of scrap steel were enough to meet their requirements. It was a drop in the ocean compared to the building of a scarab. Still, for a flea it was quite a lot, I suppose.

The quality of source materials was almost at 17%. That was a first! The venom's high concentration levels must have played their part.

I was impatient to check it all out but unfortunately, I couldn't. I had to save the new scarab for the battle.

I stepped into the opposite corner, away from my pets. This looked like a good spot. I gave it a closer inspection. Yes, definitely.

I activated the skill.

A big hulk of steel materialized next to me.

This scarab turned out to be level 10. Someone might say he was just as ugly as his forerunners. Not for me though. As far as I was concerned, he was a beauty. His stats had visibly improved and he looked considerably better. True, the unavoidable rust was still there but that was irrelevant. Just look at his Damage and Protection! They were a sight for sore eyes.

* * *

An hour's break was over before I knew it. Our Energy was back up. We could move on.

We left the barracks without further ado. An empty corridor lay before us, followed by a rather narrow spiral staircase leading down four flights. I was a bit worried if my scarab could climb it, but he managed.

We kept walking without meeting anyone on our way. We did find two stashes though: one in the corridor and the other under one of the stairs. In total, they gave us fifteen elixirs of moderate strength: five of Life, the rest of Energy.

The staircase brought us into the guardroom. A large double door in the opposite wall led into the main hall. A big heap of bones barricaded its entrance.

Intent on entering, a reckless player might have thought it just another pile of bones and step casually over it. But I knew this was the Fort's third Guardian: the Bone Golem. Who happened to have two very nasty abilities: Trap and Bone Shield.

We stepped forward, entering his aggro zone. I ordered the others to stop and wait for my command. The idea was to act in synch, fast and without hesitation.

Wait.

Don't move.

Yes! That innocuous-looking heap of bones shifted, transforming, activating the Golem's first skill.

The Trap closed.

Had I been less diligent in perusing my manuals, I would now have been lodged in the local boss' belly.

The Bone Golem. Level 27. Fifteen foot tall, breathing magic. The last stand before the final combat.

On my command, the scarab darted forward. With a deafening snap, the Golem lost his only leg and collapsed. A crit!

We couldn't allow him to transform: the moment that happened, he'd activate the Bone Shield. Then we'd be stuck in this hall until the cows come home. We could die even.

"Boris, attack! Steely Guts, move it! Turn round and give him another ramming, quick! That's right! Don't let him get back to his feet! See what I mean? Another crit, great! Boris, hit him on the head, that's a good boy! Three crits! Thirty percent Life down!"

In less than ten minutes, it was all over. We hadn't given the golem a chance to get back to his feet, let alone transform. That's team work for you. And reading manuals. Thank you, the unknown guide writers, whoever you are!

If you tackled the golem right, this awesome enemy became easy prey. The most important thing was never to switch to the defensive, otherwise you were toast.

The Bone Shield was a powerful spell indeed. Breaching it would have taken us a long time, all the while fighting off the golem who wasn't going to just stand there watching us.

> *You've killed a level 27 Bone Golem!*
> *You've received Experience!*
> *Congratulations! You've received a new level!*
> *Congratulations! You've received a new level!*
> *Congratulations! You've received a new level!*
> *Current level: 25.*
> *Reward: +20 to Knowledge*
> *Current Knowledge: 20/90*
> *Bonus points: 5*
> *Available points: 15*

> *Congratulations! You've single-handedly defeated the Fort's third Guardian!*
> *You've received a reward upgrade!*
> *New reward based on your character's class:*
> *The Armor of a Fort Guardian*
> *The Bracers of a Fort Guardian*
> *Quest Reward: a Rune Key*
> *Congratulations! You've received Achievement: Liberator of the Bone Golem's Soul!*
> *Reward: +5% to Energy Regeneration*

The triumphant scream of an eagle shattered the room. Instinctively I covered my ears. What was going on here?

One look at the hero of the day told me we had another cause for celebration. Boris had just made level 23. Which could only mean one thing: he finally got himself another skill. I wouldn't be surprised if he had just demonstrated it to us.

Boris hurried to my side.

"Good boy!" I whispered, smiling and hugging him. A boy? His chest was already level with my head! Powerful muscles rippled under his skin as he moved. A silent question filled his aquiline eyes: *So how do you like me?*

Prankster was prancing around happily next to him. Oh wow. Hadn't he grown! He was already the size of an adult lynx. Bet Master Adkhur would be surprised!

Hah! I'd been right after all:

Name of skill: The Triumphant Crow of a Night Hunter I
   Effect: Stuns your opponent.
   Duration: 10 sec

* * *

"So you're here, O mortal! Finally!" the Lich's nasty hissing voice seemed to come from everywhere at once.

He was dead right. We were there, after all. This was the Fort's main hall complete with its boss — the Fort's new owner, as large as life and twice as ugly.

It wasn't very impressive, I had to admit. I'd expected to see something more, er, gory. But this... a stock fantasy toon in a black hooded cloak, holding a long staff made of bone and crowned with some sort of animal skull.

The only scary thing about him was his level 30. I'd leveled up too fast, failing to meet their requirements. No wonder. Had I been part of a group, I'd still be level 19 at the most. Not even, considering my meager Damage.

So, Sir Olgerd, you're about to get your backside kicked big time.

Apart from the two stock spells, Weakness and Exhaustion, a level-30 boss received two more: Fury and Self Heal. Basically, I was deep in it.

Never mind. We weren't finished yet.

Besides, there was always Plan B. We could make a group. Then he'd be easy prey. But in that case, I could forget the full Guardian kit.

"I have to admit, O mortal, that you surprised me," the Lich moved slowly to the center of the room.

His hissing sent shivers down my spine. "Did I?"

"Oh yes," the undead wizard said, approaching slowly. "Firstly, you've survived. Judging by your, ahem, clothes, you should have died even before you entered the Fort. Secondly, you're crafty."

"Am I? How did you work that out?"

"By the ways in which you killed my soldiers. Only a very crafty warrior could do that. But that's not important. What amazes me is that you managed to pull it off on your own."

"Thanks," I mumbled as I warily watched his movements. He was a mere fifteen paces away from me now.

"Mortal, you know what? I think I'm gonna

keep your soul. We'll find you a new body. You can stay here and serve me."

"You know what we say back where I come from? Don't sell the bear's skin before you catch him!"

"*We say!* What a stupid notion," he emitted a nasty giggle. "After you're dead, the only thing that will matter to you is what *I* say!"

He finally stopped some ten paces away. His arms flew into the air like black wings.

Now.

"Boris, scream! Steely Guts, attack! Prankie, cast the Shield!"

Boris' Triumphant Crow assaulted our eardrums. The wizard froze on the spot like a black statue.

One second.

Three.

Five.

Come on, now! The scarab didn't seem to move. But I could see he was doing his best.

Yes! He made it!

Another ramming and a crit!

The wizard's motionless body flew to the opposite wall like a rag doll.

"And again! Don't let him recover!"

As if! In one wave of the wizard's winged black arm, a powerful air current threw the scarab to our left.

You've been cursed! Name of curse: Weakness.
Effect: -30 to Damage

You've been cursed! Name of curse: Exhaustion.
Effect: -50 to Life every 10 sec

Had I completed the Sarge's quest as I should have, I'd have received all sorts of useful goodies from local NPCs. Like Cleanse scrolls, for instance. Activating one of them could disable any debuff. Why did I always have to do it my own way?

The scarab had recovered and was gaining speed again. Then suddenly his body swung round. The Lich reached his skeletal arms out in front of him, casting some nasty attack spells.

My turn. My slingshot popped time and time again, sending a burst of three copper beads thudding into the wizard's head. I'd used the vials of Power with each shot. They were awesome. Had it not been for the debuff, the damage might have been truly impressive. I'd disrupted the wizard's spells but I'd also pulled the aggro to myself.

"Prankie, prepare to heal me! Steely Guts, get him! Boris, stay where you are!"

That was all I had time to do. A powerful blow to my chest sent me flying. I'd never been hit by a car but this was what I imagine it must feel like. For a split second, everything went black. This was apparently the Lich's minor spell: Arrow of Death.

Minor, yeah right. Was it really? Those forum wizzies should have had their heads tested.

Prankster's shield managed to absorb 20% damage. The rest was absorbed by my fragile virtual self.

A warm healing wave flooded over my body:

Prankster knew his job. I gulped an elixir, bringing my Life back into the green.

I was ready for the Lich's next attack but he didn't make it. The scarab had gotten to him first, critting him with another ramming blow.

I scrambled to my unsteady feet and staggered toward the scene of combat. The Lich's punch had been good. It had thrown me a good ten feet through the air.

By the time I made it there, the tables had turned. The scarab was lying on his back, his legs wriggling awkwardly in the air. The Lich stood next to him, his staff enveloped in a dark haze. He raised it sharply in the air.

"Boris, wait. He's casting Fury."

The dark shadow escaped the staff's top. Ignoring a long and wordy system message, I hurried to gulp another Life elixir. I could see very well that the scarab had had it.

The wizard turned his head to me, solemn and dignified. I could have bet my bottom dollar there was a triumphant smile lurking in the black depths of his hood.

"This is it, mortal!"

I winced. Not that hissing voice again. I was well and truly fed up with the guy.

"Surrender, and your death will be quick. It won't hurt, I promise!"

"Don't hold your breath," I shouted, then turned to Boris. "Now."

An explosion shattered the room just as the wizard stepped toward me. That was powerful! I could feel the floor vibrate underfoot. The room's walls and columns quivered dangerously. The ceiling showered us with stone dust.

The explosion sent the Lich flying — but immediately he was trying to scramble back to his feet. His Life was in the red. He was one die-hard sonovabitch.

"Boris, go!" I shouted, hurrying to summon the second scarab.

The Fix Box was 100% full. Clever provident Olgerd! I must have known one scarab wouldn't do it.

Boris — who'd all this time been hanging upside down from a ceiling beam — dove down, squawking fiercely.

The wounded wizard froze, statue-like. We only had ten seconds. Boris was already upon him, tearing him apart. The new scarab was level 12. His Protection was greater but he was too slow.

"Move it, tin can!" I wheezed, gulping elixirs by the vial and purposefully ignoring the avalanche of system messages.

Boris cried out in pain as the Lich began to recover.

My heart clenched. My little Boris was hurting! I'd long stopped pretending this was a computer game. For me, it was all real now.

I'd buried every single bead and pebble in the wizard before the scarab could even join in the fight. I now was empty. All I had left was close combat.

"Everybody!" I yelled, whipping out my rusty dagger — the only weapon suitable for my class.

Strangely enough, the scarab proved faster

than me. He got to the wizard before I could, ramming him down.

The last seconds of the fight barely registered, dreamlike. I think that me and my dagger had managed to get to the wizard a couple of times too. Luckily for us, he hadn't had the chance to use his last spell.

Got him. Dead as a dodo. Over and out.

Chapter Sixteen

I rubbed my sleepy eyes, forcing them open. Wake up, Olgerd! This wasn't the right moment to relax. Once I logged out, I could sleep all I wanted. Business first.

I reopened all the unread system messages.

As I studied them, my heart beat faster and harder. I hadn't expected this at all.

You've killed the level 30 Cursed Wizard!
You've received Experience!
Congratulations! You've received a new level!
Congratulations! You've received a new level!
Congratulations! You've received a new level!
Congratulations! You've received a new level!
Current level: 29.
Reward:
A Teleportation Scroll
+20 to Knowledge

Current Knowledge: 56/90

Congratulations! You've single-handedly defeated the Fort's Master!
You've received a reward upgrade!
New reward based on your character's class:
The Helmet of a Fort Guardian
The Charm of a Fort Guardian
Quest Reward: a Charmed Key

Congratulations! You've received Achievement: Liberator of the Cursed Wizard's Soul!
Reward: +20% to your chances of avoiding magic attacks.

Congratulations! You've received a Heroic Achievement: a Lone Zombie Slayer! Everybody already knows about your fearless deeds!
Reward: the Order of the Zombie Slayer

Congratulations! You've received a Heroic Achievement: A Lone Liberator of Captive Souls. Everybody already knows about your fearless deeds!
Reward: a Scroll of Great Initiation

Congratulations! You've received a Legendary Achievement: One Against Death. You're a legend!
Reward: The Order of Heroic Strength

My drowsiness was gone in a blink. I was shivering with excitement. The Blue kit paled in comparison with all these rewards and achievements.

Having studied the rewards' descriptions, I cast a bewildered look around me. Was this really happening to me? In disbelief, I decided to double-check my acquisitions.

All the rewards' icons were ruby red: the sign of their highest class.

The Order of the Zombie Slayer gave -40% to any damage dealt by undead classes.

The second Order, the Legendary one, gave +30% to Strength. *But!* This applied not only to me but also to any other players fighting alongside me. In other words, this turned me into a walking buff for any kind of raid or group I joined.

As for the scroll, it came with a restriction: I first had to attain level 50 to use it. But that was nothing compared to its potential. By activating this seemingly useless scrap of paper, I received +2000 to any Reputation of my choice. And that was a good year's worth — probably more — of doing stupid pointless quests which would otherwise have cost me a lot of time and money. Such a shame it was non-transferable. I dreaded to even think how much it might have fetched at auction.

Right. This much was clear. What next?

Two more Blue items and a bonus key. Oh. I'd been 2% XP short of making level 30.

Never mind. Another battle, and I'd be all kitted out.

Now the charmed key was interesting. According to the description, it opened a "secret room". I looked around me.

Aha. A narrow door had appeared in the

opposite wall. I could have sworn it hadn't been there before.

Bedazzled by all the Christmas presents — there was no other name for it, really — I'd failed to notice that the glowing icon of my only skill showed a number 2.

I scrolled through the logs just to make sure I wasn't imagining it. Apparently, my summoning of the last scarab had raised Control as well. Yes! No-Man's Lands, just you wait!

I cast another glance around the room just to be on the safe side and headed for the wizard's stash.

The key turned smoothly and soundlessly. I got the impression the lock had been oiled regularly — weekly even. The narrow secret door opened inward. What kind of treasures might he keep here?

Aha! I'd seen this before! A bejeweled box. No level restrictions, thank God for that. Just sitting there for anyone to open. Which was what I was going to do.

Congratulations! You've opened a Box of Treasures!
Contents:
Cleanse scrolls, 10
Antidote scrolls, 10
Potion of Absolute Fury, 1
Strength: High

Excellent. I could read more about them later. Now it was time for us to leg it.

I toyed with the idea of using the teleportation

---

scroll but decided against it. I wanted to double-check my battle path. You never know, I might just find something else I could use.

* * *

Another hour of walking through the instance hadn't garnered anything. I'd poked my curious virtual nose into every nook and cranny I could think of: dark niches and stairs, touching and searching everything that looked even remotely promising. I'd even made Boris check out the ceiling.

Nothing.

Either I'd already found everything there'd been to find or I was ignoring something pretty obvious.

"Never mind," I mumbled, studying the walls of the barbican. "We've done all we could. More, even."

Heh! I could still see my bare footprints in the dust: my first step into the scary unknown.

Funny, isn't it? It had only been a few days but I was a different man now. Had someone told me a few months ago that I might be stuck inside some computer toy chopping up the armies of the undead for a living, I'd have declared him totally crazy.

As I'd walked, I'd sorted through the wizard's treasures. Admittedly they were quite useful. Take a Cleanse scroll, for instance: it could remove any nasty debuff. True, it came with a 30-minute cooldown but this wasn't much for top league battles.

And as for the Potion of Fury... drinking it gave

me +50 to Fury for 6 hours. I remembered Grryrsch telling me about it. Apparently, it also affected your chances of dealing an injury. This was a very peculiar thing tailored to damagers: players who'd chosen to level up Damage. Definitely indispensable for executioners... but pretty useless for me. It must have cost a lot though. I might have a chat with Rrhorgus. He must know these thingies' value better than I. But scrolls I might keep... I had a funny feeling they might come in handy one day.

Right! Here we were, facing the Fort's exit. We'd done it. We'd actually done more than one could have ever imagined.

I pulled out the teleportation scroll and unsummoned my pets. They promptly disappeared, leaving the scarab standing by my side.

"Now what do I do with you? No idea! Just stay here by my side, okay? That way you might get ported with me."

Silently the scarab stepped closer. I lay one hand onto his steel shell just to be sure and activated the scroll.

Warning! In order to activate the scroll, you need to leave the instance first!

Oh, great. Now we'd have to walk out into the rain. At least this way I knew these things didn't work inside instances.

I walked through the Fort's gate and froze in disbelief.

What the hell was going on? Both my chat and

my inbox were flashing like crazy. The unread messages counter kept bleeping non-stop. Five hundred and growing! Was this some kind of spamming attack? Had I somehow managed to pick up a virus? Trust me to do that. What an embarrassment.

I opened my inbox. Aha. Wish it were a virus!

Our dear Sir Olgerd,

I thought we had an agreement? What a shame. I believed you to be a man of sense. Now I'm afraid you might need to see some proof of our commitment to you.

Tanor didn't mince words, did he? The carrot stage was apparently over. This was the stick. I was quite curious.

I checked the chat too. The reason for all this turmoil lay in my heroic achievements, apparently reported all over the Glasshouse.

Hello, fame. Just when I least needed you.

I was about the check Uncle Vanya's last message when I heard,

"There he is! Hi there, handsome! Since when can zombies leave the Fort?"

Gloom himself stood cross-armed in the middle of the bridge, his fanged jaws stretched into a smug grin.

"Check out his pet, chief."

Aha, this was our Miss Spitfire. Last time I hadn't had the chance to see her. As Bonny to this virtual Clyde, I'd have thought she'd have looked somewhat different — probably an Alven girl with a modeling body and a stock anime-pretty face.

I'd been wrong.

She was rather short and mousy. Race: Human. A gray robe, staff in hand. First impression: a pious pilgrim. Her nickname was the most striking thing about her, warning anyone to steer clear of her despite her understated appearance.

Her level was quite high, too: only one below me. She was probably Dark's second in the group. And where were Sting and Gray? Could they be stealthing toward me right now?

Slowly I stepped back, giving way to my steely tank.

"Now I see. That's how he managed to do the instance on his own," Spitfire said, curiously studying my scarab.

You bet, girl. You don't know half of my secrets yet.

As I thus got acquainted with the local criminal world, an idea struck me. Shouldn't I be grabbing my teleportation scroll? Or soaring up into the clouds astride my faithful Boris? I wasn't even scared, come to think of it. Even when I'd read Tanor's letter earlier, my heart had failed to miss a beat.

What was happening to me?

I remembered what Dmitry had said about me finally growing a set of teeth. This wasn't that. I didn't feel invincible, not at all. This was something else. I was simply looking at two players who didn't stand much chance against my little menagerie. Dmitry had been dead right there.

Gloom wasn't even a tank. The worst newb could see that. All he had was two bone axes slung behind his back. His armor too was too light for heavy weapon combat. His race's high levels of Life must have allowed him to pull mobs' aggro to himself for a while, but he wouldn't last long in a decent scrap.

Spitfire was a buffer. Her job was to cast spells supporting her allies and weakening her enemies. And if Gloom were left without her magic, then...

I was definitely thinking in the right direction. Damagers weren't suitable for drawn-out fighting.

The biggest problem in this situation was that I couldn't see the other two group members. And that was quite unsettling.

"When I asked you to get yourself some new togs, I did mean *new*," Gloom guffawed. "What am I supposed to do with this Torn Boot?"

Spitfire smirked, too. Her nickname actually suited her a lot. With her sharp face, prickly spiteful eyes and thin lips she looked like the epitome of an evil sorceress.

What's with all the smooth talk? Why didn't they attack? Why hadn't they immobilized me yet? Was I out of her spells' range?

Hah! I was right, wasn't I? As Gloom tried to distract me in conversation, Spitfire kept inching toward me. Inconspicuously, like. Yeah, right.

My scarab must have really upset their plans. Had it not been for him, Gloom would already have been on top of me while the sorceress would have cast her Air Web. But now they were forced to proceed with care.

Besides, all the chat reports of my heroic exploits must have warned them I wasn't the gullible level-12 Digger they'd first met. Now they had to be doubly cautious.

Spitfire's tense glare was filled with mistrust.

But Gloom... talk about the unpredictable human factor. No wonder engineers feared it so much, doing their utmost best to prevent it in their designs.

His beady little eyes betrayed careless disdain. He couldn't have been the one who'd suggested the "keep it clean" approach. He kept casting impatient eyes at his partner. If he could have had it his way, he'd have already attacked the ragamuffin newb that I was in his eyes.

Which was a good thing. The more your enemy underestimated you, the better your chances against him.

"And by the way," Gloom growled, "don't even think about activating your scroll, you idiot. Won't work. Give us all your loot nice and quiet and we might let you go back to your kindergarten. I'm not even going to take your zombie kit. I wouldn't touch it with a barge pole."

He guffawed. Spitfire winced, apparently unhappy with his soliloquy. No wonder: he'd just offered me some important intel I wouldn't have otherwise known.

They'd have loved to catch me with my pants down as I tried to activate the scroll. In combat, every second is priceless: they could have used it to cast the Air Web on the uncomprehending noob while I struggled through the system messages in search of the answer why I was still here and not a thousand miles away. End of story.

Thanks for the warning, buddy!

Spitfire watched my face closely for my reaction. She winced again, realizing I'd known nothing about this particular restriction.

Funnily enough, her body language had just betrayed some even more important intel. They were here alone. The other two weren't with them. No stealthed cavalry coming. They would have long attacked me otherwise.

"Everything's clear with you, guys," I whispered, pensive.

My brain helpfully offered a potential combat tactic. I did a quick check of my weapons and elixirs. The Fix Box was 100% charged. Both my pets were high on Energy. The scarab still had 70% Durability in him.

I smiled at his motionless steely shape. "So what do you think? Should we ruin these goons' day?"

Strangely enough, my inner voice preserved an encouraging silence. It too must have been fed up with all this constant running and hiding.

"Gloom!" Spitfire yelled, second-guessing my intentions.

She was clever, wasn't she? She might go far... provided she lived to see it.

Right, enough of this staring game. Let's do it.

"Out you come, guys! Boris, immobilize the big guy! Prankie, cast the shield! Prepare to heal! Steely Guts, take care of the big guy!"

You've built the simplest mechanical creature: a Swarm of Fleas!
Number of swarm members: 3

I had no time to look into their stats but their levels were good enough. Three fleas the size of a toaster each leaped toward Spitfire. She was already casting her magic, promptly reacting to the scarab's attack.

Boris' scream immobilized Gloom whose tiny eyes seemed to be popping out of his head.

"Surprise!" I said with a vindictive grin.

Almost simultaneously my steel tank rammed into him, sending him flying like a bag of potatoes.

"*Progress is a wondrous thing,*" I began crooning the old ditty from a Russian children's movie, "*it can do most anything. It can fly you to the skies, it can make you rich and wise...*"

In two powerful wingbeats, Boris soared over Gloom's head. "Give us another one, Steely Guts," I ordered, pulling the slingshot. "*No more worries, lots more shirk... Let the robots do your work.*"

The sorceress was a terrible sight. Judging by the fleas' rhythmically moving bellies and the woman's eyes bulging with fear, they weren't going to leave a single drop of blood in her. One of them had bitten into her neck while the other two hung onto her arms. Black gangrenous spots were rapidly growing around the bites. This was the Venom of Swamp Monks in all its terrible glory.

Both her arms were already black. They looked scorched. A lump blocked my throat.

Her already short Life was dwindling rapidly. With a blood-curdling scream, Spitfire tried to pull the flea off her neck. As if! She was only a buffer, not a tank. It would be all over soon.

As she died, she looked up and stared me in the eye. Her glare was filled with so much pain and desperation... and hatred. It looked like I'd just made myself another enemy. Apparently, she'd spent all her mana reserves on Gloom who was now getting his sorry backside kicked by my two pets.

Well, at first glance her gesture deserved every respect. Sacrificing oneself to save a team member was a noble deed any way you looked at it. But-

This was a game. In a couple of minutes, the sorceress would resurrect at her respawn point and continue playing. Somehow I doubted she could repeat her gesture in real life.

Gesture? More like cold calculation. In the real world things might have taken a totally different turn. She might have simply legged it at the first opportunity.

Someone might say this wasn't the way to treat a lady. Point taken.

Still, I had to defend myself. She'd already robbed me once, leaving me naked in the middle of the road. But here, a thief didn't rob a player — he robbed his family, taking their hard-earned real-world money away.

How many players had already become victims to Gloom and his gang? How many had he managed to pick clean?

Each and every one of them were real human

beings who'd invested their own savings into the game; some might have even taken out loans like I'd done. All of them had husbands and wives, children and old-age parents. They had their share of problems, too. Some were trying to save for a down payment on a house, a car or college fees. Others could be raising money for medical treatment — either for themselves or for their loved ones. People came to Mirror World hoping they it might help them solve their problems — only to walk into the likes of Gloom and Spitfire. Bastards like them had already leveled up and gained some group experience. Which they then used to tear their victims apart like the pack of hyenas they were.

This time it hadn't worked, though. Their victim had happened to have teeth too.

The scarab managed to lunge at Gloom again like a steel rhino, dealing him another ramming blow and stripping him of a nice big chunk of Life.

You've killed a player: Spitfire.
Congratulations! You've received a new level!
Current level: 30

Finally Gloom awoke from his slumber. He whipped out his two axes from behind his back and threw himself onto the scarab. My steel pet's Durability began to dwindle at a frightening speed. Gloom's body was enveloped in a red haze: this must have been Spitfire's posthumous buff. I couldn't quite make out its stats but it was some sort of damage boost.

Which gave me an excellent chance to use an Antidote.

I hurried to activate one of the scrolls. The ancient parchment crumbled to dust.

Success!
You've deactivated a damage buff-

Gloom roared his fury. I didn't read on. His damage had dropped considerably but it wasn't going to help the scarab anymore. His Durability was rapidly dwindling, approaching zero. Boris soared into the sky, knowing what was going to happen next.

"That's it, you bastard!" Gloom growled triumphantly, posing his foot onto the scarab's mangled shell. "First," he turned to me, "I'll cut your bird's wings off and then it's your turn. You have a lot to tell me-"

He didn't finish. An explosion shattered the ground. Gloom's shredded gray body flew through the air.

"Boris, don't let him recover! Fleas, get him!"

As Gloom was scrambling on all fours shaking his head like a horse, I hurried to change into my new kit.

Congratulations! You've assembled the full kit of a Fort Guardian!
Reward:
+55 to Survival Instinct
+35 to Range
+150 to Anti-Cold Protection

+150 to Anti-Humidity Protection
+150 to Anti-Sun Protection

The first thing I felt once I'd put my new gear on was a remarkable lightness over my whole body. It was as if I'd instantly shed the hundreds of pounds' worth of junk I'd been lugging around. I can't describe it. It felt like... entering a superhero's body?

A new system message awoke me from my bliss. The Swarm of Fleas was no more.

What, already? Gloom had made quick work of my little helpers! Now he was gulping some elixirs, preparing to face Boris. Still, the fleas had managed to poison him: his right leg and shoulder were turning black slowly but surely.

"Boris, wait! Let me distract him first!"

I didn't even feel the tension as I pulled the sling. It made the familiar popping sound. Gloom's giant knee snapped. Some damage this was!

He cried out in pain. Leaning against his axe, he tried to scramble to his feet.

Another shot.

And again.

I showered him with bursts like a machine gun, critting him time and time again.

With a desperate roar, Gloom hurled his axe at me.

Oh really? That's what he could do, was it?

Why hadn't he tried it before?

The explanation was simple: I stood too close.

As if in slow motion, the bone monstrosity flew past. Still, what with my current levels of speed, I would have been utterly clumsy not to have ducked in time.

I was about to loose off another slug when Boris beat me to it. Gloom didn't survive my birdie's heavy fall from the sky.

You've killed a player: Gloom.
Warning! Gloom and Spitfire have blacklisted you!

Whatever. They'd probably sent me a nasty email, too. They wouldn't be the first, though.

I cast a blank glance at the clock. The combat had lasted all of two minutes. It had felt like an eternity. My heart was about to spring out of my chest. My arms were shaking as if I'd spent all day loading sacks of cement. Still, I wasn't tired. My body felt light. I had a small adrenaline rush, that's all.

I checked the two chests left after Dark and Spitfire's respective demises. So! Apparently, my Blue set was akin to the arrival of a heavy-duty cannon at a medieval village.

The two PKs' Gray items sported some quite impressive stats... for a newb location, that is. The bone axe alone was a beauty, as was the sorceress' charm. Where had they managed to get them from? What a shame my Digger gear wasn't there. They must have stashed it away somewhere... or even sold it, which was much more likely.

I could only imagine how happy they'd been to read all the chat messages about my exploits. They must have known that achievements like those came with rewards to match. I just didn't understand why they'd come here alone. Had they had the two others with them, their chances might have been better.

Having said that... who was I kidding? Whether two or four, they would have stood no chance against my pet army, period. And once I'd put on my new Blue kit... nah, they could forget it.

But still. Why had they been alone? Had they been too greedy to share the loot with two more group members?

Having said that, the two others could have simply been offline and failed to contact the gang leaders in the time it had taken me to walk back to the entrance. In which case they might still arrive any minute to defend their boss' property.

I left the loot alone, stood up and cast a studying look around me. Nothing seemed to have changed. The area looked the same: the rain, the lightning, the Fort's foreboding walls, the thick undergrowth...

Wait a sec. The undergrowth.

I shook my head. Impossible. I of all people knew it. After all, I'd spent some time hiding in those thickets myself. Could it be a system glitch? Or a hallucination even? My brain was definitely in overload after all this fighting.

Yes, a hallucination. It had to be. There was no other explanation for the fact that the bushes seemed translucent now, allowing me to make out Vitar's crouching outline lurking in the thicket.

I rubbed my tired eyes. Oh. Apparently, not a hallucination. There he was, my treacherous fisherman friend. He nearly jumped when I gave him another look.

But what if... of course! How stupid of me. This was my new characteristic working! What was it called now? Survival Instinct. How awesome. One more thing I'd have to look up on the forums.

"Boris, you think you could fly closer to him so he doesn't notice?" I mouthed inconspicuously, pretending I was checking the loot. "Immobilize him to save him the trouble of escaping. Me and Prankie here will act naturally, won't we, Prankie?"

Playing along, Prankster set his front feet onto the edge of a chest and looked curiously inside. What a cheek!

Boris soared up and disappeared amid the clouds. Almost immediately we heard his victorious roar.

He hadn't left Vitar any chance. The guy froze in the bushes like a pillar of salt, his eyes bulging as if he'd just seen a UFO.

"Not you again," I said, studying his immobile frame with interest. "From what I can see they never gave you your stuff back, did they?"

He was dressed in some miserable rags. If the truth were known, even I'd looked better after finishing the instance. He was still barefoot, clad in some excuse for a jacket and a pair of canvas pants. He was shuddering — whether with fear or cold, I couldn't tell. The guy was a sorry sight indeed.

Had he really been so gullible as to believe Gloom's promises? Either he was stupid or he'd hoped to get into the gang leader's good books. He hadn't had a hope in hell of getting his old gear back — but he could get himself some new stuff, even if low-level. Judging by his looks, the former scenario was more like it.

The ten seconds' immobilization had finally elapsed. Vitar stirred weakly.

"Don't try to escape," I warned him. "Once you answer my questions, you're free to go."

"O-o-k-k-kay," he stuttered, glancing at the bounty chests his ex-bosses had left behind.

I shook my head. "There was nothing of yours there. Nor mine."

His eyes filled with pain. Had he really hoped to get his stuff back? For a moment, I even felt sorry for the idiot.

"They might have stashed it away somewhere," I suggested.

He lowered his head. "I don't think so. Sting and Gray left for the continent last night. They took all the loot with them. A month's worth. It must have been a lot if they had to go together."

"Clever," I rubbed my cheek in contemplation. "What are the admins thinking of?"

Vitar shrugged. "This is gameplay. They aren't breaking the rules, are they? Besides, no one really cares about this newb backwater. Smart players come here to form groups, do the main quest, hit level 10 and go directly for the instance. At level 10, mobs are quite doable there. Such players avoid PKs as best they can."

"These two, how far is their resurrection point?"

"Who knows? You really think they would tell me something like that? If you're afraid of them attacking you again, I don't think they'll do so. There's no one on the Isles who could take you on now. Besides, all their gear's gone."

"And how about those two from the village?"

"You mean Blue Beard and Catatonic? Nah, they can't come here. They've fallen out with Gloom."

"How about Dreadlock?"

"They're over there now," he nodded at the Fort. "They left to do the instance right after Gloom had robbed them."

I sighed. "I see."

Now I could understand why Dreadlock hadn't been replying to my messages. "Very well, then. You're free to go, as promised."

Vitar shrank toward the bush in disbelief.

The state he was in! Those bastards had really put the fear of God into him. He seemed to be seriously afraid of me taking it out on him. Strangely enough, I felt sorry for him despite all his treachery.

I watched as he scrambled into the woods, then went back to finish checking out the chests. As I packed the loot into my bag, I kept sensing his stare on me.

"Ah, whatever. I would have dumped it anyway," I mumbled, scooping up my entire Guardian kit and throwing it to the ground.

I added a few rings, bracelets and a fishing rod. Someone might say the traitor wasn't worth even that. Maybe not. In any case, it was my decision and my stuff. I could do whatever I wanted with it.

Now I was well and truly finished here. Time to bid my farewell to these hospitable lands.

Chapter Seventeen

Herbalists needed to harvest the Southern Meadow! Payment negotiable! Bonus resources paid separately! Food, protection and Reaper buffs on the house! Priority will be given to players with runes!
WTB everything you don't need! Price no object.
An Eastern Breeze kit available for hire!
FREE elixirs from your source materials!
An experienced player will take newbs to Midget Dungeon. PM me for the rates and other information.

Gosh, I missed this crazy gaming bustle. My prolonged solitude was beginning to show. This little seaside town, eloquently dubbed Balmy Bay, was peaceful and sort of welcoming. Although a far cry from the Maragar Citadel with its frantic chatrooms, it was exactly what I needed at the moment.

Because I'd chosen this location beforehand, it hadn't taken me long to activate the teleportation scroll. But first, I'd logged out.

Surprisingly, I hadn't felt at all tired. For several reasons. My Bronze account, my current level, my gear and the state-of-the-art capsule — all that had made my recuperation a breeze. I'd stayed twelve hours offline, eight of which I'd spent sleeping, followed by a nice hot shower and a long conversation with my family.

Naturally, they all celebrated my success. Dmitry for one seemed especially surprised. He said he hadn't expected me to take his words so seriously. If the truth were known, now that I'd had some rest and a chance to replay the events of the last four days in my head, I couldn't help wondering if I was indeed the person who'd performed all those feats.

In any case, I was done with newb locations. I had new heights to conquer.

Now, Balmy Bay. Why this town? The reason was simple: the clan which happened to control it.

Tanor's main argument was that the Steel Shirts had their fingers in every pie. He might even have been right: who was I to argue? But somehow I doubted that everybody was prepared to accept this state of affairs. Wherever there was a strong clan's hand controlling the area, there were bound to be those unhappy about the situation.

I was right. As soon as I logged into the forum and opened its Clan Wars archive, I had all the information I needed and then some.

Apart from the winners, all wars also have losers, if you know what I mean. Quite a few of them, as I'd found out. Predictably, most of the clans that used to participate in bygone wars had long ceased to exist. Some of them had joined the Alliance while a few others had holed up in their respective backwaters and kept a low profile. Still, in their heart of hearts they secretly hated the winners.

I managed to locate a few names. The Fearless, The Steel Fists, the Power of Heaven, Thor's Hammer, the Predators. Once top clans, they now counted among those dethroned by the Alliance.

Logically, their territories would be much safer for me. Having checked the latest forum messages, I decided on Balmy Bay: a quiet beachside town in the Southern part of Mirror World, part of the Predators' territory. I couldn't have found a worse backwater if I'd tried.

No, I wasn't thinking of defecting to the Steel Shirts' defeated enemy. That would be swapping one set of troubles for another. I just needed a place where I could do my thing without being disturbed. And the Predators' lands seemed to be ideal for my purposes.

Balmy Bay was a total of twenty-three houses. Talk about a one-horse town. Even Leuton was a megalopolis in comparison. Was this the only thing the once-strongest clan had left to its name? They must have been really pissed off about it. Then again, some other clans didn't even have that.

I had to give them their due: the place was cozy and well thought-out. The town walls were in excellent condition; powerful fortifications surrounded the clan's citadel. The streets were neat and clean. They even had a port although it still seemed to be a work in progress.

Actually, they had a lot of building going on. The huge hangars by the port were definitely being erected there for a reason. Workers were busy clearing new building sites by the South gate. I wouldn't be surprised to soon see all sorts of little inns, shops and taverns there.

I had a gut feeling that while the strongest clans were busy conquering No-Man's Lands, the Predators decided to stake a claim on Water World. Very soon all port cities would be packed with players in need of work, hotel rooms, customers and warehouses. I could see the Predators' point. I would have done the same thing.

In the meantime, Balmy Bay was still a sleepy fishing village awaiting its transformation into a virtual Shanghai or Rotterdam. Which suited me just fine.

My appearance was my biggest investment. This time I didn't even need to visit a barber. My Bronze account and my level 30 considerably simplified the process.

So I ordered a new character template online and entered the town a new man. Or rather, a new dwarf.

The stylists had really done their best. Apart from installing a new image, they also had the option of "dusting" your name tag. Now everyone who wanted to see my name would have to really strain their eyes. Even I struggled to do that. The letters of my name indeed looked "dusted" so you couldn't quite work out what they said. And considering the fact that I wasn't going to stand still, that should work out just fine.

Admittedly, this was only a 2-hour buff and quite costly, too. Still, a couple of hours was plenty for my purposes. And as for the money... safety was much more precious.

And so it happened that one fine day a black-bearded dwarf walked down the Balmy Bay's main street, looking totally part of the furniture. Just a dwarf like any other. They all looked the same, didn't they?

First off, I had to sell the PKs' gear. It wouldn't cost much: all levels 20+ were already wearing Green items. Still, it was worth a try. I didn't want to get Rrhorgus involved: he still had to sort out all the loot from the little chests which I planned to open after checking out the market square.

The marketplace was in the town center. It was a standard-issue location with two or three buildings forming a circle presided over by the town hall and a monument to some becloaked guy at the center. I stood too far away to make out his name on the pedestal.

The market was quite neat, come to think of it. Stalls and stands formed orderly ranks separated by rather wide passages, allowing shoppers to walk comfortably without stepping on each other's toes. I could see a few Predator clan members patrolling the market, making sure order was maintained.

I was beginning to seriously like this place.

"Excuse me! Sir?"

Were they addressing me?

I turned round. That's right. A burly red-cheeked man was leaning out of a wide dark-brown stall, its counter overflowing with various tools, runes, bags and clothes.

"Greetings, Sir!" the vendor began, squinting at my name tag.

"Morning," I said, then hurried to add in order to distract him, "What can you surprise me with?"

"Oh!" he immediately forgot all about my name and turned his attention to his goods, praising them to high heaven.

I was stuck there for a good five minutes listening to his sales pitch. I even had to pretend I was interested in some Gray tools, asking him all sorts of pointless questions. I ended up promising I'd be back as soon as I sold my own stuff, just to acquire "that absolutely awesome bag over there".

"You have stuff to sell?" he asked me.

"Yeah. It's my nephew's actually," I showed him my trophies. "He asked me if I could sell all this stuff for him."

He gave it an appraising look. "You need to see Mickey with this. He's over there in the next row. You can tell him I sent you. He'll sort you out."

It didn't take me long to get there, considering I had to stop several times for polite exchanges with other vendors. You shouldn't ignore this kind of market ritual. The more people you see, the more you learn.

Oh. This was quite a queue! Mickey was popular, wasn't he?

As I waited in line, I had time to study his stall. Compared to the humble tents around it, this was a palace.

A long wide counter was heaped with all sorts of things. Knives, swords, spears, scissors, shields, bags, hats; some unidentified bones, coils of rope and string in every possible size, not to mention all sorts of boxes, crates and sacks. A burly gnome presided over his treasures, sporting a cute *Mickey* name tag. He had a helper: an Alven salesman, tall and gaunt. What an odd pair.

"Sir! How can I help you?"

Oh, it was my turn already.

Mickey stared at me calmly, making no attempt to read my tag. His gaze glowed with understanding. He must have seen tons of guys like me here. I liked his tact.

"Morning," I said, pouring the PK's ex-property onto the counter. "What do you think of this?"

He spent some time going through it, then concluded, "Seven hundred gold. Can't offer you more, sorry. Apart from this charm, there's nothing of much value here, really."

Spitfire was full of surprises! And I used to think that Gloom's axes were the best bet. Lesson learned: never judge people by appearances.

I decided against showing him my Fort loot. This gnome seemed a bit too shrewd for comfort.

"Sounds good," I said. "It's a deal."

Shame. The gear that Gloom had stolen from me was at least twice the price of all their stuff. Never mind, at least I'd ruffled their feathers a bit. It would take them a while to come round. The thought alone warmed my heart.

"Agreed," he smiled to me.

We shook hands. The money dropped into my account.

"Anything here you think you might like?" Mickey asked.

He'd beaten me to it. I'd been about to ask him the same thing. I pretended I was considering his question, then reached into my pocket for one of the few surviving beads. "You don't happen to have something like this, do you?"

He glanced at my hand. "This looks like a slingshot slug. Used a lot by Dwand snipers. Wait a sec."

He dove into his giant storeroom and reappeared with a leather pouch. "Here. There should be about thirty of them. All different sizes and different quality."

"May I?"

He nodded, "Be my guest."

I loosened the knot and looked inside. Yes! He had all sorts there: beads made of steel, copper and stone, some round, others tear-shaped, a few spiky ones even. But most importantly, these weren't slapdash DIY jobs but purpose-made projectiles with Durability to match. Some of them seemed a little too large for my slingshot but most of them would work just fine.

"Like it?" he asked.

"Sure. I'll take them," I paused, then added, "Do you have any Intellect runes, by any chance?"

He fell silent for a moment. "I don't think so. First time I hear about them. What class are they for?

Actually, I shouldn't even ask. Too many classes these days, can't remember them all."

"True."

"I could sell you something for standard characteristics, if you want. It'll be cheaper than at auction. Would you like that?"

I'd already ordered some combat runes. All I could use at the moment was a Green double set, so I'd chosen Stamina+Protection. I'd also been toying with the idea of installing the Purple Master Digger runes but they only boosted one stat, not two. So I'd decided against it and ordered some combat ones from Rrhorgus instead.

The reason I'd asked him about Intellect was a hunch I had. The thing was, I'd found nothing about Intellect online. They had Wisdom, Concentration, Focus, but nothing about Intellect anywhere. Never mind. I might have to use all available points to level up Knowledge.

"I'm all right, thanks," I said. "All I need is these beads."

"Shame."

"You don't by any chance know a master who could make more of these for me?" I asked him as I shelled out.

"Sure," the gnome replied. "Lance the Rightie is the best smith in the whole of Balmy Bay. His shop is in Green Lane. He'll be happy to see you."

"Excellent," I shook his powerful hand. "Thank you."

"Thank *you*," he replied cheerfully.

As I left his stall, I thought I heard someone

say my name. Or was it my imagination playing up?

Green Lane was bathed in calm. It greeted me with a pleasant coolness. I wasn't used to warm weather anymore. This town was a bit on the hot side; still, I really didn't want to go back to rainier climes. Better sweat for a bit than get soaked to the bone.

I had no problem finding Lance the Rightie's shop although it was strangely devoid of any noise. Not typical for a blacksmith. Normally, these kinds of workshops were situated on the outskirts or even beyond the city walls. Still, this was a game. It changed a lot of things.

The massive steel-reinforced door opened with surprising ease. That was probably normal. You wouldn't expect a Master Blacksmith's door to creak or screech, would you?

The moment I stepped inside and shut the door after me, I was overcome by the typical racket of rattling and clattering. Work in the smithy was in full swing. And outside you couldn't hear a thing!

"Funny, eh?"

I turned to the voice. A man stood in the doorway of the noisy room. He wasn't tall, but the span of his shoulders more than compensated for his lack in the height department. This was Lance the Rightie himself.

"Actually, yeah," I admitted, looking around me.

"It's my partner, he had the Veil of Silence installed," Rightie explained, his voice ringing with pride. "It costs a fortune but lasts a whole week. This way we can work right in the city center without upsetting the neighbors."

"Good investment," I agreed.

"Thanks. How can I help you?"

I stepped toward him and opened the pouch of beads. "You think you could make something like this?"

"What's it for? A sling?"

"Not exactly. These four, for instance, are too big for my purposes."

He nodded. "There're two ways of doing it."

"Tell me."

"Either standard issue or tailored to your weapon," he replied with an apparently prepared phrase. He must have said it many times before. He probably had a lot of slingers among his clients.

"The second option, what does it require?" I asked.

"Nothing serious. You show me your weapon, I take all the measurements, we agree on the price and I make them."

"Deal," I reached into my pocket and produced the Minor Pocket Slingshot.

For a second he froze. Not a trace of sarcasm in his eyes. He looked dead serious as if I'd just shown him something truly special. You could tell he was very meticulous in his approach. A real professional.

I'd been lucky to come here.

"Got it," Rightie's voice betrayed excitement. "I've taken all the measurements. I can offer you two types of projectiles. The things in the pouch you've just shown me, only four of those will actually do."

"Oh really?" I produced one of those I'd made

myself. "What can you say about this? Any good?"

He gingerly took the tear-shaped bead. It looked like a speck of dust in his mitts. Still, despite their deceptive clumsiness, Rightie's fingers moved with remarkable dexterity.

He chuckled. "It is and it isn't."

"Oh," admittedly, I was surprised.

"The item is still unfinished. The source material is atrocious. But the finish on it is actually quite decent. This is something a beginner Apprentice might have done. Did he use some sort of Durability-enhancing design?"

Oh wow. He'd looked right through it, hadn't he? Or was it his professional level that allowed him to see these sorts of things?

"You're dead right there," I said. "He used whatever he had at hand. Adlibbed, basically."

"Did it work?" he asked, curious.

"Absolutely."

"That's the main thing," he nodded his approval, then hurried to change the subject. "I can offer you two different types of shot: lighter ones that improve Accuracy and heavier ones with a bigger chance of a crit. It's up to you."

"What about Durability?"

"Both are 30."

That was good news! "Excellent. I'd like two hundred of each, please."

"I have something else, too," he added.

"Yes?"

"Burrs — I mean crit-boosting ones — my partner could cast a spell on them too. But there's a problem with them."

"The price," I nodded my understanding.

"Not only that. Charmed bullets — or tagged, as we call them — have no Durability."

"Sounds logical. Do they explode on impact?"

He chuckled. "On the contrary. My partner studied water magic. He can cast the Ice-Bound debuff onto your burrs. Very useful to fight large mobs with. You're gonna love it."

"I already do. I'd like him to treat all two hundred of them."

"Good," Rightie said, visibly relieved. Then he added in a shaky voice, "And one more thing... probably the most important..."

"Really? You're full of surprises, aren't you?"

"Yeah," his forehead erupted in beads of sweat. "When I studied your slingshot, I saw I could make a couple of improvements to it."

I stared at him in disbelief.

"You shouldn't be so surprised," he hurried to add. "That's my job. The system shows me what I can improve. Besides, if it's something new and unusual, a master can expect to receive various achievements or skill points. And in the case of your slingshot, I might also be able to create two unique blueprints."

"Okay," I scratched my beard, contemplating his offer. "This is a decision and a half."

His eyes glowed with hope. I had very little idea of what the creation of a unique blueprint might mean for the designer. But judging by Rightie's suddenly pale face, it was quite a lot.

"Please, Sir Olgerd. Listen to what I have to

say."

I nearly jumped.

"Yes, of course I know your name," he said soothingly. "We've been talking for quite a while. I had plenty of time to work out your name tag. You shouldn't worry. If you want to remain anonymous, my lips are sealed."

That's why he'd kept dropping hints about "large mobs"!

"I can offer you a deal," he went on. "I'll improve your weapon at no cost to you. Besides, I'm not going to charge you anything at all for any of the slugs, including the charmed ones. I might even throw in another hundred of each. What would you say to that?"

Oh. Actually, what did I have to lose? Nothing. This was a win-win situation. I couldn't sense any catch here. I'd never have been able to pull off something like this myself. If I could, the system would have already told me so. Apparently, this wasn't within my Engineering Designer work remit.

Very well. Let's make his day. "Sounds good. Just please make sure you don't tell anyone about me."

"Absolutely not! I'll get to work straight away," he said cheerfully. "It'll only take ten minutes. Please grab a seat. We have some very comfortable chairs in the corner over there. Would you like something to drink?"

"No, thank you. I'd like to sit down though."

Rightie had told me the truth. Ten minutes later, he re-emerged from his shop with a victorious look, carrying two pouches and some bits of equipment.

"Three hundred with Accuracy and three more Ice-Bound," he handed me the pouches.

His face was lit up with a happy smile. His eyes glowed; his cheeks twitched with excitement.

I smiled back. "It worked, by the looks of you."

"You could say so! Take a look at this!"

Two items lay on the table in front of me.

Name: a Truss for a Minor Pocket Slingshot
Effect: +15% to Accuracy

Name: a Stabilizer for a Minor Pocket Slingshot
Effect: +5% to Damage

"Both items are Green," he explained. "This is all I can do at the moment. Besides, I managed to make their blueprints too. Apparently, this weapon hasn't been around for long. It might actually be one of a kind."

I had nothing to say to that.

"But that's irrelevant," he flashed me another happy smile. "Reputation is key! The more blueprints a master makes, the bigger his Reputation! I'll be honest with you, these are the first blueprints I've ever made. So tonight I'm celebrating! I'm taking some of my friends and workmates to the Starfish tonight. You're invited!"

"I'd love to, but... unfortunately, I have to go. I really appreciate your thinking about me."

"As you wish," he lowered his head slightly.

"Well, then! Let's put your wonder weapon together!"

Congratulations! Your weapon has been improved!

Once we were done with all the formalities, I headed for the exit. Rightie scurried along to see me out. He was already reaching for the door when he froze.

That's weird. I felt a knot forming in my stomach.

"You can't go there," he said, frowning. His voice was hoarse. His hands began to shake. "Who sent you here?"

"Mickey," I said, beginning to realize what was going on.

"It was him, then. He reported you to the Predators," Rightie said with a sad shake of his head. "One of their men has just contacted me. He asked questions about you. I'm very sorry."

"Do you have a back door?"

"Sure!" he nodded. "Follow me!"

He hurried toward his workshop.

He had a proper little factory back there! I counted three workers, each of whom had his own worktop. He even had a shop sweep! Rightie definitely planned to stay in game for the long term.

"Over there," he pointed at a small door under the stairs. "Hurry up. I told them you'd left five minutes ago."

"You shouldn't risk it."

"Don't worry about me. They know better than

to screw with me. This place isn't exactly paved with Experienced blacksmiths. Just one last piece of advice, if I may."

"Please."

"I don't think you realize how well-known your nickname is. Otherwise you wouldn't have showed up in a public place unprepared. I suggest you give it some thought. Good luck!"

I nodded my gratitude, then ducked into the dark doorway. It opened into a side alley.

I cast a look around. No one. Aggravation from another clan was the last thing I needed now. Rightie had a point. What an idiot I was! Then again, how had I been supposed to know that the brief mention of my name in the chat would have created so many waves?

I was about to summon Boris when a voice came from above,

"Sir Olgerd? Mind talking to me for a moment?"

I looked up. A level-90 Warrior stood on a small fancy balcony. Nickname: Leosant. His clan logo sported the head of a panther baring its teeth. A Predator.

I cast a quick look around.

"You don't need to worry. We're alone. My men are waiting for you by the front door."

"What do you want from me?" I asked, my mind rushing. It looked like I might need to summon my entire menagerie.

Leosant leaned against the balcony, looking relaxed. "That's funny. That's exactly what my leaders wanted to ask *you*."

"You can tell your leaders I'm just visiting. I

came here to sell some loot and do a bit of shopping."

"I see," he said, sounding bored. "Is that it?"

"It certainly is."

"Good," the Predator stood up.

I felt like a coiled spring, ready to jump into action.

"In that case," he continued, "my leaders have a message for you, just in case: *'No, you can't.* Know what I mean?"

I actually did. The Predators probably thought I'd come to seek their protection.

How funny. They must have known that the Steel Shirts were looking for me. They could probably guess why, too. They weren't going to help their old enemies, but neither did they intend to attack me. Staying neutral was their best option. Which made sense: the Predators had just invested a lot of time and effort into their town's infrastructure. They had better things to do than challenge Mirror World's strongest clan; besides, they had their dignity too.

I nodded. "Sure."

"In which case, we're done here," Leosant said grimly. "Don't let me keep you any longer. Oh, and one more tip. The sooner you happen to leave this town the better."

"This I can promise," I said, reaching for the summoning charm.

Chapter Eighteen

I remembered an episode of my childhood —
when all of my family had still been young, happy and
alive, full of energy and plans for the future. I was
eight then: a boy who'd just managed to grasp the
meaning of a major event called "moving house".

Prior to that, I'd already known the Russian
expression, "Moving house is worse than losing it to a
fire." At the time, I couldn't quite grasp it: how could
it be? All we'd be doing is moving our stuff to another
place. What's that got to do with completely losing all
your possessions in a fire?

But judging by my grandfather's constant
grumbling, he'd much rather "all this junk had
burned to hell", as he'd put it.

I still remembered taking pictures off the wall
in my room. And finding some loose change behind
the bedside table I'd moved. I'd scratched my name in
tiny little letters just under the window sill, by way of

saying goodbye. I still remember how sad I was to part with my old den.

It was our next-door neighbor, Aunt Zoe, who bought our apartment allowing us to move to a bigger one closer to the center. Despite the change of address, my Mom stayed in touch with our old neighbors. When many years later Aunt Zoe's husband had died, we went to their place for the funeral. That's when I saw my old room again.

It felt weird to know this was the same place. It was crowded with very dark bulky furniture. A ceiling lamp hung low, casting a dim light on the center of the room and leaving the rest in the dark. The ugly new wallpaper was covered in huge tasteless purple flowers. Strange faces stared at me from the pictures on the walls. Potted cacti were lined up on the window sill, bristling their needles as if informing me this wasn't my place anymore.

I decided to try an experiment. I walked over to the window, closed my eyes and reached below the window sill, my fingers searching for the tiny inscription.

I felt it. *Oleg*, it still read.

A lump formed in my throat. Tears welled in my eyes. At the time of my making this inscription, both my grandparents had still been alive. My dad had still been living with us. My mom had been full of life and energy...

Now as I sat in my room in Tronus' tower, I was saying my goodbyes too. It didn't feel as strong as when I'd been a child but you wouldn't call me cheerful, either. This place and I, we went back a while. Boris had been born here; he'd taken his first flight from this tower roof — accidentally giving me one hell of a fright.

Was I going to miss it? I looked around me. A wardrobe, a table, a chair, a bed, a window that opened to the constant drizzle outside... no, I didn't think so.

"You look as if you're saying goodbye to this old wardrobe!" Tronus stood in the doorway, leaning against the wooden lintel.

"Maybe," I mumbled. "You never know."

"I can't agree more with you, my friend," he said. "Too many things have happened just lately. You just can't keep track of it all."

"Why, has it been busy here?"

"Oh," he waved his hand at me. "Busy is an understatement. Fancy a glass of wine in my lab?"

"With pleasure," I rose from my seat.

As I walked out, I cast an inconspicuous glance back. How weird. Just by stepping out of the room, I didn't belong here anymore. I wasn't coming back. And considering what I was about to do in the near future, I doubted I'd ever be welcome again in Tronus' abode.

"Now," Tronus lowered himself into an easy chair. "You're apparently a new legend!"

I chuckled. "Just happened to be in the right place at the right time."

"That's funny. But still, how did you manage to defeat the Lich on your own? From what I hear, he's one strong sonovabitch. Always has been."

Now it was my turn to be surprised. "Why, do

you know him?"

"We used to study together. But that's irrelevant, anyway. Come on, tell me!"

"Yeah, sure. I'm going to tell you everything in a moment. Even better, I'll show you."

I opened the bag, pulled out the Pocket Book of Blueprints and offered it to him. "I inherited it, sort of. I even managed to work out a couple of designs."

He took the book and began leafing through it with an occasional chuckle or shake of the head, continuously raising his eyebrows. I even stood up in my seat, trying to see what he found so fascinating. Don't forget that I only had access to the first few pages while he, as far as I could see, was already halfway through it, apparently having no problems reading it.

Could he help me with opening more pages, maybe? This would be too much to hope for but-

He slammed the book shut and proffered it back to me.

"So what do you think?" I asked.

He cringed. "Mechanics. I was never into the Highlanders' craft or their inventions. But there're quite a few rather elegant solutions there, I have to admit... especially in the final pages..."

My heart missed a beat.

"All I can say is — congratulations!" he continued. "Now I understand how you managed to survive in the Fort."

"In actual fact, I've only just started looking through them. Now if someone could explain-"

"Sorry, my friend," he interrupted me. "As I've

just said, mechanics just aren't my thing. I've gleaned very little from what I've just read. And in any case, there's no way I'm going to explain any of it to you. That would be doing you a big disservice. I'm afraid, you'll have to learn it all yourself, slowly and gradually."

Oh well. Apparently, you couldn't outsmart the system. Never mind. It had been worth a try. Now, next thing on my agenda.

"Thank you, Master. Mind if I in turn ask you a question?"

"Absolutely. Fire away," he agreed magnanimously, taking a sip from his silver goblet.

"It's about Crast stones."

His nonchalance was gone in a flash. He tensed up. "Do I understand correctly you've finally decided on a swap?"

I nodded. "You do indeed."

"Excellent!" he happily jumped off his seat. "Follow me!"

AN HOUR LATER, I was already flying astride Boris to meet Rrhorgus.

The only things I'd accepted from Tronus were magic Teleport Crystals even though he'd offered me lots of useful goodies. I'd been dying to get my fill of freebies but they weren't really an option. I was bound to outgrow whatever items he could offer me quite soon. Elixirs weren't the answer, either. So the twenty crystals had to suffice: my strategic stocks for when the going got really tough.

The beauty of the crystals was in the fact that

they offered a teleport to any point in Mirror World provided I'd been there before. And considering the fact that the process of Boris' flight training had already taken me pretty much everywhere in the Lands of Light not to mention some far-off Dark locations, the choice of potential exit points was truly impressive. These crystals had been a very good acquisition indeed.

As I'd paid, I'd received a New Achievement message. Apparently, I'd been the first player to ever receive the crystals. You bet! It would take other players a while to lay their hands on Crast stones.

Tronus, my dear friend... what a shame we were about to become enemies. I couldn't do anything about it: this was gameplay. But I sure was going to miss this intelligent NPC and our long unhurried conversations.

"Trust you to get into trouble," Rrhorgus slapped my armored shoulder. "Our chicken shed hasn't seen such a stir in quite a while. Even the colonization of No-Man's Lands pales into insignificance in comparison. The forum is absolutely flooded with *Olgerd this, Olgerd that.*"

"I can imagine," I chuckled, admiring the sun setting over the ocean. "According to Dmitry, newb locations are trending like hell. I had to shell out for an email client. My inbox in absolutely blocked."

"I can imagine the kinds of letters you receive."

"Oh," I grinned back. "At first I opened a few. I thought my brain would explode."

He laughed.

"Well, what did you want me to do?" I shrugged. "The things they offered me... how could anyone even think of something like that! All right, all those invitations to join a raid or a clan are only logical. As are questions about the Fort and the kind of loot you can expect there. A few loan requests are a bit of a stretch, but still understandable. But asking to marry me! That's a bit over the top, isn't it?"

"You'd be surprised," Rrhorgus replied, serious. "They are in fact the most sensible ones."

I stared at him in surprise. "In what respect?"

"In terms of marriage. It comes with so many perks you can't imagine. If your Sveta ever joined the game, I'd have told you to get married in Mirror World straight away. It costs, but it's definitely worth it."

"Now you've got me curious. How is it worth it?"

"Even the wedding rings, if you think of it. Firstly, they boost a lot of stats. Secondly, you can wear them on the same finger with any other ring. And thirdly, they can port you to your spouse, provided he or she is not inside an instance. There's a daily limit though: three or four teleports, I think."

I scratched my head. "Sounds good. Like a mini-portal that you can carry around with you."

"And that's only a fraction of all the advantages offered by Mirror World to its married couples. So whoever proposed to you knew what they were doing.

Only I suspect they're probably all low-level players."

"Not necessarily. Some of them were higher levels than me."

He grinned. "They sense your potential! Or most likely, they simply don't know much about you."

"You're dead right there. You're the only person I went to see. I'd hate to create problems for my friends."

"I know, I know. Tanor is beginning to apply pressure. To me, as well. What did Uncle Vanya say about your escapades?"

"He seemed all right. He warned me that he didn't want Liz to have problems though. Aren't you afraid?"

"Who, me?" Rrhorgus bared his fangs in an ominous grin. "I'm a legless cripple already. What am I supposed to be afraid of?"

"How about Max?"

"They'll never get to him."

Judging by his confident smile, he was probably right.

"In any case, they don't need to find out about our little partnership," he rubbed his hands. "But if you don't make me a few millions, I won't invite you to my funeral, remember that!"

"If I only knew how to do that..."

"It's all right," he gave me an encouraging slap on the shoulder. "I'm sure you'll think of something. Just look at you! Level 30! A personal Blue set! Pocketfuls of useful beasties! You're a legend, man. Mirror World's very own hero. It's only been a few weeks since I sold you the Goner kit!"

I chuckled. "Those were the days! Life seemed to be so much easier back then. Talking about selling, I've opened whatever loot I got from the Serpent instance. All of it apart from the Red chest, I mean."

"You don't mean to say you've been to Mellenville, do you?"

"Not yet, but I'm going to. I had my stuff delivered to the Balmy Bay bank. I had to pay extra but it was worth it."

"I bet it was. Way too risky. Why the hell would you want to go back to Mellenville? Tanor has his eyes and ears everywhere there."

"I need to get to the Armory," I said. "I have lots of Reputation saved, don't forget. I lost some of it doing the quest but still."

"I see," he agreed reluctantly. "Lots of good stuff in the Armory. So if I understand correctly, you might need to leave a down payment."

I made a helpless gesture.

"Oh, well. If that's what you want... just don't say I didn't warn you. What have you got? Show me."

"Just a sec," I nodded, hurrying to open the bag. "Now! I opened twenty-four boxes and ten pouches in total. They mainly contained transferable Reputation resources. Claws, eyes, feathers, crystals, bits of coal and whatnot. Quite useful stuff, if you know what I mean. Then I have nine Purple and sixteen Blue runes. Plus two more Blue items: a bow and a saber. All items fully transferable with no restrictions on them. I have high hopes for the Red Wrought-Iron Chest but to open it, I have to be level 50. Besides, I found this Potion of Fury in the Fort.

Someone might offer a good price for it."

I pulled the Red vial from the bag and offered it to my friend. Rrhorgus didn't react. What was wrong with him? He zoned out, open-mouthed, as if I'd shown him the Holy Grail itself.

"Hey dude," I gave him a poke in the ribs. "What's with playing the salt pillar?"

"All riiiiight," he finally managed. "That's getting interesting. If the Serpent dungeon is supposed to be easy, I dread to think what you might bring from a really difficult one."

I puffed out my chest. "D'you like it?"

"You bet," he gave me a happy slap on the shoulder. "Now they'll be lining up outside my shop. Transferable Reputation runes and resources with no level restriction? You bet! Or would you prefer to keep the runes?"

I shook my head. "I'd love to but I can't. Having Purple runes installed at level 30 sounds almost too tempting, I agree. Still, most of them boost Damage and Speed while what I really need is Stamina. Besides, I don't think it would be wise to keep them. I need the money. Don't forget I have my monthly loan payments to keep up with."

"I see," he nodded. "I've actually brought you some Green ones. Admittedly they're not Purple but they'll give your gear some boost. It's only to get you going, anyway. I'm sure you'll get yourself even better ones."

"If only Lady Luck could hear you!"

"It's all right. We'll do it," he reassured me, then switched his attention back to the loot. "These weapons are quite rare. You can make good money by selling them. But the Potion of Fury is rather common. It might fetch you fifty gold if you're lucky. Did you say Uncle Vanya owed you some loot?"

I nodded. "Yeah. He sent me the money instead. He valued my tip at eight hundred."

"It's probably easier this way," he agreed, then added with a chuckle, "A tip! If only he knew the truth! He'd have quickly changed his tune, I assure you. Okay, I'm sending you three grand as a down payment. The rest after sale."

"Excellent. I also have all sorts of junk from the Fort. I didn't want to sell it at Balmy Bay. Too many prying eyes there."

Rrhorgus gave it a quick once-over. "This is your typical nursery loot. I could give you fifty gold for the lot."

"Really? I didn't think it was worth so much."

"Considering the sheer bulk of it, yeah."

"Just imagine how much of it I used to have," I added meaningfully.

He rubbed his chin. "I'd love to have a look at your insects. Ah, good job I remembered. Here, take it. You won't find something like this in an auction."

He offered me a weird-looking black oblong item about three fingers thick.

I read the item's description. "The Charmed Scale of the Ylean Pangolin. So what am I supposed to do with it? I thought I asked you to bring me some top quality steel ingots?"

"That's exactly what I did, didn't I?"

"Wait a sec. You don't mean-"

"Oh yes I do," he gave me a wink. "This scale is the strongest metal known in the game. And it's charmed, too! It can be used to make some very interesting items."

My eyebrows shot up. "Really? In this case, it's a gift worthy of a king! Mind if I try to insert it into the Fix Box? Let's see what it can do..."

Rrhorgus rubbed his hands, impatient, as I fiddled with the ingot. "And? How's it going?"

I read the Fix Box's stats. "You'd be surprised."

"Come on, don't drag it out!"

"This one scale fills it up 50%. Quality of source materials: 87%-plus!"

"I see..." he rubbed his green chin, suddenly pensive. "Does that mean that there's something better than this around? You're our walking metal detector, aren't you?"

"Don't forget its readings depend on the future item's quality. A scarab can't be made with soft metals. So yes, there must be something harder than this."

"Your class is something else! Just wait till I tell Max. He's gonna love it. Promise me to make a video of your next scarab."

"I will. How many scales do you have exactly?"

"A dozen with the one you already have," he hurried to produce the rest. "I also have twenty ingots of shardelithic steel and ten vials of Venom of the Stonehead Adder. The quality is a dream!"

"Excellent, thanks! It must have cost you a lot."

"Don't mention it," he waved my words away in an old man's gesture. "We'll work it out. Don't you know how medieval merchants used to send their younger sons to war? They'd club together to buy them some armor, weapons and stuff. Give them some food and a bit of money. Hire an old experienced merc to keep an eye on them. And off they went to pillage and plunder, followed by a wagon train to bring all the loot back home."

"You've got some sick imagination! So that's what you think I am, a plunderer?"

"Why not?" his left eyebrow shot up in a mocking surprise. "Can't you see the similarities here? You could be my son. Okay, maybe not a younger one."

I chuckled. "All we need to do is get a wagon train to follow in my wake. Problem is, where I'm about to go, they'd be gobbled up wholesale: drivers, carts and the loot, right down to the last wagon wheel. As easy as that."

"That reminds me," he said in mocking seriousness. "My Granddad used to say to me, *'You'll do it, sonny boy! A bit of a push goes a long way'*. Admittedly he said it every time I used the potty. But that's irrelevant, isn't it?"

We laughed.

"Right," I finally said. "I don't want to keep you. No idea when I'll see you next."

"You take care, man. I know you can do it."

I gave him a hug, then leaped onto Boris' back. As we took off, I noticed Rrhorgus' eyes widen in amazement. But of course. Last time he'd seen Boris he'd still been a baby. And now he was level 28 and bigger than a horse. A dream!

We turned a farewell circle over the clearing. I waved my hand to Rrhorgus one last time. Then we took to the skies. We had too many things to take care of.

Below, a village lay, its lights glowing. We left the ocean behind. Today it had been quiet as a mill pond. The weather was warm and dry. Just what I wanted to see, to tell you the truth. I'd had the rain and damp up to here.

I was curious how the launch of Water World would affect this peace and quiet. Most likely, these little villages would cost their weight in gold.

The Predators had done the right thing, setting down in Balmy Bay. I wouldn't be surprised if their scowling panther logo would top our clan rankings soon.

I nudged Boris to rise above the clouds, just in case. The huge moon illuminated the clear sky. I could reach out and touch a star. It was so quiet here. So peaceful. At the moment, this seemed to be the only safe place for me.

Admittedly, Tanor had been busy. He'd spoken to everyone I knew. Even Dan and Saash had written to me saying they didn't want problems with the Steel Shirts. What had those two got to do with me? I'd long forgotten all about them.

To be fair, my friends hadn't appreciated the pressure. You had to give them that. Resistance to authority is in our genes. Everyone had written encouraging letters to me, offering their help. Naturally, I wasn't going to go for that. They didn't need problems. Still, it felt damn good to know someone did care.

Now we were approaching Mellenville, the capital of the Lands of Light. Despite the late hour, it was all aglow. Here, life never stopped, bustling with players completing quests, farming resources or just sightseeing, roaming its countless streets and squares. What an amazing place!

Had it not been for my current level and Reputation, I wouldn't have been able to even enter its airspace. Ditto for the ocean. I couldn't advance further than a few dozen feet away from the shore. Every time I'd tried to do so, I'd received a system warning.

It didn't take my satnav long to locate the Armory.

We circled it for a bit, then landed on the roof of the house next door. The roof tiles crunched their protest but endured nevertheless. The local police wasn't going to appreciate our methods. Still, it wouldn't have been too clever to land in the Armory square. This part of the city may have seemed sleepy and deserted but as the saying goes, even walls have eyes and ears.

I spent another ten minutes lurking in the shadows keeping an eye on the square. If Tanor had sent someone here to intercept me, they'd have to be at least level 100. Even my enhanced Survival Instinct wouldn't allow me to see a high-level stealther.

At least I had my teleport crystals.

Now that I thought about it, Tronus' tower was probably the safest place for me. Still, it was too late. If everything worked out, very soon the situation would change. I'd have no friends left in the Lands of Light. Which meant I had to milk my Light-side Reputation for all it was worth while I still could.

Ten minutes had expired. Everything seemed hunky dory.

Rrhorgus had been right, of course. Coming to Mellenville was the worst thing I could have done. Even though duels were banned and severely punished, Tanor's henchmen could always find a way to kidnap me somehow.

Time to do it. I unsummoned Boris. He could use some rest. I absolutely couldn't afford to lose him now. His three-hour respawn time could ruin all my plans. Better be safe than sorry.

I gulped down a Potion of Gust which gave me +40% to Speed for 5 minutes. That should be enough.

Now the Smoke and Mirrors elixir, giving me a 2-minute invisibility. What a shame you couldn't use all these potions in battle: an opponent's attack annulled their properties. They cost an arm and a leg, too.

Let's go! In two long leaps, I landed on a second-floor balcony. Before I knew it, I stood on the sidewalk below. Talk about Spider Man. Had I been wearing my old Digger duds, it would have taken Tanor some time to scrape me off the pavement. In game, gear was everything, you had to agree.

I moved in short bounds, hiding in the houses' shadow. It wasn't easy to do, you know. Mellenville was one well-lit city.

In one last sprint I reached the Armory's front door.

No guards in sight. Could they all be indoors? In any case, I'd made it here without a problem, excellent.

I was about to regret my wasting money on the precious potions when a system message appeared in my view,

Warning! A player Tipitop has attempted to cast a Freezing Hand on you!
Success! Magic attack repelled!

I pulled the door toward me as hard as I could and dove inside like a mad hare. Yes! I'd made it.

I could hear shouts coming from the street,

"You bastard! He's gone, look!"

"He's probably high on potions."

"Tipitop! I thought you were going to freeze him? You call yourself a Necro?"

"That's not my fault! I got a system message! He's immune to my magic!"

My heart was about to explode. What the heck had it been? So fast, too!

I leaned against the wall and covered my eyes with my hand, exhausted. Talk about a close shave. I'd been lucky their Tipitop was level 90. But Tanor! Clever bastard! He'd second-guessed my movements, hadn't he? He must have put two and two together, realizing I was bound to turn up here.

Aha, and here was a message from him in my inbox...

Dear Olgerd,

I suggest we have a friendly talk. Please vacate the building. My men have overreacted and will be punished accordingly.

Yeah right. Like, I can't wait. After such a valiant demonstration of their friendly intentions? Oh no, thank you very much.

"Sir Olgerd! Are you all right, Sir?"

I looked up. Two level-200 guards stared down at me from their natural height. Their expressions betrayed silent adoration. What's with all the puppy eyes? But of course! So stupid of me! I was a hero and a legend, wasn't I?

Very well, then...

"I'm fine, thanks," I replied, gasping. "I was about to enter the Armory when those idiots attacked me right by the front door."

This wasn't a lie, was it? A magic attack was technically still an assault. And if it had been logged in, the guards were bound to know about it. Who in their right mind wouldn't believe a Zombie Slayer?

"They're too much!" a bearded guard growled, stepping toward the entrance.

The other one knitted his eyebrows. "It's all right, Sir Olgerd. We'll sort them out."

The door closed behind them. The sounds of a scrap reached me from the outside.

Another message from Tanor came,

Don't you think you're overdoing it?

I just loved it. So he hadn't been overdoing it by

sending his best heavies to kidnap me, had he? And the moment I sought protection from local law enforcement, it turned me into a goon? This guy had some sick ideas. Then again, why should I be surprised? Most people do develop reality check problems once they come to power. Or rather, they begin to view their own actions as the only correct ones. Double standards, dammit...

The noise behind the door kept growing. Apparently, Tanor's boys weren't so keen on spending a stretch in the cooler. A squad of ten more guards hurried to the scene, their armor rattling, each of them saluting me as they ran.

That'll teach them to upset Mellenville's legendary hero!

What a shame I had to leave all this behind. I was beginning to enjoy it.

Would you like to talk?

It was Tanor again. This reminded me of a joke where a guy refuses to open the door to the police who ask him to "have a talk". Instead, he asks how many of them are there.

"Five," the brave cops reply.

"In that case, you can talk between yourselves, can't you?"

Oh no, I had absolutely no time to talk to anyone at the moment. Especially because the Armory's keeper had already arrived. One of the most important NPCs in the whole of Mellenville.

"Greetings, Sir Olgerd!" the distinguished man

lowered his gray head to me.

I answered his bow. "Greetings, Sir Dreyfus!"

Despite his advanced years, he gave the impression of someone ready to bare his sword at a moment's notice, joining the thick of a battle.

His posture betrayed an officer's training. His face was covered in a fine web of old scars. His sapphire-blue stare seemed to pierce right through you. Add to this his steely composure: he didn't bat an eyelid at the sounds of the melee outside. You could tell straight away this was a man hardened by many a battle.

Really, why would he care about a run-of-the-mill street fight?

"I reckon you have your own reasons for visiting our place," he said.

"I do," I nodded. "I've heard a lot of good things about it."

"Oh have you? I wonder who from?" he squinted his right eye at me. "Don't get me wrong, please. The Armory is no secret to anyone. I just thought that someone might have referred you."

"Sure," I bluffed. "Captain Gard of the Maragar Citadel."

His rugged furrowed face expanded in a good-natured smile. A rare sight, probably.

"Gard's always been an expert in weaponry," he assured me, still grinning. "You know why?"

I shook my head. "No."

"Easy. I taught him everything he knows!

He guffawed, so unexpectedly for his stern comportment. A hearty slap of his broad hand on my shoulder made me crouch. A clip around the ear from such a hand might kill you outright.

"So what do you have in mind?" he finally asked.

"Anything you can show me," I blurted out.

"Good attitude," he commended me. "Worthy of a warrior. Very well! No good us standing here. This way, please."

* * *

A couple of hours later we stood on a large balcony overhanging the Armory, celebrating a deal.

"To new company!" he toasted me. "I appreciate your Fort story. Rest assured I'll communicate it to the Council. We really should pay more attention to that part of our lands. What was the name of their sergeant again?"

"Crux," I said. "They're desperate for any help."

Judging by the fact that no system messages had come up during our conversation, it was just that: a conversation. A welcome change from the furious haggling session we'd had earlier.

Haggle? You could say that! Dreyfus could outbid a seasoned market trader. I hadn't expected this from a hardened soldier at all. Now I could understand the Council's decision to post him in the Armory. Firstly, to keep their own butts out of trouble: soldiers and politicians didn't mix very well. Guys like Dreyfus wouldn't keep any dirty secrets under wraps. You might even get a sword between your ribs for your filthy little practices.

Secondly, this penny-pincher was perfect for the job. He'd almost ripped my soul out. But at the end of the day, we were both happy with the deal.

"Oh yes," the old man said, admiring my little menagerie. "Now that you've told me about the zombie fort, I understand why you needed that particular type of armor. And with these beasts... oh man."

I shrugged. "Them and I, we're one. I'm strong only as long as they are."

I'd had to put my hand in my pocket nice and deep. Still, it was worth it. Both Boris and Prankster had become twice as strong. I'd got them both special "Arsenal-mark" helmets, breastplates, greaves and other bits of armor which made them look like some mythical beasts from ancient legends. What was I saying? They *were* mythical beasts, weren't they?

I had one last visit left to pay before setting off for No-Man's Lands. But I had to buy some presents first.

Chapter Nineteen

"Here they are, the Woods of Lirtia!" I said under my breath as I patted Boris' neck. "I can imagine old Master Adkhur's face when he sees us!"

I'd just left the auction after having stocked up on a tasty cornucopia of treats for Master and several chunks of juicy high-level salmon for the kitty. I'd love to know if the level of presents affected the resulting buff's quality. That would be really good if it did.

We were flying over one of Mirror World's largest locations — and undoubtedly one of the most popular. The tiny figures of players were everywhere: scurrying amid the trees, crowding the numerous clearings and bustling along the snaking river banks.

Everyone was busy here: cutting, chopping, farming, hunting, fishing, grinding and sifting. Was it my imagination or the players' numbers had at least doubled since I'd been here? As far as I remembered from my first visit, it hadn't been as crowded.

Then again, why shouldn't it be? Mirror World was trending, its top players becoming media celebrities overnight. I wouldn't be surprised to see them in commercial breaks soon advertising everything from beer to panty liners.

The black backs of the local wolves appeared below. I trapped a smile in my beard, remembering how huge they'd seemed to me on my first trip.

As I approached the familiar grove, I realized something was wrong. "Boris, let's land here!"

Once large and emerald green, the head of a giant tree looked like the scorched skeleton of a magic beast. Had they had a fire here? Apparently not. This was something else. The tree trunk was pitch black, twisted as if someone had been trying to squeeze the juices out of it.

The clearing had become a burial site filled with ash. I could see mummified bodies lying everywhere, their outlines hinting at the forest animals they'd once been. Wolves, elk, bears and deer... I saw a few large feline bodies and peered anxiously at them. Big sigh of relief. No Lita. No wonder: you had to go some to smoke a pet like her.

Master Adkhur's hut stood split like a walnut, its walls destroyed by the same weird magic. By now I had no doubts this must have been a magic attack.

And not just that. This had nothing to do with players. I was the only person with access to this particular location. More than likely, it was some new development — a yet unknown playscript — surfacing.

This must have been one hell of a scrap as the

forest animals had tried to defend their master. Still, the owner of the murderous black magic had proved the stronger. Which meant that Master Adkhur was either dead or captured.

Alternatively, he might have escaped. I couldn't see his body anywhere which was good news, sort of. He just might be alive somewhere.

The longer I lingered, the more I wanted to leave the place. Once a peaceful haven of beautiful magic, it now resembled an A-bomb site littered with scorched remains.

Boris didn't seem to like it here, either. Scowling, he spread his legs wide ready for takeoff, his tail swishing nervously.

"We won't be long," I assured him before heading for the hut.

A thorough check of its remains produced nothing. Judging by the walls melted by the weird witchcraft, there was nothing intact left inside.

I heaved a disappointed sigh. "All right, let's move it."

Boris looked relieved. I was about to leap into the saddle when I glimpsed something at the edge of the clearing.

"Wait a sec... what have we got here?"

A cowering animal was trying to hide behind a thin tree. My newly-acquired Survival Instinct had allowed me to notice it. How strange. I'd never seen any living thing here before, apart from Master Adkhur, Lita the lynx and myself. This wasn't right.

The creature was bigger than a fox but smaller than a wolf. While I was considering my options, it decided to make the first move.

The leaves rustled, parting. The creature walked out into the opening and headed clumsily but confidently toward us. It looked very much like a wolverine.

Name: Smooth-Haired Growler, the system reported. *Level: 10*

He was no threat to us. Boris calmly watched the visitor who seemed to be quite nervous. Still, he continued his advance, baring his teeth, his hackles on end in a cautious warning, as if saying, *I have to approach you but make sure you don't do anything stupid.*

Wait a sec... what was that tied around his neck? Wasn't that one of the funny green ribbons that Master Adkhur used to decorate his robes with?

That's right! And dangling on it was a small square package!

"Come here, boy," I urged the beastie. "It's all right. No one's gonna hurt you. We're friends. Gosh, you *are* skinny, aren't you?"

The Growler approached us sideways with his tail between his legs, suspicious, his hackles still bristling. He kept casting wary glances at the crouching Boris who tilted his head sideways like a dog, studying the weird visitor.

In the meantime, I removed the ribbon and broke the seal on the package wrapped in leather. Inside was a single scrap of paper covered all over in small hasty handwritten scribbles,

---

Olgerd, if you're reading this, then you must have seen what they've done to my temporary abode. The enemies of our clan attacked me in the dead of night. They managed to break the powerful charm that my friend Master Satis had cast over the grove.

I had to flee. Those bastards killed so many of my animal friends, dammit! Had it not been for them, I wouldn't be writing this now. They sacrificed their own lives to save mine.

I'm not going to tell you where I'm hiding now. You should understand: anyone can intercept this message. Let me just tell you it's time you do what you were planning to do all along. Restore the Twilight Castle to its old glory! Wake up the Gray Obelisk resting deep within Brutville Halls!

Oh, and one more thing. Please give Clumsy something to eat, will ya? I told him to wait for you here. He must be absolutely starving.

This is it, my friend! Until we meet again!

The letter wasn't signed. Still, it was perfectly clear it was from Master Adkhur.

As soon as I finished reading, a new system message appeared grandly before my eyes,

Congratulations! You've been entrusted with the fate of an entire race!

Time to fulfil your destiny!

You must reach the Twilight Castle and go down the Brutville Halls to activate the Gray Obelisk.

Reward: Unknown

Warning! You can't complete the task at your current level! You need to grow stronger!

Optimal leveling conditions:

An extended immersion for a minimum of three months.

Preparation time required: 24 hrs.

Aha, this was Vicky sending me a discreet message. Like, it was time to make good on my promise. Apparently, they were up to something out there in the real world, seeing as they'd openly told me to go for an extended immersion.

Oh well. If they say so. So much for my daily gym and pool sessions. Here I go again, lying flat in a capsule feeding through a tube.

With a sigh I reached into my bag for a fish and handed it to Clumsy. Unhesitantly he dug his claws into its fat scaly side and darted for the woods.

As I watched him leave, I heard excited voices behind my back,

"Whoa! What do we have here?"

"Have you been to this location before?"

"What, is this an event or something? Why is there nothing about it in the chat?"

"See that black bear? Yesterday we tried to smoke one exactly like that! Our group couldn't do it!"

"Did he do it all by himself?"

"Are you filming?"

"Do I look like I am, stupid?"

"Why not? Everybody else is!"

I turned around. There were about twenty of them, mainly grinders and low-level warriors. No, not twenty. A whole crowd of them was hurrying in their wake.

"Hi, man!" a red-bearded dwarf shouted, pointing at the dead animals. "What did you do it with?"

"It's so awful!" a slender-limbed Alven girl shuddered, holding a fancily decorated sickle in her hand.

They must have thought that I was the one responsible for the massacre.

"Just look at his mount!" a Dwand exclaimed. "I've never seen anything like it!"

"Where did you get it from?"

Without saying a word, I turned to Boris and leaped into the saddle. ""Let's go, kiddo."

The threatening toss of Boris' head made the more curious shrink back. Spreading his wings, he kicked off gracefully, raising a cloud of gray dust. In two powerful wingbeats we were soaring high in the sky.

I hid a grin in my beard as I circled the clearing one last time. While most of the players had frozen below open-mouthed, some of the more daring ones were already checking the dead animal bodies for loot.

I tried not to think what was about to happen. I had a funny feeling it might end in a nice big scuffle.

"That's it, kiddo. We're done here. Time to head to No-Man's Lands."

Chapter Twenty

The sun was setting slowly, little by little, taking its own sweet time like a small boy trying to cadge another half-hour of playtime before bed.

Not a thunder clap in the sky. Occasional clouds were soft and fluffy like pink cotton candy, floating somewhere minding their own business.

It was quite windy though. Still, I wasn't cold. No wonder: this Protection of mine was better than any amount of Purple elemental runes. The first time I'd been here, I'd frozen to the bone. The Ardean Range is no place for hothouse flowers. But now I didn't feel a thing. I was lying in the snow as if it was the most natural thing in the world, rereading my and Sveta's letter exchange.

Everything's going to be all right, Oleg darling. Our girl is strong and brave. She must have taken after her Daddy.

And Mommy. You're an incredibly strong woman, sweetheart.

I'm her mother. That says it all. It'll be fine, trust me. We've done the hardest part. And it's all thanks to you! You're our Daddy, our champion! Aren't you afraid of going there? I keep watching all those No-Man's Lands raid videos. It looks so scary. The mobs they have there! And that's virtually a stone's throw from the Citadel. I dread to think what they're like where you're heading.

Nah. I'm done being afraid. Come what may. In any case, I go there prepared.

I saw it! Christie saw it too!

Saw what? What do you mean?

The video! It's trending now! The mysterious Fort hero! Your Boris is sooo cute! He's grown so much! And he's wearing armor!

What video are you talking about?

The one in the scorched woods. With all the dead animals. Did you really do it all by yourself?

Aha. I see. No, it wasn't me. It's part of the script.

Everybody thinks it was you. But you know

what? It's probably for the better. At least those bastards will keep out of your way.

The sound of snow crunching underfoot distracted me from reading. It came from the bottom of the cliff where I'd set up my lookout.

I peeked out from behind the rock.

"Hey, Lightie! It's all right! It's me, Droy! Remember?"

I recognized the sarcasm in the voice. This was the Caltean advance team leader I'd met here last time. So his name was Droy, then.

I rose to my feet and peered openly down.

A Caltean warrior stood at the center of a small plateau. Same dark beard, same furs hugging his stocky frame. He had a spear and a short sword.

He'd grown several levels since I'd last seen him. Did that mean that Caltean NPCs could level up just like players did? Having said that, it was only logical. Citadel guards leveled up, too — slowly but surely. Apparently it was done to preserve the game's balance.

"How did you know I was here?" I shouted.

He suppressed a smile. "Our scouts had their sights on you already this morning. They wanted to smoke you themselves but when they mentioned your flying beast, I knew straight away they were talking about you. Hah! Don't forget to thank your Gods of Light for your miraculous delivery! Now go back to where you came from! Next time I might not happen to be around!"

"Don't call me a Lightie. I'm not one of them."

I had to stick to my Ennan cover story. If Adkhur had accepted it, it just might work now too. As long as I followed it, adlibbing if necessary, I might be all right.

"Ah, an outcast? What have you done, killed your neighbor? Heh! That's good! One Lightie less!"

Congratulations! You've just completed a hidden quest: True Face

Reward: +5 to your Reputation with the Red Owls clan.

Warning! You need to watch out! Now the clan's enemies will double their efforts in pursuing you wherever you go!

Excellent. It looked like I'd done everything right.

"What are you doing in our clan's lands?" he sharply changed the subject.

"Looking for a new home!" I blurted out.

The thing was, right until now I'd had a rather clear plan of action. I had no business in the Twilight Castle quite yet, not with my current level. Still, the Ennans Map had had two hidden prompts: the locations of the two remaining Masters to the north of No-Man's Lands.

That's how I used to think before: I'd go visit them and have a talk... all the Masters were like the links of one chain, weren't they? Otherwise, why all the wealth of information about them? But once I'd visited Adkhur's desolated abode, it had all gone downhill. He'd disappeared from the map, together with Satis the Mage and Axe the Warrior. That's the way the cookie crumbles...

So it had been back to the drawing board. Dmitry and I had picked each other's brains and come up with this idea of leveling my Reputation with the Calteans. Seeing as the whole of No-Man's Lands was packed with potential prompts, all I had to do was walk into one of them. Which was exactly what had happened to me on my first trip here.

At the moment, my flimsy relationship with Droy was my only foothold this side of the Citadel. And judging by my Rep growing and by the thoughtful expression on Droy's face, I should persevere in this direction.

Finally he shouted, "Can you come down? Not a good idea yelling all across the Ardean Range. You never know who might be listening. You'll be safe, I promise!"

I was prepared to do this. I'd already created a resurrection point nearby. Sooner or later, I was bound to start interacting with the locals.

I took a deep breath and began descending. It didn't take long. Soon I stood opposite Droy who nodded to me, his face friendly.

Congratulations! You've just completed a hidden quest: Trust is the Road to Success.

Reward: +5 to your Reputation with the Red Owls clan.

Warning! You need to watch out! Now the clan's enemies will double their efforts in pursuing you wherever you go!

Excellent. I smiled and nodded back to him.

I'd have never been able to tell him from a dwarf. His skin was a dark ashen color, that was the only difference. His clothes weren't much. Apparently, the Red Owls were on a lean streak.

"You've changed, Lightie," Droy finally announced, studying me with interest.

"So have you," I replied, hinting at his levels.

He shrugged his burly shoulders. "You could say that."

Only now did I notice a bandage on his right hand: a dirty gray rag spotted with familiar reddish brown.

He'd been wounded. He must have spent a lot of time fighting. That's how he'd gotten his current level.

I peered at the wound tag. This was a Green poisonous debuff! And what if...

"I can see you're wounded," I said.

His eyes squinted threateningly. "What's that got to do with you?"

I raised my hands in a conciliatory gesture. "Sorry. I didn't mean any disrespect. I just might try and help you, that's all."

I could see his eyes gleam with hope. His wound must have hurt a lot. Still, this expression disappeared as soon as it came.

"Light magic!" he spat on the ground.

"Light, Dark, red, green, what difference does it make? If it helps, why not try it?"

"Good question," he growled. "You can ask our

shaman what he thinks about it. He knows the answer to that."

He cringed. I could see there wasn't much love lost between these two. This was a good moment to press on, "Why didn't he heal you then?"

"Good question, Lightie," he replied with a sad chuckle.

This wasn't a healthy attitude. "Let's do it this way. I'll try to help you. If it doesn't work, then apparently this wasn't the will of... who is it your shaman normally asks for help with his healing?"

"The Higher Beings," he hurried to offer.

"Thanks. So if it doesn't work, then it wasn't the will of the Higher Beings. But if it does..."

"Okay, okay, then this *was* the will of the Higher Beings too!" he grinned his understanding. "Very well, you've talked me into it! Go ahead, heal me!"

Trying not to betray my excitement, I reached into my bag for one of the Purple Cleanse Scrolls. I'd bought a whole shedload of them at the auction last night. They were costly but worth every penny.

I'd actually stocked up at the auction very nicely. Apart from all sorts of scrolls, stones and elixirs, I'd also got myself a good pickaxe and a capacious new bag. Plus some clothes: a cloak, a shirt and a pair of pants. In other words, I'd willingly parted with every bit of money that Dreyfus the Armory keeper had failed to relieve me of.

Right, let's have a look. The moment of truth. Could I use a scroll to heal this guy here?

It worked no problem. It had two options: to

either heal myself or another character. I chose the latter. A new box promptly appeared, inviting me to enter Droy's name. I pressed *Activate*.

A golden shimmer enveloped Droy's arm.

Success! You've healed a character: Droy.
Would you like to remember this action: Yes/No

I quickly pressed *Yes*. Now whenever I needed to heal someone, all I had to do was point a scroll at them.

Yesss! It worked!

Overjoyed, Droy studied the spot where his old wound had just been. Our eyes met.

He proffered his hand to me. "Thank you, Lightie."

Congratulations! One of the most respected warriors of the Red Owls Clan considers you his friend!

Reward: +100 to your Reputation with the Red Owls clan.

Warning! You need to watch out! Now the clan's enemies will double their efforts in pursuing you wherever you go!

"My pleasure," I answered his strong handshake. "Please call me Olgerd."

He nodded. "Do you think you could do this again?" he asked, his voice filled with hope.

"Only if it's the will of the Higher Beings," I said with a sly squint.

He grinned his understanding. "Follow me."

Chapter Twenty-One

Uh-oh. This wasn't how I'd imagined a prosperous Caltean settlement to be. I'd thought it would be a nice little town or at least a village. Nothing of the sort. This was just a temporary camp — and a badly fortified one at that. It was situated even worse, deep down in a mountain gorge. This was a trap if ever I'd seen one.

How weird. If even I with my total lack of military training could see that, then who was in charge of this disorderly tribe?

The place looked like a Gypsy camp crowded with tents of every size made with animal pelts, bones and pieces of wood. You could see straight away that the Calteans were new to the nomadic lifestyle. There was no system to their camp. Tents blocked everybody's way. Had I wanted to cross it from one end to the other, I should need a whole team of cartographers — provided they could find their way around.

The camp was a smoke-drenched riot of noise, animals bellowing and humans shouting everywhere I turned. I really couldn't understand how I'd managed to have missed it from the air.

Judging by the small numbers of livestock — which must have been either buffalos or yaks by the looks of them — the Calteans were finishing off their last dwindling supplies.

"Droy, you sly bastard! You did capture him on your own after all, didn't you?"

Three Calteans stood in our way, their levels slightly lower than that of Droy's. Their gear was even worse. All three were similarly burly, with identical beards. They must have been the scouts that had noticed me first.

"He's not my prisoner," Droy snapped. "He's my guest," he pulled my hand, dragging me deeper into the camp.

I glimpsed his men's long faces. They watched our departure open-mouthed.

Our arrival hadn't gone unnoticed. Children, women, men, young and old — they all dropped whatever they'd been doing and stopped to get an eyeful of the stranger. The further we went, the less happy I felt.

Strangely enough, I didn't notice any malice in their faces. They stared at me with a rather curious interest. This was Reputation for you. Mirror World had taken care of that. How strange: here of all places I didn't feel like I was in the game at all, in this nomadic camp surrounded by these stocky gray-skinned savages. I had a funny feeling I might spend a lot of time in occupational therapy once I was finally back.

We stopped in front of a rather large tent which looked considerably better that the rest — not because it was richer because it wasn't; but it was quite cleverly put up. Apparently, the same principle applied here as in the real world: show me your home and I might tell you who you are with a 90% certainty.

"In you go," Droy lifted the curtain made of animal skins. "Welcome to my home."

Congratulations! You've just completed a hidden quest: A Friend's Welcome!

Reward: +100 to your Reputation with the Red Owls clan.

Warning! You need to watch out! Now the clan's enemies will double their efforts in pursuing you wherever you go!

I stepped inside, preparing to adjust my eyes to darkness. Not at all. The inside of the tent was rather well-illuminated. Daylight was coming through a hole up in the ceiling. A neat open hearth had been installed underneath it. The air wasn't stale: the tent must have been well-ventilated. Whoever had built this place knew what they were doing.

To our right was a small altar. Upon entering, Droy bowed to it. I hurried to copy his movements. The main thing was not to goof up. A new congratulation message appeared, indicating I was on the right path.

To our left lay a bed. A wall above it was hung with Droy's numerous trophies. I did my best to express my delight under Droy's watchful gaze. He must have been really proud of his victories.

Another bed, slightly smaller, was set up a bit further on. Droy was already there, beckoning me to approach.

Okay, what did he have there?

Not *what*. *Who*. A broad-shouldered young fellow, skinny as a rake, his eyes closed, his hair matted with sweat. He was asleep. No, not really. Unconscious. He looked a lot like Droy.

"My son," Droy's quivering voice confirmed my suspicions. "Look."

He turned back the blanket of animal pelts and pointed at the young man's chest.

Jesus. Where had they gotten all these debuffs from? I took a closer look. The youngster was in a bad way. His Life bar barely glowed at 2%.

"Hold on, man," I said softly, reaching for another scroll.

"Don't move, you wretched Lightie!" the angry voice made both me and Droy jump.

I swung round. A skinny Caltean stood in the doorway. He was dressed in a long muddy-colored robe hung with bone charms. A long white beard, a hooked nose, spiteful gray eyes and a perfectly bald scalp: not a pleasant individual to look at.

Figures of warriors hovered behind the shaman's back (no points for guessing who it was). They had a rather guilty look. Apparently, my new friend was a respected tribe elder.

Droy frowned regally. "Who said you had the right to enter my house, Laosh?"

"And who said you had the right to bring a stranger to the camp without my permission?" the shaman retorted.

"He's not a stranger to me! Twice he saved my life!"

That was admittedly good to hear.

"And you, Laosh — where were you when my wife was dying?" Droy continued. "And why won't you help my son now, seeing as you're already here?"

"You know very well there's no cure for Lithron venom," the shaman frowned, shaking his long gnarly staff in the air.

"No cure? Are you sure? What's this, then?" Droy victoriously bared his arm.

Everybody gasped. Even the shaman looked slightly taken aback.

Then we were showered with questions. "How did you do it?" "Tell us!" Lots of people seemed to have the same problem here.

"I know what it is!" the despicable old shaman finally announced, pointing a crooked finger at me. "It's Light magic!"

Rather than yelling at the host in his own house, he'd have better clipped his fingernails once in a while.

The others recoiled. They didn't seem to like alien witchcraft here.

"This was the will of the Higher Beings!" Droy announced, sticking out his chest.

I glanced at the sick youth. His Life was at 1%

already. While the others were engaged in their pissing contest, the boy could die.

"Droy," I said under my breath. "Your son is dying."

He bared his sword. "Heal him! Whoever tries to stand in his way, I'll personally wrap his guts around my sword!"

I hurried to activate the scroll. The poisonous debuff disappeared in a cascade of golden glow.

The crowd heaved a collective sigh behind my back.

"And? Olgerd? Did it work?"

I stepped aside. "Take a look."

The happy father leaned over his son's bed and ripped the bandages away, exposing his perfectly healthy chest.

"Now he needs some sleep," I said in the patronizing tone of a doctor. "Make sure there's enough food at hand. By sunset, your son will be capable of eating your biggest bull."

Droy ran his shaking hand over the youth's hair. It was probably my imagination but I thought I saw his eyes well with tears.

A light touch to my shoulder distracted me from the happy scene.

I turned round. The shaman had already made himself scarce. A few of the warriors stood behind me, hope in their eyes.

"Listen, Lightie... any chance you could heal me too?" the tallest one asked.

"Me too..."

"And me too, please..."

"And my son..."

I nodded my agreement. I just hoped I had enough scrolls. In any case, I could always pop back to the Citadel and buy some more.

Oh wow. My Reputation was definitely going up.

* * *

My fears had proven true. Sick Calteans started coming in their droves. I barely had time to produce new scrolls. Droy's tent had turned into some sort of field hospital. My popularity had truly soared by the evening when Tim, his son, had finally come round and asked for something to eat.

I had to send a lot of them back though. Not because I didn't have enough scrolls but simply because I didn't know much about healing.

All sorts of people kept coming, asking me to heal their broken legs and crossed eyes, sore throats and missing arms. It had taken Droy some time to explain to his fellow kinsmen that I wasn't a healer and that all I could do was extract Lithron venom.

As I did my healing bit, I kept an ear out for any useful information. Admittedly, the Calteans didn't conceal anything from "the doctor". They turned out to be a chatty bunch.

So what had I gleaned? The Red Owls used to live in the Silver Mountain Valley behind the Ardean Range. Then one day they'd been attacked by some

Nocteans who forced them off their lands.

Fear and loathing filled the Calteans' voices whenever they mentioned the Nocteans. According to the warriors, they were invincible by their sheer weight of numbers. That's how it had come to pass that their Clan Council had decided that in order to survive, the Calteans would have to leave their valley.

The Calteans were actually a settled nation. They weren't used to nomadic lifestyle. Add to this the fact they'd had to leave their dwellings in a great hurry, leaving behind a wealth of hard-earned possessions.

Some had decided against leaving: those were mainly the old and sick. Basically, this was the local apocalypse of an entire nation. My heart went out to them.

Having listened to their stories, I'd come to the conclusion that the main reason behind the Calteans' defeat was their lack of unity. Integrity was an alien word to them.

Firstly, the Calteans counted several dozen smaller clans, each ruled by a shaman chief — who was considered the ultimate power on earth. Imagine the scope of his ambition.

Secondly, the clans were constantly feuding with each other, their vendettas sometimes erupting in long-term military conflicts. Even though the Noctean invasion had happened during a hiatus of relative peace, none of the shamans had even considered the advantages this fact offered. Basically, they didn't give a damn about their neighbors.

That's how the Calteans' old grudges had

played a nasty trick on them. Even when they absolutely had to unite in the face of a mutual enemy, those pig-headed pagans refused to bury the hatchet.

As a triumph of their diplomatic efforts, they'd managed to call up a Council of Chiefs. After a prolonged high-tension, air-blue-with-cussing dispute, all they had achieved was agreement on their exodus' general direction. But they'd gotten so hot under the collar in the process that it was decided best if every clan went their own way.

Predictably, the strongest clans got the best pick and moved southward without even realizing they were heading directly for the Citadel walls.

The weaklings had to make do with the locations situated to the east and west of their old homes. Trust the Red Owls — the poorest of the poor and the weakest of the weak — to get the worst pick. Strangely enough, the Caltean Council hadn't even considered the northern direction, which was exactly where the Twilight Castle stood.

All this offered a lot of food for thought.

It had taken the Red Owls a long time to get to the Ardean Range. They had kept stubbornly walking like a herd of migrating bison, suffering constant attacks from predators which took out their best warriors.

Poisonous debuffs were part of the same story. During one of their recon missions, the Owls' scouts had come across a Lithron nest in a deep mountainous gorge. My patients described them as "stinky, bitey, furry beasts". Many a warrior had died that day; the survivors had all been "rewarded" with the debuffs.

By my estimation, had I not interfered just in time, the clan could have lost about another fifty of their strongest men. No wonder my Reputation had soared. The sheer fact that they'd stopped calling me Lightie was already a victory.

It looked like we might need to have a talk. I had a few things to tell my new friends.

When the flood of the sick by the tent began to dwindle, I called Droy aside.

"You wanna talk?" he asked.

"Yeah," I mouthed. "Somewhere no one can hear."

He nodded at his tent. "Let's go in."

As we entered, he pointed at a trestle bed by the fire. "Sit down," he said. "And speak freely. No one can hear us here."

"Before I say anything, I need to ask you something."

"Go ahead."

"Where exactly are you heading?" I ventured.

He grinned. "Had you asked me this morning, I'd have had to kill you. But you've saved my son. I owe you."

"Is it so serious? Well, I'm sorry..."

"It's all right," he brushed my apology away. "Laosh the shaman had a vision. We must go south west."

"South west, where exactly?"

"Dunno. That's what Laosh said."

"Why south west?" I tried to find out more.

"Spirits told him there was a valley on the other

side of the Ardean Range. Lots of grass for the cattle, lots of game to hunt. We'll be safe there. That's what he said."

I could almost see this Laosh the shaman's pantomime at the Council of Chiefs. Everybody must have simply ignored the old boy. In the meantime, he'd already come up with a Promised Land story for his clansmen.

I nodded. "I see. What else did the spirits tell him?"

"Nothing. That's it."

"So you don't know what lies on the other side of the range, do you?"

He shook his head. "We sent out some scouts but they haven't been back yet."

I heaved a sigh.

"Have you seen them?" Droy's voice filled with hope. "They were our best warriors. The best hunters."

'Sorry. I haven't seen them. But I do know what lies on the other side."

He sat up, his glare glowing, his mouth slightly open. "Speak up."

"There's no valley on the other side of the Ardean Range."

It took him some time to take this in. Then he sprang to his feet and began pacing the tent. His hand kept rhythmically closing around his sword hilt. He knitted his bushy eyebrows, his black beard standing bolt upright.

"I knew it! I knew something wasn't right!" he whispered furiously without stopping. "Old fart!

Spirits talking to him! What a skunk! I just can't believe it..."

He froze. "Wait here!" he snapped and darted out of the tent.

In the following few minutes, the tent became crowded with angry bearded warriors levels 200 to 270. Apparently, none of them had needed a special invitation.

Finally they all sat down in three semicircles in front of me. Droy stepped into the center of the tent and raised his hand, stopping their talking and whispers.

He went on with a brief opening speech on the subject of his sacred brotherly friendship with all those present, interspersed by occasional statements whose meaning was best described as "You know me!" and "You've fought with me!", giving me ample opportunity to study the newcomers.

Their rugged faces were furrowed with scars, both old and new. These guys had been through a lot — and they'd survived to tell the tale. The clan's elite. Besides, it turned out I already knew most of them. Earlier that day, I'd healed many of them or their family members. This was encouraging. I had a funny feeling I knew why Droy had called them all up.

"Olgerd, tell them! Tell them what you know!"

What did I say?

Slowly I rose to my feet and took Droy's place at the center of the tent. "Ask your questions. I'll answer them if I can."

"Droy says there's no valley on the other side of the Range," the red-bearded Arrum began. "He says the shaman's prophesy was wrong. What is there then?"

"A huge river. It's called the River Quiet. It's seething with monsters this big."

"And behind it?" demanded Seet, a guy who resembled a large weathered boulder.

"The Rocky desert. Nothing grows there," I replied patiently.

"Anyone live there?"

I nodded. "I didn't get a chance to have a good look at them. They're too fast and there're lots of them."

"And what lies beyond the desert?" asked the mountainous Orman.

"The Quartan Valley."

At the word "valley" they perked up.

"Don't hold your breath. The place is absolutely packed with giant spiders."

"How big?" the bald-headed Shorve asked.

I cast a look around me. "They're about as tall as this tent is high."

They were a sorry sight. The good thing was, they believed me. My Reputation kept working in my favor.

"Beyond the Valley lies the Blackwood," I said. "But it doesn't matter. Even if you manage to survive crossing the river, the Rocky Desert, the Spider Valley and the Blackwood, you won't be able to advance much further."

"Why not?" they asked almost in unison.

"Because you'll walk right into the walls of Maragar Citadel where you'll share the fate of all the other clans."

Dead silence hung in the tent.

"Do you mean that-" Droy began, shattered by the news.

"Exactly. I can even venture a guess that those of your clans that headed east must have eventually walked into some Dark fortress, too. I'll tell you more: I'm pretty convinced that at the moment, the Red Owls are the biggest and strongest among your clans. Both Light and Dark fortress defenders are very well armed. They have high walls defended by the best warriors and wizards."

Bang! I'd just lost 200 pt. Reputation with Mellenville!

Then again, it was only logical. I'd just revealed some of the Citadel's secrets to its potential enemy.

My path as the outcast had begun.

Chapter Twenty-Two

"You stupid idiots! Who did you believe? A stranger, a snake oil salesman? He's only been here a few days and already you believe everything he says? By doubting my words you doubt the will of the Higher Beings! Have you ever thought that he might have come here on purpose? What if his Lightie bosses sent him here deliberately, to talk us out of crossing the Ardean Range? In which case, Droy, you're an idiot! Did it ever occur to you that Lighties might have captured our scouts and tortured them into disclosing our plans?"

I was witness to a local revolution. In just a few days, Droy had managed to stir quite a kerfuffle. Still, the shaman hadn't been born yesterday, either. The old schemer hadn't wasted his time. While Droy was simple-heartedly trying to tell his clanmates about the looming danger, Laosh the shaman had managed to secure support from the clan's strongest members.

He'd promptly managed to call up the council and every time Droy had delivered his passionate yet unarticulated speech, the shaman would tear his arguments to bits.

He really was on a power trip, that one. Oh how he loved every win he scored over his inexperienced opponent! How smug he was, playing with words and choosing just the right expressions to illustrate his point! Droy had nothing left to do but watch forlornly as his only hope to save his people dwindled to nothing.

Oh, yes. My friends had lost this round, that much was clear. All of them were warriors, hunters, shepherds and craftsmen: simple-hearted folk unschooled in the fine art of scheming and politics.

It takes a different mindset to battle someone like this Laosh. You need to know when to play along with them, when to offer a baksheesh or even to receive it. Men like him stop at nothing — and strangely enough, this is also their biggest weakness. Sooner or later, people's trust in them tends to erode, forcing them to seek support from weaker — albeit just as hungry — allies. That means sharing your hard-earned power with your new friends, closing your eyes to their appetites — until the moment when they shed their masks of humble anonymity to overthrow the ruler reckless enough to share the precious resource of his power with them.

Besides, Droy tended to press his point too hard. Once the first excitement had died down, no one seemed to care that much. When you spend too much time waiting for a disaster to strike, you sort of get used to the thought and aren't that afraid anymore.

Same thing had happened to the Calteans. At first they'd been really scared, desperate to do something ASAP. But then their everyday concerns had sort of dulled the initial shock. Subconsciously all the clan members wanted to hear their chief's speech — and Laosh had delivered, giving them exactly what they wanted to hear.

Admittedly, no one was skeptical of Droy's story. He was no village idiot either: to the contrary, he was a respected commander and a great warrior. Which was a big fat plus to our cause.

Laosh didn't realize it yet. He was too busy enjoying the sound of his own voice. In the meantime, the grains of doubt sown by Droy were bound to germinate.

All we had to do was bide our time. We needed to send out another scout group and wait for their report. As soon as the Calteans realized that their precious shaman was taking them for a long and pointless ride, I would be ready to offer an alternative.

Laosh' fierce voice distracted me from my musings. Wait a sec. Was he talking to *me*?

"Speak up! Cat got your tongue? Have you got nothing to say to us?"

That's right. He *was* talking to me. Was it some sort of speaking duel?

I knew what he was up to. But I equally knew I was going to lose this game. My Reputation just wasn't up to it yet. Laosh had had all the time in the world to level his own up.

Very well, mister. Thanks for the opportunity,

anyway.

I wasn't going to try to convince the rich and powerful. They were unlikely to sacrifice their comfortable lifestyle for some weird stranger and his ideas. I had to target those who were already on the fence. I had to improve their trust. Off we go!

I gave the gloomy Droy a wink and walked out of the crowd, facing the council.

"You're wrong, Laosh," I said calmly. "I have a lot to say to you all. You've just accused me of lying. You're very welcome to think so. There's nothing I can do to convince you otherwise so I'm not going to try. You also said that I want to talk your people out of going west. And you're dead right there!"

Whispers ran through the crowd. Droy and his supporters stared at me in disbelief. Laosh stuck out his chest, looking like a winner.

"You're right, Shaman," I repeated. "You only got one little thing wrong. You said that the people of Light are afraid of you and that's why they sent me here. What a ridiculous thing to say. The people of Light can't wait for you to come. With every Caltean they kill, they get stronger. I saw what happened to another Caltean camp. It was razed to the ground by the forces of Light. Their best wizards and warriors stormed it, destroying the trebuchets so prized by your Caltean neighbors."

Oops. Another system message and another - 100 to my Reputation with Mellenville.

"How do you know about the trebuchets?" a white-haired elder wheezed.

I smiled. "The ones that launch Rock Erezes

onto enemy cities? You said it. How would I know about them, really? I'm an enemy spy and a liar, aren't I?"

Many a warrior's face darkened. Women gasped. Children instinctively clung to their parents.

"That proves nothing!" Laosh spat.

"No, it doesn't," I agreed. "I'm not trying to prove anything here. I'm just telling you what I saw myself. Your trebuchets are powerful weapons. I once saw an Erez kill all of Droy's warriors in one clean sweep. But I also saw a warrior of Light kill an Erez with his own hands back in the Citadel. The armies of both Light and Dark have scores of soldiers like him."

Okay, so I'd exaggerated a bit but not too much, really.

"And what's more," I added, "their armies are heading this way — and very soon, too. There'll be a big war. For you it'll be over quickly. Which is why we need-"

"Enough!" Laosh butted in. "We've already heard your tales! Go back to your seat, stranger! The council will decide your fate!"

Oh, well. If you say so. I shrugged and took my place next to Droy.

I had some idea of what Laosh and his henchmen would decide. Still, that was irrelevant. I'd done what I'd wanted to do. The crowd followed me with grateful stares: the lowborn Red Owls had believed me, judging by the flicker of system messages and the spinning of my Reputation counter. A bit more, and I might receive a Gray order.

After a quick deliberation, the council

announced their decision. Droy was allowed to extend his hospitality for one more week. Once it elapsed, I had to leave the camp. In other words, I received a conditional banishment.

The Red Owls didn't look happy with their chief's decision. That was good news.

The crowd began to disperse when Laosh announced, "One more thing! Tomorrow a team of forty warriors will leave the camp. And just to dispel your doubts, I'm going to lead it myself. Those remaining should begin to break camp. Stranger, you're coming with us!"

His cunning face dissolved in a smug smile. Clever bastard. If I declined, it would mean he'd been right all along. If I agreed, he'd be free to swat me like a fly at his first convenience.

I nodded, accepting the offer.

It made him happy no end. I had a gut feeling he'd already thought of some nasty trick to play on me.

"Cheer up," Droy gave me a hearty slap on the shoulder. "You'll come with us. We won't let him get to you."

Great minds think alike...

A non-player character has sent you an invitation to join his group!
Accept: Yes/No

Oh really? Okay. I pressed *Yes.*

You've just joined an NPC group!

From now on, you'll receive 1% of the group's combat experience.

For your information: as the holder of an Order of Heroic Strength, you bring +30% to Strength of all group members.

As I tried to weigh up all the pros and cons of joining an NPC group, Droy and his friends inconspicuously surrounded me and guided me back to camp.

Flames danced in the night, dispelling its viscous gloom. Sparks shot out toward the starry sky like so many lightbugs, expiring on their journey and turning into tiny ashes.

We sat around the campfire: Arrum Red Beard, Seet the Burly, Horm the Turtle, Orman the Bear, Shorve the Hasty and Droy the Fang. And myself.

It turned out that Droy wasn't just a warlord. He was also the elder of a small clan of his own. That's why he enjoyed so much authority. And that's why I had known nothing about it earlier. I hadn't had the right access yet.

But now as my Reputation with the clan grew, new details continued to come to light. Like the men's nicknames.

They were preparing for the journey. Some were checking their weapons, others mending their clothes. A few like myself sat leisurely enjoying the dance of the flames.

"Olgerd," Orman the Bear turned to me, busy rubbing some nasty-looking substance into the tip of his spear. "Is it true what you said about wizards and warriors who can defeat an Erez?"

"Unfortunately," I said. "Not one but many even."

"Wow," Seet the Burly said slowly. "I'm not a coward but now I start to think that the Nocteans weren't the worst enemy."

"You can say that," Shorve the Hasty agreed.

"Can't we make a deal with them or something?" Horm the Turtle suggested.

No idea why they'd nicknamed him Turtle. True, he was a bit on the slow side but he was a very clever man, that's for sure.

"I don't think so," I said.

"Why not?"

"Because for the warriors of both Light and Dark, killing a Caltean is a feat of valor. They get rewarded for your heads."

The men sat up straight, proud of themselves. Their opponents thought them valuable trophies! That meant that their enemies had respect for them!

I immediately thought of the medieval Russian Prince Svyatoslav who'd died in battle against the invading Pecheneg tribes while crossing the Don rapids. They said that his enemy Khan Kurya made a chalice out of his skull believing it to be the greatest honor to Russia's slain ruler. Afterwards, both the Khan and his wife used to drink wine from the chalice hoping that the dead Prince's spirit would grant his strength to their future son.

Somehow I didn't think anyone would pay the Calteans' bodies the same kind of respect. At best, their scalps, clothes and weapons might serve as evidence when someone claimed his or her Reputation upgrade.

I understood of course they were only a bunch of game scripts. Still, my heart refused to accept it. I couldn't bear the thought of the fate that awaited my new friends once they met some of the top players. I didn't doubt for one moment that only the top players would venture into No-Man's Lands. This wasn't the place for the weak.

"What, even trebuchets don't work against them?" Droy the Fang asked, sounding insecure.

Shorve the Hasty had already told me how Droy had received his nickname. He'd been still a small child when a pack of wolves had attacked their herds. Little Droy had had enough presence of mind to confront them and even assaulted one with a stone, knocking out a few of the wolf's teeth. He would have died for sure had it not been for his father and uncle who'd come running to his aid.

So it looked like my Droy was a warrior from a young age, literally.

"Not really," I replied. "Last time I saw members of your tribe in action, they destroyed a few houses and set free a few Erezes. Still, the Lighties rebuilt everything they'd destroyed in three days. May I ask you something?"

"You can try," Droy said.

"Where did you get the trebuchets from?"

I'd been racking my brains over this ever since I'd seen the Caltean camp. They just didn't look capable of building such complex machinery. They were a primitive tribe living in tents and clad in animal skins. Many of them still used spears with either stone or bone tips. It just didn't sum up.

Horm the Turtle shrugged. "They aren't ours, those things. Never have been."

"What do you mean?" I turned to Droy. "How about the trap your warriors caught the Erez with before it killed them, remember?"

Droy fidgeted on his mat. He heaved a sigh. I must have touched on a very sensitive subject.

"Yes, those machines... and the traps... and lots of other things. The Black Axes procured them."

"Where did they get them from?"

"The Forbidden City."

"Their survivors told us it was only a fraction of all the treasures they'd found there," Horm added.

The group emitted a collective sigh, their expressions dreamy, their eyes glowing. This place must have been some kind of local El Dorado.

"Do I understand correctly that those Black Axes are the strongest clan among you?" I asked an uncomfortable question.

"They are," Droy replied matter-of-factly. "They're the only ones who can assemble the ancient machines."

How interesting. A nomadic clan capable of handling complex machinery. They wouldn't have come across some blueprints, by any chance?

"They were always into mechanical things and stuff," Seet said. "They were constantly busy inside that Silver Mountain of theirs like it was an anthill!"

Aha. This was starting to become clear.

"Traps and trebuchets! That's nothing," Shorve

hurried to butt in. "I heard that the City Palace dungeons are absolutely packed with all sorts of stuff. Lots of weapons there, they say. And steel monsters. They're huge. Only they're asleep. Or maybe dead, I dunno."

Curiouser and curiouser.

"Had it not been for the Forbidden City's guards, the Black Axes would have had a ball..."

The warriors grew long faces.

"Are there guards there?" I asked.

Orman nodded. "They wiped the floor with the Axes. Lots of great warriors died that day."

Others began eulogizing the names of their friends who'd died in that battle. This was the system's all-too-subtle message: enough info for the time being.

"And the trap you saw," Droy added, his face drawn, "I swapped it with one of the Axes for five buffaloes. Still, I failed to save my brothers. Had it not been for you, I wouldn't be here to tell the tale. Damnation! I rue the day we did it."

"What do you mean?" I asked.

"Our shaman needs trapped animals for his magic tricks," Seet replied. "He offers a good price for them. Leave it, Fang, don't beat yourself up. The guys knew what they were into. At least you helped their families out by selling the Erez. Everybody knows that. We all respect you for what you did."

Droy was about to reply when the shaman's messenger arrived.

"Laosh orders you to go first," he said calmly. "The main group will set off in three hours."

"Tell that old far-" Orman began.

"Okay," Droy butted in. "You can tell Laosh we heard him. Now go."

Once the messenger left, Seet put in words what everybody was thinking, "The old bastard knows we're the best scouts around."

Everybody looked at me expectantly.

I chuckled. Sure. The shaman was obliged to know that my skills made the scouts' job a breeze. He knew they could count on my aerial recon support. What a cheek!

"Everybody hit the sack now," Droy ordered. "We're setting off at daybreak."

* * *

The next morning was cold and cloudy. The sky was completely covered. It might actually snow by lunchtime.

Boris and I soared just under the clouds studying the area. Below, a group of six warriors hand-picked by Droy himself was busy negotiating the cliffs. Hand-picked was an overstatement: same old faces, their levels exceeding 250. They were a force to be reckoned with.

Nothing had happened... yet. Our progress was quiet and peaceful.

What a shame NPCs didn't have a chat of their own. That way I could warn them about the unsafe parts of their trek. As it was now, I was obliged to descend every time I saw something suspicious. Now too, I'd noticed a few long shadows in a gorge and hurried to cruise lower.

"What is it?" Droy asked me the moment Boris landed.

'I can't really tell," I said, removing the helmet. "I only saw their outlines. There're about six or seven of them."

"Sounds like the Shaggies," Arrum Red Beard suggested.

"How far are they?" Droy asked.

"Around that bend over there," I pointed.

Droy gave me a slap on the shoulder. "Good. Go back up now and keep your eyes peeled."

I put the helmet back on and leapt into the saddle. Sensing my excitement, Boris took off like a missile.

Having said that, why not? Just look at him shining in his brand-new suit of armor. A fine monster he was!

Considering our levels, as warriors we were pretty useless. Still, it was our rightful job to give the enemy a bad hair day.

I'd forgotten to mention that as soon as we'd left the newb location, I'd received the system message lifting the ban on air-to-ground. Which meant we could now deal 100% damage!

Oh, and talking about weapons, my Minor Pocket Slingshot had left a lasting impression on the Calteans. The way they'd guffawed I thought they might trigger an avalanche. The advice they'd given me! According to them, I could use it to kill sparrows, to scratch my feet or to launch fish food into the pond. I should have made a list. Even my pretty accurate skull-cracking practice had failed to impress them. Then again, what did I expect, with my level and all?

The sun poked out from behind the clouds. Excellent. It made me harder to detect in the sky.

The Calteans fanned out. They showed good training. Droy definitely knew what he was doing.

Aha! Now I could really get a good eyeful of the local beasties. So that's what they looked like, then.

There were six of them. Judging by their body shapes, I could describe them as giant hairy lizards the size of large alligator, with sharp triangular teeth and long curved claws. They froze, holding their breath. They definitely knew we'd be using this path and had taken up strategic positions all around it.

I told Boris to fly over the cliff. As soon as I reached its north side, I knew my gut feeling had been right all along. How many of them were there? Twenty, thirty? Fifty? Had we just walked into an incubator or something? I had to hurry back and warn the others!

I returned to the sunny side, searching out Droy's figure amid the cliffs.

Warning! Your group is engaged in battle!
Reminder: you're a member of an NPC group!
You receive 1% of the group's combat experience.
For your information: as the holder of an Order of Heroic Strength, you bring +30% to Strength of all group members.

Engaged, already? What about the lizards they were fighting? Let's have a look... the strongest one was level 220. Uh oh. Way too much for humble me. Arrum Red Beard, the weakest warrior in the group, was level 255.

So it looked like this unexpected bonus wasn't meant for me. My presence, however, had given the Red Owls the boost they needed. They were making mincemeat out of the poor beasties.

Olgerd, what are you waiting for? You still have personal XP to take care of!

My slingshot began cracking off in rapid fire as I tried to deal as much damage as I possibly could in the time I still had.

You've attacked a level 220 Hairy Pangolin.
Damage dealt: 455
Keep on fighting!

In a couple of minutes, the melee was over. My group had smoked the whole six-strong pack.

Your group has killed a Pack of Hairy Pangolins!
You've received Experience!
You've received a new level!
You've received a new level!
You've received a new level!
You've received a new level!
You've received a new level!
Current level: 35
Reward:
A Teleportation Scroll

+20 to Knowledge
Current Knowledge: 196/340
Available points: 5

I loved it. Five levels just like that!

Seeing as I'd failed to find any Intellect-boosting runes or items, I had to invest all the available points into it. By now I had no doubt Intellect was my priority. Growing my Knowledge bar was indispensable for my "Army Mechanic's" further development.

I couldn't wait to see what my Pocket Book of Blueprints would surprise me with this time. If scarabs and fleas were considered "simple beings", I could only imagine the kind of complexity these blueprints had in store for me.

Apparently, the more valuable a blueprint, the more Knowledge its study required. I was only a few points short of 200 Knowledge. Had the Pangolin pack counted seven beasts instead of six...

A thought stirred somewhere in the deep recesses of my darker self. Wouldn't it be good if Droy's group "accidentally" came across the large pangolin pack I'd just seen on the other side of the cliff?

But the existence of dark thoughts is to be ignored. I shook my head free of them. Some idea! I could only explain it by the excitement still ravaging my blood.

"Droy! You can't go north!" I shouted. "We'll have to make a detour! Turn onto that path over there!"

"Why?" he hadn't even broken a sweat in battle.

I pointed north. "There're many more of them there. At least twenty times more. Big ones, too."

Droy frowned. "In that case you're right. We'd better make a detour. If they're too many, they might kill my warriors. Seet! Leave a sign for those who'll follow."

Then he turned to me. "Thank you, friend."

The game engine seemed to be having a generosity day. Reputation, XP, loot — I had plenty of everything. I cheered up. And I knew somebody else who'd be more than happy to see all the Pangolin claws, teeth and hair — Rrhorgus. Purple resources were always in demand.

What a shame there was no email access in No-Man's Lands! Even the auction and the info portal were unavailable. I might have to use Boris to take me to see Rrhorgus — which would be a shameful waste of time.

None of the Calteans seemed to notice me collecting the loot. Even when the monsters' bodies dissolved into thin air, they just accepted it matter-of-factly. The game mechanics is a sobering thing indeed.

Well, that was a good start to the day. Let's wait and see what else it might bring.

Chapter Twenty-Three

"Olgerd, what takes you so long?"

"Sorry Arrum, I won't be a moment," I said, hurrying to take another swing with my pick. "Five more stones, then I'm done."

Arrum Red Beard shrugged. "You and your stones! Well, suit yourself. If you like your backpack heavy..."

I hid a smile in my beard. They may be "useless stones" to him, but as far as I was concerned, they were very useful. How can Master-level Purple quartz rock be useless? Someone was bound to need it and this someone might just be prepared to shell out a nice fat sum for it.

We'd discovered the quartz rock deposits early in the afternoon. Or rather, we'd discovered the cave that housed the said deposits. The group had decided to stop and investigate... and man, was I happy they had.

In one final swing of my pick, I became the proud owner of two hundred of the choicest quartz rock stones. The exercise felt nostalgic. It had been a while since I'd used my Digger tools. Okay, it was only two hundred stones, but they'd added 9 pt. to my skill. How good was that?

Then again, what was I talking about? Even one extra point was welcome in my situation. Master-level craftsmen didn't have it easy, oh no. Clans kept all high-level resources under their own control. And here they were literally scattered under your very own feet.

"Olgerd! Come here, quick!" a shout came from within the depths of the cave.

I awoke from somewhat smugly admiring my stat chart. What now?

I found all the Calteans in one of the side tunnels. They stood there frozen. The hissing of torches was the only sound in the gloom.

Once I pushed my way through, I finally saw what had silenced these usually chatty characters.

The cave's rocky floor was littered with bones, picked clean and whitened.

These had been Calteans, no doubt about it. Their spears and rusty swords were still lying around. Judging by the bodies' position in relation to each other, it didn't look as if they had died in battle. The local mice — or rats, or whatever other petty scavengers they had here — had made sure the cause of their death wasn't easy to determine anymore.

We saw traces of old campfires. These men must have decided to spend the night in the warmth of the cave — never to wake up again.

"Olgerd? What do you think?" Droy's voice made me jump.

And not only me, apparently. Orman even shuddered as if he was suddenly cold.

No wonder. The place was spooky. The torches' light didn't reach the cave's walls nor ceiling, making it look enormous. It felt as if something ancient and utterly terrible was watching us in the dark. The dancing flames of our torches made the skeletons appear to stir, trying to get back to their feet. Even back in the Fort swarming with zombies I'd never felt so uncomfortable.

I cleared my suddenly dry throat. "They didn't fight. You can see that, can't you? And still something killed them."

"But what?" Arrum asked.

"I'd venture a guess they suffocated in their sleep," I said, casting wary looks around me. "It smells funny here, don't you think? We really shouldn't linger here if we don't want to share their fate. I'm pretty sure of that. Did you know them?"

I'd lied about the smell. I just wanted to get out of this place ASAP.

Droy nodded. "Yes. These are our scouts. This is the sword of Camus the Fingerless..." he heaved a sigh, picking up a rusty sword that lay next to the campfire.

"And this is my uncle's spear..." Shorve whispered.

Their words seemed to open the warriors' eyes to the scene. Almost every one of them discovered a kinsman among the dead.

They realized they couldn't leave the bones lying around in this God-forsaken cave. They had to bury their brothers with due honors. Still, they also knew they had no time to do that.

So the warriors swore a solemn oath to come back one day, provided they survived, and perform all the necessary burial rites.

The cave didn't look as if it could harbor anything I could use. Besides, I wasn't in the mood for treasure hunting. The other guys might misunderstand it.

"You told us the truth, my friend," Droy said once we came out into the open air. "You were right what you said at the Council. Our warriors would never have surrendered without a fight to anyone — be they servants of Light, Dark or the demons of Inferno itself. You're doubly right in saying they died peacefully in their sleep. The cave's breath must have killed them. I had a Black Axe friend who told me about these things."

The warriors continued in silence, only exchanging occasional words when they absolutely had to. How I understood them. Even though their scouts hadn't been heard from for a long time, their families had still harbored the hope that they might see them again one day. Now, knowledge had replaced the old hope — accompanied by sorrow.

And so we kept going until we stopped for the night.

"Does that mean they didn't even cross the Ardean Range?"

We were sitting by the fire. The men had had enough time to digest the tragic news. It was time for them to get it off their chests.

"Shame we've got no ale," Droy sighed.

"Your orders," Horm said. "No one's taken any. That way we could have at least drunk to their memory..."

A collective sigh rustled over the campfire.

"Listen, guys," I said. "Basically... How can I say it... I didn't know alcohol wasn't allowed on the march. It's not ale that I've got, anyway. Just some light swill. But it's enough for us all to celebrate your kinsmen's valor."

I reached into my bag and produced the two wine flasks I'd prepared for Master Adkhur.

"Brothers," Orman said with a faint smile, "now what would we do without our Olgerd here?"

Everyone turned to their leader. Droy chuckled and rolled his eyes.

With his silent approval, the others reached for the drink. The flasks began changing hands, emptying quickly.

"Smells good," the bald-headed Shorve announced, sniffing his cup. "Must be a good wine."

I shrugged. "I got it for a friend."

"Well done!" Arrum slapped my shoulder. "Friends deserve the best, always!"

Everyone hummed their approval. The noise stopped quickly enough though, as Droy rose from his place.

He spoke unhurriedly about honor and valor, naming his friends, teammates and comrades one by one. He hadn't forgotten to mention a single one of them. That's a leader for you. This is the kind of person everyone would follow. It's people like him who become the founding fathers of whole nations.

I studied the Calteans' faces, realizing that now they'd follow Droy to hell and back.

He hadn't forgotten to mention me, either, and said a lot of good words about me which made my Reputation grow another few hundred points. Finally we drank our wine. We didn't get the chance to talk though, as Seet who kept first watch came to the fire. He looked worried.

"What's up?" Droy asked.

"There's some movement on the path," Seet reported.

"Who are they?"

"I couldn't see."

Droy turned to me. "Olgerd-" he stopped, seeing that I'd already summoned Boris. "Be careful," he added instead.

As Boris took to the sky, I watched the Caltean camp, amazed at their discipline. They kept quiet. No one was fussing about. Everybody seemed to know what he was supposed to be doing. Some were putting out the fire while others were already scaling the cliffs. Only once safely above did they begin stringing their bows and readying their spears. You could see that each knew his role in the group.

We didn't have far to fly. Our potential enemy was moving quite fast: soon it would walk right into the Caltean ambush.

The sky was starless, shrouded by black rain

clouds. Doubtful they'd see me. My Ennan eyesight, however, was perfect for this setting.

When I approached the enemy, I realized that we might get away without a fight.

A single Caltean was scampering down the path.

He was making good speed, casting constant looks behind him — apparently being followed.

He wasn't a Red Owl, either. None of that animal-skin-and-wooden-spear nonsense. He was clad in quality armor, with a round shield slung on his back and an axe in each hand. Even without screaming or hollering, he was making an awful lot of noise running. Red Owls would never do something like that.

Well, well, well. Let's have a look. I told Boris to go down a bit.

Aha... Just look at this monster behind him! How had the guy managed to have aggroed it?

I took a better look. A creature the size of an adult lion was following in the Caltean's wake.

A Spike-Headed Banther.
Level: 280

The banther's powerful body was all covered in quills. Especially his head. He looked very much like a spiky-maned lion. Why was he chasing the guy? The Caltean must have accidentally triggered his aggro zone.

Oh, yes. This place was no sunny Leuton. The local mobs aggroed you for a single careless sneeze.

I had to warn the group before they smoked both the monster and his hapless quarry.

"It's a Caltean!" I shouted, hovering over Droy's head. "He's alone running! Doesn't look like an Owl! He'll be here soon! He's chased by a dangerous monster!"

Droy nodded his appreciation and made a circular motion with his right hand over his head, signaling to me to stay overhead.

Yessir! Affirmative, Sir! In the meantime, let's get our slingshot ready.

Almost immediately, the Caltean came running out to our campsite.

"Hey, Scraggie!" Droy shouted to him. "Get to the cliffs, quick!"

Heh? Did they know him? In any case, he obediently darted for cover.

He did so just in time. The monster raced out into the opening. He looked even uglier up close. His powerful feline paws ended in long claws; his massive chest was covered with an ugly spiky growth. His large jaws sported a pair of impressive saber teeth.

"Attack!" Droy shouted, launching his spear.

In a split second, the monster was studded with spears and arrows like a pincushion. The new Caltean added his two cents — or rather, his two axes — to the picture. I too was doing my best, loosing off slugs in rapid-fire succession.

The spiky bastard didn't survive our hospitality. His impressive Life bar emptied in a few seconds.

You've received a new level!
You've received a new level!
Current level: 37.

I was beginning to like it here.

The icon of the Pocket Book of Blueprints didn't blink though. Oh, well. I'd have to gain more Knowledge, wouldn't I?

Silence fell over the scene. This had been an impressive battle — or should I say a turkey shoot?

"Scraggie, you alive?" Droy exclaimed cheerfully.

"Droy?" the man's hoarse voice came from the dark. "Is that you?"

"Who do you think? You know anybody else who'd bother to save your sorry ass?"

The warriors guffawed. Grinning, they emerged from their positions. The new Caltean too exited his hideout.

They restarted the fire, allowing me to get a better look of the slain mob.

Wait a sec... this wasn't a mob! It was someone's pet!

How had I managed to misread his tag?

What was it, then? Did that mean players were already so close? My back erupted in goosebumps. If that was the case, then we were about to face the choicest of the top players. The best of the best.

I had to locate the monster's owner ASAP.

Slowly his body dissolved into thin air. I turned around. The new Caltean was already shooting the breeze with the group.

I'd been right. He wasn't a Red Owl. You didn't have to be an expert on Caltean culture to see that.

He was level 310, wearing steel armor, a closed helmet, a round shield and battle axes. Droy's warriors looked like cavemen next to him. His shield was decorated with a picture of two black crossed battleaxes — apparently his clan's logo.

"You've always been an ambush expert, old vagabond!" Scraggie shook Droy by the shoulder. "It didn't take you long to set it up! Can't believe you recognized me!"

I could see that Droy felt flattered by this praise. Apparently, this Scraggie guy was a respected individual.

"Well, what did you expect? It's not as if you've changed a lot!" Droy replied. "You should thank *him* for us being so quick."

Scraggie squinted shortsightedly in my direction. I was forced to walk out of the shadows and nod a greeting.

As soon as he realized who it was standing in front of him, he reached mechanically for his weapon. His eyes lit up with hatred. His mouth curved in a smirk.

Oh. Sorry, man. This wasn't the agreement.

Boris materialized next to me and hissed a warning at the scowling newcomer.

"Nobody move!" Droy shouted. So frightening he was in his anger that even Scraggie shrank back.

"What do you think you're doing, you old fart?" Droy growled at him. "You wanna kill my man?"

Surprised, Scraggie looked around himself at

the Red Owls encircling him. "Droy, are you nuts?" he shouted. "He's a Lightie, for crying out loud! They kill us! You don't know!"

"I do," Droy replied in a calmer voice. "He told us everything. Both about your group and the Lighties. Everything. I'll tell you more: he's already saved our backsides several times. And yours too, as you've just seen. I don't give a damn which side he's on. He's my friend."

"Mine, too."

"He's our friend."

"Sure."

My friends' voices made my heart flutter: an incredible feeling.

"So let's just cool it and have a talk," Droy raised a conciliatory hand. "Do you believe me?"

Scraggie gave me a moody look. "Yeah."

I could see the word had cost him a lot. "I know what you mean," I decided to add my two cents. "If it'll make you feel any better, I never took part in the killings of your kinsmen. Last time they attacked the Citadel, I was still working in the mines."

"I know you were," Droy said placatingly. "Let's go sit by the fire. Then we can talk."

"Wait, chief," I stopped him. "I have a question for Scraggie."

The warrior frowned.

"It's about the monster that was chasing you," I hurried to explain, "Or rather, about his master."

Scraggie's mouth opened in amazement. "How did you know?"

"I'll tell you later. We don't have much time. Is

he dead?"

"He is," Scraggie replied grimly. "He killed my two best scouts."

"Was it far from here?"

"No. Wasn't far at all. But just before he died, he'd managed to summon the beast. Just like you've just done."

That player must have been overly optimistic. He'd probably hoped to handle the Calteans on his own without having to summon his pets. Still, it hadn't quite worked that way. The Calteans had proved tougher than he thought. And still he'd managed to smoke two of them! Two to one, that was quite a ratio. Had he summoned his pet earlier on in the fight, Scraggie wouldn't be having this conversation with us, that's for sure.

"Was he a Lightie of a Darkie?" I asked.

"Darkie."

"Droy," I turned to my friend who'd been anxiously following our exchange. "I need to see the playe- er, the guy's death site."

"There's nothing there," Scraggie said. "His body already disappeared."

"I can see certain things you can't," I said.

"He's right," Droy said, then turned to me, "Go now. Just keep your eyes peeled."

I grinned darkly before jumping onto Boris' back.

"It's by the dead tree near the path!" Scraggie shouted from below.

IT HADN'T TAKEN me long to get to the site.

First I saw the path, then the dead tree.

There! I could see the dead Calteans' bodies. And the chest left after the player's death. He was probably on his way back here now, hurrying to collect his stuff. I had to be quick.

Boris circled the site several times before landing. I let Prankie out. He cast his Shield over me, then began inspecting the surrounding shrubbery.

No one around, by the looks of it.

Let's check it out.

"Enjoying yourself?" a cheerful voice made me jump. "Stealing from a fellow player, nice one, dude!"

I swung round but saw no one. The voice sounded quite near though. Then again, I should have known better. This was probably a high-level rogue or assassin with Stealth to match.

"Well, well, well! Who do we see here? The legend of Mellenville!" the voice sounded quite close. "Your scalp must cost a fortune! Aren't I the lucky one? But first we need to talk."

Finally the Dark player materialized less than twenty feet from me.

Name: Furius
Race: Alven
Level: 290
Clan: The Lords of Chaos
Class: Black Ranger

Never heard about this class before. And judging by his level, the Steel Shirts' Romulus wasn't the top player anymore.

The Colonization seemed to have been advancing nicely, and so had the players.

What was he doing here, anyway? Then again, why would I even ask? This had to be a clan scout on a recon mission.

"Good idea, dude," the player grinned. "Flying your pet over No-Man's Lands monitoring any potential battle sites, then looting them if you're lucky. Not bad at all. Definitely worth it."

Okay, if he said so. Although if the truth were known, I didn't feel guilty in the slightest. This was war. *A la guerre comme à la guerre.*

But it looked like this philosophy might just backfire on me now.

Oh, no. I wasn't going to surrender without fight. Furius was wearing nothing but his starting pants. Having said that, he could easily smoke me with his bare hands if he wanted to. But at least this way I had a chance of legging it.

"I love your pets," he continued. "Where did you get them from?"

"That's my business."

He tut-tutted. "No need to be so rude, man."

Warily he inched toward. Was he afraid of me or something? WTF?

The I remembered what Sveta, my wife, had told me. They all must be thinking it had been me who'd scorched Master Adkhur's location. Furius had admitted he'd recognized me. Which meant...

"Your beastie wasn't bad either, was it?" I said, playing for time as I stole a furtive step back.

"Did you see him? Yeah sure! You must have

picked up all of the scraggy Caltean's loot. Saves me the trouble of looking for it. You're something, you!"

"You didn't hear me. I said, *was*."

He looked confused. "What about the Caltean?"

"What about him?" I bluffed.

He frowned. "I don't understand."

"It's okay," I said. "Take your time. I'm off now."

"You what? Wait a sec, dude! Where d'you think you're going?"

"Sorry, man. Got lots of things to do. Nice meeting you."

"You have a cheek!"

"Listen, dude," I said, trying to keep my shaking voice level. "I really need to go now. It's been nice talking to you. But now we both have things to do."

He paused, thinking. Yes, he definitely was wary of me. I'd love to know what they were saying about me in the forums.

"I think you're right, dude. We both have things to do."

Aha, so he'd decided to attack me anyway. Perfectly understandable. A high-level player afraid of a newb? I don't think so.

Still, it was probably a good idea to attack him first. What a waste of resources... but it was well worth it.

You've built the simplest mechanical creature: a Swarm of Fleas!
Level: 120
Number of swarm members: 5

Wow! Five of them, all level 120! Quality of source materials at 70%, too! Each flea was the size of a microwave.

They went for the player all at once. If even one of them managed to bite him, it would be of great help.

In the meantime, I hurried to activate a teleport crystal.

Warning! You can't activate the scroll in the course of battle!

Excuse me? What was it now?

A powerful blow threw me back a good dozen feet.

Warning! The Swarm of Fleas has been destroyed!

Wow. Already? Prankie's Shield too had been deactivated, his Life barely glowing at 3%. And the guy was virtually naked!

I glimpsed some ash crumbling to the ground from his hand. Was it some kind of scroll spell he'd just used on me?

His long face betrayed amazement. Apparently, I wasn't supposed to have survived the blow. *Graveyard Wind:* judging by the name, it must have been some Necro magic.

They liked these zombie shticks here, didn't they? Had I not been protected against it, I'd have been heading for my resurrection point already.

I gulped a vial of Ale of Life and jumped to my feet. Leaping onto Boris' back, I unsummoned Prankie.

The player darted toward his chest. No points for guessing he had a bow waiting there.

Boris soared up — unfortunately, not fast enough.

I kept snapping my slingshot non-stop, clueless as to how many slugs I'd already loosed off. They did less damage to him than mosquito bites.

Some Ranger this guy was! Normally, they're low on defenses. Not this one. Even naked, he completely ignored my hits.

I created five more fleas and sent them down after him.

The player had already slung his bow. For him this was just target practice.

Look at the damage he'd dealt! He killed a flea with two arrows. Then again, why would that surprise me?

I could see his smug grin. It looked like we might die, after all. Oh. So stupid of me.

I dropped five more fleas.

But no. He didn't even look at them, the bastard! He was aiming directly at Boris.

I'll never be able to forget what I did next.

I unsummoned Boris right there in the air.

And we'd already climbed a good hundred feet.

At first it felt like zero gravity. The system must never have come across such unorthodox use of the summoning charm before. The next moment, however, the forest below began to shoot toward me.

A loud whooshing sound a few feet overhead told me that Furius had missed.

Up yours, mister!

I span through the air until a series of impacts stopped my descent, knocking all the wind out of me. I landed.

Warning! You've been injured!
Injuries sustained:
Dislocation of your right shoulder
Lacerated wound of your left thigh

Could have been worse, I suppose. Luckily, tree branches had cushioned my fall.

Excellent. I'd managed to save Boris and even survived in the process. All I had to do now was make myself scarce. The fleas were doing a good job distracting Furius but I had a feeling it wouldn't last.

I quickly picked up the greaves and a pauldron I'd lost in my fall, summoned Boris and told him to make his way through the woods. Judging by my injury counters, it didn't look like I might be doing much running in the next twenty-four hours.

And as far as looters went, I wasn't much better, either. That was a fact.

Boris was doing his best, barging through the bushes without slowing down.

A few moments later, I received another system message, telling me I'd "lost the fight for the reason of fleeing the battlefield" and removing a few XP percent.

Had we really made it? Somehow I didn't think

so. I whipped out the teleportation crystal.

Please choose your destination.

Yes! "Hold it, kiddo," I whispered, casting furtive looks around.

Boris stopped, then promptly disappeared as I unsummoned him.

"We have some growing to do ASAP," I said, selecting my last bind point.

Chapter Twenty-Four

The shaman was a sorry sight. Every word uttered by Scraggie hammered another nail into the coffin of his "Higher Beings theory".

On one hand, it worked in my favor, improving my authority. But on the other, we had a big problem now. Namely, Scraggie himself.

The shaman's main group had caught up with us by midday. Almost straight away, an impromptu rally started up, demanding Scraggie speak.

My injuries had healed overnight. I was fresh and ready for new challenges. Now I was standing slightly aside from the others, watching the shaman lose face in public.

The warriors listened to Scraggie's speech intently. Every now and then, heads turned to check me out. Their grim faces betrayed one single thought: *The Lightie told us the truth. He hadn't lied to us.*

Scraggie was enjoying the audience, spinning a

glorious yarn about the Black Axes' campaign southward. He didn't spare praise describing the epic battle by the Citadel walls, mentioning their defeat but fleetingly. He didn't forget to thank Droy's group for rescuing him. He hadn't mentioned me though, for obvious reasons.

That wasn't what I was interested in. Why all the hoo-hah? What was he up to?

Having duly warmed up his audience, Scraggie finally moved to the point. As it turned out, his group had been chased by a Dark raid. And weren't good neighbors supposed to help each other out in times of trouble?

He delivered all that in a rich, flavorful language. Had Droy been able to speak like that, we wouldn't be standing here now.

It turned out, I was right. The Black Axes — once the strongest clan Under the Mountain — had been reduced to a handful of refugees, mainly women and children plus about twenty warriors and their shaman chief. All of them much the worse for wear.

A lot of them had perished on their way south. These were uncharted lands, and the Axes had had no nomadic experience. Sickness. Monsters. Battling the Lighties. Then a long and exhausting way back... I was surprised some had survived at all.

Those Dark players were smart bastards! They sent the Calteans in front to give them a free ride through No-Man's Lands! All the Darkies had to do was follow in their slipstream picking up the loot.

Now my encountering a Dark scout so far from their original habitat seemed perfectly logical.

But that wasn't the problem. The problem was, the Red Owls had bought Scraggie's speech hook, line and sinker. They agreed to help the Axes battle their way back.

So stupid.

This Scraggie was a piece of work, really. He'd put up quite a show. No wonder: charity begins at home, as they say.

Laosh the shaman was the only person who in theory could talk his kinsmen out of it. But unfortunately, by now his authority had waned.

Just when everything was coming together so nicely! The Red Owls would have reached the River Quiet, seen for themselves that there was no land of milk and honey lying beyond it, and promptly turned back, having suffered no losses. As it was, we didn't even have to continue to the river as by now everybody realized I'd been right all along. But then there was this loud-mouthed Scraggie ruining the whole picture.

Just look at the warriors hanging on his every word, their eyes glowing with righteous anger. They just couldn't wait to offer their neighbors a helping hand, completely forgetting it had been the Black Axes who'd unceremoniously walked all over them during the initial choosing of the route.

There was something else I realized as I tried to assess the situation. At the moment, the only person who really wanted to avoid confrontation was myself. All the others profited from fighting.

The admins earned their living selling combat gear: all that costly armor, resources and combat spells. Players needed the loot, the fame, the adrenaline rush, not to even mention Reputation leveling. Even the Calteans, for some reason of their own, seemed to need the upcoming battle.

It didn't look as if I could prevent it, no matter how hard I tried.

Wretched computer program! Why should it care that this battle might become the last for most of my new friends? And I, in the meantime, had some really grandiose plans for them.

I had no doubts that the Dark raid was strong. But there was no way I could explain to the Calteans that their opponents were immortal, capable of resurrecting time after time and rejoining the battle.

It wouldn't have surprised me if the news of a new mega event had already been advertised in every chat and forum. Things like *"Bring 20 ears of Caltean warriors to earn 1 Rep point!"* Bastards.

Still, it didn't look as if I could stop them. No one was going to listen to me, as simple as that. If anything, they might even bear a grudge against me as if I were trying to strip them of their rightly-deserved glory.

Just look at Droy puffing out his chest in pride! A life saver! Had he only known...

There was only one chance left.

I had to talk to Laosh.

* * *

"Ah, it's you," the shaman said as I entered his tent. He sounded tired.

Admittedly, he hadn't played too hard to get. He'd agreed to meet me almost straight away.

I cast a quick glance around. I didn't expect this at all. I'd thought his tent would be packed with luxuries and creature comforts. Nothing of the kind.

It was Spartan. A small table and a stool stood in the corner. Animal skins were heaped by the wall further along — apparently serving as his bed. The tent itself was small. Very modest. The old man was full of surprises.

"Have you come to gloat, Lightie?" he asked, apparently misunderstanding my expression.

"No. I've come to you to prevent your warriors from going to a certain death."

"Oh," he stared at me with interest.

How funny. His gaze was free of enmity or hatred. It was tired — almost apathetic.

Whatever had happened to the Laosh who'd used to dictate his will to the council? Where were his confidence and charisma? I was looking at an old-age pensioner who'd been short-changed by a cheeky marketwife.

"And how are you going to do it?" he asked.

I shook my head. "I won't. You will."

* * *

"So?" Droy nodded at the direction of the river.

"They're coming," I said. "Ten of them. And a supply train."

His face brightened up. He must have thought that ten Dark players against his sixty warriors was a good ratio.

Well, well. Don't hold your breath, man. One Dark wagon driver could easily smoke ten of our warriors. At least.

Had I just said "*our* warriors"?

I seemed to have fallen into my role. It probably had something to do with the fact that the place was quite poor on game details. An occasional system message reporting new Reputation points, the combat logs which I didn't bother to check anymore, and a few other bells and whistles, that was the extent of it. It felt as if I was in some sort of a parallel real world.

"They must be an advance party," Droy said.

Somehow I didn't think so. "Remember what I said about their best wizards and warriors?"

"Why, you think that's what some of them are?"

"They *all* are. You need to be very careful."

All the players belonged to the Lords of Chaos. A top clan, all of them level 250-plus. This was one hell of a strong group.

Their leader was Sub Zero, a level-270 wizard. I'd often come across his name in the Glasshouse news. An experienced and clever commander.

"You think our women and children are far

enough back by now?" Seet asked me.

"I do," I nodded. "They're safe."

We'd sent our "civilians" back to the main camp already several hours ago, keeping only experienced warriors.

Having said that, Black Axe children had been scared witless of Boris. They must have seen their fair share of terrible monsters in their travels. The other clan members hadn't appreciated my arrival, either. For that reason I tried to stick with the Red Owls.

When I'd returned from my recon flight, I'd been faced with the fact that Laosh had failed to talk his warriors into retreating. The Black Axes' commander had quickly taken over the leadership. Little wonder: apparently, this had always been his modus operandi.

My friends had even congratulated me on getting rid of my arch enemy, saying that Laosh would never recover from the blow. They even added they might elect another shaman now — the Black Axes' Ameret sounded like a good alternative to them. They were deliriously happy. This was the dawn of a new Caltean era! They were about to teach the Darkies a lesson!

Poor bastards.

The Black Axes, however, didn't seem to look forward to fighting the Darks. They apparently already knew enough about their enemy. The Owls had even been "offered the honor" of going first into battle. My friends naïvely celebrated the new respect their highland neighbors seemed to have for them. As an old client of mine used to say, they'd been "taken for a nice long ride".

I hadn't hesitated to share my concerns with Droy but found little support from him. He was too fascinated by Scraggie's unexpected show of friendship to pay attention. All I'd managed to procure from him was a promise not to rush headlong into battle.

Laosh had refused to talk to me. He took his defeat really badly.

Basically, I'd done my best. How did that Schiller quotation go? *"The Moor has done his duty..."* There was precious little I could do against some of Mirror World's best players. I'd just had a miraculous escape from Furius — and only because he'd rather conveniently been in his birthday suit.

Had I made a mistake joining the Red Owls, then?

Experienced players might disagree. They might even call me an idiot.

Indeed, this was probably a highly advantageous position, especially considering the recent developments in the Caltean army. Now that our little group had joined the Black Axes' raid, I was going to receive XP by the bucketful.

Someone might have considered this a gift from the gods: being rushed through levels by a few dozen NPCs, what's there not to like? In which case, why did I feel so rotten?

"There're coming!" the sentry's voice awoke me from my sad musings.

"Olgerd, up you go!" Droy shouted. "Keep your eyes peeled! Stay out of it unless you can't help it!"

"You too!" I shouted from above. "Don't stick your neck out! You promised!"

He waved my warning away and turned to his soldiers.

There was nothing I could do. What a shame.

The Calteans had decided to meet the enemy on a small hill. No idea whether that was the right thing. How could you even talk about tactics when your enemy could burn the whole place to ashes in a matter of seconds?

Still, fear takes molehills for mountains, or so they say. I just hoped I was overreacting.

On seeing their enemy, the Dark players stopped. Their "supply train" was comprised of two wagons exactly like those used by my old friends the Guiding Eyes. They unhurriedly lined it up across the path like a mini siege vehicle.

How interesting. Had I been wrong thinking that I couldn't second-guess their actions?

Even the dumbest of strategists would have used the wagons as a cover for vulnerable group members such as healers, buffers and archers. That way they could support the damagers without having to waste magic resources on their own protection.

Five tanks, two archers, a buffer, a healer, Sub Zero himself and two wagon drivers both under level 200 — that made twelve players in total. Still, I had a gut feeling there were more of them there. You couldn't disregard any potential stealthers. And considering every player also had a mount and a pet... oh. I felt very sorry for the Calteans.

The tanks moved forward, falling into line. The

others took cover behind the wagons. I was right, wasn't I? Sub Zero knew what he was doing. This was a foolproof tactic against mobs or NPCs. I'd have done the same.

Come on, Olgerd, use your head... What did I know about tactics? Tanks aggroed mobs. Buffed to their teeth, tanks were virtually unkillable — with all the support from the buffers, healers and archers, they turned into regular killing machines. Mobs or NPCs, it didn't really matter. The tanks' job was to stubbornly aggro those with higher damage counts.

So basically, this battle against sixty Calteans was going to become a pleasant end to the Darkies' hard day.

Now that I had a pretty good idea of their tactics, I also knew what the Calteans should be doing. Question was, who was going to listen to me? I'd tried everything already. The Calteans were chomping at the bit like battle horses, deaf to the voice of reason. All I could do was watch helplessly from above as the tragedy unfolded on the river bank.

The distance between the two groups had shrunk to a mere hundred paces. That was no range for wizards and archers. Still, Sub Zero seemed to be lingering. Why?

In the meantime, the Calteans' ranks were promptly regrouping, shield-carrying warriors encircling the Black Axes shaman. He was about to cast his magic. I couldn't see Laosh anywhere. Was he going to stay in his tent?

The Red Owls lined up in front, shouting and spitting at their enemy. I couldn't hear what they were saying but somehow I doubted they were wishing the Darks a good day.

This lull before the storm sent shivers down my spine. I suddenly realized I wanted it to be over quickly. This was like watching your team play while knowing the final score all along — still hoping it had been but a typo in the news stream.

I was about to climb lower when something totally unexpected happened.

Two nimble figures materialized within the circle of shields and assaulted the Black Axes' shaman, shredding him on the spot.

Before his bodyguards could even react, I received the system message reporting the shaman's death.

That was it. One of the most important and highest-level NPCs in the entire Caltean raid had died within a few seconds.

So much for our magic support.

I could see a smirk on Sub Zero's face. How cool was that? He'd just stripped his enemy of their most powerful player.

The Calteans' ranks fell into disarray. The late shaman's bodyguards attacked the two assassins which resulted in their losing three of their own men. Furius was one of the two stealthers, brandishing his short sword like it were a fan blade. Only now as I watched him did I realize how lucky I'd been.

The other rogue was using his two swords to make mincemeat out of the bewildered bodyguards. Even from above I could see blood gushing everywhere.

The two stealthers' gear wasn't that great. They must have known they were going to die like some wretched kamikaze.

Finally the bodyguards came round and struck back.

Congratulations! You've received Experience!
Congratulations! You've received a new level!
Congratulations! You've received a new level!
Congratulations! You've received a new level!
Congratulations! You've received a new level!

At first, I didn't even realize what had just happened. Then I knew: this was Furius and his raidmate biting the dust.

I was level 42 now. And once the battle began in earnest... I dreaded to even think.

Another system message followed, informing everybody that Scraggie had been appointed the raid leader.

Why not Laosh? He was second in seniority in our little army!

Wait a sec. And what if...

Of course! I should have known! A character with the highest Reputation became leader by default. Did that mean that Scraggie had somehow outdone both Droy and Laosh in that particular department?

What followed next must have answered Sub Zero's expectations perfectly. Scraggie led the infuriated warriors into battle.

How I understood them! A handful of Darkies had just inflicted an unforgivable effrontery upon them. These kinds of things could only be washed away with blood.

It was a good job Scraggie had left ten archers behind as reserves. He should have started by employing archers first thing though. True, they wouldn't have dealt much damage but they'd have worn out the enemy's magic shields.

The distance between the enemies shrank dramatically as the Owls hurried to deal the first blow. What an honor for a warrior!

Fifty paces.

Forty.

Thirty.

Dramatically Sub Zero threw his hand in the air, summoning a whole menagerie of beasts out of thin air. They had all sorts: panthers, rhinos, pangolins, buffaloes and tigers. The pets' levels matched those of their owners'.

I whistled in amazement. The pets' gear was mainly Red. I dreaded to even think how much it must have cost their owners. Each mount was probably the equivalent of a luxury car.

I slapped Boris' neck. "Sorry, kiddo. Can't afford it quite yet. We still have some growing to do to qualify for these kinds of toys."

Before the Calteans could get properly scared, the monsters were already making quick work of them, dishing out crits left, right and center. Badly equipped, the Red Owls met the gigantic pangolins and rhinos with their bare chests. Screams of fear and agony came from everywhere. The clatter of steel and the roaring of wild beasts filled the air.

I had to close my eyes for a moment, so lifelike it was. So graphic. Blood gushing everywhere from severed limbs. Bodies squirming in agony from mortal wounds. This didn't look like a game anymore.

The pets had done their job, nipping the Calteans' attack in the bud only some dozen paces away from the tanks' position.

Once again Sub Zero theatrically raised his hand. A flight of arrows showered us from behind the wagons. I also noticed a few icicles and fiery crossbow bolts among them.

Earth reared up under the Calteans' feet. Some of them were burning alive; a few others exploded in a cascade of ice. A Black Axe warrior grabbed at his throat and began sinking to the ground, his face melting like a candle made of blood and gore.

It might have ended very badly for the Calteans, had Scraggie lived. Luckily, he didn't. I watched a panther rip him apart. That was the end of his war. I had to give him his due though: he'd fought at the forefront and died a hero.

The moment the system informed me of the new raid leader's name, I knew not all was lost. Surprisingly, it turned out to be Laosh. I actually thought the system would go for Droy but apparently, the old shaman still enjoyed enough of his old popularity. If only I knew their Reputation counts! That would have made dealing with these stubborn bastards so much easier.

The moment I received the message, a blue aura enveloped the Calteans' bodies.

A magic shield! Laosh was in!

The Red Owls' battle cry echoed over the field. Their warriors perked up.

Soon the first XP and level messages started coming. The Darkies' pets were dying one after another. I, too, had loosed off a few shots but only scored one hit, with negligible damage. Oh, no. Pointless wasting ammo. My bullets couldn't make a dent in their hides.

Annoyed, Sub Zero screwed up his face. So you didn't expect this, mister? We still had plenty of shot in the locker!

I couldn't see Laosh anywhere. He must have been still in his tent, casting his magic. Good. That was exactly what he should be doing. Now I understood why Sub Zero tried to take out the shamans first. They were a power to be reckoned with.

Finally the Owls reached the enemy ranks. A battle ensued, best described as "let's see who can remove the magic shield first".

I watched them in silent desperation. To say it looked stupid was an understatement. A thirty-strong Caltean crowd surrounded five tanks and tried to deal them some damage while getting in each other's way, apparently oblivious to the enemy wizards and buffers casting their supportive magic from atop the wagon roofs.

Laosh wasn't going to last forever, you know. The Caltean shield would collapse any minute now!

Finally the enemy stealthers joined in. They reminded me of sharks awaiting their hour. I'd love to know where their resurrection point was. Couldn't be too far, judging how quickly they had recovered. They must have used some portable resurrection point — an altar or something. Forum posts sometimes mentioned these sorts of things. If that was the case, I could only imagine how much something like that might cost.

Strangely enough, Laosh had outmagicked the Darks' buffer. His shield was still holding.

Now the Owls began dealing damage in earnest, showering the enemy tanks with the blows of their spears, poleaxes and swords. The damage numbers were actually quite decent. It felt good to know I too was playing my part.

You had to give the Darks their due. Their ranks hadn't buckled.

A giant Horrud was especially impressive. It was the first time I'd seen one in full armor. At least ten foot tall, he was holding a huge club in each hand. His helmet was completely closed. Mist billowed from its mouth slit. Nickname: Dimax. Level: 272.

Laosh' shield wasn't going to last much longer. The moment it was down, these two clubs were going to do some very bad damage to the Calteans. I dreaded to even think about it. Rrhorgus might want to check this guy out, just to get some prospective.

Funnily enough, the short-legged Calteans had chosen this giant as their prime target. They must have thought that smoking him would be a truly valorous deed. So stupid. They should be targeting the wizards instead.

That was it. The bluish glow surrounding the Calteans had expired. Once again they were sustaining losses. Predictably, the Horrud jumped at his chance. Forgetting his place in the ranks, he began advancing, brandishing his clubs, until he found himself in the thick of the attacking Calteans.

He'd taken it too far, hadn't he? His Life bar had shrunk considerably. Even the healers' magic couldn't help him anymore. No wonder: his body was studded all over with arrows and spears.

He paused momentarily, apparently reaching for a vial. As if! The tiny but militant Calteans jumped at his feet and assaulted him from behind until finally the Horrud lay sprawled on the ground, Gulliver-like.

The Alven healer perked up but Sub Zero raised a prohibiting hand. I had to agree with him. Pointless wasting mana on someone who'd disobeyed orders. The more disciplined soldiers were the healers' priority, especially because as soon as their wizards recovered, the Darks would counterattack. And I had a feeling this attack just might become the last one for my Caltean friends.

Wow! I got three levels for Dimax. He had been awesome.

It looked like I was right after all. They definitely had a portable resurrection point hidden in one of those wagons. A field altar or something. The good news was, thingies like those didn't last forever, either. They took one hell of a lot of energy.

Dimax barged out from behind the wagons like a raging rhino. He paused next to Sub Zero, shouting something, mist billowing from under his helmet. He seemed unhappy with their leader. Sub Zero didn't bat an eyelid though. He nodded at the battlefield as if saying, *go and do your bit, and then we'll talk.*

By the time Dimax made it to his raidmates, two more of them had gone to their respawn points. Even from where I was, I could make out the scarlet-red chests they'd left behind.

Soon they were already scurrying back from behind the wagons. Judging by their and Dimax' not-so-special armor, the tanks were using their standby gear kits.

Once again there were five tanks — but the Calteans' ranks had thinned out considerably. There were barely twenty of them left standing. I saw Droy, covered in blood but keeping a safe distance, barking orders. Had it not been for him, this battle would have already been over.

Sub Zero seemed to realize it too, casting impatient glances at Droy. I just hoped he wouldn't use some heavy-duty spell on him — one of those with long cooldown times.

How could I break through the Calteans' prejudices? How could I explain to them that as long as the buffers and the healers were alive, the tanks would just keep coming back?

Sub Zero was smart. He didn't engage his archers, knowing he just might pull the aggro to the rest of the raid. So at the moment, his tanks were taking the brunt of the attack. Plus Furius and his stealthers — but they were clever, reappearing here and there and pulling absent-minded lone warriors.

The Calteans were on their last legs. I didn't even count the handful of archers in the back. Their shots made virtually no difference.

Admittedly, the enemy tanks didn't enjoy it either. Their initial derring-do had been long forgotten. They were slow on the uptake, their reaction times considerably worse. Even their faces betrayed exhaustion. Only Sub Zero seemed to be cast from a slab of granite, apparently up to something really nasty.

The Red Owls still had a few trump cards up their sleeves. Like the stuff Orman had smeared his spear with. According to him, that was the venom of the very creatures I'd healed with my Cleanse scrolls. The Dark tanks seemed to have already gotten the taste of it — and they hadn't liked it.

I had to do something while the Dark wizards had their hands full with other things. But what?

Actually, where was Laosh now? I could see some kind of scuffle by his tent. My heart clenched.

Had the Darks finally gotten to him?

I told Boris to land. In a few heartbeats, I was already standing next to the shaman's tent. The guards obediently let me in: the Red Owls trusted me.

Jesus. The place was a right mess. Laosh lay on the floor with his eyes closed. His face was sunken, his bony arms lying listlessly along his body. His gray skin had turned noticeably pale. Poor old man. He'd overstrained himself.

His servants rushed around the tent like headless chickens, fear and desperation in their faces. They didn't seem to notice me at all.

I walked over to Laosh and crouched next to him.

His ancient lips quivered. "You were right...

Lightie..."

His body was still conscious!

"I was blinded by false pride... I should have listened to you..." he choked on his words. The servants hurried toward him but he raised his hand, stopping them halfway.

Laosh struggled to open his eyes. "Do you know how to stop them?"

"I do," I said firmly. "But-"

I was about to explain to him the intricacies of the Darks' tactics when my gaze chanced on the shaman's table. Lost in the paraphernalia of yellowed scrolls, bits of leather, small animal bones and tangled ribbons and string, lay two items that looked very familiar.

My heart missed a bit. I knew how to do it.

* * *

I'd been a young boy then. Every time our crowd finished watching yet another samurai flick, we'd get together to make wooden swords all of our own.

The stealthiest among us were sent off to procure some wooden planks. Normally, they either came from our neighbors' fences or lone park benches.

The ideas of private or communal property were alien to us then. We needed the swords ASAP to join in the great battles.

Naturally, the sword-making process involved production expenses, like Uncle Greg's boxing our ears for the rolls of insulating tape we'd taken without his permission, plus all sorts of cuts and splinters we suffered in the process.

Splinters! They were a must: a rite of passage. I always wondered why I, now a tall grown-up guy, couldn't abide the pain from the tiniest of those microscopic splits.

Extracting them had been just as painful and difficult. It hurt your feelings too: while other guys were already winding the insulation tape around their swords' hilts for a better grip, I was still picking my finger trying to pull out the annoying sliver.

Now too, as I circled the Dark players' fortifications astride Boris, I felt like I was a tiny microscopic splinter that didn't allow them to finish off what they had so successfully started.

The battlefield situation hadn't changed too much in my absence. That was good news. I still had time, then.

I met Droy's stare. I could see he agreed with my idea now.

Instead of attacking headlong, now the Red Owls had hunkered down under the flimsy protection of the few remaining shields. Finally their archers could support them with their arrows. Still, that was way not enough.

All the members of our small recon group were still alive, keeping close to Droy. I really wanted to hope I'd been instrumental in their survival too, thanks to my Order of Heroic Strength.

"It's all right, guys," I whispered, directing Boris into the Darks' rear. "Help is coming."

Boris headed for the cliffs at some distance from the Darks' positions. Once there, he dropped down and dove for their wagons almost touching the ground. They noticed us too late — and by then, we'd already soared back up.

An Alven archeress hurried to string her bow... sorry, lady. Too late.

Would you like to activate the trap: Yes/No

Yes, please. Both.

Two fiery yellow flashes blinded the pretty archeress. Two giant bundles the size of an elephant dropped directly at the center of their makeshift fortification.

The blow was so powerful that both wagons bounced and dropped to the side, crushing players and draught beasts alike.

A familiar furious roar echoed through the air as the two Rock Erezes broke free from their confinement. I congratulated myself. Those two shimmering marbles on Laosh's cluttered table had caught my eye just in time.

Boris banked a steep turn over the cliff and began descending. I craned my neck, hoping to see what was happening below.

A new system message popped up,

Warning! Furius, a level-295 Black Ranger, has just attacked you!

Chapter Twenty-Five

"*R*ational use of resources, you say," a ginger-headed Dwarf took a sip from his enormous mug. "There was this woman in my old firm..."

"Oh no, here he goes again," a black-bearded gnome screwed up his face as if he'd just eaten a lemon.

"No, you really should listen," the gingernut insisted. "There's a lesson in it for you too."

The gnome heaved a sigh. "All right, all right, just keep going."

"So we had this woman in our department. Our wages weren't up to much, as you well understand. She was married. So one day she tells us they just won a lottery."

"Lucky bastards."

"Sure. We thought they might want to buy themselves a house. The place where they lived was a right hovel. But what do you think? The next day, she and her husband arrive at work in this latest Audi, a luxury model with all the options, bells and tooters. They just picked it up from the dealer's. She told us, they had thought long and hard and finally decided to invest all their winnings into that car."

The gnome frowned. "And? What's the point of your story?"

"The point of my story is, before splurging on the runes for your next skill level, you really should replace your old pick first! You still have another year working with Gray resources!"

"All right, all right, so I made a mistake," the gnome admitted grudgingly. "No need to rub it in every five minutes. Can happen to anyone."

"Not to me, it can't," the dwarf retorted. "This isn't the right place to make mistakes, man. This isn't some dumb computer toy. Everything that happens here is for real. You either get serious or quit the team. No one's gonna do your work for you here. You have to use your own Gray gear."

In the silence that fell, the dwarf wheezed his indignation.

"Oh, come on, man," the gnome finally said. "I learned my lesson! I understand now. You don't have to be mad at me."

"I vouched for you to the others," the dwarf said bitterly.

"I know!" the gnome moved closer to the dwarf and shook him amiably by the shoulder. "I'll make it worth your while! You're gonna see! I'll level up good, just like Pilot! Then money will start flowing in!"

"Yeah right," the dwarf snorted. "Until the next

time."

"No, really, I promise! I know now. You'd better tell me if you've heard anything about Pilot. I've been too tired to check the forums just lately. I just don't get enough shut-eye."

The ginger-headed dwarf nodded. "Pilot! Apparently, the Lords of Chaos have blacklisted him. They say they've put a reward on his head."

"The Lords of Chaos? Not them too?"

"Yeah. Nobody says much about it, you understand. The only thing I know for sure is that he's ruined their No-Man's Lands raid."

"No way!"

"Well, there you have it. Take my advice: don't be too quick on the draw. You have a lot of leveling to do before you become one like him. Some guys said he used to work in the mines with them. They said he had the worst possible gear and had to lug the rocks all the way up from the lower levels — and still he outperformed them hands down!"

The video stopped. I looked up at Rrhorgus. A cheerful smile lit up his green face. His eyes laughed.

"I taped this a few hours ago in a tavern in Leuton," he said. "I thought you might like it."

I heaved a sigh. "You can say that. That was quite an eye-opener. Pilot! When did they come up with this moniker?"

"A few days ago," he said. "I'll tell you later. Your turn to talk."

The story of my latest escapades didn't take long. Rrhorgus listened to me open-mouthed, unblinking, gulping occasionally whenever I mentioned my loot or the resources I'd farmed.

"And once you dropped the Erezes onto their wagons, what happened then?"

"Nothing. They took me out before I could even get properly scared."

"They smoked you?" he asked in disbelief.

"Sure. Took Furius two arrows to get to us. Both me and Boris."

"Vindictive bastard. And what happened then?"

"Then I came round in a nice secret cave stark naked. I'd made it my resurrection point just in case."

He nodded his approval. "Good idea."

"I thought I'd die there in the three hours it took," I shuddered at the memory.

"Were you waiting for Boris to respawn?"

"Yeah."

"Why three hours? Shouldn't it be six?" he asked, surprised. "But of course! He's Relic, isn't he?"

I nodded. "Exactly. So we hurried back ASAP, right across the mountains."

"How did you manage to keep your gear?"

"Oh," I smiled. "By accident."

He giggled. "You and your accidents!"

I grinned. "Furius, if you remember, shot us down when we were directly above the cliff. So that's where the chest with my stuff landed, isn't it?"

"So he failed to rob you! Good. And you know what? I have a funny feeling you took his gear in the end."

I shrugged and said with a deadpan face, "Sorry about that."

The glee on his green face gave way to sadness. "Dammit. What a shame."

"For him, yeah."

"You bastard!" Rrhorgus beamed, his vast brow breaking into a happy sweat. "Come on, don't drag it out!"

"So basically, I came down to the battlefield. It was empty already. Both the Darks and the Calteans were gone."

"So who won the fight, then?"

"I discovered the traces of a Caltean funeral pyre on the river bank. Which means they must have. I didn't get any XP while waiting in the cave. You probably must be present at the battlefield to earn it. Still, I managed to do a few levels in the time it took me to launch the traps and the Erezes."

"I can see that! 52 already! Well done!" he patted my shoulder.

"Thanks."

"So what have you got for the old man?" he moved on to business.

"The Darks' chests were already gone. But their wagons were still there."

Rrhorgus rubbed his green hands. Was it my imagination or he'd smacked his lips — exactly how cartoon frogs do when seeing a nice fat fly.

"They'd been farming for several days already," I said. "Lots of stuff in those wagons. The way I see it, the Darks' scouts must have collected their chests as well as the most valuable stuff from the wagons. They couldn't have had enough place in their bags to retrieve it all. My backpack is about to burst. Only you know... I don't feel good about it. It's not my stuff..."

"Oh, give it a break," he interrupted me. "You're the winner. These are your legitimate trophies! That's how it works here. This is gameplay. It's either you smoke them or they smoke you. Besides, they knew very well what they were doing crossing into No-Man's Lands. It's every man for himself there. No skin off your nose."

"I understand. But still it doesn't feel right."

Rrhorgus spent the next hour checking the trophies, tut-tutting his approval. Judging by the look on his face, we were doing well.

"It might be a good idea to hold on to these thingies for a while," he said, closing his bag. "Too many conspicuous items. Either that or I'll have to auction them anonymously — but this, as you well understand, is not exactly the same kind of money as selling them through a legitimate vendor."

"I always thought the auction brings up the best money."

"To sell regular stuff, yeah maybe. Definitely not rare items. At auction, the buyer you need might not have the necessary sum available."

What a strange notion. "Then he's not what I need, is he?"

"Olgerd, dude. Good job you're not a vendor."

"Why would I need to be? I have you, don't I?"

"There're many ways of getting a good price for an item. You could sell it on credit. Or just loan it out. It's just like in real life. Yes, you might need to wait for your money but in the end it might be well worth it. All right, so some dude doesn't have the funds readily available. But he might be able to pay in installments plus the few percent interest. I do him a favor and he pays for it. Fair enough."

"All this is way over my head," I admitted.

"Good for you. In any case, here's a detailed list of all my services including the interest. Just to keep you on top of it. Would you like me to transfer the money to your account or do you prefer cash? Oh, and here're some scrolls for you, a few bits of steel and some other odds and ends."

Finally we sorted everything out. I leaped into the saddle. Rrhorgus dramatically wiped an imaginary tear. "Off you go, my golden goose!"

I rolled my eyes. With a farewell wave of my hand, I took to the skies.

* * *

As I returned to the Caltean camp, I had plenty of time to think over a few things. The biggest of which was, *What now?* Or to put it more precisely, *How am I supposed to pull this off?*

The trade routes map was perfectly blank now. The Ennan Masters' locations were gone. The only point still marked on it was the Twilight Castle.

How could you expect me to storm its dungeons — with only a rusty scarab and a couple of fleas for company? Somehow I didn't think so. There, it was a totally different ball game. True, the scarab wasn't rusty anymore and I'd even doubled the number of fleas — but still I was far below the level required to tackle that part of the world.

What if sacrificing myself for the Calteans' victory had been a stupid thing to do? Should I have kept my distance instead, loosing off slugs at the combatants from the safety of some cliff? I could have summoned both Boris and Prankie — that way they could have gotten their share of XP, too. All three of us could have leveled like a dream — I could have been level 70 now at least. Boris and Prankie could have gotten themselves a new skill each.

What about the dead Calteans, you might say? Oh... for some people that might not even be a problem. This was only a game, after all. Besides, there were plenty of Calteans still left in the camp: warriors, women, children and elders. I could have continued using them to aggro various mobs and receive the XP without having to lift a finger.

And then what? What was I supposed to do next, once I'd dispensed with the entire Caltean tribe? What a stupid question. Furius had already given me a tip, albeit unwittingly. All I had to do was fly over No-Man's Lands monitoring any potential combats, then looting the victims. How difficult was that? No risk, definitely no expenses. Just pure profits.

My blood ran cold with the prospect. If the game developers really thought I was capable of any of that — well, then they had another thing coming.

Dmitry had been right, though. The Calteans were my only lead. Then I'd have to play it by ear.

I couldn't help thinking about everything that

had happened just lately. No more lying low. I'd given myself too much exposure. They'd even hung a nickname on me! Lance the Rightie had a point: I'd had no idea how popular the wretched Fort trip had made me.

The Steel Shirts, the Lords of Chaos... I was in it deep now. The Dark players had put a price on my head. I'd forgotten to ask Rrhorgus how much it actually was. Then again, what difference did it make?

Tanor's letters had stopped. For a few days already, he preserved a dignified silence. Apparently, the period of the proverbial carrot was over.

I'd had to delete myself from all of my friends' lists — Rrhorgus being the only exception. I didn't want to hurt anyone. Once I was out of this mess, I might reconnect with them, so that we could all get together and have a good time. They were all smart enough to understand. Especially because this wasn't the first time I'd had to do this.

BY THE TIME I GOT to the main Caltean camp it was already dark.

And a beautiful night it was, too. Not a cloud in the sky. The boundless deep heavens were bestrewn with billions of stars like some celestial lightbugs. The Moon was going off the scale.

The sheer novelty of it felt like a warning. It was as if the skies of Mirror World had been chosen to deliver a message, announcing new changes due to arrive.

Finally, the camp. The cliffs around it resembled the jaws of a giant monster about to devour the tiny bugs crawling at its base.

Way below, dozens of campfires illuminated the foot of the cliff. The one in the middle was especially large. Even from where I stood, I could make out the many Caltean figures surrounding it.

Boris and I began our descent.

I could hear voices from below, multiplied by the echo. Although I couldn't make out the words, I got the impression they were addressing me.

That's right. More voices joined in.

Finally, I could see. They were the Owls' sentries waving to me.

I was about to wave back when a new system message popped up into view,

Warning! You've encroached on a Caltean Clan Union camp!

Wow! A union, already? That was quick!

There was definitely something going on in the camp. Something important. I'd only just noticed that everybody seemed to have already packed up. That's right. Hadn't Laosh ordered everyone to get ready by the time we came back from our recon mission?

The big question was, where were they supposed to go? Or where *we* were supposed to go, rather. That was the million-dollar question indeed. It was probably what their elders were discussing now by that large fire in the middle. Good timing.

I soared over the camp, seeing their faces smile as they turned in my direction. Kids were screaming their excitement. They were happy to see me back, weren't they? Really happy. This was night and day compared to my first visit here. Admittedly it felt awesome.

Sensing my good mood, Boris flew low above the ground, his broad wings spread wide, his ashen-color armor emitting a dull glow in the light of the campfires like a dragon's scaly hide. He was showing off, the bastard!

The Calteans actually seemed to like it. They reached out without fear, hoping to touch the regal animal. He was truly handsome: a Night Hunter any way you looked at him.

The elders by the main fire gave me a standing greeting. Just as I'd thought, I saw all of both clans' leading figures. My friends were beaming. Was it my impression or Droy's face was about to erupt in a happy smile?

I met Laosh's gaze. So he'd survived, after all. He'd lost some weight and looked older — but he'd come back, that was the main thing. We exchanged friendly nods. I just hoped he could forget the old grudges and look forward to our new cooperation.

Droy opened up his arms to me as I sprang from the saddle. My shoulders were plastered with hearty slaps.

"Hey, give it a break, guys. You're gonna beat me to death!" I croaked. Not much chance of that, though. They apparently would much sooner have smothered me with their bear hugs.

"He's alive!" Droy eased me aside, his hands still on my shoulders. "How is it possible? I saw you fall to your death on the cliffs!"

That explained it. "Yeah right, dream on," I replied.

The Calteans guffawed, doubling their shoulder-slapping efforts. Each and every member of our group wanted to tell me everything they thought about my miraculous return from the dead. Shame they did so using expressions one can't repeat in polite society.

Had they known how right they were about my return from the dead...

The constant jingling of system messages accompanied their show of affection. Only when they'd finally left me alone and seated me at a place of honor by the fire, was I able to open the chat window.

Every word I read took my breath away. My heart was about to explode.

Congratulations! You've been awarded the Order of Recognition for outstanding services rendered to the Red Owls Clan!

For your information: the Order of Recognition is awarded to a player who has collected 500 pt. of the Reputation in question.

Congratulations! You've been awarded the Order of Friendship for outstanding services rendered to the Red Owls Clan!

For your information: the Order of Friendship is awarded to a player who has collected 1000 pt. of the Reputation in question.

Congratulations! You've been awarded the

Order of Respect for outstanding services rendered to the Red Owls Clan!

For your information: the Order of Respect is awarded to a player who has collected 2000 pt. of the Reputation in question.

Congratulations! You've been awarded the Order of Recognition for outstanding services rendered to the Caltean Clan Union!

For your information: the Order of Recognition is awarded to a player who has collected 500 pt. of the Reputation in question.

Warning! For your assistance to the enemies of Mellenville you've been stripped of all its Reputation points, awards and signs of merit!

The warning was followed by an impressive list of all the major Mellenville NPCs whose friendship I'd lost. Gard and Tronus were on it too.

My heart missed a beat as I glanced at my Awards tab.

Phew. Big sigh of relief. The Orders of Heroic Strength and Zombie Slayer were still there, untouched. Apparently, they were awarded regardless of a player's affiliations. My Reputation with Mellenville, however, that I had so laboriously been piecing together, glowed a discouraging zero.

That was it, then. There was no way I could go back to the capital. Any Mellenville guard would consider it his sacred duty to smoke me.

Did I feel disappointed? Not really. I'd known it

would happen sooner or later. I would simply have to be ready to face the animosity of their office workers, that was all. Then again, what office workers? All they had was machines and terminals.

Still, it didn't look as if I was going to get any more discounts from their NPC shop owners. I could still use the auction, however.

That was logical. I hadn't swapped sides. I'd only lost my Reputation with the capital city. Could happen to anyone.

The Black Axes weren't as enthusiastic in meeting me as the Owls had been. Still, they seemed quite happy to see me. My crazy stunt over the Darks' wagons had had its effect: I was now the proud owner of 300 pt. Reputation with the Black Axes clan.

The ice was broken. Time to look deeper into the situation.

I closed the chat window and tried to focus on what the clan's best warriors were saying.

"We need to send out scouts back to the Silver Mountain Valley," a large Caltean said. His name was Latis.

Judging by the clothes he was wearing, he was neither a warrior nor a wizard. He didn't look like a farmer, either. Was he a craftsman? He was broad-shouldered, with spadelike hands and a hammer stuck under his belt. Yes, a craftsman, definitely.

"What about the Nocteans?" Amcy the Rake objected.

He was one of our guys, skinny and wrapped head to toe in animal skins. Definitely a reindeer breeder.

"Nocteans don't stay long in the areas they conquer," a short guy pointed out. His name was Pritus.

So! Just look at him! He was a bespectacled intellectual just like myself! He looked admittedly alien next to the rugged warrior and cattle-breeder types.

A long black cloak shrouded his figure. A large beret framed his long face. His intelligent eyes studied everyone from behind the glasses of his small pince-nez. I was dead sure he had a whole pile of books in that backpack of his. How interesting.

The others engaged in a heated discussion. Apparently, the short Pritus guy enjoyed a considerable authority here.

Could he be the one responsible for putting the trebuchets together? There had to be a reason for him being invited to the council.

"Pritus is right," the gray-bearded Crym boomed. "We shouldn't have left our old home at all. It was this constant shamanic squabble. They're never happy, always fighting between themselves, and we pay the price."

The Black Axes hummed their approval, casting unfriendly glances at Laosh who shivered under their stares.

Surprisingly, Droy jumped to his defense. "You're dead right there, Crym. May I only add that it was the shamans from Under the Mountain who kept winding him up. To the best of my knowledge, Laosh wanted us to unite and face the Nocteans with weapons in our hands. It was your leaders who chose otherwise."

Droy's authority had considerably grown. Both clans' eyes were upon him, their expression very similar to adoration.

"As far as us going back to the Silver Mountain Valley," Droy continued, "I disagree."

"Why not?" Crym challenged him. "Has the old warrior Droy the Fang lost his fighting spirit?"

The Owls frowned. An angry hum sped along their ranks. This was a serious accusation.

"Yes, I have," Droy replied.

Silence fell over the campfire. I watched their long faces and open mouths.

Laosh alone smiled his understanding. Our eyes met. Fighting the Darkies had really brought those two together: Droy and the shaman seemed to read each other's thoughts these days. Which was a good thing. Their clan's wellbeing was more important than their own ambitions.

"You heard it right," Droy said. "I'm not going. You can't fool me a second time running. A smart warrior warned me about the trouble ahead. I didn't believe him. I was blinded by false pride. I put my own interests before the clan's. Scraggie told us about you fighting the Lighties. According to him, you performed wonders of valor. In fact, the Lighties drove you out by the scruffs of your necks like mangy dogs! Sit down! You're men — so you'd better face the truth when your friends and allies tell it to you! My men gave their lives at the River Quiet so that you and your families could live: your wives, mothers and children. And you too! You knew that the enemy was strong and still you didn't warn us. Now you're trying to do the same. Sorry, it's not gonna work."

He turned to Crym. "You wanna fight the Nocteans? Good. Take your men and off you go. I'll be the first to call you a hero. My Owls aren't coming. Why? Because all they'll do they'll die ignominious deaths. The Valley isn't our home anymore. We need to find a new one. You either follow us or take your families back to die at the hands of the Nocteans. It's up to you."

He fell silent.

What happened next could best be called a "well-choreographed play". Laosh rose from his place and announced,

"I suggest we vote! Those in favor of the Black Axes joining the Red Owls, raise your hands!"

Excellent move. Still, this wasn't checkmate yet.

A pregnant pause hung over the campfire. Then it exploded in a multitude of angry voices.

You should have seen that! Respectable gray-haired elders jumped from their places and screamed over each other's heads in the shaman's direction.

Laosh sat calmly on a large rock strewn with animal skins. Not a single muscle twitched on his furrowed face. He resembled a bronze statue. His proud dark stare focused on the flames as if he had nothing to do with any of this.

I cast a quick glance at Droy. Conspiring bastards! Droy — who was still my commander as technically I remained his raid and team member — tilted his head calmly to one side, listening to a warrior's report: his back straight as a ramrod, his hands resting in his lap. The Axes around him were gaggling like geese in a farmyard but he didn't seem to give a damn.

Soon the angry outcry began to subside. The situation moved to Stage Two: the Axes' elders put their heads together and began discussing something between themselves, occasionally screaming out and spitting at their opponents' feet. One old guy even spat another one in the eye; a few more tugged at their opponents beards, then continued to discuss the situation. Talk about art (or a computer game, as the case may be) mirroring life!

They all seemed to realize that their joining the Red Owls was inevitable; still, each one of them was trying to profit from the situation. I wouldn't be surprised if Laosh had already spoken to each one of them in private, promising them exactly what every one needed, and what I was watching now was just a show for the sake of appearances. The Axes just didn't look too upset. The idea of a clan merger must have been already in the making for quite a while.

Sentient beings just can't help it. Our politics are just one big show where every actor knows his or her place in a prearranged setting.

Finally the performance was over. Gray-haired elders stepped out one by one into the center, heads lowered and their right hands pressed to their hearts, and delivered a proud and dramatic speech about the Calteans' kinship and loyalty.

I counted nine of them. Crym was the last one to step into the circle.

Now it was time for checkmate.

Warning! The Black Axes clan has ceased to exist!
You've lost 305 pt. Reputation with the Black Axes clan!

Warning! The Caltean Clan Union has ceased to exist!
You've lost 530 pt. Reputation with the Caltean Clan Union!
You've lost the Order of Recognition awarded by the Caltean Clan Union!

Congratulations! You've received Achievement: Reluctant Onlooker.
Reward: +3% to your chance of receiving Knowledge in battle.

There you had it. I'd just become a "reluctant onlooker" of a historical event. Smiling, the Owls began rising from their seats to give new clan members a hug.

Once their show of fraternal affection has subsided, Laosh rose from his place and raised his hands in the air, calling for attention. "Brothers! Brothers!"

Once everyone quietened down and went back to their seats, Laosh went on,

"We still have the most pressing question to answer. Which direction should we go?"

Another pause hung over the campfire. Laosh

looked around him. Finally he said, "I have a proposition."

"Yes!"

"Go ahead!"

"Spit it out!"

With a regal nod, Laosh went on, "There is a warrior amongst us who many a time has warned us against looming danger. It was only thanks to him that our group managed to defeat the enemy."

Dozens of stares alighted on me. I could physically sense them. It took all of my self-control not to shudder.

"He's been through a lot. He knows much," the shaman continued.

Well, he was a bit over the top with praise but...

"Let him speak."

The crowd hummed its agreement. The funny thing was, the moment the Black Axes had become Red Owls, I stopped sensing their cold animosity. They simply accepted me, viewing me as a friend. Reputation was an excellent tool any way you looked at it.

"What do you think, Olgerd? Which direction should we go?"

For a moment, I didn't know what to say. What would my advice mean to them, anyway? Okay, so they accepted me, but that was the extent of it. My suggestion would be just that: a suggestion. It wouldn't be me who would make the final decision. The tribal and clan leaders would decide for their people.

Wait a sec... I froze as if struck by lightning. How could I have forgotten! And what if...

I dug a shaking hand into my bag. My fingers closed around a coarse parchment scroll.

Would you like to activate the scroll of Great Initiation?

For your information: your sudden surge in Reputation may gain you some very powerful enemies!

Accept/Decline

My heart missed a beat. Was this the decision I was meant to make?

Accept!

Thank you. Please choose a Reputation you would like to increase.

I scrolled through the list until I found what I needed and pressed *Activate.*

The Red scroll crumbled to dust. System messages flickered before my eyes,

Congratulations! You've received 2,000 pt. Reputation with the Red Owls Clan!

Congratulations! You've been awarded the Order of Merit for outstanding services rendered to the Red Owls Clan!

For your information: the Order of Merit is awarded to a player who has collected 3000 pt. of the Reputation in question.

Congratulations! You've been awarded the

Order of Veneration for outstanding services rendered to the Red Owls Clan!

For your information: the Order of Merit is awarded to a player who has collected 4000 pt. of the Reputation in question. No more Reputation can be awarded.

Congratulations! You've received a Legendary Achievement: The First Among Outcasts! You're legend! Reward: the Order of the Outcasts' Right Hand.

In accordance with the Reputation ranking rule, you've become the new raid leader!

For your information: Currently your raid counts 296 non-player characters.

Light warriors, 16

Lancers, 50

Archers, 60

Military engineers, 6

Miscellaneous nomads, 164

The shaman's voice distracted me from reading,

"Olgerd! Which direction should we go?"

I forced myself to focus. When I finally managed to do so, I was stunned by the change in the Calteans.

Firstly, the expressions on their faces. I could barely recognize any of the men. Droy's warriors, Droy himself, Laosh and all the others — they all looked at me as if I was their clan's last hope. The one who would take them to the promised land. Oh. The Order of Veneration, did you say?

Apart from that, a new pop-up window appeared in my mental view, containing some kind of graph: a clan ranking table. It wasn't static: the clan members' names shifted up and down all the time. Now I could find out each clan member's Reputation with a single click. And not just that, but also his or her level, abilities and other stats.

My hands began to shake. My heart felt as if it was about to explode.

I raised my head and slowly looked over the silent clan leaders. My friends. I met Laosh's gaze. He was second after me in Reputation. The old man gave me a solemn nod, as if saying, *Speak up — we're ready.*

Oh well. I'd have to live up to my new kinsmen's expectations.

I stood up to my full height and said in a loud voice,

"We can't go south. Nor can we go back to retrieve your old home that you lost. Trust me. Both west and east are out of the question. We only have one direction left, and it's the only right one. We're going north! Our new home awaits us — the Twilight Castle!"

Chapter Twenty-Six

We'd already been trudging for a week across the huge location known as the Icy Woods. It wasn't some fairy-tale Christmas forest enveloped in glittering snow — oh no. This place seemed dead. No birds singing, no animal prints in the snow: only row after row of black tree trunks looking like giant thorn bushes, their gnarly branches reaching out for you, trying to scratch you, to draw blood, to delay unwanted newcomers. Only when an occasional breeze disturbed their black tops, might one hear a sudden crackling noise — the only sound this spooky forest was able to make.

Admittedly, it wasn't my first time in northern climes. I'd always had a huge respect for them. It had been my uncle — my Mom's brother — who'd used to work building the city of Novy Urengoy in Arctic Siberia. Later, I'd been to visit it myself and seen it with my own eyes. No idea where the Mirror World designers had drawn their collective inspiration from, but this location was very lifelike. I mean, *very*.

Even back in Mellenville when I'd first studied the Ennans' map sitting in a warm hotel room in my cozy bathrobe, I'd already shivered imagining what it was going to be like. And here I was now, experiencing all the pleasures of an Arctic hike in my very own albeit virtual skin.

That was nothing! Here're a few location names, just to give you an idea.

Frozen Fang, Icy Woods, the Desert of Seven Snowstorms...

The cold was such that our gear began losing its Durability already on the third day of our trek. My kit's Protection wasn't going to make it, I could see that. Luckily, Droy reacted just in time, issuing me a fur coat made of the skin of the local long-haired breed of buffalo. According to him, I looked "frozen to the bone".

The coat proved awesome. No level restrictions, tons of Durability and 15 pt. Cold Protection. An item like that could fetch a lot of money at auction.

We were seven in total. Same faces, minus Arrum Red Beard. He'd earned himself an arrow in the shoulder in that last battle with the Darks, so he'd been forced to stay with the clan, replaced by Crym the Hammer — the burly gray-bearded Black Axe who'd been all for going back to the Silver Mountain Valley.

I had this hunch that they'd been itching to get back there for a reason. And a very good reason, too. I'd have to give it some thought.

Crym was definitely not cut out to be a scout. He slowed our advance up quite a bit. Even I showed better results, considering my level.

All his stats pointed at the fact that Crym was much better suited as a tank. There was a reason though why I'd agreed to accept him into the group. Quite a hefty reason too, which outweighed all other inconveniences and made the group respect my decision.

Crym the Hammer was the only Caltean alive who'd been to the Twilight Castle.

Even though he'd only managed to see the Ennan city from a distance, it still made this grim man a real find for me.

I suppressed a smile, remembering the events from a week ago.

My brief speech by the campfire had triggered prolonged debates. Oh yes. Despite the fact that my Reputation was going through the roof, I'd had to listen to each and every leader and raid commander — and the shaman, of course. None of them could wait to speak their mind, showing off their quick thinking and sharing their respective points of view. Speeches... the Calteans seemed to live for them.

After a prolonged and boring discussion we'd finally come to the conclusion that it would probably be best to send out Droy's scout group first, like they'd done the last time. The remaining Calteans would follow suit, guided by Laosh.

I liked their plan. Really, why not? They'd already accepted the direction suggested by me and it wasn't as if I was trying to snatch the tribe's leadership. As our manager used to say, *'Specialization is key'*. So basically, I was quite happy with my current position.

Admittedly, as I watched their debates, I was dying to open the clan stats and change everything. The only thing that stopped me was the sheer complexity of clan control. All those constantly varying graphs and stats and a gazillion descriptions... oh no, I decided not to go there, at least not at the moment. How had they managed before me? I gave myself a solemn promise to look into clan controls at a later date.

Droy's anxious voice distracted me from my musings.

"Are you sure?" he asked, looking grimly at Shorve the Hasty who'd just jumped down from a tree.

Shorve nodded. "Absolutely. I could clearly see the smoke in the west."

"Who might that be?" Orman asked, exhaling a cloud of mist.

Shorve shrugged. "Could be anyone."

"Olgerd? What do you think?"

Six pairs of attentive eyes focused on me. The men's beards and eyebrows were covered in frost. Clad head to toe in furs, they looked twice as broad. I didn't differ much from them, either: the same frosted beard and my bulky fur coat.

Admittedly, apart from the biting cold, the spooky woods and yesterday's snowfall, our hike was rather uneventful. The Ennans' map led us, avoiding any dangerous areas. But it looked like our luck had just run out.

"What do you want me to say?" I asked. "I need to take Boris and go take a look. Then we can talk."

They nodded their beards in agreement.

"In that case, we'll be waiting for you over there on top of that hill," Droy said, pointing with his mitt. Then he added, "Be careful, okay?"

I rearranged my fur hood and leaped into the saddle. "Don't worry," I smiled to him. "It's gonna be all right. Boris, up we go!"

Boris' muscles tensed up. He kicked himself aloft, lifting us both into the air. Immediately, hundreds of microscopic ice fragments bit into my face. My eyes watered.

The frost kept getting fiercer.

"Come on, kiddo. Let's see what kind of problem they have over there."

If only we had a Hugger mount for each group member! No harm in dreaming, is there?

This past week had tested us to the limit, what with the deep snow, angry magic trees and the cold that chilled you to your very bones.

Admittedly, I'd been trying to walk most of the way. I didn't want to spend too much time away from the other guys. Team spirit was paramount. True, they were only NPCs, but still you never knew what they might be up to. You wouldn't want to force your way through thorn bushes only to discover that another team member is soaring in the sky astride your own mount.

The good news was, we were almost there. According to my calculations, the morning after tomorrow we would see the walls of the Twilight Castle.

Remembering Furius and his arrow's range, I tried to stay as high as I could. It was unlikely any players had already managed to get this far, but still.

I was flying over the Icy Woods, the snow below blinding white next to the gnarly outlines of the dead trees.

Finally I saw the smoke of campfires. How far was that? Ten minutes of flight max. If anything happened, our group had virtually no lead time.

What were they doing there?

The day before yesterday, I'd checked all the road before the snow had begun to fall. There had been no one there. Could it be a new surprise from the admins? Or even players, after all?

I saw them before I'd even got close. They were definitely not players. Oh, no. These had to be game developers having a laugh. They were probably sitting there now by their computer screens curious how I was going to get myself out of this mess.

How many of them were there?!

"You've got to be kidding me!" I grumbled. "Do they have to be so many? A couple of dozen I could understand, but *this*? Those developers have got some nerve!"

I decided to descend a notch to take a better look at them.

"Nocteans," I whispered, my voice breaking with emotion.

Any hopes I might have harbored of peacefully parting our ways with this new mysterious enemy had now been shattered. These guys wouldn't leave us alone. As simple as that.

The Calteans' sworn enemies looked very much like Rock Dwandes in a picture I'd seen in the info portal. Not the most popular race in Mirror World, I had to admit. Their looks were *very* special.

The Nocteans were covered in long tufts of dirty gray hair. Their ears were pointy like those of bull terriers, their similarly froglike jaws packed with very sharp teeth. Height was the only difference: these guys stood a good head taller than the Dwandes. As for the rest, they looked the spitting image of the latter. The overworked admins must have decided to use a template they'd had at hand. They had a point: why try to invent a plastic fork when it's already being produced by all and sundry?

Their group's levels averaged 280. They were very badly armed, though. Only about twenty of their warriors boasted some sort of gnarly bone-topped sticks and primitive stone axes, that was the extent of it.

They were clad in loincloths. Savages with clubs.

How many of them were there, really?

I counted twenty-three campfires, with at least a dozen warriors sitting around each. Rounded off, that's about three hundred. It was pretty clear that the Red Owls wouldn't survive any potential engagement, weapons or no weapons. We had a hundred-fifty warriors at most. The rest of the clan were women and children. So if they stayed here for another day, Laosh might lead his clan directly into the enemy's clutches.

I made another circle over the enemy camp and headed back.

"So what is it?" Droy asked, his voice shaking with worry as I landed.

The others surrounded me, their faces grim, their eyes anxious.

"Nocteans," I said. "About three hundred of them. No idea how this could have happened. Last time I checked that direction, there was nobody there."

Droy's face darkened. Orman spat on the ground. The other warriors commented on the news in a less-than-acceptable language.

"How did they get here?" Seet the Burly asked.

"Where do you want them to be?" Crym grumbled, pointing around him. "These wretched Woods just might be their home."

"It's not your fault, Olgerd," Droy said. "Those bastards can move really fast. They must have arrived with yesterday's snowstorm. You'd better tell me... do you think they'll stay there long?"

"It doesn't look like it. They didn't have tents, only campfires."

Orman smirked. "Tents! Those savages don't need tents, do they? They sleep in their filthy holes in the ground."

I shrugged. "I didn't notice any holes, either."

"Did you check the direction they came from?" Droy asked.

I nodded. "Judging by their footprints, they arrived from the north west. If they continue in the same direction, they will walk right into our path..."

"To discover the rest of the clan," Droy finished my phrase for me.

"They're too many," Horm the Turtle said. "No way we can win. But we'll have to face them if we want to keep going. The rest of the tribe is too slow — and noisy. By tomorrow night, the Nocteans will know they're coming."

The air heaved with the sighs that surrounded me. Everybody understood that.

"And what if they decide we're too many? Can they just give it a miss?" I asked.

Judging by the warriors smirks, this wasn't very likely.

Droy decided to explain it to me in more detail. "Why do you think the Nocteans arrived in our valley to begin with?"

"No idea," I shrugged. "Could be lots of reasons. From what I hear, the place was good. Plenty of food, too."

Orman bared his teeth in a grin. "Olgerd sees right through it. Only he doesn't seem to realize how right he is."

I frowned and looked up at Droy.

He lay a reassuring hand on my shoulder. "Don't get angry with the guys. These monsters have taken too much from us, you see. And you're dead right about food. They're always hungry. With one correction. They feed on *us*."

Now it was my turn to cuss. Admittedly, I rarely do so but when I do... This time I managed to really excel at it. Crym and Shorve even slapped my shoulder with approval.

"Now you can see our predicament," Droy said. "Any ideas?"

I'd already given it some thought on my way back. "As I already said," I replied unhesitantly, "there's only one direction we can take. We can't go south, west nor east. There's no place for Calteans there. Crym is my witness."

Crym nodded his agreement.

"The Twilight Castle is already within reach," I went on. "And if we-"

"Are you trying to suggest we distract the Nocteans?" Droy interrupted me.

"Exactly," I said. "I'd rather they follow us than attack the clan."

"And once we reach the Forbidden City, we'll have better chances of survival there," Crym agreed. "And I don't think the local dwellers will appreciate a horde of Nocteans enter their city."

"First we need to get there," Horm the Turtle grumbled, cautious as usual. "Who can guarantee the City guards won't start by killing *us*?"

At these words, all eyes turned to me.

"There are no guarantees," Droy replied for me sternly. "That's why we're the advance team! It's our job to investigate everything! And if we have to die, so be it! You knew what you were getting yourselves into."

Strangely enough, the men didn't look unhappy. On the contrary: they seemed inspired by their noble task.

Droy cast a formidable stare over his men.

"Shorve the Hasty is the fastest among us. I suggest we send him back to the clan to warn Laosh. He'll know what to do."

The warriors hummed their approval.

"Follow in our tracks," Droy instructed Shorve. "I don't need to tell you, do I? Avoid engaging with the enemy. Your job is to survive and give them our message."

Shorve nodded.

"We really should send Olgerd instead," Droy said slowly. "But I have a feeling we might find it hard without him."

"We need to get going now," I said. "It doesn't look as if the Nocteans are going to stay where they are for much longer."

"And what if they do?" Horm asked. "That's not what we want either, is it?"

He was right. Our group needed a head start, but if the Nocteans lingered in their current camp for much longer, it would be a catastrophe. Luckily, this was a game. I could always aggro the wretched things. The rest would be a matter of skill.

"Don't worry," I grinned. "Leave them to me."

I DIDN'T HAVE TO AGGRO THEM, after all. By daybreak, the Nocteans had picked up our trail. By midday I knew they were going to catch up with us before we reached the city. That's considering our group had been doubling all through the night and for the most part of the morning. It looked like I'd underestimated our enemy.

There was another thing, too.

"So how is it?" Droy gasped, breathless from the run, when I finally landed.

The other men took the brief break as a godsend, collapsing into the snow on the spot.

Crym suffered the most. He was puffing like a steam engine but soldiered on.

"Don't play the hero," Droy told me. "Your place is in the saddle. At the moment, you're the group's eyes and ears."

I agreed. There was one problem, though.

"Guys," my voice broke. "I'm a lousy scout, I know. This is my second screwup in as many days."

"What now?" Droy stepped toward me.

"A few four-legged beasts have left the Nocteans' camp," I said. "I swear they weren't there last night!"

As if confirming my words, the foul wind which had been right behind us all that time brought a blood-curdling wolflike howl.

The warriors jumped to their feet as one man.

Orman spat in the snow. "Werewolves!"

"It's not your fault, Olgerd my friend," Droy reassured me. "You're the best scout I've ever met. You can't have known that some Nocteans can shapeshift. So stupid of us. We should have warned you."

"How many are there?" Horm asked.

"Twelve."

"That's all right," Crym said. "They want to tie us up in combat."

"How much time do we have?"

That was Seet.

"They should catch up with us by sunset," I said.

The warriors exchanged grim stares, apparently realizing the group might not survive the engagement. Wretched Nocteans!

What could we do?

But what if...

'Well, brothers," Crym the Hammer hid a smirk behind his gray beard, "it looks like my journey ends here. I'm fed up with all this constant running. Besides, I'm too old to turn my back to the enemy. Go! I'll delay them!"

Excuse me? What the hell was going on here?

No one tried to talk him out of it. No shows of drama or protest followed. Silently the warriors came over to him one by one, touching his shoulder.

What, was that it? Had they already decided? I beg to differ! Now was the moment to use my Reputation.

"That's right!" I said out loud, attracting their attention. "Good decision! We need to delay them! Still, you seem to forget one very important point. I'm the one responsible for it. So it's up to me to sort out this mess."

Crym opened his mouth to speak out but I motioned him to stop. "Sorry, friend, but you're not staying here."

I looked over their grim faces. "None of you are."

Chapter Twenty-Seven

Arctic sunsets are awesome and fearfully cold. Today, the fiery-red disk of the sun seemed especially hasty as if it knew what was about to happen and was scrambling out of our way back into its celestial halls. Like, it had seen enough for one day.

Shame about that. We were about to have a nice party here. Or rather, I was. By my estimation, the rest of the group had already left the Icy Woods and were now crossing the Frozen Hills — the last location before the Forbidden City.

The howling of the Noctean werewolves was already almost upon me. They were looking forward to their meal.

Yeah, right, dream on. I wasn't such an easy prey, sorry guys.

You've built the simplest mechanical creature: an Armor-Plated Scarab!

Current level: 170

"There!" I said proudly, studying the brand-new shining beetle which had materialized on the snow. "Now we're cooking!"

The beetle (the size of the German car of the same name) stood still in the small clearing surrounded by trees.

What a difference! Gone were the rust and the lame leg. And the size of him! His golden scales glistened predatorily in the rays of the setting sun, the crests on his head studded with foot-long spikes. If he rammed you, you'd know all about it.

Apart from his eye-pleasing size and stats, the Charmed Scale of the Ylean Pangolin had also given the scarab a new skill. It had a simple, unassuming name: Bone Crusher, giving the scarab +30% to his chances of injuring his opponent.

The approaching sound of the werewolves' expectant howling didn't sound so scary anymore. How funny. Still, I was admittedly quite weak at the knees.

"Let's give these whiney dogs a warm welcome," I slapped the scarab's armored flank.

It felt like I'd punched a cliff.

I placed two of his scales into the Fix Box straight away. This way I could promptly build another scarab when I needed to. Then I climbed aboard Boris' back and told him to stay behind our tank. Prankie made himself comfortable on Boris' neck. We could always use his shield spell if the mobs got to me. His levels weren't up to ours, anyway.

"Looks like we're ready," I whispered, racking my brains for every potential scenario of the upcoming combat.

My heart was about to leap out of my chest.

A new bout of howling made me jump. It sounded very close this time. Mechanically I whipped out my slingshot and gripped it hard, trying to stop my fingers from shaking. Its support sat snugly on my forearm. A burr, one of those cast with the Ice-Bound spell, lay in the pouch.

"Come on now," I grumbled. "The sooner we start, the quicker we're out of here."

All I heard back was silence, disturbed only by the chattering of my own teeth. I was frozen to the bone.

I looked this way and that, about to check the scarab's settings one last time. No chance. Something gray and huge came from behind the trees with a blood-curdling growl.

A Noctean Werewolf

I glanced at the scarab. He didn't look so big anymore compared to the shapeshifting monster.

The werewolf stopped and began sniffing around, peering around him shortsightedly. Mountainous muscles rippled under his matted gray hair.

Finally his black glare stopped, focusing on us.

His hackles stood on end. The beast bared his long sharp fangs. Viscous saliva dripped off his jutting lower lip onto the snow.

Having gotten an eyeful of the miserable idiots stupid enough to challenge his pack, the werewolf tilted his head up in a very doglike gesture. His heavy — and eerily cheerful — howling assaulted our eardrums.

More beasts leapt from the woods, answering his call. Hot with the chase, their tongues hanging, they fell upon us like a school of hungry sharks.

On my command, the scarab accelerated forward, too. In contrast with the leaping wolves, he barged forward like a snow plough, raising a wave of snow in his wake.

I should have summoned him a week earlier, shouldn't I? That way he could have made our progress through the Icy Woods so much easier. Just look at the lovely track he was leaving behind him, all straight and clean!

A second later, my scaly tank had rammed his first opponent. An agonizing scream echoed over the clearing. The scarab had caught the werewolf in midair, piercing the beast's belly with the sharp spikes studding his crest.

The snow turned dark crimson. The wounded wolf's packmates jumped onto their attacker, entangling him in a swirl of gray bodies. I couldn't see the scarab at all anymore, the constant flash of system messages the only sign he was still going strong.

The scene of the bloody battle had become a mess of crimson slush. The scarab's Bone Crusher skill actually worked *very* well. Three werewolves were seriously injured already. As opposed to the scarab's previous versions, this one was a real swiftie. Just look at him spinning around, dealing out blows left, right and center!

He had it hard, too. Even from where I stood I could see the terrible dents in his armor. His shell, so smooth only a minute ago, was now covered in pits and ragged holes. One of his antennae and two of his legs had been ripped off.

I shuddered, imagining the damage these werewolves could have wreaked on our little group. Crym the Hammer was a hero, and no mistake. Still, his sacrifice would have been in vain. The werewolves would have made quick work of him.

Never mind. Now!

You've built the simplest mechanical creature: an Armor-Plated Scarab!
Current level: 170

"Quick, go help your brother," I motioned the newly-arrived second scarab to the battle scene.

Unhesitantly he took off and scurried along the cleared path toward the canine melee.

A fierce agonizing scream announced the pack's displeasure with the new arrival. Seven injured werewolves already!

The snow around was spattered with blood and flecked with tufts of gray hair. Despite this, the pack's life was still in the green. In order to kill one werewolf, I'd have to simultaneously release a good dozen scarabs like these two. The level gap was just too big. My slingshot was useless in this situation. Shooting it would just be wasting ammo. In any case, I'd achieved my goal: my group had gained a considerable head start.

I didn't want to waste all of my precious Pangolin Scales. I wouldn't win, anyway. The two scarabs were going to stand their ground for a while, delaying the werewolves.

Time to make myself scarce.

Boris soared up into the sky with a rather hasty effortlessness. He can't have enjoyed sitting there on the ground within twenty paces of the monsters. Admittedly, neither I nor Prankie had enjoyed it much, either.

Boris circled the clearing one last time and headed north.

"Go, kiddo," I whispered. "We can't do much here anymore."

As we were crossing over from the Icy Woods into the Frozen Hills, I finally received a system message reporting the scarabs' complete loss of Durability. It also stripped me of a few XP points for "fleeing the battlefield".

As I was taking all this in, two crystal clear sounds reached me from afar — like two balloons popping.

I swung round in the saddle, trying to discern this new development. Then I realized. My scarabs had self-destructed!

I could only imagine what the epicenter of their combined explosion looked like. I just hoped it would take the werewolves quite a while to recover from this last surprise.

---

* * *

I flew over the Frozen Hills following our group's trail. Unlike the never-ending Icy Woods, this particular location was over in a blink. Nothing special, really: the hills below looked quite ordinary. Still, I told Boris to climb over the clouds, just to be on the safe side. You never knew what kind of mobs might inhabit these places.

Some fifteen minutes later, my satnav informed me of an approaching city below. I told Boris to swoop down. I wasn't going to miss this sight for the world.

We welcome you, O traveler, to the glorious Twilight Castle and its environments!

Unfortunately, I didn't get the chance to celebrate. Immediately we were consumed by a fierce snowstorm.

This was another one of No-Man's Lands' unpleasant features. You'd travel across a nice quiet location, and just as you were about to cross over into the next one, you'd get caught in a snowstorm; alternatively, a sharp drop in temperature would attempt to freeze you solid. I still thought that these were the admins busy fine-tuning No-Man's Lands. Because if players encountered such rapid changes, they'd bury Customer Support in letters and complaints.

Screaming out in surprise, Boris dove down.

"Hold on, kiddo!" I shouted over the howling

wind. It threw us around like a feather, the prickly snow lashing my face, blocking my ears, my mouth and even my eyes...

I couldn't see anything.

I clung to Boris' neck and closed my eyes, feeling his powerful muscles ripple under my hands as he continued to combat the elements.

I pried my eyes open. The land was approaching rapidly. My jaw was locked — I must have been screaming non-stop.

I braced myself for the impact. It took all my self-control not to squeeze my eyes shut like a scared little boy.

What happened next was probably what paratroopers call the "opening shock". Just as we were about to hit the ground, Boris threw his wings out wide. We felt a slight jerk upwards. The next moment we were embraced by a soft, deep heap of snow.

I struggled around in it for a while, finally scrambling back to my feet. I cast a quick look around but couldn't see past my own nose in the howling snowstorm.

"Boris!" a weak croak escaped my throat.

A light nudge in my back made me swing round. "There you are!" I threw my hands around his neck. "Are you hurt?"

I began anxiously running all around him like a mother hen looking for possible injuries.

Phew. He was all right. His Energy was nearing zero, though.

"Take a break, kiddo," I said, producing the

summoning charm. "I'll try to find out where we are exactly."

The snowstorm had long buried the Calteans' trail. It looked like we'd have to get to the city separately. I just hoped they were okay. Droy was an experienced scout, no doubt about it; still, stronger men had been known to succumb to these brutal elements. Me, I had nothing to fear in this respect. All I had to do was open the map and follow it. Especially as I already knew the best way of traveling across snow banks.

You've built the simplest mechanical creature: an Armor-Plated Scarab!
Current level: 170

Hiding behind his steel flank and wrapping myself tighter in my fur coat, I opened the map.

I'd actually thought it would be worse than this. Even though I'd been diverted quite a bit from our original route, it wasn't that terribly far. According to the map, the walls of the Western Bastion were supposed to be over there and I was over here. With the scarab's help, I'd be able to get back to the main road quickly, then use it to get to the city walls. The group was supposed to wait for me there.

If the truth were known, I was even glad the weather was so rough: it meant that our pursuers would have to battle through it too. So even if they somehow managed to pick up our trail, the snowstorm would considerably slow up their advance, allowing us plenty of time to get ready to face them.

I just hoped we survived until they arrived. Only now, when I was virtually in sight of the city walls, my doubts and emotions began to get the better of me. The Twilight Castle's mysterious guards worried me a lot. Which was why I had to be the first to enter the city. And then... come what may.

I slapped the scarab's scaly flank, nudging him to get going. He staggered and listed, getting stuck in a snow drift. Just when I was about to regret having wasted a precious Pangolin Scale on him, the scarab stirred and lunged forward, gaining speed.

With a sigh of relief, I followed. Much better! We should have done this before we'd even entered the Icy Woods. The guys would have loved it.

After a quarter of an hour, we'd already reached the Market Road leading to the city's main gate. Every now and again, grim statues of ancient heroes that used to line the road loomed out of the snowstorm. I couldn't see them very well. Not the right moment for sightseeing, anyway: the wind forced my head down. Having said that, some of the statues definitely reminded me of something...

Yes! Of course!

The massive scene carved in the rock that I'd seen back in Spider Grotto — that's what it was!

The warriors surrounding the king: his bodyguards. Same helmets, same full-height shields and poleaxes. One guy seemed to be holding something that looked like a crossbow... wretched snowstorm! I couldn't see anything! The fact that the sun had already set didn't help, either — but my Ennan eyesight helped me somewhat.

I probably advanced a hundred paces when a new message glowed red before my eyes,

Turn back, O trespasser! This is a sacred place guarded by ancient spirits!

Warning! This location can be too dangerous for players of your level!
Please refrain from visiting it.

I know, I know.

More messages followed, but I didn't get a chance to read them. The snowbanks on each side of me exploded, releasing dark silhouettes that came for me.

"Here we go," I whispered, aloof.

My left hand reached for the slingshot. My right hand had a spiky burr ready. The scarab was awaiting my orders.

"Wait till they come closer," I told him.

Two of the silhouettes stopped: they were probably archers. The rest continued their advance. I couldn't make out their levels yet, but you had to be stupid not to realize the City guards had to be at least 300+.

I pulled the sling taut, aiming it at one of them. He was by far the biggest. Admittedly, this was waste of good ammo. Maybe it was better to start thinking about how I was going to do my own corpse run once I'd died.

The nearest silhouette was less than twenty feet away when I remembered the Teleport Crystals.

My hand jerked toward my bag.

Orman's sarcastic voice reached me through the snowstorm,

"Finally! Where the heck have you been?"

I peered at the approaching predatory silhouettes, recognizing my friends. The two archers turned out to be Horm and Seet. The big guy was Crym the Hammer and the one next to him, Orman the Bear. And the one who looked as if he was about to break every bone in my body with his bare hands was... Droy!

"You cunning bastard!" he repeated, giving me a bear hug. "We thought that was the end of you!"

"He's not that simple," Crym nodded at the scarab. "I bet those drooling dogs regret ever meeting him!"

I faked a shudder. "I still shake when I think about it."

"Are they dead?" Horm the Turtle butted in.

I shook my head. "Unfortunately not. They're not easy to kill. But I gave them a good hiding."

"Good," Droy nodded. "That gives us some time to get ready."

"Come on, let's go then," I said. "Where are the city gates? Show me."

They exchanged funny glances.

"Let him see for himself," Droy said, then turned to me, "Come along, then."

As it turned out, we'd been standing right next to the city gates all along. Or should I say, the ex-city gates.

"Is this some kind of joke?" my quiet voice

shook as I took in the unfolding vista.

Everywhere I turned I could only see ruins. It was as if some giant had razed the city to the ground just for fun. Even the ruins of Ancient Rome looked better in comparison.

Where were the city walls? Where was the citadel? The gate, for crissakes? Was this their fabled Twilight Castle?

Chapter Twenty-Eight

"There was a time when this world was ruled by Wizards and Masters. The former controlled the elements while the latter created crafts. This period is called the Golden Era for a reason, for no one has ever managed to repeat what they did in those days."

Crym's level voice, the gentle warmth of a small campfire, a hot meal and the finally calm weather — no wonder I felt drowsy. Still, I shouldn't sleep. We had visitors arriving at any moment.

"The pinnacle of their art was the Eselmord, or the Golden Gate," Crym went on, staring at the fire. "Few now can explain their reasons for building it. Could it be the Masters' pride? Or the Wizards' thirst for new knowledge?"

Orman chuckled. "Or, as my Dad used to say, they had an itch in the backside. What was it they needed? More gold? More glory? Or power? Idiots! They thought they'd be able to control the gate to

Inferno!"

"And what happened next?" I asked Crym, curious, but he was deep in thought.

Droy replied instead, "The Black Era began, that's what happened. Countless bloodthirsty monsters escaped from the portal, devouring everything that moved."

The men descended into grim silence, staring at the flames. Finally Horm continued,

"If legends are to be believed, the Forbidden City was built by the descendants of those ancient Masters," he announced confidently.

"I believe you. Just look at this," in a dramatic sweep of his hand, Droy pointed at the collapsed city. "Even in this state, the ruins are still impressive, aren't they?"

I had to agree. Even though the city looked as if flattened by a massive blitz, it still gave you this, how can I put it... this sense of *unwavering*. Take this ramshackle house we'd taken cover in, for instance. Its walls were as thick as my arm. This was more of a mini citadel than a house. And judging by the ruins, there were hundreds of them there.

I thought of Mellenville, sun-drenched and filled with laughter. The Ennans' objectives when building their city had been slightly different. Its narrow streets and thick-walled houses with arrowslits for windows — everything pointed to the fact that this was a stronghold meant to sustain numerous enemy attacks. I didn't yet know what the center of the city looked like but the outskirts were well-fortified. Or should I say, *had been* well-fortified.

There was nothing left there now but rubble and debris.

Could that mean there were no guards left here, either? We'd been lying low in this old house for a few hours already — and no one had troubled us yet.

"From what I heard, the Nocteans arrived during the Black Era, too," Holm added.

"You're right," Orman spat on the ground. "They probably escaped that wretched portal with all the other monsters."

He was about to add something else when Seet the Burly appeared noiselessly from behind a collapsed wall. Seet was our lookout. His face was strained, his left hand tense on his taut composite bow.

"They're coming," he said.

Orman cussed under his breath.

"Talk about the devil," Horm said.

"Back to your positions," Droy commanded calmly. "Seet, put out the fire. Olgerd, you ready?"

"Yes," I summoned the well-rested Boris and leapt into the saddle.

Like a monolith of steel, the scarab froze in a small passage between the heaps of rubble. The men scattered to their positions, bows at the ready.

We'd chosen this particular house for a reason. The layout of its ruins offered only one approach route while allowing us to retreat to the ruins of the house next to it... and then to the one next to that one... so that theoretically we could get to the city center.

I tried to imagine what the city used to look like still undamaged, when its walls and the main gate could sustain enemy pressure and the complex maze of its fortified houses had still been ready to face any opponent. How many armies had broken their teeth on this particularly hard nut? Even now, although admittedly a sorry sight, the Twilight Castle seemed to instruct us on the best retreat tactics we should be using.

"Olgerd — now!" Droy commanded.

Boris spread his wings and took to the sky. Uh-oh. The bird's eye view of the city was rather sad. It gave you the impression it had been trampled by a crowd of angry giants.

Judging by the map, the Brutville Halls where I had to land in order to activate the Twilight Obelisk had to be somewhere in the center, lying amid the ruins. Never mind. I had plenty of time to think about it. I had more important things to worry about now.

In a few powerful wingbeats, Boris gained altitude and began circling over the city gate. The snowstorm had long subsided. The enormous disk of the Moon appeared from behind a dark foreboding cloud. Visibility was excellent.

I could see that the Nocteans had already entered the city too. Mission accomplished! We'd managed to lure them away from the clan. I just hoped Laosh had received our message and knew what best to do. We, for our part, had only one option: engage the Nocteans and try to exhaust them before our main forces arrived.

One look at the Nocteans' progress through the

city showed me that they were scared of the ruins. They advanced gingerly, weapons at the ready. Had it not been for that big Noctean guy over there, they might not have ventured into the city at all. I could see no werewolves — either they were walking in their human shape or were still busy licking their wounds back in the Icy Woods.

Actually, they weren't so numerous now. About fifty of them were missing. Had they died on the way? Or gotten lost in the snowstorm? In any case, that was good news.

The giant Noctean emitted a loud growl. Four of the others reluctantly left the group and moved in the opposite direction.

I'd love to know what they were so afraid of. Could it be us, by any chance? Somehow I didn't think so.

Admittedly, it made me feel uncomfortable.

The Noctean recon group began moving toward our positions. They proceeded cautiously, casting wary glances around them and jumping at every shadow. Another thirty or forty feet, and they'd be within our kill zone.

A scrawny Noctean walked in front, crouching — they must have let the weakest one lead the way. He'd been in a scrap or two, I could see that. His right ear was missing, his hairy hide covered in bald patches, his wide wrinkled nose sniffing the cold air.

A few more steps, and he'd smell the campfire.

And so he did. He took in a deep breath and froze, pressing his only ear to his neck. His fanged head turned toward our positions.

He didn't get the chance to warn his packmates about it. Pierced with black Caltean arrows, the four scouts died quickly and soundlessly. Not that it helped us very much. The others saw their bodies amid the debris and raised the alarm.

Their leader emitted a threatening roar which echoed over the ruins, raising a unanimous screaming reaction among his people.

Here we go.

The Nocteans acted exactly as we'd thought they would. They were too stupid to live, really. The one narrow passage leading to our positions was immediately packed solid with their squirming gray bodies.

The scarab darted forward, adding to the havoc. Accelerating, he rammed the hairy Noctean mass, blocking their way like a wine cork blocks the narrow bottleneck.

Black Caltean arrows showered their exposed bodies, taking their deadly toll.

I tried to keep up, my slingshot firing non-stop. The chat window kept blinking, trying to report something apparently important, but I didn't care. I was too busy. The scarab was about to pack up. I was waiting for the explosion.

I'd already got the Fix Box set up. This would be my fourth scarab. I had enough Pangolin Scales left to build two more.

Just as I thought that we could use another thirty bowmen firing from those walls, a powerful explosion shattered the air.

That was one hell of a bada boom. Powdered

snow hung over the narrow passage. My ears were so blocked that my eyes watered.

When the smoke had dispersed somewhat, I realized what a major blunder I'd made back in the Icy Woods when I'd left the battlefield before the fight was over. I could have made a good ten levels in one go — at least.

The scene was a total mess. The passage which only a second ago had been blocked with Nocteans was now heaped with gory bits of flesh. I felt sick and dizzy. Would I ever get used to the sight?

I took in a deep breath to suppress the gagging reflex. The icy-cold air burned my lungs, bringing relief and clearing my mind.

"At least now I know why the werewolves weren't back," I whispered, giving Boris a light slap on the neck.

In the meantime, the Noctean leader below kicked and roared, trying to stop the panic. When he'd succeeded, he decided to take the next party in himself. The explosion had actually widened the passage somewhat, allowing the Nocteans to double their efforts.

On my command, Boris dove down. The next moment a brand-new steely tank rose in the attackers' way and ploughed toward their leader.

Before the giant Noctean could prepare to repel his attack, I dropped five fleas directly onto his head. Judging by his furious roar, he didn't like it.

"Enjoy," I murmured. "There's more where they came from."

Boris banked a steep turn and shot upward.

The Noctean leader was a terrible sight. Stabbed in the stomach by the fleas' sharp mandibles, he was rapidly erupting in black ulcers. The other Nocteans jumped onto their leader's attackers as one man.

I flashed a bloodthirsty grin. "Too late, guys. Your general is toast."

The ruins cheered with Caltean voices. Droy and his men had seen the whole show. Admittedly, that felt good.

Black arrows showered the enemy again, coming thicker this time. The Calteans must have realized that not all had been lost.

What happened next is best described as a complete washout. The body of their already dying leader convulsed and began shapeshifting.

A couple of dozen Nocteans did the same.

Werewolves.

"Retreat!" Droy shouted.

Good decision. Once the second scarab exploded, the passage would become even wider. Time to move to the next house and start everything all over again.

Unfortunately, we didn't have time.

The Calteans had underestimated the Noctean leader. While we'd been busy defending what we'd thought to be the only access route, another Noctean group had approached us from the rear, taking cover behind all the debris and snow banks.

How could this have happened? Why hadn't I noticed it? And what the hell was wrong with their fabled game system? The passage in front was the

Nocteans' only possible aggro direction!

The Calteans engaged in a hand-to-hand. Closing their shields, Orman and Crym met the Nocteans' first blow, with Droy brandishing his spear from behind their backs. Seet and Horm were loosing off arrows non-stop.

What was I supposed to do? My knees began to shake. My heart froze like a scared bird.

As if understanding the state I was in, Droy raised his head up, "Try to deter them! As long as you can!"

Got it.

Strangely enough, my friend's voice and — most importantly — his prompt clear-cut order had had a calming effect on me. "Yessir!"

Not a moment too soon. The Nocteans were busy taking my scarab apart. Another explosion shattered the air. Without waiting for the billowing snow to set, I released another scarab, followed by a new swarm of fleas.

While their leader was busy fighting off this new obstruction, I turned to the Caltean positions.

Oh.

We had casualties.

Seet lay face down in the snow, pinned down by a large slab of rock. A dark spot kept growing under his body, its color unclear at this distance. No points for guessing what it was, though.

Horm sat on the ground next to him clutching a knife, his chest heaving. A broken spear stuck out of his left shoulder.

Crym's shield was long gone. Like an ancient

god of war, he was brandishing two axes, reaping death wherever he turned. Droy and Orman fought by his side, equally awesome.

Still, I could see they had only seconds left to live.

No idea what had prompted me to do what I did next. Could it be the understanding that we'd lost this battle? Was I angry with myself — or was it guilt feeling for having led them into a trap? I don't know. I just couldn't sit there in the safety of the sky watching my friends die.

The system reported the fleas' death just as I landed next to the dying Horm.

"Watch out!" I shouted, summoning my last scarab.

The armored behemoth skirted the fighting Calteans, outflanking them, then accelerated and rammed the attacking enemy.

"Go!" Droy shouted. "Fly away! You can still survive!"

I shook my head. "Oh no. If I do, I'll never be able to forgive myself."

Strangely enough, I didn't even think that I wasn't going to die *for real*. I completely forgot I'd promptly resurrect in my nearest bind point.

In the heat of the battle, I was perfectly prepared to give my life for my friends, fighting shoulder to shoulder. I was beginning to understand what Uncle Vanya had told me by the Citadel walls all that time back.

For me too, this wasn't a game anymore.

The scarab pulled the aggro to himself,

allowing the Calteans to step back and take a breather.

Good. They needed it.

Droy heaved Seet onto his back and dragged his body toward us. I did the same with Horm. Both seemed to be still alive — not for very long but still it was good news.

"When your steely machines are dead, the Nocteans will flood this place," Droy croaked, heaving, as he lent against his spear slippery with blood.

I glanced at Crym and Orman, both gasping and covered in blood. Or was it enemy blood?

Before I knew it, the break was over. An explosion thundered behind my back. In less than a few heartbeats, a victorious Noctean roar echoed from the ruins.

The werewolves would be here now.

There they were coming.

Their greedy jaws showed through the gaps in the collapsed walls. Their leader was here too.

Orman spit out a clot of blood. "Unkillable bastard."

A second explosion followed, accompanied by the yelping of wounded Nocteans.

We stood back to back. On my command, Boris soared up into the sky with Prankie sitting on his neck. I didn't want them to join the fight but they sure could use the XP.

"Brothers!" Crym growled, clutching his predatory axes. "Fighting with you is an honor!"

"Barraah!!" the warriors roared at the approaching Nocteans.

I think I shouted too, joining in their battle cry.

My heart was about to explode — but not with fear. I was quite prepared to rip the enemy apart with my teeth!

Was it my imagination or did the leader's ugly jaws stretch into a crooked grin? He seemed to be amused by what was happening.

The werewolves surrounded us, awaiting their leader's command. They were ready to fall upon us.

The leader didn't get the chance to issue that last order. A strange commotion began in the monsters' ranks. They cast scared looks around themselves, losing all interest in us.

Dark silhouettes rose on the city walls.

"The Forbidden City guards," Crym whispered sadly.

"How many are they?" Orman swung around, peering at the walls. "There're dozens of them! No, hundreds!"

He didn't get the answer. The dark shadows charged.

The Noctean leader died first before he could even move. Blood-curdling screams of agony echoed in the ruins. The high Moon cast its light on the massacre, making it appear doubly awful.

The city guards killed silently, their every movement swift and practiced, as if they had done it a million times before. No matter how hard I looked, I couldn't make out their levels. The situation seemed much worse than I'd originally thought.

We turned back to back, shuddering with every new scream of agony. Everyone seemed to have forgotten all about us.

In less than fifteen minutes, the Noctean pack had ceased to exist. The mysterious shadows closed in around us.

"Honestly," Orman said, "I'd rather die from a guard's sword than in filthy Noctean jaws."

Everyone nodded their agreement.

An invisible grumbling voice broke the silence,

"Satis, this ragamuffin — is he the Chosen One we've been waiting for?"

We startled and looked at each other in confusion.

"He is, Master Axe," another invisible voice replied, soft and gentle. "He is the first of the descendants of the Ancient Race who managed to reach this place in the last five hundred years."

I almost thought I knew the voice. That's how our logics lecturer used to speak back in college.

"And these scruffy dogs, are they his army?" the first voice grumbled again.

"Who are you calling scruffy dogs?" Orman barked. "Come out, so I can teach you some respect for Caltean warriors!"

The invisible creature grunted. "Satis! I think I like them!"

The shadowy veil parted, letting out two figures. The one to the right was a burly warrior clad head to toe in gold armor. To his left stood a gray-bearded old man in a long silver cloak and a large beret on his head.

The Calteans tensed up. I, on the contrary, heaved a sigh of relief and stepped forward.

"Greetings, Master Satis and Master Axe the Terrible!"

The gold-clad warrior grinned. "He might actually go far. He's quite good with Brolgerd's toys. He even managed to tame a Night Hunter."

"Adkhur was right," the old man said. "He is the one we were waiting for."

"I'm too tired," Axe said mournfully. "Satis, let's finish it all."

The two masters exchanged meaningful stares. "Greetings to you, O Keeper of the Twilight Castle!" they said in unison.

"We've been waiting for you for a long time, the last of the Der Swyors," Satis began. "We're happy you've finally arrived in your ancestors' home city."

He must have read the understandable skepticism in my face as he hurried to add, "It's true that the city has fallen into certain disrepair these last five hundred years but you have the power to change it all."

"Wait a sec!" I exclaimed, disappointed. "What do you mean, change it all? I only agreed to activate the obelisk!"

"This mortal has a cheek!" Axe fumed.

Master Satis winced and lay a soothing hand on his shoulder. "Wait, my friend. The new Keeper doesn't yet seem to understand what 'activating the obelisk' actually implies."

I frowned. "If the truth were known, I don't understand any of it. I expected to come to a city — but this is only a pile of rubble! And now this Keeper stuff and you dropping hints about the obelisk. What's going on?" I turned, seeking support from the

Calteans.

They froze, open-mouthed. Even Seet and Horm had come round, sitting on the snow staring unblinkingly at the scene with saucer eyes.

"Satis, I've had enough of his nonsense!" Axe growled, stepping forward. "What's going on, you say? It's that as of now, you're the one in charge of all this caboodle! Here, the key to the city! Take it! Satis, we don't have much time! Give him the Sphere!"

The gold-clad warrior shoved a large bunch of keys into my hand and hurried to step back. Immediately his figure began to ripple like a reflection in a pond, dematerializing before my very eyes.

The wizard floated toward me. His invisible hand touched my shoulder, a benign smile on his gray-bearded face,

"We're sorry, Olgerd. We've been trapped in this world for way too long. Our people are waiting. Here, take this magic sphere. It will protect you for the time being, but its powers won't last for very long. Take this scroll, too. In it, you'll find the answers to whatever questions you might have. Fare thee well, O Keeper of the Twilight Castle! Be brave!"

His outline dissolved into thin air like a whiff of blue smoke.

I stood there silent, holding a bunch of keys in one hand and a small glass marble and a yellow scroll in the other.

A bright red system message hovered before my eyes, its every word confirming my worst suspicions. I was in it deep and proper.

Congratulations! You've become the new Keeper of the Twilight Castle!

You must restore the ancient Ennan home city to its old glory!

Your job is to keep and defend it!

Be brave and strong of spirit!

Watch out! From now on, the world knows that the ancient city is being restored!

May your ancestors' blessing be with you!

More messages followed: new levels received... my doubled Legendary status... more great Achievements... I wasn't really in the mood to peruse it all.

Why should I? Everything was pretty clear, wasn't it? Very soon the area before the city walls would be absolutely packed with greedy loot seekers.

A new war had just started in Mirror World.

End of Book Three

About the Author

Alexey Osadchuk was born in 1979 in the Ukraine. In the late 1990s his family moved to the south of Spain where they still live today.

Alexey was an avid reader from an early age, devouring adventure novels by Edgar Rice Burroughs, Jack London and Arthur Conan Doyle.

In 2010 he wrote his first fantasy novel which was immediately accepted by one of Russia's leading publishing houses Alpha Book.

He also used to be a passionate online gamer which prompted him to write the story of a man who joins an MMORPG game hoping to raise money for his daughter's heart surgery. In 2013, the first book of *Mirror World* was published by EKSMO, Russia's largest publishing house. The original Russian series now counts three novels. The second book of *Mirror World, The Citadel,* is now being translated into English.

Want to be the first to know about our latest LitRPG, sci fi and fantasy titles from your favorite authors?

Subscribe to our **NEW RELEASES** newsletter:
http://eepurl.com/b7niIL

Thank you for reading *The Way of the Outcast!*
If you like what you've read, check out other LitRPG
novels published by Magic Dome Books.

Dark Paladin LitRPG series by Vasily Mahanenko:
The Beginning
The Quest

**The Dark Herbalist LitRPG series
by Michael Atamanov:**
Video Game Plotline Tester
Stay on the Wing

The Neuro LitRPG series by Andrei Livadny:
The Crystal Sphere
The Curse of Rion Castle

**The Way of the Shaman LitRPG series
by Vasily Mahanenko:**
Survival Quest
The Kartoss Gambit
The Secret of the Dark Forest
The Phantom Castle
The Karmadont Chess Set
The Hour of Pain (a bonus short story)

Galactogon LitRPG series by Vasily Mahanenko:
Start the Game!

Phantom Server LitRPG series by Andrei Livadny:
Edge of Reality
The Outlaw
Black Sun

**Perimeter Defense LitRPG series by Michael
Atamanov:**
Sector Eight
Beyond Death
New Contract

Mirror World LitRPG series by Alexey Osadchuk:
Project Daily Grind
The Citadel
The Way of the Outcast

AlterGame LitRPG series by Andrew Novak:
The First Player

The Expansion (The History of the Galaxy) series by A. Livadny:
Blind Punch

Citadel World series by Kir Lukovkin:
The URANUS Code

The Game Master series by A. Bobl and A. Levitsky:
The Lag

The Sublime Electricity series by Pavel Kornev
The Illustrious
The Heartless
Leopold Orso and the Case of the Bloody Tree

Moskau *(a dystopian thriller)* by **G. Zotov**

Memoria. A Corporation of Lies
(an action-packed dystopian technothriller)
by Alex Bobl

Point Apocalypse
(a near-future action thriller)
by Alex Bobl

You're in Game!
(LitRPG Stories from Bestselling Authors)

The Naked Demon (a paranormal romance)
by Sherrie L.

In order to have new books of the series translated faster, we need your help and support! Please consider leaving a review or spread the word by recommending *The Way of the Outcast* to your friends and posting the link on social media. The more people buy the book, the sooner we'll be able to make new translations available.

Thank you!

Till next time!

Made in the USA
Middletown, DE
29 November 2018